THE
MILLS & BOON®
Centenary Collection

**Celebrating 100 years of romance with
the very best of Mills & Boon**

DID YOU PURCHASE THIS BOOK WITHOUT A COVER?

If you did, you should be aware it is **stolen property** as it was
reported *unsold and destroyed* by a retailer. Neither the author nor
the publisher has received any payment for this book.

*All the characters in this book have no existence outside the
imagination of the author, and have no relation whatsoever to anyone
bearing the same name or names. They are not even distantly inspired
by any individual known or unknown to the author, and all the
incidents are pure invention.*

*All Rights Reserved including the right of reproduction in whole or
in part in any form. This edition is published by arrangement with
Harlequin Enterprises II B.V./S.à.r.l. The text of this publication or
any part thereof may not be reproduced or transmitted in any form
or by any means, electronic or mechanical, including photocopying,
recording, storage in an information retrieval system, or otherwise,
without the written permission of the publisher.*

*This book is sold subject to the condition that it shall not, by way of
trade or otherwise, be lent, resold, hired out or otherwise circulated
without the prior consent of the publisher in any form of binding or
cover other than that in which it is published and without a similar
condition including this condition being imposed on the subsequent
purchaser.*

*® and ™ are trademarks owned and used by the trademark owner
and/or its licensee. Trademarks marked with ® are registered with the
United Kingdom Patent Office and/or the Office for Harmonisation
in the Internal Market and in other countries.*

*First published in Great Britain 2008
by Harlequin Mills & Boon Limited,
Eton House, 18-24 Paradise Road, Richmond, Surrey TW9 1SR*

© Sharon Kendrick 2002

ISBN: 978 0 263 86639 1

76-0408

*Harlequin Mills & Boon policy is to use papers that are
natural, renewable and recyclable products and made from
wood grown in sustainable forests. The logging and
manufacturing processes conform to the legal environmental
regulations of the country of origin.*

*Printed and bound in Spain
by Litografia Rosés S.A., Barcelona*

Promised to
the Sheikh

by
Sharon Kendrick

MILLS & BOON
Pure reading pleasure

Sharon Kendrick started story-telling at the age of eleven and has never really stopped. She likes to write fast-paced, feel-good romances with heroes who are so sexy they'll make your toes curl!

Born in west London, she now lives in the beautiful city of Winchester – where she can see the cathedral from her window (but only if she stands on tip-toe). She has two children, Celia and Patrick, and her passions include music, books, cooking and eating – and drifting off into wonderful daydreams while she works out new plots!

Don't miss Sharon's sizzling new book available from Mills & Boon® Modern™ in May, *The Greek Tycoon's Baby Bargain*.

CHAPTER ONE

THE man silhouetted against the shuttered window was not known as the Lion of the Desert for nothing. His skin glowed with tawny good health and his black hair was as thick as an ebony mane. The magnificence of his honed, muscular body had left countless women sighing with wistful longing and he carried about him an air of leonine grace and stealth.

Sheikh Rashid of Quador was a man few would have the folly to cross, and consequently his mood was usually as lazily unperturbed as a lion who was master and king of all he surveyed.

But for now his eyes glittered with icy displeasure.

'Repeat yourself, Abdullah,' he commanded, his deep voice as tightly controlled as a coiled whip.

His manservant swallowed nervously. 'Forgive me, Excellence—'

'Repeat yourself!' rang out the cold instruction.

Abdullah cleared his throat. 'There are…er…rumours sweeping the city, Sheikh.'

A pair of jet eyebrows were raised in silent yet imperious question. 'You dare to speak to me of rumours?'

'When they concern you, Excellency, then, yes—it is necessary that I should do so.'

'And?' he clipped out.

'Your people are growing restless, Sheikh.'

The black eyebrows were knitted together and fierce possessiveness gleamed like steel from the narrowed eyes. 'There is more rebellion underfoot? Insurrection that I must quash?'

'No, no—nothing like that, Sheikh. Your people accept that you rule them with an iron fist. The people of Quador live happily. They have food in their bellies and the security of knowing that our profile in the modern world is a shining one—'

'Enough of compliments!' snapped Rashid. 'I have no need of them!'

'Indeed.' Abdullah sighed, the expression on his face not unlike that of a person who was anticipating a particularly painful visit to the dentist. 'The people of Quador wish to know why you have not yet taken a…wife,' he finished, with a weak smile.

'A *wife*?' The set of Rashid's lean body became dangerously tense and the hard, proud profile became stony. 'My people have no right to concern themselves in such matters! I shall take my bride when the time is right—and I alone will decide when that time is!' He thought fleetingly of Jenna and the black eyes gleamed anew, his voice transforming itself into a deceptively silky snare. 'But there is something else you are not telling me, is there not, Abdullah?'

'Indeed.' Abdullah swallowed. 'Reports from foreign newspapers have begun to infiltrate the internet—'

'The *internet*!' spat out Rashid. 'This internet is nothing but the work of the devil! It should be forbidden!'

'Yes, Exalted One,' agreed Abdullah placatingly. 'But if we are a member of the modern world, then it is impossible to halt progress!'

'And what *exactly* has infiltrated the internet?' demanded Rashid, his lush mouth flattening into a line of undisguised anger.

'Your…er…your relationship with a certain woman in Paris is causing some disquiet.'

'With Chantal?' Rashid felt the instinctive heavy pull of desire as he allowed his mind to linger briefly on the physical attributes of his most long-standing mistress. 'My friendship with Chantal is nothing new.'

'Precisely!' agreed Abdullah triumphantly. 'And its very endurance has provoked concern that you are perhaps planning to make *her* your wife!'

Rashid swore in French—one of the seven languages he was fluent in. 'Are my people mad?' he questioned incredulously. 'You know which woman is promised to me!'

'Indeed,' murmured Abdullah.

'Do they not know that a man has many needs?' continued Rashid. 'What Chantal brings to me has. nothing to do with marriage!' His mouth curved. 'It is not my destiny to marry a woman ten years my senior who will be unable to provide me with the many offspring I will one day desire!'

'That is as I thought, Exalted One.' Abdullah breathed a barely perceptible sigh of relief. He hesitated. 'Would you not make that message clear to the world? Has the time for offspring not now arrived?'

Rashid gave a heavy sigh and turned his face towards the window once more. Through the shutters, shafts of sunlight from the bright heat of the midday sun filtered through and illuminated his dark and golden beauty. In his tense, angry silence he was unmoving, as still as some hawk-nosed statue of a predatory conqueror.

Was the time now come? Was he indeed—ready?

He was known and feared for his resolute nature, for his steely intelligence and his decisiveness. It took him no more than a second or two to consider what had been plotted out for him since childhood, and then he nodded his dark head in answer to the silent question he asked himself.

Abdullah was his most trusted advisor, and the rumours must be gathering apace if he had summoned up the courage to alert his ruler to their existence.

And a man about whom uncertainty prevailed surely ran the risk of weakening his indomitable position...

He turned and surveyed the emotionless face of his envoy. 'So be it,' he said slowly. 'Destiny must at last prevail.' His eyes glittered with a cool acceptance and only the most lingering flash of regret, which was quickly replaced by the heat of sensual expectation. 'I will send for Jenna,' he stated softly. 'And the wedding will take place as soon as it can be arranged.'

Inside the wild and wonderful interior of her New York apartment the telephone began to shrill, and Jenna jumped.

'Can you answer that for me, Brad?' she called.

'Got it!'

Still damp from the shower, Jenna walked into the sitting room, a towel wrapped around her slim, glistening body and another draped in an elaborate turban around her head, just as Brad picked the receiver up.

The moment she saw the look on his face tiny little shivers of apprehension began to prickle at her skin. It was him; she knew it. She wasn't sure how, but she did.

Him.

Tiny beads of sweat broke out on her forehead, until she reminded herself that life had changed. That promises once made could be broken. The bond which had once existed between them had been silently yet inextricably severed. Surely it was inconceivable that he should demand what she had once most desired and now most feared.

'Jenna?' Brad was drawling in his soft American accent. 'Yeah, sure! She's right here. Hold on. I'll get her for you.' And he pulled a face as he handed her the phone.

Still trembling, Jenna took the receiver from him silently. 'Hello?'

There was a pause. 'Jenna?'

It *was* him. She would have known that voice anywhere, but then maybe that was because no other man in the world spoke like him. Steely-soft and velvet-hard. Sexy, predatory and distinctly unsettling. She swallowed, the modern woman she had become sorely tempted to say, Who's that? But she thought better of it. To affect not to know him would be to cast a slur on his character as well as denting his ego—and everyone knew that Sheikh Rashid of Quador had an ego the size of the United States itself!

'Rashid,' she said cautiously. She heard his terse exclamation in response, and knew that she had somehow angered him. 'How are you?' she asked in English.

'Who answered the phone?' he shot back—rather unexpectedly in the same language.

She considered telling him that it was none of his business, but again thought better of it. Rashid assumed that everything was his business, and that he had an inalienable right to have absolutely everything he wanted. But then he had been denied nothing from the moment of his birth—so maybe that was not so surprising.

'He's a friend of mine,' she informed him lightly. 'Brad.'

There was a moment of silence, and when he began to speak again there was not a trace of velvet—the voice was pure steel. And anger. *'Brad?'* he repeated on an incredulous note. 'A *man*? You have a *man* in your apartment?'

The irony wasn't lost on her. one rule for Rashid and another entirely different one for her. But much better to take the heat out of the situation with humour—for hadn't she once been able to make him laugh, a lifetime ago, before all her foolish girlhood dreams had been crushed underfoot, vanquished by the knowledge of just what kind of man he was? And what he did.

'I think so!' she joked rather nervously. 'Unless he's a master of disguise!'

In his stately study in the Quador palace, Rashid felt the slow burn of anger sizzle into rampant life. 'And how long has this *Brad*—' he spat the word out as if it was poison '—been your *friend*?'

Jenna clenched her fist around the receiver, so that her knuckles grew pale, but the instinctive movement brought with it a return of her resolve. Enough was enough! She was no longer his subject—not really. Hadn't her years in America and her new life here freed her from his influence?

But Rashid had the cunning of a fox—simple rebellion would not work with him. She did not yet know what he wanted, and until she did it was better to play the game. To slip into the role he would expect of her.

'Oh, ages,' she said vaguely, and then injected a note of docile interest into her voice. 'Did you just ring up for a chat, Rashid? Or was there something in particular you wanted?'

The 'something in particular' he wanted right now would have been to burst into her apartment and tear this Brad from limb to limb, demanding to know just who he was and what he had been doing... But Rashid drew himself back from expressing an emotion as wasted as jealousy, and instead allowed himself an arrogant smile. The one thing he *could* count on was that Jenna was as pure as the snows which topped the Quador mountains. Jenna...

His.

His.

Only ever *his.*

'I am displeased,' he said, with a silky and dangerous menace. 'Would you care to explain what he is doing there? Or do you make a habit of entertaining young men in your apartment?'

No, she would not care to explain herself, but she knew him well enough to realise that prevarication would be pointless. If any other man had spoken to her in that tone of voice she would have slammed the phone down. But this was a man like no other.

She thought about the dreams she had once cherished. Dreams about him which had taken on the quality of nightmares when she had learned the truth about him. At least living in America had allowed her to pretend that she was a different person from that foolish dreamer—and after a while it had become second nature to her and the pretence had become real. She *was* a different person.

And she would not let him spoil it now!

'What do you want, Rashid?' she sighed.

'I think that perhaps it was a mistake to allow you to study in America,' he observed in a hard voice.

'I disagree.'

'You *dare* to disagree with your sheikh?' he questioned mockingly, but Jenna realised that there was a hard ring of truth to his imperious question.

I dare to defy you! she wanted to shout, but if she did that then it would be all-out war—and there would only be one winner. She forced herself to put the sound of pleasure into her voice. Once it would have been genuine—there would have been delight there, too—but no more. 'At the time you put up few objections,' she pointed out.

'Because you twisted your father around your little finger!' he retorted. 'Convinced him that you should be allowed to travel. How persuasive you were, Jenna.'

'What is done is done, and the past is past,' she murmured in true Quador fashion. 'Now, come on, Rashid—do tell me to what pleasure I owe this phone call. *Such* a surprise,' she finished truthfully.

Rashid frowned. A surprise indeed, and several things had still not yet been explained. 'And where is your sister?' he questioned. 'Does she approve of this friend of yours, with whom you are so intimate that he sees fit to answer your phone for you?'

'Oh, don't be so old-fashioned!'

'But I am old-fashioned,' he told her silkily. 'Extremely old-fashioned. And you still haven't answered my question. Does your sister approve of this friend of yours?'

'Nadia approves of Brad,' said Jenna woodenly, but her eyes widened with an expression of fear as she stared into Brad's frowning face. If only Rashid knew that her sister was in love with Brad—that they were virtually living in the flat as man and wife. How his old-fashioned sensibilities would be outraged! 'He's a nice man,' she finished, and hoped that the fear had not crept into her voice.

'*Was* a nice man,' Rashid corrected coldly.

Now the fear was out in the open and she made no attempt to hide it. 'What do you mean by that?' she whispered hoarsely.

He gave a short, almost cruel laugh. 'Oh, I mean nothing more sinister than stating a fact, my sweet Jenna—simply that Brad and your life in New York will now become things of the past.'

'I think it's *your* turn to explain yourself,' said Jenna steadily, even though her heart was bashing madly against her ribcage.

'Can't you guess?' His voice had deepened into a beguiling caress. He remembered with a sudden deep ache the silken golden-brown of her hair and her deep amber eyes—so at variance with the other women of Quador. But she owed more than her looks to the inheritance of her American mother, he realised, a pulse beginning to beat at his temple. He wondered just how independent her life in New York actually *was*. And he wondered how many men 'friends' she had over there.

He should have put a stop to it long ago!

'The time has come, Jenna,' he said softly, and a sense of the inevitable began to heat his blood. He had embraced his destiny with a passion for all his life, and this particular destiny was no hardship.

Now she didn't care—she *would* affect to misunderstand him. Surely he could not mean what she suspected he was about to say next. 'Time for what?'

Rashid's mouth tightened. There had been little contact between them over the past four years, other than the formal and highly chaperoned meetings when she'd flown home to see her family, but that had been necessary for all concerned. Sensibilities had had to be preserved. And when he had gazed on the gleaming gold of her hair, and the lush, almost sinful curves of her body which even the traditional flowing Quador clothes could not disguise, he had been almost glad of the company of the chaperon. Had understood completely the need for their presence.

She had sent him dutiful letters from New York in which she portrayed a life which sounded almost dull due to overwork. And because of this he had been prepared to tolerate her short burst of freedom. As his wife she would be expected to dedicate her life to charitable works; this was surely not a bad way to begin?

And she was a highly intelligent woman... Far better to allow her a little leeway than to clip her wings completely.

He narrowed his eyes. 'I think you know very well what for, Jenna,' he snapped. 'It is time for you to return to Quador and become my wife!'

The hand that held the phone trembled. 'That's hardly the most romantic proposal I've heard!' But her laughter bordered on the hysterical and she saw Brad, who was still listening in to the conversation, stiffen with disbelief and alarm.

'If romance is what you seek from me, then better you should take the first plane home,' he instructed silkily, and he felt the blood heat in his veins, for opposition was rare enough to excite him!

Romance? She doubted whether he would understand romance if it came up and kicked him in the teeth! Gritting her own teeth together, she forced herself to stay calm with a huge effort of will.

'Rashid, you cannot still wish me to become your wife.' A note of desperation had now crept into her voice.

The heat died as her opposition began to irritate him. A little offered resistance was a game he could play as well as the next man, but enough was enough! She should be breathing soft sighs of gratitude down the phone at him by now! Planning her trousseau in her head!

'My *wishes* are not paramount,' he emphasised coldly. 'The agreement was made many moons ago, as well you know. But I will satisfy your every need as my wife, Jenna—of that you need have no doubts.'

She heard the raw, sexual boast which had deepened his voice and she shivered for all kinds of reasons—most of which she dared not even begin to analyse. Oh, yes, she knew exactly what he meant—and she *didn't* have any doubts. His prowess in the bedroom was legendary.

But Jenna had learnt much during her time in America—not least that women expected equality in a relationship. And equality with Rashid would be nothing but a distant dream.

Women expected something more, too—and that something was called love. Hopeless. For not only did she doubt Rashid's ability to give and receive love, she knew deep down that he would see such behaviour as a sign of weakness. Love made you vulnerable, and Rashid was the personification of invulnerability.

'Rashid,' she said, more weakly than she would have wished. 'You cannot mean that.'

There was an icy silence. Then, 'You may have the mistaken idea that sustained resistance is provocative, but let me tell you, Jenna, that you are wrong. You will be mine and you will return to Quador immediately. Is that understood?'

She forced herself to accept the inevitable, knowing that it was pure folly to deny him at least the second part of his command. She would return to Quador and she would be forced to play a cunning game herself. Soon Rashid would no longer want to marry her, but he must appear to have taken the decision himself. She must just make sure that he did.

The steely voice was speaking again. 'Still you hesitate,' he observed dangerously. 'Perhaps you wish for me to send someone to collect you?'

She blanched. Imagine one of Rashid's aides coming here and discovering the cosy domestic relationship between Nadia and Brad!

'No!' she protested. 'I'll book myself on the first available flight.'

'I will make sure that the first flight *is* available,' he said smoothly. 'A car will be awaiting you when you touch down in Quador, to bring you to the palace.'

And the connection was ended with a click.

CHAPTER TWO

JENNA put the receiver down with a hand which continued to tremble and looked up to see that Brad was standing there, the narrowed look of question still in his eyes.

'Jenna, what the hell is wrong?'

She stared at him. 'You do realise who that was?'

Brad nodded. 'Oh, yes,' he said grimly. 'I've heard enough stories from Nadia about his arrogant authority. I would have to be pretty dumb not to have guessed that it was Rashid. What the hell did he say to you? You look *awful*.'

It occurred to her that she was still standing wrapped in nothing but a towel, and a frisson of fear cooled her skin like ice-water being splashed on it.

What if Rashid sent one of his New York contacts to the apartment to make sure that she was obeying his command and preparing to leave? Someone could ring on the doorbell any second now, and wouldn't the situation look frighteningly compromising? She shuddered as she imagined his reaction to a report that she was cavorting half-naked in front of another man.

'Let me go and get dressed,' she said urgently, 'and then I'll tell you everything.'

In her bedroom she quickly pulled on a pair of jeans and a crisp white shirt, and combed through her long, damp hair before studying her reflection in the mirror.

She needed to act, and to act quickly! Rashid would never

marry a woman whom he did not find attractive, and she would have to do everything in her power to make sure that he didn't. She would embrace the American side of her personality with a vengeance—and Rashid's immovable conservatism should do the rest!

Nodding resolutely at her pale face and widened amber eyes, she returned to the sitting room, where Brad had made a pot of coffee. She took a mug from him gratefully, wrapping her long fingers around its steaming warmth and hoping that a little of it might creep its way into her heart.

She sat down on the sofa.

'So spill the beans,' he said quietly.

Jenna sighed, knowing that she did not have to ask Brad to keep what she was about to tell him completely confidential; he more than anyone knew how to keep secrets. 'He wants to marry me.'

Brad almost choked on his coffee. 'Say that *again*?' he demanded incredulously.

Jenna put the mug down and shook her head. 'Maybe I phrased that badly. I don't think he actually *wants* to marry me—it is just something he believes he must honour—an agreement which was made between our parents a long, long time ago.'

'Jenna—I don't have a clue what you're saying!'

She supposed that it must sound positively barbaric to a modern professional American man—and in truth didn't it sound more than a little barbaric to her? She sighed again, pushing a damp strand of hair from her cheek and fixing him with a candid look.

'I'll try to explain. Rashid's late father and my father were great, great friends—and when I was still in my cradle they decided that, provided I fulfilled certain...' She hesitated for a moment. 'Certain *criteria*, then I would one day make the perfect wife for Rashid.'

'And those criteria were what?' he questioned astutely.

Faint colour crept into her cheeks. 'Physically, I must be pleasing to Rashid's eyes—'

'Well, there couldn't be any doubt about that, surely?' he laughed.

False modesty would help no one. She shrugged. 'I understand that in that particular condition I met his specifications,' she answered slowly.

'You make it sound like the guy is picking out decor for a house!'

'Maybe it is a little like that,' she admitted, but she felt a shiver of memory as she recalled their last chaperoned meeting when she had surprised a hot, fleeting look of hunger in Rashid's enigmatic black eyes as he had greeted her. A look which had washed over her and made her skin tingle with awareness, even while the knowledge that Rashid desired her had filled her with fear and trepidation. 'The Ruler's needs must always be met. That is a given.'

'What other criteria?' asked Brad quietly.

Jenna bit her lip. 'The obvious one, of course. That I must go to him unsullied—but I really don't want to talk about that.'

Brad nodded. 'Sure,' he said understandingly. 'So what is it that you aren't telling me, Jenna? Surely the idea can't be that abhorrent to you? I've seen pictures of the guy and he sure looks like he fits the bill of conforming to most women's fantasy man!'

Jenna swallowed as unwilling images of his hard, lean body and cruel, dark face swam tantalisingly into her mind. 'Oh, no one is disputing Rashid's appeal,' she said carefully. 'Not even me. He is a most spectacular man. It's just that America has changed me—or rather knowledge has changed what I thought I once wanted.'

Brad pulled a face. 'You've lost me!' he protested.

Time had deadened some of the pain of discovery, but not all of it, and it still hurt to say it. 'When I first came to the States I had access to the free press for the first time in my life. I read newspapers with gossip columns—columns which documented Rashid's lifestyle with disturbing clarity.'

Brad nodded. 'I think I'm beginning to get the picture,' he said slowly.

Jenna splayed her hands over her thighs and curled her fingernails so that they bit into her through the denim. 'Rashid is almost twelve years older than I am,' she said. 'But when I was little he looked out for me—protected me.'

He had indulged her hero-worship of him. Taken her with him when he went falconing. And from the age of fourteen she had thought she would almost die with pleasure to see that formidable presence astride his night-dark stallion, subduing the bird of prey as if he could communicate with it by instinct alone. And maybe he could, she thought bitterly. For wasn't he a creature of prey himself?

Somewhere along the way she had acquired the rare ability to make him laugh, to gently tease him, and she had been the only person allowed to get away with what he would have regarded as insurrection in others. She had thought that the world began and ended with Rashid, and had grown to long for the wedding she knew must one day come.

'So what happened to make you hate him?' asked Brad.

Jenna lifted her head, surprised. 'Hate him? I'm not sure that I hate him.'

'You sound like you do—the way you talk about him.'

Did she? Wasn't hate too powerful an emotion to describe her feelings for Rashid? Too closely and dangerously linked to the flipside of such an emotion—love itself? A love which would never be anything more than one-sided and, consequently, never enough for the woman she had become.

Because when she had turned eighteen their relationship had changed fundamentally. Had it been the onset of womanhood which had made the magnificent sheikh grow so wary and distant in her company? she wondered. The atmosphere between them had been brittle with some kind of unnamed tension. Their earlier ease in each other's company had evaporated like the rare desert rains which sizzled beneath the intensity of the fierce Quador sun.

And she had missed that ease. Desperately. Without Rashid

as her confidant she had felt as though she was in limbo—existing and not really living at all.

'Rashid made no move to marry me when I came of age,' she said slowly. 'And my pride wouldn't let me show my disappointment. I had no wish to stay in Quador, just waiting and waiting for some distant wedding, and so I told him that I wished to learn something of my late mother's country, that I wanted to study in America. It had always been her dearest wish that I should know something of her homeland.'

Rashid had had a great deal to cope with as well. His own parents had been killed in a plane crash, and his rightful inheritance had come much sooner than anyone had anticipated. As well as coping with his grief he had had to come to terms with governing a vast country. It had not been an easy transition as power was transferred to the handsome young Sheikh. Many had doubted he would be able to stamp his dominance onto the demanding land and Rashid had been determined to prove them wrong.

She remembered the thoughtful way he had considered her request to study law in America, consulting long and hard with her father before they had both given her their consent.

'I admit that I found his blessing to leave both upsetting and confusing, but the reason for this soon became crystal-clear.' She let out a painful, shuddering breath as she remembered the newspaper clippings. 'The truth hurt,' she told him quietly.

'What truth?' Brad questioned.

'The truth about his lifestyle. How very foolish I was,' she said with a bitter laugh. 'I thought that as I was promised to him he would forsake all others. How naive could you get? I soon discovered that Rashid had been involved with super models and actresses since he was a teenager. The news had been kept from me while I lived in Quador, but I found out soon enough once I moved away. Why, he even has a mistress at the moment—it is well documented enough. He shares another woman's bed in Paris even while he summons me back for our wedding!'

'Are you sure?' asked Brad, in a horrified voice.

'Perfectly sure. Her name is Chantal and she is his favourite. No doubt she will occupy a nearby hotel even during our honeymoon—such are the customs in Quador!'

He flinched. 'So what the hell are you going to do, Jenna? Surely you aren't going to allow yourself to tolerate a union like that?'

'Oh, no,' she said with quiet fervour, and allowed herself a small smile of determination. 'I shall go back to Quador and convince Rashid that I am not the woman he wishes to marry.'

'And how will you do that?'

The smile died on her lips. She must waste no more time, and neither must she involve Nadia or Brad in her decisions—for Rashid would not tolerate collusion. She shivered. The consequences for her sister would be unimaginable. 'I'll think of something,' she said airily, and smiled as she stood up. 'Don't worry about *me*, Brad,' she said.

'But I do,' he said, with a shrug.

She looked affectionately at the man her sister loved with such a passion. 'Well, don't,' she remonstrated softly. 'I do not intend to let him bully me into doing something to which I am morally opposed.'

He didn't look convinced. 'Sure,' he said. And neither did he sound it.

Jenna tossed the golden-brown hair off her shoulders like a feisty young mare preparing for flight. 'And now I'm going to book my flight and pay a visit to the stores.'

Rashid's plane touched down in Paris and a darkened limousine was waiting to whisk him away to the luxurious apartment situated in the sixth *arrondissement*, the city's most prestigious area.

As always, one discreet bodyguard preceded him while another hovered unseen to the rear. When they reached the door Rashid nodded his head and held his hand out for the leather case the other man carried.

'You may leave me now,' he instructed.

'But Exalted One—'

'Leave me!' Rashid rasped. 'I will make my presence known to you shortly.'

The bodyguard narrowed him a look which said that he objected to the Sheikh's insistence, but he knew that such objection was pointless.

'Yes, Excellency.'

Rashid rang the bell. He had his own key, but he knew that he could no longer use it.

The door opened and Chantal stood before him. She had been expecting him—his phone call earlier that day had been rapturously received, as was normal. Just for a moment his mouth tightened as he thought how *Chantal* would have responded to his proposal of marriage. With pleasure, and joy, and with hunger. And the contrast between the almost insulting uninterest which Jenna had displayed filled him once more with the slow burn of anger.

'*Chéri*, your unexpected visit has brought me much pleasure,' murmured Chantal, and like a vixen she moved towards him, all perfume and silk and shockingly provocative experience as she held her arms out.

But he took a step back and shook his head, and although she shrugged with disappointment she still followed him unquestioningly into the huge sitting room with its spectacular views over Paris.

He watched her for one last time. As a mistress she had been matchless. Utterly matchless. Her looks belied her forty-four years and her body was sleeker and more toned than that of a woman half her age. The raven hair gleamed and moved with the careless abandon which only the finest hairdresser could construct, and the deceptively simple green silk dress must have cost a king's ransom. And what Chantal didn't know about the art of lovemaking simply wasn't worth knowing.

His mouth tightened again.

'A drink, *chéri*?' she murmured, and her voice dropped into husky entreaty. 'Or shall I run you a bath?'

In the past he might have had both. Or neither. He might rip the expensive dress from her body and it would simply excite her, make her part her pale thighs eagerly for him.

But no more.

He shook his head. 'My car is waiting.'

'So?'

'Chantal, there is something that I must tell you—'

She stilled, her eyes narrowing with suspicion as something in the tone of his voice must have warned her, and he realised that she was woman of the world enough to know that the news he had come to bring to her today would not be to her liking.

Defiantly, she reached for her cigarettes and lit one. 'Then tell me, *chéri*—do not keep me in suspense!'

'I'm getting married.'

She didn't react, just blew the smoke out in one long, deep breath, the perfect arch of her eyebrows elevating only very slightly.

'So I must offer my congratulations, must I?' she questioned coolly.

He smiled. From the almost supercilious mask she wore it was impossible to guess at her true feelings. But then, she had never shown him her true feelings—and hadn't that been one of qualities he had most admired about her? 'Thank you.'

She drew deeply on the cigarette. 'Who is she?'

'Jenna.'

She nodded, and then the mask slipped and a calculating look sharpened her beautiful features. 'The girl who is half-American? She lives in New York?'

Rashid frowned. Had he told her so much? 'The very same.'

'She must be overjoyed.'

Rashid's mouth tightened again. She *should* be overjoyed, though her attitude had been a million miles away from the gratitude he had been expecting. But Jenna would soon learn never to try to resist his wishes again!

'What woman wouldn't be?' asked Chantal sadly, before he

could answer. She stubbed the cigarette out with a vicious movement of her fingers and began to unbutton her dress. 'So this will be the last time for us, *chéri*? Or will you still have time for me once you are *married*?'

He could see the pale thrust of her breasts contrasted against the lace of the exquisite lingerie she wore and he felt his body hardening with the slow, relentless pulse of desire. But he quashed it as ruthlessly he would a scorpion which could sometimes be found lurking beneath stones in the unforgiving desert.

'No,' he said roughly. 'Stop that!'

She moved her fingers beneath her dress, drifting her fingertips provocatively against herself, and her eyes widened alluringly as she began to move her hips with slow, sensual rhythm. 'Are you sure, *chéri*?' she whispered huskily.

A muscle worked in his cheek as he dropped the leather case he was carrying onto the chair in front of her. 'Yes, I am certain!' His voice was harsh. 'Do your dress up! Now!'

She stared into his face for a long moment and began to do as he had ordered, the pallor of her cheeks the only outward sign of her distress.

'The apartment is yours to keep,' he said.

She nodded. 'Thank you,' she said heavily.

He had known that she would not refuse. 'And I have brought you something.' He indicated the box with a stabbing movement of his finger.

'What is it?'

He opened it up and row upon row of glittering diamond brooches lay there in dazzling array against a backdrop of dark velvet. He saw the look of natural indulgent pleasure as she surveyed them, before lifting her eyes to his in cool appraisal.

'For services rendered?' she enquired, with a wry smile.

He shook his head. 'As a small symbol of my gratitude for such an enjoyable relationship.'

The pleasure was replaced by alarm. 'It needn't be over, Rashid,' she said urgently. 'You know that.'

Yes, he knew that. She could be his for the taking, whenever and wherever he wanted. Jenna need never know, need never find out—he had countless people who would cover for him without question. It would be almost expected of him to behave as his father had done.

But he shook his head. 'It is over, Chantal,' he said roughly, and indicated the jewellery with a casual wave of his dark-skinned hand. 'Take your time. Choose the one which pleases you most, and I will arrange to have the remainder collected by Abdullah.'

She nodded and stared at him. 'So that's it?'

'You knew that this would happen some day. It was as inevitable as the dawn which follows night. So let us have no regrets, and let us remember the past with affection.' He glanced down at the costly timepiece which gleamed so palely gold against his dark wrist. 'It is time for me to leave. My plane is waiting.'

She nodded, and abruptly turned away from him. 'Goodbye, *chéri*,' she whispered, but he heard the hint of tears in her voice.

'Goodbye, Chantal,' he said softly.

He was almost at the door when she halted him with a word. 'Wait!'

He turned around, but he didn't need to look into her face to know what was coming next.

'If ever—*ever*—you change your mind, you know that I'll be here for you, Rashid.'

He gave a hard smile. 'Goodbye, Chantal,' he repeated, and without another word he turned on his heel and left her apartment.

CHAPTER THREE

AS SOON as Jenna emerged from the plane the blazing temperature of Quador hit her, and it was like being punched in the face by a blazing fist.

The flight had been mildly eventful merely for the fact that as soon as she had arrived at Kennedy Airport she had been upgraded to first class, and it didn't take a genius to guess who was behind that.

She had started to protest, but then her words had tailed away uselessly and she had seen the check-in girl looking at her with ill-disguised curiosity, as if wondering who in their right mind would object to flying home in unadulterated luxury on Quador Airlines.

Abdullah, Rashid's chief aide, was standing on the Tarmac waiting for her, next to the dark-windowed car which bore Rashid's distinctive crest, and he bowed his head respectfully as she approached. Though not before she had seen the small triumphant gleam in his eyes.

He knows! she thought. He knows the purpose of my visit! But Abdullah was very much of the old school of courtier, and she suspected that he thought Rashid was long overdue in taking a bride for himself.

'Did you have a pleasant flight?' he asked courteously, as the powerful car was waved straight through all the normal barriers without question.

'A wonderful, smooth flight,' replied Jenna truthfully. She certainly wasn't about to start enlightening Abdullah about the nervous churning in her stomach as she had contemplated what she was about to do.

Rashid's palace was situated in an isolated spot just outside the main city of Riocard itself, its solitary location necessary for grim and practical reasons. There had been several assassination attempts on Rashid's father, and on his predecessors too, and Jenna wondered whether Rashid had also been a target for the many fanatics who would wish to rule Quador themselves.

She turned her head to look out through the window, unprepared for the leap of distress in her heart which her thoughts caused. But she reasoned that just because she had no wish to marry the man that did not mean she would wish to see him hurt.

Rashid hurt! Jenna gave a wry smile. It seemed as unlikely and as incongruous an idea as trying to imagine Rashid being celibate!

The palace itself was centuries old, with formal terraces and magnificent pillars carved with figures of Rashid's ancestors. The grounds had been modelled on a larger scale of some beautiful English country-house garden, and the well-tended lawns were almost indecently green. A large and decorative rectangular pond glittered back the reflection of the blazing sun and Jenna found herself wishing that she could trail her fingertips through its soothing coolness.

The car slid smoothly through the vast, ornate gates which were guarded by lynx-eyed men who carried poorly concealed guns and Jenna shivered, looking around at the formal security with new eyes. If it seemed like a different world, then that was because it *was*, and she had grown accustomed to, grown to love, the freedom and ease of her life in America.

'The Sheikh is waiting for you in his private apartments,' said Abdullah. 'I suggest that we do not keep him waiting.'

Suggestion, indeed! It was nothing but a smoothly broached command, and Jenna nodded, feeling a little like the sacrificial lamb going to the slaughter.

She mounted the curving marble staircase with a growing feeling of dread, and even the sight of the exquisite mosaics in every hue of blue imaginable, the priceless chandeliers which hung in crystal waterfalls from the ceiling, could do little to quell her fears. She had always loved the palace, but today it looked like nothing more than a gilded prison.

The guard outside Rashid's apartments pushed open the heavy door.

'Your case will be brought from the car for you,' murmured Abdullah, and he raised his eyebrows. 'You have travelled lightly, I note.'

Well, of course she had—she wasn't planning on staying! 'Very lightly,' she agreed, with a tight smile.

'Very well. I will take my leave of you now, mistress,' said Abdullah, and he bowed his head.

'Thank you, Abdullah.'

Jenna stepped inside the room, praying for the serenity to see her plan through without giving herself away. But in spite of her misgivings her mouth dried instinctively as she saw Rashid silhouetted against the window. A high-born female chaperon was sitting demurely on one of the brocade window seats close by.

Had she ever thought that her refusal to marry him was going to be easy? A piece of cake? Had she simply forgotten his magnificence, and the effect it always had on her? she wondered distractedly. Or simply trained herself not to dwell on it, because then she could disregard the fact that he still had the power to fill her with a hopeless yearning?

Even now.

Dressed in traditional flowing robes of cloth-of-gold, his muscular body seemed more vital than that of any other man she had ever laid eyes on, and her traitorous heart reminded her of how much she had once adored him. And trusted him.

He heard her enter, but he did not turn. Not immediately. She had kept him waiting for two days since his telephone call summoning her here, and now he would make her wait before she could feast her eyes on the stern face of the man to whom she would soon be joined! He felt the first stirrings of desire, but he did not allow his mind or his body to linger on such thoughts. First he must dispense his disapproval!

Jenna knew what was expected of her. Reminding herself that to anger him would not help her case, she spoke one word in the demure voice she had practised in her head over and over again during the flight from New York.

'Sheikh.' It was both an acknowledgment and a deference, and there was a split-second pause before she saw him half incline his proud head. And then, very deliberately, he turned around to face her, and the dryness in her mouth increased, as did the acceleration of her heart.

How *could* she have forgotten his physical presence? For he was magnificent! Utterly, utterly magnificent! The carved face so cruelly perfect, the coal-black eyes gleaming with a fierce and icy intelligence. And something else, too.

Not anger, no. Anger would be too mild a word to describe the emotion which was sizzling its way across the room at her.

Fury.

Stark, undisguised fury.

She should have been expecting it, had told herself to expect it, but even Jenna was unprepared for her shivering response to the vision of the formidable Rashid slanting her a look of total condemnation.

'What have you been doing to yourself?' he hissed at her, like an angry serpent who had been disturbed. He spoke in French, presumably so that the chaperon would not understand, but the soft, sensual-sounding words only reminded Jenna of his mistress, and it was as though someone had driven a stake through her heart with all the force they could muster.

She lifted her eyes to his, feigning ignorance of his question. 'Sheikh?' she questioned, with a very credible line in demure confusion.

Again, Rashid felt the blood heating his veins, but this time not with desire—no, certainly not that! For the woman who stood before him bore such little resemblance to the Jenna he remembered that he scarcely recognised her.

She wore tight blue jeans and a silky amber top which matched her huge eyes and emphasised the luscious swell of her breasts. High-heeled snakeskin ankle-boots made even more of the length of her long, slim legs, where the denim clung to them so provocatively. So very Westernised, he thought, in disgust, as he let his cold and disapproving gaze travel to her head, where a wide-brimmed and flower-decked straw hat was managing to conceal all the silken splendour of her hair.

But it was the make-up which caused the little pulse to beat so forbiddingly at his temple. Quador women—and particularly high-born Quador women—did not mar their complexions with the false glitter of cosmetics!

He scowled.

There was a subtle golden glow which shimmered over the heavy lids of her deep-set eyes, and the long lashes were ebony-dark and spiked like the legs of a spider. Her full lips gleamed provocatively, highlighted with some rose-pale tint, and whilst the man in him could not deny that she looked very beautiful indeed, he also knew something else.

That she looked like a tramp!

More mistress than wife!

'How dare you come before me so attired?' he demanded imperiously.

'You don't like my clothes?' she questioned innocently.

He would like to tear them from her back! Fighting down the urge to storm across the room and do just that—for he could not ignore the watchful eye of the chaperon—he steadied himself with a deep breath.

'You look like a tramp!' he offered, giving voice to his thoughts.

'Hardly,' answered Jenna drily. 'A tramp would ill be able to afford the cost of *this* outfit!'

'Not *that* kind of tramp!' he contradicted icily. 'The kind of tramp to be found hanging around the back streets of Riocard!'

'Oh, you mean a prostitute?' she questioned helpfully.

Furiously, he ignored that. 'Why did you not come to me wearing traditional Quador dress?'

'Because this is the kind of thing I'm more used to! It's all the rage in New York!'

'Why?' he snarled. 'Does *Brad* like you to dress like that?'

Jenna realised that she was straying into dangerous and uncharted waters. And that she was supposed *not* to be antagonising him! 'I'll go and change,' she offered, but he shook his head.

'Oh, no, you won't,' he said grimly. 'You have kept me waiting too long. You will leave only when I give you leave to!' He drew another deep breath. 'Would you like some refreshment after your journey?' he forced himself to say.

She felt like asking him if he was offering tea or hemlock, but thought better of it. She shook her head, and the movement drew his eye and caused another small snarl of irritation.

'Remove your hat!' he ordered.

This was it. The moment which would confirm her conversion from Suitable Wife to Sassy American! With one easy movement she pulled the straw hat from her head, though her heart was pounding nervously as she stared at him with an expression she prayed was not *too* defiant.

For a moment Rashid was speechless. If she had suddenly started flying around the State Apartments he could not have been more profoundly shocked.

'But you have cut your hair!' he observed in a strangled kind of voice.

For one bizarre and crazy moment Jenna thought that he sounded almost *sad*, but nerves must have made her imagination work overtime. And when she met the steel of his eyes she knew that she must have been mistaken.

'Yes. Do you like it?' she asked lightly, and felt the air-conditioning cool her newly bare neck.

'*Why?*' he demanded hoarsely as he remembered the silken strands of syrup-coloured hair which had streamed down almost to her bottom. A pulse leapt in his groin. He had imagined untying it on their wedding night, had pictured it spread out across his chest, contrasting so beautifully against the dark skin. 'Why shave your head like that? To look like a man? No longer a woman?'

Something in his criticism made Jenna forget her vow not to anger him any more than was necessary. His look of pure censure offended some very elemental emotion deep inside her, and the look he was lancing her way made her fleetingly wish that she had not opted for such a dramatic cut, that she could win back his approval.

Until she reminded herself of Chantal, and of all the others. Let *them* crave his approval—she would make herself tolerate his contempt!

Or would she?

Was it feminine pride which made her draw her chin up and pull her shoulders back in haughty query? The movement caused her breasts to push imperceptibly against the silk shirt, and she saw from the sudden tensing of his body that it had not escaped Rashid's attention.

The chaperon, whose job it was to protect but not to intrude, was listening to the conversation but unable to understand it. She was not looking at them either, her hands busy with some prayer beads.

So she would have missed the look of raw, feral hunger which had darkened Rashid's eyes to pure ebony. And the dull flush of colour which crept over his arrogantly carved cheekbones.

If a look could be X-rated, then Rashid had just invented it! Refusing to be intimidated—or tempted   by the undisguised sexual hunger which emanated from his body, Jenna stared back at him, even though she was acutely aware of the stinging of her breasts and the heated rush of some honeyed feeling which was making her knees feel very weak indeed.

'You think I look like a man?' she challenged softly.

Had something in the air around them changed? For the chaperon lifted her head and frowned, but Rashid paid her no heed. She was his subject, and here only to ensure that neither the man nor the woman touched each other.

'Go back to your beads!' he commanded in his native tongue, and the woman obeyed him instantly.

He reverted to French, and gave a small nod of his dark head in the direction of the chaperon. 'You see? That is the kind of compliance I am used to, Jenna. The kind of compliance I expect,' he purred, mesmerised by the tight little buds which were pushing against her shirt.

She would be responsive, his Jenna, he thought, with a sudden heady rush of elation and power. Maybe he had always instinctively known that, but now he was certain. He would make her weep with pleasure in his arms. He would captivate and subdue her until she wanted him and only him, and he would tutor her desire until it matched his own!

'Not from me,' she said instantly. 'I am not your subordinate! I have lived too long in America not to consider a man and a woman to be equals!'

He stiffened with outrage. 'How do you dare to speak thus to your Ruler?' he demanded incredulously. 'When we are wed you will *naturally* take on the subordinate role of wife!'

His arrogant boast drew her up short. This wasn't going as well as she had hoped. In fact, that was the understatement of the year! He should be gradually going off the idea of marriage to her by now. Minute by minute, his resolve should be weakening. She decided to play the equality card a little bit more.

Defiantly, she raked her fingers through the starkly cropped hair. 'I'm pretty pleased with it myself,' she confided, and gave him a bright smile. 'So easy to manage. I can go straight to college with it still wet from the shower. Just like a man, actually!'

His eyes became cold chips of jet. *'Still wet from the shower?'* he repeated tightly. 'You go to college with your hair wet?'

She supposed that it must sound bizarre to a man whose position had always isolated him from the cares and concerns of normal everyday life—but he was making it sound as though she had committed some kind of sexual deviation. 'Of course!' she expanded. 'If I'm late.'

He expelled a low breath. 'Well, you will not have such concerns in the future, because you will not be studying from now on, Jenna! And you will grow your hair immediately!'

Jenna stared at him in alarm. This wasn't what she had intended to happen at all!

Deep in her heart she knew that her objections to him were well founded. It wasn't just the fact that he was an irrepressible seducer with great streams of women waiting to leap into his beds—his arrogance was even more breathtaking than she had remembered!

But then she had never openly opposed him before.

Imagine what kind of autocratic and overbearing husband he would make! Worse than in her very worst nightmares.

She had hoped that it wouldn't come to this, but she knew she had no choice. There was one thing and one thing only which would guarantee her a seat on the very next plane out of Quador.

Her voice was remarkably steady as she said, 'But I can't marry you, Rashid. It…it wouldn't be fair.'

The black eyes glittered with interest. 'Oh?'

She swallowed, and now her voice was not so steady. 'B-because I am no longer fit to be your wife,' she breathed. 'You see, I have already taken a lover before you, Rashid. I am no longer pure. And therefore I cannot marry you.'

CHAPTER FOUR

HELL broke loose.

Rashid harshly uttered a Quadorian curse, then added a few more in English and French and Spanish to really get the message home. Then he strode over to Jenna, his face a livid picture of dark fury, and the chaperon sprang to her feet in alarm.

'Excellency!'

'Silence!' he thundered autocratically, and the chaperon sat straight down again.

His rage was so potent that he felt consumed by it, as if it had invaded his very blood—but alongside that rage came the desire to beat his fist uselessly against the wall. Jenna! His Jenna—in bed with another man! He wanted to kill him!

'I want his name!'

And then to kill her!

'Well, you can't have it!' Jenna backed away from him, recoiling as much from the expression on his face as from his anger. And if she had thought that she had seen contempt there before, then she had been wrong. *This* was contempt—a contempt so blisteringly undiluted that it seemed to sizzle off him in hot and tangible waves.

She forced her stumbling words out with difficulty. 'R-Rashid, I realise that this means that you can't marry me— w-won't *want* to marry me—and I'm sorry if it's ruined all your plans. But I think the best thing is if I just get straight back on the plane to America and—'

'Silence!' he thundered, cutting across her babble with the gunfire shot of his voice. He controlled his breathing with difficulty. He could never remember feeling quite so outraged before. Nor so shocked. With a supreme effort of will he banished the disturbing vision of Jenna lying naked and entangled with another from his mind. His black eyes narrowed, but the gleam that spat from them was like a searchlight. 'Was it Brad?' he questioned softly.

Her eyes widened. 'No!' she gasped.

He nodded. Her reaction had been too instant to be a lie. Instinct told him that. 'Then who?' he pursued, with deadly intent.

She shook her head, wishing that her long hair was back to camouflage her flaming cheeks. 'Rashid, I must go,' she said desperately.

'Not yet,' he contradicted implacably, and traced a thoughtful forefinger along the shadowed jut of his chin.

He did not speak for a moment, and when he did his words startled her. 'It is inconceivable that you leave Quador without first seeing your father,' he murmured. 'And you really need to freshen up before you do so.' His eyes swept over her disparagingly. 'Don't you?'

Was he really letting her off so lightly? Jenna let out an inaudible sigh of relief. Maybe she had just unwittingly provided the answer to his unspoken wishes. She had let him off the hook and he could continue his playboy activities to his heart's content—without the prospect of a jealous wife watching his every move.

And he did have a point. She had come straight here after a long flight, directly into the heat of the Quador day. She was hot and she was sticky. Once she bathed and made herself respectable she could visit her father.

She shuddered. Would Rashid tell him? She met the coldness of his eyes and her tongue snaked out in a vain attempt to

moisten her dry lips. She saw his eyes darken in angry response.
'Yes,' she said quietly. 'I would like to bathe and change, and
then I will be gone from your life for ever.'

His smile was cruel. How naive she was if she thought that
she could drop a bombshell like that and simply walk away
from the devastation she had caused! But he merely nodded his
head. 'Very well, Jenna,' he agreed equably. 'Your chaperon
will show you to a private set of apartments, and you will make
use of them as you please.'

Swallowing nervously, she nodded. In truth, she had not
expected his anger to subside so quickly. She had thought that
his pride would be offended more than anything—and didn't
it almost *hurt* that he now seemed to be accepting the situation
with apparent calm? Maybe Rashid was more modern and
more tolerant than she had imagined him to be.

But one sneaking look at the unyielding face told her not to
push her luck, and to get out of there before he changed his mind.

He barked out an instruction and the chaperon nodded, beck-
oning Jenna to follow her.

Unseeingly, she left the State Rooms and walked in the foot-
steps of the older woman through a maze of palace corridors,
her heart pounding painfully with relief and an aching sense of
regret for what could now never be. It wasn't until she was
safely inside a dim, cool bedchamber, where her one suitcase
lay unopened on the bed, that her pulse began to die down to
something approaching normality.

'You wish that I should stay and assist you?' asked the
chaperon, but Jenna shook her head.

She needed solitude to get her jumbled thoughts and
emotions in some kind of order. She needed to compose herself
and present a calm façade to her father—and she certainly
couldn't begin to do that if she had an audience. Particularly
an audience with such curious eyes. She shook her head.
'Thank you, but, no. I am used to managing on my own.'

Once the woman had quietly closed the door behind her Jenna

sank with trembling knees onto the low, wide divan on which most high-born Quadors slept, and buried her face in her hands.

If she lived to be a hundred she would never forget that look of haunted disillusion which had fired Rashid's face, so that for a moment he had resembled the devil himself. And she found herself remembering with poignant longing the expression of indulgent tenderness with which he'd used to look at her, so very long ago.

But it was too late for that now. She had sealed her fate with her words, and Rashid would never forgive her. She must just pray that he would be reasonable enough never to repeat what she had told him to her dear father.

She forced herself into action. The sooner she acted, the sooner she could be out of here. She filled the deep circular bath with water and oils scented with jasmine, and stripped off her jeans and her silky top. She threw them on the bed, together with her underwear.

Then she opened the suitcase and pulled from it a traditional Quador outfit, her breath escaping in a shuddering sigh as she laid it carefully on the bed.

The soft, silken robes brought back memories of happier times. In a way she had missed their filmy respectability—the long flowing tunic and the wide trousers worn beneath. A woman could feel like a real woman when concealed in the soft, sensual caress of silk.

She bit her lip as she lowered her body into the bath and closed her eyes.

She lay there for long, timeless moments, until lethargy began to seep into her limbs, and then she washed herself with the delicious scented soap and wrapped herself in a towel. She walked back into the bedchamber to find the room filled with an unexpected presence.

A dark, powerful and brooding figure awaited her, and her heart very nearly stopped.

'R-Rashid,' she stumbled foolishly. 'W-what on earth are

you doing here?' But the look in his eyes told its own story, and her heart picked up its beat again as she shrank from the ebony blaze of his eyes.

He had come here to gather facts, or at least that was what he had convinced himself during his furious march through the palace. He had intended to do nothing more than tell her that the thought of her with another man had tainted his view of her for ever. But one sight of her curved and slender body, even the boyish haircut, had driven away reason and left him with nothing but the insistent clamouring of his senses. He was on fire with a need that consumed him.

'I'll leave why I'm here to your own imagination, Jenna,' he said, his voice menacingly soft.

To think that all the while he had been rejecting Chantal's sensual invitation Jenna had been cavorting with some unknown man on the other side of the world! The rage burned so bright within him that he felt he might explode with it.

'And I am sure it is a very vivid imagination these days, is it not? Has your American lover taught you much?' Dark eyebrows were arched in arrogant and erotic query. 'Perhaps your new-found knowledge is such that you would like to share it with me?'

She understood his meaning instantly. 'S-stop it!' she gasped, but she was speaking as much to her own body as to the sexual predator who stood so tense with expectation beside the divan.

What was happening to her?

Because, somehow, the way that he was looking at her with a mixture of desire and contempt was igniting forbidden dreams that she had thought long-vanished.

A cruel smile curved his delicious lips. 'Stop what?' he questioned, almost conversationally. 'I'm merely elaborating on what you have just told me—giving you the opportunity to demonstrate your *liberation*!' He spat the last word out as if it were poison.

'I think you'd better go, Rashid,' she said in a low voice. She dropped her gaze from his so that he wouldn't see the hot, answering hunger in her eyes, which was making her breasts tingle so intensely that it was a sensation close to exquisite pain. 'I'd like to get dressed now.'

The smile became even more cruel. 'But that would oppose the wishes of your Ruler, Jenna.'

She lifted her eyes in horrified and excited understanding. 'You can't mean—'

'Oh, but I can. I do not wish to see you dressed. On the contrary—your naked body is all I desire. I want you, Jenna—and I want you now. For too long I have played the assiduous gentleman around you. Fool! When all the time…'

He began to move towards her, and it was so close to all her illicit half-forgotten fantasies that she was frozen there, like a statue waiting to be brought to life by the man she had always desired more than any other.

He was nothing but a breath away now, all dark and golden stealth, muskily rapacious. 'If I had but known…' he continued, and reached his hand out to run his fingertips over the long, bare line of her neck, feeling it tremble in response. 'If I had but known that you were in need of a man's body, then I should have oh, so willingly complied with your wishes.'

'G-go away,' she said helplessly.

His voice deepened as he saw her body sway instinctively towards his. 'But you don't want me to. You want me, Jenna. You always did. And now you always will. You will ache with the memory of what you have thrown away for the rest of your days. That will be my curse on you!'

He pulled the towel away from her unprotesting fingers, and as it fell redundantly to the ground he sucked in a raw breath of longing as she stood naked before him, her body more beautiful than he had dreamt of, even in his wildest dreams.

Her skin gleamed as if of gold, with dark and secret shadows, and the lush swell of her breasts was tipped with dark rose. He sucked in a shuddering breath as he felt his body jerk into life.

'May the desert always bloom!' he groaned thickly, and pulled her urgently into his arms to kiss her, more excited than he had ever been in his life.

Melded tightly against him, Jenna could feel every lean, hard contour of his body through his silken robes, even while his mouth worked its predictable magic, and then she was lost from all sane thought. Many times she had imagined a kiss like this, and yet the reality blew the fantasy away in meaningless little pieces.

'R-Rashid,' she whispered shakily, lacing her fingers possessively in his hair, as she had wanted to do for as long as she had been a woman.

He groaned again as he reached down to cup one breast, feeling its ripe, warm weight nestling in the palm of his hand while his thumb teased the hardening nub with an expertise which had her almost fainting. 'Rashid, what?' he questioned unsteadily. 'Rashid, make love to me? Rashid, join me to your body? Is that what you want, Jenna?'

May God forgive her—because that was *exactly* what she wanted! She gave no answer, merely a fraught little whimper of assent, because now his hand was splayed possessively over the slight swell of her belly and was moving down between her thighs. She should have felt frightened, but all she felt was a deep, almost unbearable sensation of longing.

And then he found her, touched her where she was filled with heat, and she bucked with unexpected pleasure as the drift of his fingertip filled her with a curling sense of warmth which made her knees buckle.

He was famous for his restraint. For his ability to pleasure a woman until she could be pleasured no more. Then and only then would he take his own release. But this time there were no thoughts of restraint or finesse or of demonstration of his consummate skill as a lover. This time he would not wait. He groaned again as he tugged at the silken tie of his trousers. *Could* not wait.

Somehow she had fallen backwards onto the bed, on top of her discarded clothes which had been lying there, but none of that seemed to matter. Nothing mattered other than the sight of her dark and golden and fiercely aroused lover as he prepared to straddle her, and a sigh caught painfully in her throat.

Rashid! Her beautiful, beloved Rashid! Hers, but never really hers. Not now. Only this once. She felt the threat of tears pricking at her eyes. She wanted him. Needed him. She always had done. And just for once she would taste the pleasures of paradise in his arms. She opened her eyes and her arms to him in silent invitation though her heart felt as if it was breaking.

For with that look of raw, ill-concealed passion on his face it was so very easy to imagine that she loved him still. She made a little moan of regret and longing, and her fingertips met the rasp of his shadowed chin. He bent his head to kiss her again, and that kiss swept her away into a world that she could barely believe existed.

He moved over her, so aroused that he could barely contain himself. What had she done to him? This vixen! This desert cat! This wicked, wanton and unknown Jenna who had taken another to her bed! He lifted his mouth away from hers and bent his head to briefly suckle her breast, felt the knife-edge of bitterness as he thought of what she had thrown away. She could have suckled his baby, he thought. That joy could have been hers. And his.

But then his thoughts were overtaken by a need to possess her. A need so strong and so urgent that he was eaten up by it. Her eyes were wide and her lips were parted in gleaming invitation as he entered her.

And when she let out a stifled cry he thought at first it was because he was so big inside her. By the desert flower, he had never *felt* so big! But something warned him that this was not all as it seemed. The little tremor as her nails bit into his shoulders—as if what was happening was new to her.

He stared down at her in disbelief, watching the tears begin to slide from beneath the corners of her tightly closed eyes, and it hit him like a body-blow just what was happening.

He tried to stop himself, but it was too late for that—far too late. He felt the slow shuddering of an orgasm so deep and intense and earth-shattering that he thought he might die at that very moment, and be happy to die that way.

For a moment the world lost meaning as it shifted out of focus, and then reality began to creep back, like the first faint sun after the winter freeze.

He stifled a groan, and when he had stilled he withdrew from her as gently as he could. But he did not need to see the scarlet flowering which had spread over the clothes and divan like new blossom. He had guessed for himself.

He caught her against his bare chest. But she was stiff and unmoving in his arms as the words caught in his throat like dust and his heart pounded with something very close to pain.

'You were a virgin,' he said flatly.

CHAPTER FIVE

JENNA didn't answer for a moment, but when she opened her eyes
it was to surprise an expression of something approaching sorrow
in his own. Moving out of his embrace, she reached for the huge
towel which lay beside the bed and cuddled it over her protec-
tively, though its warmth did little to take the edge off her feeling
of naked exposure and her teeth began to chatter violently.

'*Weren't* you, Jenna?' he demanded again, but this time his
voice was gentler. 'A virgin?'

'Y-yes,' she stumbled.

'You lied to me,' he said, but it was less an accusation and
more as though he was trying to work out some kind of insolu-
ble calculation.

She bit down on her lip. 'Yes, again.'

There was a heartbeat of a pause. 'But I don't understand.'
His voice sounded dazed. 'I don't understand why.'

It was the closest she had ever heard to Rashid admitting
confusion. She opened her eyes and wished that she hadn't, for
he was lying on his side, leaning on his elbow with his chin
resting on his hand. And, although his eyes burned into her with
their jet-dark question, he seemed thoroughly unselfconscious
in his nakedness.

His body was burnished gold by the sunlight which filtered
in through the shutters, as if he had been moulded from some
precious metal. It was a very, very beautiful body, thought Jenna.

But it had not brought her pleasure, she reminded herself achingly—and now it never would.

'Why, Jenna?' he persisted, and his eyes narrowed as he saw the sudden tremble of her lips. He who had never failed a woman had failed this one!

She shook her head. 'I can't,' she whispered. 'I'm not having this conversation now. Not here. Like this.' Beneath the towel she felt more vulnerable still, worried that he might touch her again—and even more stupidly worried that he would not. How had this unthinkable situation come about? 'I'd l-like to get dressed, please.'

He narrowed his eyes, and then nodded. 'Go and get dressed, then,' he said quietly. 'But I'm not going anywhere.'

She edged him a pleading look as she moved off the bed with as much dignity as she could muster.

But he ignored her silent request. He obviously had no intention of moving. True to his word, he continued to lie there, as lazily indolent as a cat who had just sampled a particularly large saucer of cream. Couldn't he just do the decent thing, and go—and leave her with this terrible sense of regret?

She grabbed her underwear and her silky Quador clothes and, feeling his dark eyes still on her body, moved towards the bathroom, where she defiantly turned the key in the door very loudly.

She showered for a long time, washing every last musky trace of his masculine scent from her body, and then she slipped on the robes, which were coloured palest blue, and went back into the room, expecting—no, hoping—that he would be gone.

But he had not gone. Of course he hadn't.

Some time during her shower he had put his own robes back on, and now he was sprawled, silent and watchful, on one of the long, low couches which lay beneath the window.

His lashes concealed the expression in his shuttered eyes, and his face had never looked more impossibly remote as he followed her movements.

Rashid watched her. Her body was completely and decently covered now, but she still exuded an irresistible sensuality. A sensuality which had made him weak as he had never been weak before!

His mouth tightened. 'I think you owe me some kind of explanation, Jenna.'

'I owe you nothing!' she retorted hotly. Not now. She had paid her dues in full.

A glimmer of humour—the very first she had seen since she had walked into his palace that day—briefly softened the hard, dark eyes. 'You like to fight with me, don't you?' he observed softly.

She shook her head. 'No one ever fights with you.'

'You do,' he contradicted. 'Jenna.' His deep voice lingered on the syllables and made it sound like an erotic entreaty. 'Why did you tell me that you had had a lover when it is now self-evident that there has been no one?'

Except for you, she thought, with sad bitterness. And in the end she had blown it, so caught up with nerves as he had entered her that she had known no pleasure at all.

'Do you really need to know?' she asked wearily.

'Yes.'

She guessed that there was no point in evading this particular issue. What Rashid wanted, Rashid generally got— and why shouldn't he know the truth?

'It was a last desperate attempt to get out of marrying you,' she said.

He frowned as if had misheard her. '*Desperate?*' he echoed incredulously. 'You would go to such lengths not to marry me?'

'That's right.' She nodded her head, spurred on by a determination that he should know the strength of her resolve. 'I don't want to marry you, be your wife. I told you that repeatedly, Rashid but, as usual, you wouldn't listen! You ordered me over here in spite of my objections. You want your own sweet way and you're determined to get it—just like you always do!'

'You flatter me, Jenna,' he said sarcastically.

'No, I don't—and what is more I never will! Everyone else around here does, and that's half your trouble!'

'Half my trouble?' he repeated dangerously. 'And just what is *that* supposed to mean?'

'That you're arrogant!' she offered.

Black brows were raised in imperious question, as if she had just rather stupidly stated the obvious. 'And?'

His lazy acknowledgement filled her with the courage to tell him what was really going on in her mind. 'And I don't want to marry an arrogant man! I don't want the kind of marriage you are offering me!' she declared. She saw him open his mouth to object, but she shook her head and carried on, not caring that no one *ever* interrupted Rashid! 'When I get married, I want it to be as an equal!'

'An equal?' he repeated faintly.

'Yes! It's an interesting word, isn't it, Rashid? One which I learnt in America! Go and look it up in the dictionary if you really don't understand it!'

'I think you forget yourself!' he said tightly.

'I think not!' she contradicted, and for a moment her vulnerability and sense of regret were washed away by an overwhelming wave of *power*! She was no longer bound by an ancient promise to him! She was free to say exactly as she pleased—and maybe some long-overdue home truths wouldn't go amiss.

'I don't want the kind of marriage your parents had. All Quador men consider it to be their unquestionable right to...' She clamped her lips together firmly.

'To what, Jenna?' he questioned silkily.

As if he needed telling! She shivered with distaste. 'To have mistresses!'

'Mistresses?'

Her pent-up anger and frustration exploded in a fit of temper she hadn't seen in herself for a long, long time. 'Oh, please don't insult my intelligence by playing dumb with me, Rashid!'

she snapped. 'I'm not stupid, and neither is everyone else! I read the newspapers, you know!'

He noticed the ragged breathing which was making her delightful breasts rise up and down quite enticingly, and thought fleetingly that if it had been any other woman he might have taken her straight back to bed there and then.

But then if it had been any other woman he doubted he would have lost all control and left her unsatisfied. A fact which was surely contributing to her magnificent temper—a temper which was making her look fiery and beautiful and almost *formidable*.

Neither men nor women lost their temper in front of him, and in this woman the novelty value was proving highly erotic. But enough was enough; she needed to know who was the master.

'Explain yourself!' he commanded.

Jenna pursed her lips together. 'The whole world knows that you have many women,' she began, and when she saw the slight shrugging of his shoulders her blood pressure threatened to shoot through the ceiling. 'You see! There you go again! Looking as though it's something to be *proud* of!'

'Many men do it,' he commented quietly. 'But mostly they don't have the paparazzi waiting around to capture the moment on film!'

She sucked in a breath of outrage that was directed as much against her *own* behaviour as his. How could she have just let him have sex with her like that? How *could* she?

'Even in yesterday's newspaper in New York I saw that you had been pictured leaving your *friend's* apartment in Paris only the day before!' she raged. 'Cutting it a little fine, weren't you, Rashid? You must have some stamina—to have made love to her and then to come back to repeat the experience with me!'

He was contemplating giving her an insight into the *real* extent of his stamina, when he saw the faint glimmer of tears which had turned her eyes into liquid gold and he cursed aloud. What right had he to make any kind of boast in view of what had just happened?

His voice was as soft as she had ever heard it, and it soothed her as if it were a lullaby. 'I had not intended to make love to you today!' he murmured. 'As my bride, you would have come to me a virgin—and I would have been so much slower with you. So much more gentle! And now I have ruined your first experience of making love.'

'Maybe we both ruined it,' she argued quietly, and then turned her eyes up to his. 'Oh, why did you have to follow me here, Rashid? Why didn't you just leave me alone?'

Not follow her? Rashid shook his head. His anger and his desire for her had reached a point of total combustion that could not have been denied. He hadn't asked himself what had guided him so inexorably towards her room because he had been eaten up with a gnawing kind of jealousy which had blinded him to all thought and reason.

Until he had walked into this bedchamber and seen her wrapped into nothing but a towel. And then a primitive hunger had taken over completely.

'But I could not let you go just like that,' he declared heatedly.

'Why not?'

'And let you take your leave of me with those your final words?' His question was incredulous. 'That you, as my betrothed, had taken another lover?'

She bit back the obvious remark that he had not *acted* like her betrothed for the past few years—that might smack of desperation of a different kind. And, whatever else happened today, Rashid would remember her as having some kind of innate pride.

'But there remains a question, Jenna,' he continued quietly. His deep voice sounded reflective, though the hooded black eyes told her precisely nothing of his true feelings. 'Just what do we do next?'

She stared at him, then shrugged. 'As planned,' she said steadily, 'I would like a car to take me to my father's house, please.'

His lips compressed together and he threw her a look of impatience. 'As if this had never happened?'

'I think that is probably best, under the circumstances.'

'Best?' He gave a short, hollow laugh, and then spoke in a low, urgent tone. 'I think that you must be talking out of the back of your head—as you say in America—if you think that this matter can now be forgotten.'

There was a steely determination underpinning his voice which made her regard him with wary eyes. 'Just what do you mean by that, Rashid?' she whispered.

'I have taken your honour,' he said simply. 'Taken it in a way which grieves me bitterly to think of, and there is a price to be paid for that action.'

A price to be paid. He made it sound as if she were a diamond on sale and up for the highest bidder! 'Don't be ridiculous—'

'I am *never* ridiculous!' he lashed back, and then drew a deep, laboured breath. 'Jenna, you were always intended to be my bride, and that situation will still stand. For how can I send you home to your father, knowing what has happened between us?'

'But he need never know!' she protested, desperate now.

There was an infinitesimal pause. 'Not even if there is a baby on the way?'

Her heart missed a beat. 'A baby?' she whispered hoarsely. 'A *baby*?'

'Well, of *course* there could be a baby!' he exploded impatiently. 'Did you not learn biology at school? I used no form of contraception—and I assume that, as a virgin, you were not protected either!'

The repercussions of what they had just done began to seep into her consciousness, like blood falling onto a stone. And it hurt. 'Do you normally go around taking the risk of impregnating a woman?' she questioned huskily, but her hands were shaking as she imagined him with other women. 'Don't you ever take any responsibility for your lovemaking? Just exactly how many children have you sired—?'

'Jenna!' he thundered. 'I have never, ever spilled my seed into a woman before today! The royal blood of Quador cannot be squandered in such a way!'

'Then what was so different about this time?'

A pulse beat relentlessly at his temple. This he could not answer—except to tell himself that he had been out of control in a way which was completely alien to him and had shown him a side of his nature he had not known existed.

'I have no need to explain my actions to you, Jenna,' he said softly, his eyes as hard and as bright as diamonds. 'But I see no need why the marriage should not now go ahead, as planned.'

'Couldn't we just wait to see if there's a baby on the way?' she beseeched him, knowing in her heart that it was useless, for she recognised that steely determination of old. 'And if there isn't—then couldn't we forget the whole thing?'

He knitted his dark brows together in recognition of her sustained reluctance to be his bride. 'No,' he said flatly. 'We cannot.'

'And if I refuse?'

No one refused him anything. Ever. And whether he got what he wanted by negotiation or coercion—he always won in the end. 'Perhaps you wish that I should inform your father of what has just occurred?'

Warning bells threatened to deafen her, and all she could see was the cold ebony light gleaming from his eyes. 'Rashid! You w-wouldn't d-do that!' she breathed.

'Wouldn't I?' He smiled, but the smile sent a shiver down her spine. 'Oh, I would, Jenna—believe me, I would.' The eyes glittered again. 'And what do you suspect your father would say if I told him?'

Jenna flinched. She knew very well what he would say. And feel. For a Quador man, her father was remarkably in touch with his feelings. Unlike this beast of a lion who sat so mockingly before her now! He would be hurt and angry that she had lost her honour before her marriage. He would feel her to be compromised, as indeed she now was. Quador had such black and white views on a subject like this, she thought. Oh, why had she ever agreed to come back?

'He would make me marry you,' she said woodenly. 'You know he would.'

'Correction. He would be *delighted* for you to marry me. It was always what he wanted.'

She shook her shorn head distractedly. How *could* her father, her sweet gentle father, possibly have agreed to let his daughter be given to this…this…? 'Barbarian!' she spat at him.

He gave a low laugh. 'Oh, how I enjoy your protestations and your defiance, Jenna,' he murmured. 'Your capitulation will make a worthy prize, and you, my sweet, will make a most stimulating partner!'

Defensively, she locked her long fingers around her neck. 'Partner!' she echoed. 'I can't believe you have the nerve to use an expression which describes some kind of *sharing*!'

'We will share many things,' he promised. 'And I will show you how much lovemaking *can* be enjoyed.'

She felt sick.

Sex.

That was what this was all about. Sex and pride and bloodlines and showing her just why he was considered one of the world's greatest lovers. Whatever had happened to the mention of love? But more fool her for wishing for the impossible. It had never been anything other than a business arrangement, and one which he had been happy to avoid for as long as possible.

And when he tired of her, as he inevitably would, what then? For Rashid had known many women in his life—why on earth should he settle for a life of marital fidelity when he was used to variety in the most exotic sense imaginable.

Could she bear it? She imagined some not-too-distant day when he would go abroad on 'business'—but in reality would no doubt be seeking out the experienced warmth of Chantal, or women just like her?

But what else could she do?

She asked herself what alternative she had, tried to imagine the scenario of thwarting his wishes and risking her father's wrath. She thought of Nadia, too—and her loving but clandestine relationship with Brad. What if Rashid followed her back to New York, determined to get his own way, and discovered the truth about her sister and her American lover, as doubtless he would?

He would put a stop to *that*, as well—she wouldn't put it past him. And how could she threaten her dear sister's very obvious happiness because of a bizarre sequence of events which had culminated in her losing her innocence to Rashid?

She had no choice—she was doomed if she did and doomed if she didn't. Her fevered mind could not see any alternative to the one which lay so darkly in front her.

She nodded her head, her face full of resignation, but she did not flinch from his piercing gaze. 'You may take me as your bride, Rashid,' she said, with quiet dignity. 'But you cannot make me a willing partner! And here is something else that might make you change your mind—I will never enjoy sex with you. Never, ever, *ever*!'

By the shafts of his silken-clad thighs he clenched his fists with anger, but only for a moment. He must maintain control—at least until after the ceremony. But it wasn't easy—not with her lips parted in protest and just begging to be kissed.

Resisting the urge to crush her into his arms and to prove her wrong in the most unequivocal way possible, he stood up and towered over her, like some dark, avenging statue.

'You must know that I like nothing better than a challenge, my impetuous Jenna,' he said softly. 'How I will take pleasure in making you take those words back, in having you sigh my name over and over again as you beg for more, and yet more.'

'Never!' she said again, but that look of dark intent in his eyes was difficult to challenge.

'We shall see,' came his cool retort. 'Now, come. Let us go to your father. Let us break the happy news to him.'

CHAPTER SIX

'YOUR Sheikh awaits you, mistress. The wedding draws near.'

The words seemed to come at her from a long way away, and Jenna forced herself back into the present from out of the wistful thoughts which had occupied her mind for much of the last week. And one thought alone had dominated.

There was to be no baby.

The discovery had not surprised her, for physically she had not felt any different—and surely she would have felt profoundly and completely different if Rashid's child had been growing inside her womb?

But she had been unprepared for the primitive swamping of despondency when she had learned that she would not start her married life as a pregnant woman. At least a baby would have given her some reason for being. Some *reason* for being married to a man who did not love her.

She had spent sleepless nights weeping silently into her pillow as she mourned something which all common-sense told her was the best thing which could have happened.

Yet Rashid, too, had not reacted as she might have expected. There had been none of the expected exultation and relief. She had quietly told him and he had taken the news in silence, his dark eyes hooded, and then he had nodded his dark head.

'It is as destiny wills it,' he had said, his voice sounding cold and toneless.

Yet wouldn't a pregnancy have reassured him that his all-important bloodline would continue? Wasn't her fertility the most vital aspect of this union?

'Mistress,' said her lady-in-waiting again. 'Your Sheikh awaits you.'

Jenna stared into the floor-length mirror as if scarcely believing the image which was projected back at her.

She did indeed look fit for a king!

She wore a heavy gold satin gown, richly and lavishly studded with jewels, which weighed almost as much as she did. Her hair had grown a little in the weeks leading up to the wedding. Rashid had not demanded it—he had not needed to. She had seen the unmistakable glitter of disapproval every time those dark eyes had surveyed her long, bare neck. Quador women wore their hair long—and now that she was the public representative of those women she would have to do the same. And, in truth, she had missed the weight and the silken caress of her waist-length locks.

Today, her hair was adorned with tiny jewelled clips—and every jewel was the real McCoy. She was wearing a king's ransom on her head!

Diamonds. Sapphires. Rubies and emeralds. All gleamed with multi-coloured splendour—dazzling and bright—making her face look pale by comparison. Her amber eyes glittered back at her, huge and haunted and distracted, and the fingers which were clasped together by the heavily encrusted belt which lay low over her hips were trembling like the first leaves of spring.

And no wonder. For the day she had so been dreading had finally arrived.

Her wedding day.

For the past forty-eight hours world leaders had been flying into Riocard, as had film stars and models and moguls—rich and powerful friends and acquaintances of the man who seemed like a cold-faced stranger to her.

The world's press were camped along the wedding route and glossy magazines from just about every country in the world had been sent to cover the 'wedding of the year'. She had received countless requests for interviews, but she had refused them all—for surely perceptive journalists would easily be able to detect her uncertainty. And her insecurity about the future.

From outside she could hear the sounds of the jubilant crowds lining the main streets of Riocard, in the hope of catching a glimpse of their Sheikh's bride as she travelled with her father to the palace for the ceremony which would make them man and wife.

Rashid's wife.

Jenna shivered, trying not to think about what lay ahead. First there was the ceremony itself—with all the eyes of Quador on her, along with the eyes of the world. They would be expecting a bride who was rapturous with joy at the thought of marrying one of the world's most eligible bachelors.

She allowed herself a wry smile. If only they knew! What would they say if they discovered that she and Rashid had barely spoken a word to each other in the intervening weeks— let alone loving words. They had discussed only what had been absolutely necessary.

Only once, with her father in proud attendance, had she summoned up the courage to ask Rashid about what her future 'role' as his wife would entail.

And Rashid had narrowed his black eyes and fixed her with a look of bemused tolerance.

'Why, Jenna,' he had responded softly, 'your role is to support your Sheikh.'

'But I have been studying law, Rashid,' she had pointed out. 'Could that not be put to some use?'

Her father had shaken his head and smiled. 'Your role as consort will leave you little spare time, Jenna.'

And Rashid, murmuring his agreement, had risen, his silken robes flowing, signalling that the discussion had come to an end.

The chaperons had put paid to all but the most formal communication between them. Like questions from Rashid about her preferences for the wedding feast—and, on one memorable occasion, a drawled query about where she would care to spend the honeymoon.

As far away from you as possible, her eyes had said, but she had given him a sarcastically submissive smile. 'That choice must be yours, O Sheikh,' she had answered softly, and had seen his mouth tighten in response. 'Perhaps Paris?' she had questioned, with mock innocence. 'I believe that the Sheikh knows the city *very* well?'

He had drummed his long fingers on the exquisite inlaid desk at which he'd sat, and his dark eyes had frosted her a look of pure ice.

'Perhaps we should stay right here in Quador,' he had murmured in a little-spoken Quadorian dialect which he knew full well that she alone in the room understood. 'After all—one bed is pretty much the same as any other!'

Jenna shivered again. After the wedding and the feast would come the wedding night itself, and that was the part she was dreading most. She had declared that she would not respond to him, that she would tolerate his caresses but not enjoy them. Yet over the last few headachy days she had begun to wonder whether she would have the resolve to withstand his raw and heated sensuality.

But even if she didn't there was no guarantee that she would enjoy it—not if that single, frantic bout in the bedchamber was anything to go by. And if she was worried that Rashid would be unable to resist the lure of mistresses past, present and maybe future—then she was almost certain that a frigid wife would send him running straight to their beds.

She stared into the mirror one last time and fixed a practised smile onto her lips. She would go forward towards her future, and put her trust in fate.

There was little else in which she could trust.

* * *

Rashid stood with narrowed eyes as he surveyed the horizon for the first sign of her carriage.

'Exalted One?'

Rashid didn't move, his heart unaccustomedly heavy. 'What is it, Abdullah?'

'The woman—Chantal—she has been leaving messages for you, O Sheikh.'

Rashid *did* turn round then, his narrowed eyes growing even more flinty than usual. 'You dare to speak to me of such matters on the day of my wedding?'

'I merely pass on messages, Sheikh, just as I have always done.'

'Then pass them on no longer,' said Rashid tonelessly. 'I instructed Chantal not to contact me. She knows that I am a man of my word.'

'Indeed.' Abdullah nodded.

'Did she choose one of the pieces of jewellery I left?' Rashid enquired, as an afterthought.

Abdullah shifted uncomfortably. 'She said that making a choice was impossible, Excellency.'

'And?'

'She kept them all.'

For a moment the Sheikh was still, and then he smiled a cynical smile. 'So be it,' he murmured. 'Then there is nothing more to be said.' He stilled once more as bells began pealing loudly in the palace courtyard. 'She is here,' he breathed. 'Jenna has come.'

Moving stiffly in the heavy wedding gown, and surrounded by her women-in-waiting, Jenna made her way slowly towards the Throne Room, where Rashid awaited her.

And with her first glimpse of him a small, instinctive sigh escaped from her lips—for he looked as perfect as it was surely possible for any man to look.

He wore robes of silver, far plainer than her own, and from his belt hung the priceless Quador sword which was never far from his side. He turned around and his carved face was stern, but for one brief moment the dark eyes softened as he bowed his head with imperial grace.

He had got what he wanted, she thought as she moved across the crowded ornate room to his side—while her own wishes had been cast aside in the tide of his arrogant determination.

'You look exquisite,' he murmured.

And so did he. She bowed her own head, because, stupidly, the appreciative blaze from the black eyes had made it seem like the most wonderful compliment she had ever received. A tiny morsel thrown to a starving dog. 'Thank you.'

The ceremony passed in a blur. Ancient words were spoken. Heavy crowns placed upon their heads. The wedding vows were quietly made—vows of love and endurance and fidelity. And, staring into the onyx glitter of his eyes, Jenna found the words all too simple to say. A wave of sadness rocked her, for she *had* loved him with all her heart, and deep down she suspected that she still could.

But as Rashid echoed her words of undying fidelity they sounded hollow and empty in her ears.

He placed a circlet of rubies on her finger as the words of the ceremony echoed around the high-vaulted Throne Room.

They were married. Man and wife. Jenna felt faint as her eyes were drawn to a sudden cloud-like spectacle outside the window—the blur of wings as a thousand white doves were released into the skies.

How free they looked, she thought wistfully. How carefree.

Rashid felt her tremble beside him as she watched the birds fly away. 'What troubles you, Jenna?' he whispered.

He did. She turned to face him, her brow criss-crossing with concern. 'Will the doves not fly straight into the desert and perish?' she questioned worriedly.

He gave a brief, hard smile. Did she think so badly of him? 'I am not such a barbarian as to condemn such living beauty to death,' he demurred. 'No, they will be carried on the warm thermals to more hospitable climes than Quador. Who knows? They may settle where no dove has ever settled before—a new beginning for them as well as for us, sweet Jenna.'

Jenna suppressed a sigh of longing. He could make his words sound like poetry—if only he meant them!

After the wedding came the feast in the Banqueting Hall, and there were murmurs of approval from the glittering assembly as they looked around, observing for themselves the vast wealth of Quador.

Meats were turning on vast spits. Huge bowls of jewel-bright and glistening fruits tempted the eye and the palate. But Jenna had little appetite for food and she felt dazed in the spotlight of so many curious stares.

She drank some strong wine from one of the carved golden goblets, and the fiery liquid burned into her stomach, filling her with a welcome warmth.

Rashid bent his head to her ear. 'And now we must move into the Grand Ballroom, my sweet bride,' he murmured softly. 'They are awaiting our first dance.'

'Duty calls,' she responded with a nod of her head, and the thumping in her head only increased as she saw him frown.

A string quartet had been flown in from New York and they played quietly in one corner of the ballroom as Jenna moved into her new husband's arms.

For a moment she saw the envious eyes of an international starlet fixed on them—a woman whose tiny, glittering dress showed off every perfect inch of her body. And then she was aware of nothing other than the scent of the man who was now her husband, and the lean, hard body beneath the fine silk he wore.

He touched his lips to her ear, and she shivered. 'You are pale, Jenna mine,' he observed. 'Has your wedding day not pleased you?'

She lifted her head up, dazzled by the piercing black light from his eyes. 'It has all been so…bewildering,' she said truthfully. 'I hadn't thought…hadn't realised just what a big show it was going to be.'

His eyes narrowed. *'Show?'* he questioned, his voice sultry, but underlaid with a faint note of impatience. 'The trappings are necessary, but a wedding is a wedding is a wedding—and tonight I will show you just how fulfilling married life can be.'

She quickly turned her face into his shoulder again, for fear that he should see the foreboding in her eyes.

Rashid felt the stiff tension in her body, but kept his face relaxed, knowing that every eye in the room was on them, and that every nuance would be observed and reported back.

What had happened to the easy warmth which had once flowed like honey between them? Should he ever have let her leave? Was he to blame for this frosty state of impasse? He allowed himself a small sigh. He bitterly regretted the way he had taken her, with such fervour and such little consideration for her innocence. He had believed her rash declaration. Had thought that she was a woman of sexual experience—and oh, how wrong he had been.

He drifted his mouth to the jewelled hair, remembering her angry words to him. So she would not enjoy sex! He smiled. Let her say that when the morning sun washed its first golden rays over their naked bodies!

It was almost eight by the time they took their leave of their guests. They were to spend that night in the Palace, before travelling to the west of Quador the following day, where Rashid had a hunting lodge and only a bare skeleton of servants.

They would be almost alone, she realised—or as alone as a man in his position could ever be.

'Come now, Jenna,' he said softly, and, taking her hand, he led her past the clapping guests towards his quarters. 'Let the wedding night begin.'

It was a journey which seemed to take for ever, and all Jenna was aware of was the pounding of her heart and the powerful presence of the silver-clad Sheikh by her side as they mounted the marble stairs.

At last he drew her inside the door of a room which was indisputably the room of the Ruler. The floors were also of marble, and priceless paintings of his ancestors clothed the walls. At the far end, looking almost a car journey away, stood the wide, low divan—hung with embroidered canopies, a coverlet of pure gold silk spread smoothly across its surface.

He could feel her trembling as he turned her to face him, and he stared down for a long moment into her heart-shaped upturned face.

'Do not be afraid, Jenna,' he murmured. 'For you have nothing to fear.'

Save for her own shortcomings and being at the mercy of a man who knew everything there was to know about the art of love, while she knew almost nothing.

He began to draw the tiny jewelled clips from her hair almost absently, and placed them on an inlaid table. The style was far less severe now, he thought, and framed her face with soft waves of silky golden-brown.

He bent his lips to hers and for a moment she tensed, but the brush of his mouth was as light and as drifting as a feather, and it was barely there before it was gone again.

Rashid sighed. 'You look as though you are just about to enter the lion's den,' he observed.

She felt a smile wobble its way across her mouth. 'How very appropriate,' she observed drily. 'Since you are known as the Lion of the Desert!'

He laughed, and the white teeth gleamed in such contrast against the olive skin, and Jenna was startled by how long it had been since she had seen him laugh like that.

He tipped her chin upwards and looked down into her eyes. 'You are tired,' he commented wryly, and took her hand to lead her to the divan. 'Come, let me undress you, and then you shall sleep.'

'Sleep, Rashid?' she echoed disbelievingly, and saw him knit the dark brows together.

'Believe it or not, I am not the barbarian you once called me,' he responded coolly. 'Perhaps you have reason to fear my advances—presumably that is why you vowed never to enjoy sex. I will not force myself upon you, and neither will I beg you, Jenna,' he asserted softly. 'You will come to me willing, or you will not come at all. There will be no demands made on you which you do not wish to fulfil.'

Now she felt utterly confused. He began to deftly undo all the tiny buttons which adorned the front of her wedding gown, and his words set up a nagging feeling of doubt and insecurity. What did he mean? It was his right as her Sheikh and her husband to consummate the marriage, surely?

She threw him a look of challenge. 'I feel as though I could sleep for a week,' she admitted.

'Then so be it.' The last of the buttons was freed and he helped her step from the heavy dress, sucking in an instinctive breath as he saw what she was wearing. For the gown might be traditional Quadorian, but the undergarments beneath were sheer Hollywood.

An underwired bra in fine gold lace—which curved her breasts upwards into two exquisitely pale mounds—and an outrageous G-string in matching material which emphasised the darker triangular shadowing which blurred so tantalisingly before his eyes.

'Who bought these?' he questioned unsteadily.

She lifted her eyes to his. 'My ladies-in-waiting instructed me to be beautiful for my wedding night. I sent to…to… America for them.'

And beautiful she most certainly was—but the haunted look in her eyes was no spur to making love to her. He turned away abruptly, afraid that the reined-in control he could feel tightening his face would only add to her trepidation.

'Get into bed,' he said, more harshly than he had intended, and went to stand by the window.

She did as he instructed, and some of her apprehensiveness

was relieved the moment her body sank into the welcome softness of the divan. She stretched beneath the coverlet, and the tension began to seep away.

She was here and she was Rashid's wife, waiting in his bed, and the doubts which had nagged her all day suddenly crystallised into certainty. Had he not just been gentle and considerate with her? And would she not fulfil her own worst fears if she held him at arm's length? Wouldn't that almost certainly drive him into the arms of another woman?

From beneath her long lashes, she stole a look at him. His lean physique exuded the same kind of restrained power as a caged tiger, and a tiny throb of aching warmth made her limbs feel suddenly fluid.

'Rashid?' she questioned tentatively.

He turned around, but his face was so impassive that it appeared almost indifferent.

'I am going to take a shower,' he stated.

Jenna nodded, and swallowed down another doubt. Shouldn't she have bathed herself? Come to her Sheikh scented and shining? For one mad and impetuous moment she opened her mouth, about to offer to wash his back, just like a modern, liberated woman.

Except she must remember that she was not—that her independence had only ever been an illusion. And besides, he had already stalked off into the bathroom and banged the door behind him.

Rashid stripped off his wedding clothes with a grim and ruthless efficiency and turned the shower on full; standing beneath it for long, countless moments.

When he returned, with only some of his ardour dampened by the cool jets of water, she was fast asleep.

CHAPTER SEVEN

JENNA awoke late the next morning, blinking her eyes in confusion as her sleep-befuddled mind struggled to work out exactly where she was, and when she did her eyes flew open.

In Rashid's bed.

His wife!

Slowly she turned her face to the empty space beside her, and saw that the pillow lay as smooth as untouched as it had the night before.

'Fear not, my beauty,' came a mocking voice from what seemed like a long way away, and she narrowed her eyes to look at the far end of the room, where Rashid stood like an imposing statue suddenly brought to life as he began to walk towards her.

He was fully dressed in silken robes of creamy buttermilk, against which his dark and golden looks appeared all the more startling. But his face was hard and impenetrable, with a certain edge to it, and there was nothing of the appearance of the eager groom about him.

Her hand flew to her heart, feeling its wild fluttering as he continued to walk towards the bed. 'Rashid,' she said breathlessly, 'you are up very early.'

He made a small murmur of dissent. 'It is almost ten, Jenna—and soon the sun will be high in the sky. We must make haste for the lodge before that happens.'

She had to know. She *had* to. 'Where did you…where did you—?'

'Sleep?' he interrupted, his dark eyes flashing with cruel humour. 'Why, I slept on the divan beneath the window, Jenna—for fear of disturbing your sleep.'

Beneath the silk coverlet her body trembled, her other hand moving towards her breasts. She was still wearing her fancy bridal underwear, she realised, her cheeks growing pink. She must have fallen asleep without remembering to take it off.

And Rashid had not removed it either—in fact he had not wanted even to share a bed with her. What she had been half-dreading and half-longing for had failed to materialise, and yet the fact gave her not one moment of pleasure. Better that he should have ravished her than treat her this morning with such insulting indifference!

She forced herself to meet the mocking black light of his eyes. 'There was room for two, Rashid,' she said quietly. 'You didn't have to sleep over there and be uncomfortable all night.'

'On the contrary,' he responded coolly. 'It was not in the least bit uncomfortable.' He hadn't achieved much sleep, all the same—but he suspected that it was more than he would have gained if he had subjected himself to the torture of lying beside her sleeping body without touching her.

'Oh. Well, I'm glad you had a good night's sleep,' she said, rather woodenly.

He allowed the faint drift of a smile to glimmer at the corners of his mouth. 'That wasn't what I said at all,' he offered obliquely. 'But you certainly did, didn't you?'

She nodded. 'Yes, I was very tired.'

Or just eager to lose herself in the safety net of sleep? His mouth tightened. 'Now get dressed, Jenna, and we will leave as soon as you are ready.'

She waited until he had left the room and then distractedly

showered and put on silk trousers and a slim-fitting matching tunic, which were more suited to travelling along the bumpy roads to the lodge than one of the more formal and elaborate outfits which comprised her trousseau.

When she went downstairs to where he was breakfasting a sudden dark gleam of approval softened the hard eyes and he motioned for her to come and sit beside him.

He poured her coffee and handed her a dish of fruit, and his hand suddenly reached out to trace the skin beneath her eyes.

'All those dark shadows gone,' he observed quietly.

'Yes.' The shadows beneath her eyes were only being replaced by the shadows in her heart. But the tender gesture disarmed her, and Jenna found herself smiling in response before tucking into the exotic fruits with something approaching her normal appetite.

He refilled her coffee cup and she found herself relaxing. Yet his consideration and his restraint both charmed and alarmed her. This Rashid was more like the Rashid of old, she thought—and that was dangerous. For he was not the same man at all. The Rashid she had loved had been the ideal fantasy man of her dreams. The perfect man and the perfect lover—forsaking all others and loyal only to her.

But the true man had been as much of an illusion as her own hard-fought-for independence. And if a man like Rashid had known many pleasures of the flesh—then how long before he was tempted into tasting them again?

Especially a man who had not even spent his wedding night in the same bed as his wife…

She pushed her cup away and looked up to find him watching her.

'Shall we leave immediately?' he questioned softly.

Jenna nodded. 'As you wish.'

Outside stood a gleaming four-wheel drive, and Jenna's mouth curved into an instinctive smile. 'No ancient Quador chariot, this,' she observed.

'You don't approve?' he murmured.

'Of course I approve! I know only too well how treacherous the unmade roads can be! It's just that in America these vehicles are used on suburban school-runs—I'm sure that many of my friends over there would be surprised to learn that it is also the honeymoon car of the Sheikh and his wife!'

He narrowed his eyes. 'You mean that they wouldn't think it romantic enough?' he mused.

'Possibly.'

His eyes glinted. 'But comfort can be very romantic, Jenna—as you shall discover for yourself when you let me escort you in air-conditioned splendour!'

He was right, it *was* romantic. Beguilingly and misleadingly so.

Closeted together on the back seat, speeding through the sweetly familiar countryside, it felt almost like old times. They passed places where he had taken her riding as a child, and the past somehow became inextricably bound up in the confusing state of the present.

The child in her had dreamed of a moment such as this, and yet the woman she had become seemed less certain of anything than the child had been.

He watched the play of emotions which chased over her face as they drove deeper and deeper into Quador, forcing himself not to take her into his arms and kiss away all the barriers between them. She would come to *him* or not at all, he reminded himself grimly.

'Will you miss America?' he asked suddenly.

She turned to face him. His dark handsome face sent a spear of longing through her, surprised by an unfamiliar look of disquiet there.

She shrugged her shoulders a little. 'I thought I would,' she admitted. 'But this is home—and home occupies a part of your heart that no other place ever can.'

'That is a good start,' he mused. 'For a honeymoon.'

But what kind of honeymoon? she wondered as the car bumped along an unmade track to the hunting lodge she had not visited for years, and a small sigh escaped from her lips.

'What is it?' he questioned.

'I—I'd forgotten how beautiful it was,' she sighed, as the long, low building which stood in the shadow of snow-peaked mountains came into view.

And he had forgotten how beautiful *she* was—even with her magnificent hair all shorn off. He had allowed her perfect profile and those high, delicious cheekbones to fade from the forefront of his mind. He had allowed the two of them to become worlds apart. And now surely they *were* worlds apart?

'It's been a long time,' he agreed. 'Too long since I was here, also.'

'Seriously?' She squinted her eyes to look at him. 'But you used to come up here whenever possible!'

His smile was rueful. 'You think that extended breaks go hand-in-hand with ruling a country the size of Quador?'

'You don't delegate?'

'Delegate?' He gave a short laugh. 'Delegation is a luxury I can seldom afford, Jenna. Being accepted by my people means that my profile always needs to be high.'

'But you *are* accepted by your people!' she said, with sudden passion. 'You know you are, Rashid!'

He smiled. 'Careful! That sounded very nearly like a compliment!'

She laughed back, caught in the dark cross-fire of his eyes. 'Hold your horses—I wouldn't go that far!'

For a moment they shared the compatibility of days gone by, and Rashid felt his heart thunder like the pound of equine hooves. 'Speaking of horses—are you hungry?'

Hungry? How could she be hungry for anything other than the taste of his lips on hers once more? She shook her head. 'No, not a bit. I had a big breakfast. Why?'

'Then shall we ride together, Jenna? As we used to?'

There was a heartbeat of a pause, but she hid her disappointment. 'Yes, Sheikh,' she answered quietly. 'I would like that.'

The driver had come round to open the door of the car. 'Let us go inside and change,' Rashid said, and his voice had deepened.

Shown inside by a delighted servant, Jenna felt a peculiar mixture of relief and disappointment to discover that she had been allocated her own separate room, complete with a large divan and a luxurious *en suite* bathroom. She guessed that Rashid had a mirror image, only larger—and she also guessed that this meant that they could spend nights apart should they wish. She told herself that royal custom decreed it, that it had always been so and that she must just accept it.

And wasn't it easier to slither into her jodhpurs and a long-sleeved white shirt without those mocking black eyes fixed on her—reminding her that in every way that mattered this was not a *real* marriage.

But all her anxieties and fears were washed away when Rashid led her into the stables and she was confronted by the sight of the Arab mare whose golden-brown and gleaming skin did, as Rashid had once commented, so cleverly mimic her own.

For a moment she was speechless, and then she turned to him, her eyes wide and brimming with tears which were not just about the horse. 'Pasha!' she whispered. 'Can it really be so?'

'Of course.' His voice was very soft, but his heart beat strangely as he saw the luminous amber gaze she directed at him. 'Did you think that once you had left for America I would let your father sell her to a stranger?'

Jenna put her arms around the horse and pressed her face close to its warm neck, breathing in the scent of a long-forgotten youth. 'Why, Rashid?'

'Because the horse belongs to you, Jenna, and always shall.' His voice deepened into a sultry caress. 'Just as you shall always belong to me.'

She thought that the words sounded more like a stamp of possession than any declaration of affection, but at least he wasn't seducing her with false promises. Still with her arm draped around the horse's neck, she stared into the irresistible dark glitter of his eyes. She didn't *want* to be only half a wife, she realised.

His words to her came filtering painfully back. He would not beg her, and if she came to him it must be as one who was willing.

Should that moment be now?

But the eyes of the bodyguards who stood discreetly in the shadows of the stables were upon them, and Rashid would not approve of a display of feelings in front of his staff.

Instead, unaided, she swung herself up into the saddle and flashed him a smile of challenge.

'Race you, then,' she said.

And with a small exultant laugh he mounted his own night-dark stallion with the grace of the born horseman. 'Done,' he murmured, and trotted out of the stable before she had time to gather her reins.

'Cheat!' she called after him, but her cry was lost on the desert wind. And suddenly nothing else mattered other than the pounding movement and graceful strength of the animal beneath her. The sand flew up in fine clouds from beneath Pasha's hooves and Jenna gave a whoop of sheer, unadulterated pleasure as she raced to catch her Sheikh up.

With the purity of the desert spread out before them, they rode for hours, but always within sight of the mounted body-guards. Every now and then Rashid made them stop to drink from cool flagons of water, the sweat sheening their skin as they greedily tipped the liquid into their parched throats.

'You look happy now,' observed Rashid. Achingly, he noted a drop of water which had trickled down from her mouth and now fell with an enticing splat onto the shirt which clung to her breasts, and the heat which invaded his veins was hotter than the desert sun.

Not completely happy. But happier. She passed the flagon back to him. 'So do you,' she said softly.

'It's easy to be happy when you are unencumbered by the burdens of state,' he said wryly, with a shrug of his broad shoulders.

'If you're trying to tell me that you'd be more contented as a nomad, living out here all the time—then I would challenge you, Rashid!'

She challenged him in more ways than she would ever know. He shook his head. 'That isn't what I'm saying—I'm just making the observation that a man is the sum of many parts, and that the carefree part of me can rarely be allowed to break free.'

It was odd that he had used that word. *Carefree.* Hadn't she thought the same thing about the doves which had been released on their wedding day?

'Well, it's free enough now,' she observed mischievously. 'So why not make the most of it?' And she galloped off to the sound of his soft laughter.

The sun was sinking in the sky by the time they returned to the lodge, and the mountains had grown mysteriously darker in shades of deepest blue and green.

Jenna was uncomfortably aware of being hot and sticky and covered in dust—but even more aware of being closed in. The vast open space of the desert had guaranteed them a certain freedom and ease, but now they were inside the lodge once more the tension was back.

And how.

Rashid's face had taken on that cool, forbidding mask once more, and his words were almost clipped as he turned to her. 'Dinner will be at eight,' he told her formally. 'I will see you then.' And he turned on his heel as he headed for his own room.

Telling herself that she would *not* be disappointed by his abrupt change in attitude, she took herself off to bathe, then she slept for a while before changing for dinner. Just before eight she arrived in the dining room to find Rashid waiting for her. Her heart sank to see that his face was as darkly enigmatic as before.

It was an informal room compared to its counterpart in the

palace in Riocard, but its relative simplicity did nothing to detract from the magnificent carved table and the equally magnificent chairs. It was unmistakably a royal room, made all the more so by the sight of a brooding Rashid, who was standing by a roaring log fire, for the mountain nights could be bitter.

He watched her as she walked in, all grace and sensuality in a long, white dress whose bodice was embroidered with tiny sprays of jasmine. With her face completely bare of make-up, he thought that he had never seen a woman look more lovely.

Or more untouchable—which was ironic in view of how she had behaved with him the other day. But that passionate and responsive woman seemed like a world away—and, whilst the memory filled him with the constant ache of longing, he could not deny that he was captivated by the first woman in his memory who was not using every feminine wile in the book to seduce him.

But then, why would she? She wouldn't know how to play the games of feminine seduction. She had been a *virgin*, he reminded himself with a bitter pang of guilt.

'Hello, Jenna,' he said softly.

When he looked at her like that—with a mixture of awe and hunger and fascination—she felt both shy and secure, and completely at a loss as to how to handle things. She couldn't just walk straight into his arms, could she? Especially not as a servant was bringing in a steaming platter of Quador chicken and another dish of spicy rice.

'Hello,' she said simply.

'Are you exhausted after your ride?'

She wondered whether that was a leading question. If she said that she was, then wouldn't that give him the excuse to sleep alone again? And anyway, she did not feel in the least bit tired; she felt *alive*, exhilarated—as though anything could happen on this night.

She shook her head. 'Not a bit—I'd forgotten just how relaxing riding could be.' She looked at him from between slitted lashes. 'And you?'

His smile was tight. 'I have never felt less tired in my life,' he said, his voice pure velvet.

It wasn't easy to concentrate on anything other than the dark and proud face, but she made a big effort. Somehow she forced herself to eat something, for she had eaten nothing since breakfast, and to drink the iced juice which was poured for her.

But they chatted like old times, and as some of the apprehension left her body it was replaced by the certainty of what she must now do.

Because it was up to her.

She knew that Rashid had a will of steel—and, much as she suspected that he wanted her, the first move must come from her. Her bitter words could not just be unsaid; she must show him that she was willing to be a wife to him in every sense of the word.

They had finished their coffee and the fire was very low when he lifted his dark head and fixed her with a glittering stare.

'And now, Jenna?' he questioned softly.

This definitely *was* a loaded question. Her lips felt like parchment as she stared into his dark chiselled face.

'I think it is time for bed,' she managed.

He needed to be crystal-clear about her expectations of him. Or her lack of them. 'Alone?'

She shook her head. She would *die* if he left her alone tonight.

'Not alone, Rashid,' she murmured quietly. 'Together.'

CHAPTER EIGHT

HER heart was pounding as he closed the bedroom door, and she thanked heaven that the room was lit only with the soft light of the lamps. She wanted to see him, but not in too much detail, for she was terrified that she would disappoint him and prove as hopeless a lover as she had done before.

He stood in front of her, surveying her with an unmoving face, the ebony glitter of his eyes and the rapid beat of the pulse at his temple the only outward sign of life.

Her lips parted. 'Rashid,' she breathed threadily, hoping that he would not want more than this to signal her assent. He had told her that he would not beg—well, neither would she!

He saw her raise her chin in defiance and he almost smiled at her gesture of pride. But the moment was far too intense for humour or for battles of will. Because the look in her eyes and the way she had whispered his name told him everything he needed to know.

'Come to me, sweet Jenna,' he commanded softly. 'Come to your Sheikh.'

It was only a few steps, but her legs felt so weak that she feared they would not carry her that short distance. And only the fact that he was standing there, his eyes inviting her into his embrace, ensured that she found herself where she most wanted to be.

She gave a little moan as he pulled her against him, and,

catching her face between his hands, bent his head to kiss her in a kiss which was sweet and as potent as strong wine. She felt so dizzy with the sensation of his mouth against her mouth, his tongue flicking an erotic little entry inside, that she barely registered time passing, barely even registered the moment when he slid the zip of her dress down and gently removed it from her body.

The white embroidered dress pooled in a luxurious heap by her feet and she was left in nothing but the extravagant white lace of her lingerie. He made a fierce imprecation beneath his breath as his eyes observed the provocative swell of her breasts, before lifting her into his arms and carrying her across the room like a victor with his trophy, to where the divan awaited them.

'Rashid,' she half protested, but it was a wonderful sensation to be locked in the powerful arms of such a man.

It wasn't until he had lain her down that he looked at her with an expression as close to tenderness as she had ever seen, and her heart came close to melting. Because in that moment she recognised that her love for him burned as strong as it ever had.

'Shall I undress for you now, my sweet Jenna?' he questioned quietly. 'Would you like that?'

The blood thundered in her ears as she nodded, knowing that she would be far too shy to undress him herself. 'Y-yes. Yes, I would.'

With a fluid movement he swept the silken tunic over his head, dropping it carelessly on the floor, enjoying the way the tip of her tongue flicked its way along her lips as his muscular torso was laid bare.

And then he untied the sash of his trousers and heard her tiny gasp as he kicked them away from him.

He saw the startled direction of her eyes, and he looked down at himself and then shrugged. 'You see the effect you have on me, my sweet Jenna?' he mused, but then his voice gentled. 'It will not be as before. I will make you taste pleasure tonight, my sweet desert flower,' he promised softly. 'I will satisfy your each and every need, and when the sun rises in the morning you will have known the rapture and the joy that your beauty and your virtue merits.'

She didn't doubt a word of it, and something in the velvet caress of his voice allayed her fears, so that when he came to join her on the divan she wrapped her arms around him tightly, with greedy possession.

He laughed softly as she pressed her breasts so eagerly against his hair-roughened chest, and he kissed the top of her head before gently pressing her back against the bed.

'Stay still,' he commanded, and then his eyes glittered with irresistible challenge. 'If you are able.'

She stared at him in confusion, but by then he had taken her bra off, was bending his mouth to her nipple, and she felt such intense pleasure flooding through her as his lips closed around it that she moaned his name aloud.

'Rashid?'

'Shh,' he whispered against the tightened nub, and licked it as luxuriously as he would a lollipop.

And while he suckled her he began taking off her lace panties, very, very slowly, sliding them indolently down over her knees.

'Rashid!' she moaned, for the panties were off and she was as naked as he was, and now he was drifting his fingertips up inside her leg to find the silky flesh of her inner thigh.

'Shh,' he said again, only now his fingertip was no longer on her leg, but touching her very intimately indeed, teasing and moving against the moist skin in a way which was making it impossible for her not to move her hips in a silent yet agonised plea for she knew not what.

'Rashid,' she whispered in mystification. 'What is this?'

He tiptoed the finger with precision against her honeyed flesh and felt her shudder helplessly in response. 'Mmmmm?'

The powerful sensation which was creeping inexorably through her veins made her forget the question she had been asking, and she opened her eyes distractedly to find him watching her. And still he touched her, only now the movement had quickened, and he was bending his head to kiss her…and she felt as though she was going to die…to die or to…

It came upon her with the shock and force of a thunderbolt, her back arching and her legs splaying indolently as wave upon wave of pleasure rocked through her and she moaned against his mouth.

And only when she was completely still did he stop kissing her and raise his head to look down at her, a slow smile lifting his mouth as he saw her look of dreamy contentment, the flush of roses to her cheeks.

She smiled back at him. 'I liked that,' she said shyly.

He laughed with pleasure. 'Yes, I know you did. But that was only the very beginning, my sweet Jenna. There are many, many variations on the act of love, and I intend to explore each and every one with you.'

Just for a moment she felt her heart sink as she thought of all the other women he had known, but ruthlessly she pushed the thought away.

He was her Sheikh and her husband and she was here in his bed—far better to seize the moment and enjoy it than to sadden herself with regrets and hopeless longings for words of love.

He stroked away a damp strand of hair from where it had been glued to her cheek. 'Shall I make you pregnant, Jenna? Would you like that?'

Her heart thudded with disappointment against her ribcage. Was that all part of the deal—a son and heir just as soon as possible? 'W-would you?'

He shook his head. 'Pregnancy changes a woman's whole life. It is not for the man to decide.'

'Well, then I would like to wait for a while,' she ventured. 'To give ourselves a chance to know one another.'

'Mmmm.' He leaned over and pulled a packet of condoms from a secret drawer in the inlaid locker, then slanted her a lazy smile. 'Starting tonight.'

It wasn't what she had meant, but her doubts were soon for-gotten because Rashid had begun to make love to her, and who on earth could think at a time like that?

CHAPTER NINE

'RASHID?'

Rashid paused in the act of tying his sash and looked over at where Jenna lay, her naked body so golden against the snow-white of the sheet. It wasn't easy being married to her—he never wanted to get out of bed in the mornings!

He raised his dark brows quizzically. 'Yes, my sweet?'

She squinted at her watch. 'You are up very early. Are you…are you going away?' She nearly said *again*, but she bit the vulnerable word back.

He nodded his gleaming dark head and glanced at the time. 'I am afraid so, Jenna. I must travel to the eastern region with haste.'

'Why?'

His eyes narrowed. 'Oh, nothing that need concern you, my sweet.'

No, of course not. Politics was not the business of a wife. It was always the same. Her heart lurched. 'And will you be away for long, my Sheikh?'

'For as long as it takes, Jenna—no longer.'

She could tell from his voice that the subject was closed and she must be satisfied with his rather curt explanation—except that satisfied she most certainly wasn't. No way. Except in the purely physical sense, of course—Rashid seemed able to fulfil her every wish and her every desire, and invent a whole lot more into the bargain.

But ever since they had returned from their honeymoon she had discovered for herself just what was expected of the wife of the Sheikh—how she herself was nothing more than an isolated figurehead. And how their two worlds barely touched.

She had her charity work and he had his affairs of state—a demanding and taxing role as Ruler which took him away from her far more than she would have dreamed of.

So much for putting off having a baby so that she could get to know him—why, she barely saw him! The closeness which had been reawoken between them during those two glorious weeks of their honeymoon seemed to have vanished into nothing once they returned to the busy life of the palace.

Everyone wanted him. His advisors wanted him. His politicians wanted him. Foreign countries wanted him. She wanted him, too—but the only time he was ever completely hers was in their marital bed, when he took her to paradise and back again without fail.

But even that seemed strangely empty once the pleasures of fulfilment had receded and he had fallen into an exhausted sleep by her side. The words of love she longed to tell him remained unsaid—for Rashid was a man who seemed to have no time for terms of endearment. He told her that she was beautiful, yes, and he told her that her body pleased him greatly—but the lavish compliments only served to emphasise that she did not have what she most desired.

His heart.

'Can't I come with you, Rashid?' she asked plaintively. 'Just this once?'

He frowned. 'That will not be possible. You have your committees, Jenna, and I am told that your contribution to them is invaluable. Do you not wish to serve your country, my sweet?'

She heard the unmistakable disapproval in his voice and suppressed the sigh which would anger him further. She was not his partner. Nor his equal. Only when she had accepted that would she ever be able to find the inner peace she yearned for.

'Then at least come and kiss me goodbye,' she murmured.

He did as she asked, feeling the sharp tug of desire as he bent his lips to the softness of hers and then ran his fingers through her hair. 'It is almost down to your shoulders now,' he murmured. 'Much better.'

'Thank you. I am glad that my Sheikh approves,' she said demurely, and sat up, and saw his eyes darken as her bare breasts were revealed.

'Do you know how much you tempt me?' He sighed regretfully. 'All my officials are waiting for me, but how I wish I could lose myself in you.' He moved away from the bed before he was lost in the weakness of that temptation.

With an aching heart she watched him leave and then lay back down on the divan again, staring sightlessly up at the high ceiling above her.

It was not as she had hoped it would be—in fact it was a million miles away from how she had hoped it would be. He didn't *talk* to her. Or confide in her. Or ask her advice. In six months of marriage he had seemed preoccupied the whole time, and Jenna felt like just a tiny, tiny fragment of his life. Yet deep down she had known and feared that it was going to be like this, for was it not the royal custom? Separate lives. His father had had a marriage which had been very similar, and his father before him—everyone in Quador knew that.

Her own parents' marriage had been exceptionally close, but that had been a rarity. High-born Quadorian men usually took mistresses. She knew that, and yet it did not stop her from yearning for that same kind of closeness with Rashid—a closeness he did not seem remotely interested in giving her.

He was gone for five long days, with two crackled and annoyingly brief telephone calls their only communication.

And then the very thing she had been most dreading happened.

She was just emerging from a committee she had been chairing which had discussed setting up a hostel for battered

wives, when one of her ladies-in-waiting gave her a message
from Rashid.

It was stark and to the point.

*I have to fly straight to Paris on urgent business and
will probably be away for the week. I will ring you the
moment I get the opportunity.*

Paris?

Paris? Where Chantal lived and no doubt waited for the
dark Sheikh.

Her face blanched and she crumpled the paper with a
whitened knuckle.

'It is bad news, mistress?' asked the lady-in-waiting anxiously.

The very worst. Rashid had been given the perfect excuse
to meet up with his mistress. Unless that was the real purpose
behind his visit—and she had no way of finding out for
Abdullah would tell her nothing. She shook her head. 'No, it's
nothing,' she lied painfully. 'I will be—I will be in my office
should there be any call from the Sheikh.'

In her office she paced up and down and her heart pounded
with fear and jealousy. It was only what she had expected, and
yet the actuality was a million times more disturbing than her
fevered imaginings.

He was a man of relentless sexual appetite with a taste for
the exotic. And he was used to variety. His stream of lovers
had been legendary—so why on earth should that have
changed? His father had taken mistresses—it had been an open
secret at court. Six months of marriage had probably left
Rashid feeling jaded and bored, no matter how much she tried
to please him.

Her hand trembled. She couldn't share him! She would *not*
share him! She would sooner be without him than be able to
bear the thought of him in another woman's arms!

Her fingers still shaking, she picked up the telephone and
rang her sister on the other side of the world. 'Nadia?'

'Jenna, is that you?'

'Of course it's me.'

'But you sound *terrible*—what on earth is the matter?'

'R-Rashid has flown to Paris.'

'And?'

'Nadia—he has a mistress in Paris.'

'*Had* a mistress,' Nadia corrected gently. 'He's married to you now, remember?'

As if she could forget! 'I have to know if he's seeing her, Nadia,' she said urgently. 'I can't live my life like this—I *have* to find out!'

'Well, can't you just fly to Paris and surprise him?'

Jenna shook her head. 'Oh, sure—he's surrounded by minders and aides who would lie through their teeth for him! If I announced that I was taking a plane to Paris he would probably hear about it before the airline did!' An idea began to take root in her mind. 'Unless I was arranging to meet *you* for a holiday in London, of course!'

'London isn't Paris,' Nadia pointed out.

'I know it isn't—but I could catch a train from London straight to Paris.'

'And what about your bodyguards? Can you really see *them* letting you do that?'

Jenna gave a small tight smile at her strained reflection. 'You know how people always say how similar we look?' she queried softly. 'Why, if you were wearing my clothes and I was wearing yours—well, anyone could easily mistake us for one another!'

'Jenna—you aren't suggesting what I think you're suggesting, are you? Are you going to pretend to be *me*?'

'How long have I covered up for you and Brad?'

'That's blackmail,' her sister objected jokingly.

'Or you could say that one good turn deserves another.' There was a pause. 'So how soon can you fly to London?' Jenna asked crisply.

Her plans proved almost ridiculously easy to execute. She arrived in London accompanied by a lady-in-waiting and two bodyguards and went straight to the large penthouse suite at the Granchester hotel, which Nadia had booked.

She hadn't seen her sister since the wedding, and the two of them embraced tearfully.

'Jenna, what on earth are you going to *say* to Rashid?' asked Nadia worriedly. 'Won't he go mad if he finds out you've been checking up on him? And won't someone tell him that you've left Quador?'

'I don't care. I have to find out the truth,' said Jenna urgently. 'The man I married is like a stranger to me.'

'Already?' asked Nadia sadly.

'Except during our honeymoon, when we seemed as close as a couple could be.'

'But you love him? You do still love him, don't you?'

'As life itself,' answered Jenna simply. 'That much has not changed. But I can't live a lie, Nadia—and my love for him will be eaten away if he intends to be free with other women. I would sooner divorce him than have that happen.'

'He would never allow it, Jenna—you know that.'

'We shall see. We're in the twenty-first century now, not the Dark Ages—he cannot keep me a prisoner to his will!'

Jenna sent one of the bodyguards out with her lady-in-waiting to pick up a coat she had ordered from one of London's most exclusive department stores and then she dressed in some of Nadia's unashamedly American clothes.

And by nine o'clock that evening she found herself safely alone in Paris, speeding along in a taxi towards the Splendide, where Rashid always stayed when he was in the city.

Unless he was at Chantal's, she thought, with a painful lurch of her heart.

She went straight up to his suite and the door was opened by Abdullah, his look of confusion quickly becoming one of

wariness as he registered just who it was standing there, in blue
jeans and a black leather jacket.

'Mistress,' he said slowly, and bowed his head.

'I have come to see the Sheikh.'

There was a pause. 'The Sheikh is not expecting you.'

It was unmistakably a reprimand, but Jenna forced a smile
onto lips which felt as though they had been carved from ice.
'I want to surprise him.'

'The Sheikh is not here, mistress.'

'And I suppose you're not going to tell me where he is,
Abdullah?'

'You know that I cannot do that, mistress.'

Her skin prickled and her smile faded as she marched past
him. 'Then I shall wait.'

She didn't have to wait long. She had only been slumped in
an armchair for less than ten minutes, watching a French soap
opera in a vain attempt to try to keep her heart-rending thoughts
at bay, when Rashid entered the luxury suite.

She heard him before she saw him. Heard the urgent words
spoken to him in an undertone by Abdullah. And then suddenly
he was there, filling the room with his magnificent and rather
daunting presence. She searched his impassive face for any tell-
tale signs of betrayal. Where had he been? Had his naked limbs
been entwined with Chantal's? Where had he *been*?

He stood looking at her, his face as dark and as unforgiving
as thunder, but she was too angry to care.

'Would you care to explain the meaning of this unwarranted
intrusion?' he hissed.

Intrusion! 'And would you care to explain just where you
have been until this hour?' she retorted furiously.

'I'll tell you where I have been, you little fool—I have been
at the British Embassy in an attempt to find out your where
abouts!' he stormed. 'I have had half the police force in London
scouring the city. And your sister—who I gather you were
supposed to be meeting—is nowhere to be found either! What

the hell are you doing *here*, Jenna? And where the *hell* are your bodyguards?'

'I gave them the slip!' she boasted, blithely ignoring the look of dark menace on his face. 'I dressed as Nadia and took the shuttle from London!'

'You did *what*?'

'You heard!'

He was almost beside himself with fury as he strode over to confront her, and he very nearly hauled her angrily into his arms—until he reminded himself what would happen if he did *that*. 'You fool,' he grated again. 'Didn't you stop to think about the danger you were placing yourself in?'

'I can take care of myself, Rashid! I did without bodyguards for most of my life and I can function perfectly well without them!'

'Not as my *wife*, you can't!'

'Oh, your wife!' she scorned. 'What's in a name? What kind of a *wife* am I, Rashid? And, more importantly, what kind of a husband are you?'

He went very still. 'And just what is that supposed to mean?'

'Think about it!' she stormed, but at least she felt alive again. At least the tiptoeing around his feelings and trying to guess at his needs had been replaced by a vivid but liberating *honesty*. 'What have you been doing since you've been in Paris?'

The black eyes glittered dangerously. 'What do *you* think I've been doing, Jenna?'

The bitter words came tumbling out before she could stop them. 'Making love to your mistress, I expect! *Chantal*! I expect it's nearly *killed* you to be faithful to me for six long months, hasn't it, Rashid? Assuming, of course, that you *have* been faithful?'

His dark skin paled. 'How *dare* you speak to me this way?'

'But I'm your wife now, Rashid! Aren't I entitled to my opinions—?'

'Not if they are a complete fabrication!' he snapped.

'Well, how about a few answers, then?'

He controlled his breathing with difficulty. 'You really think that I've spent the evening making love to Chantal?' he questioned incredulously.

'Don't ever speak her name in front of me!' She shot him a blistering look, conveniently forgetting that *she* had been the one to bring the woman's name up. 'Were you?'

'Of course I was not. I told you—I've been at the damned embassy!'

'There's no "of course" about it, Rashid. You haven't spent the last two days at the embassy, have you? What else am I to think? You could easily have made love to her! And don't try to tell me that she wouldn't still want you to—because what woman wouldn't?'

He very nearly thanked her for the compliment, but resisted. He had never seen her in such a rage! 'But *you* are the woman I make love to. *You* are my wife, Jenna,' he stated softly.

'Except that I'm not—not really. Am I?' she finished in a small, broken question.

He saw all the fight and the anger leave her, to be replaced by a sadness which smote him like a blow from a sword. 'You want the truth?' he questioned huskily.

She shook her head. 'I *don't know*!'

'Well, whether you want it or not—you *need* to know it, Jenna.'

'Rashid—'

'The day after I asked you to marry me, yes, I *did* come to Paris—'

'Don't!' She shuddered, but he did not heed her plea.

'I told Chantal that it was over, that you were to be my bride and yes, she wanted me to make love to her—'

'Oh, *don't*!' she begged again, but he shook his dark head resolutely.

'I told her no,' he continued inexorably. 'I have not spoken to her since and I have no intention of doing so.'

Her eyes opened very wide. 'Really?'

'Really.' His voice softened. 'Jenna, what makes you think that I would betray you? Do you think that the vows I made on our wedding day were meaningless?'

She shook her head. 'How do I know *what* you would do,' she asked in frustration, 'when you won't let me near you?'

He frowned. 'But we share a room each night—'

'When you're *there*!' she argued. 'And I'm not talking about physically, anyway, Rashid—I'm talking about emotionally!'

'emotionally?' he echoed, as if he was unfamiliar with the word.

'Yes, emotionally,' she said tiredly. 'Apart from on our honeymoon, I feel as though I might as well be living with a robot!'

'You have many, many insults for me this evening, don't you, Jenna?' he observed quietly.

'I don't mean to insult you—I'm just telling you how I feel. And don't glower at me like that, Rashid! I know you've had a lifetime of people revering you and only ever speaking to you when you initiate the conversation! But what is the point of being married if we aren't going to be close to one another?'

The black eyes glittered. 'You have complaints about our marriage, Jenna?'

'Yes, I do!' She drew a deep breath, knowing that she might never have another chance to say this. 'You never *talk* to me, do you? You never tell me about your day! Half the time you won't say where you're going, or what you're doing—or who with—so of course my imagination works overtime! And you never seem to stop working, either! When was the last time we spent some quality time together that wasn't in bed? I'll tell you when—on our honeymoon, and that was six months ago!'

He stared at her with eyes which were filled with a sudden, dawning comprehension. 'I once told you that I had a problem with delegation,' he mused slowly. 'And now it seems that this is a skill which I must embrace more wholeheartedly.' He sighed. 'No, I do not confide affairs of state to you, it is true,' he agreed. 'But do you not know that knowledge can be a dangerous weapon, Jenna? That if you were aware of all the ramifications of what goes on in Quador I would be putting you at risk?'

'How?'

His black eyes were very sombre. 'Do you not know, my sweet, that there are still factions in the country who would wish to overthrow your Sheikh? When you asked if you could accompany me to the Eastern region the other day, I said no. I didn't say why—that there were very real dangers at play at that time.'

'Then why didn't you just *tell* me that?'

'Would you not have worried about me?'

'Of course I would!'

'Well, then.'

'It isn't just about the not confiding, Rashid—you never…'

She had her pride, but pride itself could be dangerous if it prevented you from discovering the truth, and she had to know. She *had* to.

'I never what?' he prompted softly, for her mouth had taken on a tremulous shape that made him want to kiss it.

'You never tell me how you feel.'

'About what?'

'About *me*!' she burst out. 'You never tell me that you love me, which can only lead me to assume that you don't! And if you don't love me, then it's obvious that you will stray eventually.'

His mouth hardened. 'What right do I have to speak of love to you?' he questioned bitterly. 'When I took your innocence so brutally and then forced you into marrying me?'

'You didn't rape me, Rashid,' she pointed out.

'But I might as well have done!' he raged. 'I showed no restraint! No control! I have never behaved like that in my life before!'

'And neither have I! We both got carried away in the heat of the moment—it wasn't anybody's *fault*!'

'But *I* was the experienced one,' he asserted harshly. 'I should have stopped in time. And I couldn't,' he finished harshly. 'I just couldn't.'

'So what? Is it such a major crime that just for once in your life you failed to live up to your own exacting standards?' she demanded. 'If you really want to know—I feel quite powerful that I should have been the one to make you lose control like that. If it's forgiveness you want, then I've forgiven you, Rashid—if only you could forgive yourself.'

He stared at her for a long moment. 'But I still forced you to marry me, didn't I, Jenna?' he said slowly. 'When the idea was clearly so abhorrent to you.'

'And don't you know why?'

He shook his head. 'Because your feelings for me had died?'

'They never died, Rashid,' she said, and a small, rueful smile broke through. 'Even though I tried like anything to kill them off.'

He reached out a fingertip and smoothed it down the smooth surface of her cheek. 'And why would you do that?'

'Because I kept reading about all your lovers in the newspapers,' she admitted brokenly. 'And I was as jealous as hell of them.'

He gave up trying to keep her at arm's length and pulled her into his arms, staring deep into her amber eyes. All along he had tried to protect her, but he saw now that by doing so he had only succeeded in making her insecure.

'There have been lovers, yes,' he said quietly, and he saw her flinch. 'But not nearly so many as the newspapers reported.'

She flinched. One would be too many! 'Why any?' she whispered. 'Why not just me?'

He shook his head and tried to explain. 'Jenna, my father's marriage was not one I intended to replicate—but I am a pragmatist, and a realist. I knew that when I married you I intended to be utterly faithful, but I was unable to offer you my fidelity until then. We couldn't marry before you left—I had only recently come into the Sheikhdom, and I needed to give myself wholeheartedly to my country.'

He stared at her, and his voice grew quiet and serious. 'I needed to live a little, to experience something of the world—

to give in to some of the temptations of the flesh so that those temptations would not haunt me for the rest of my life. Does that sound incredibly selfish?'

She thought about it. 'Yes, I suppose it does,' she said honestly. Jenna had a pragmatic streak herself, and she was now beginning to see why Rashid had acted as he had. She might not like it, but she could understand it. Not that she was going to let him know that. Not yet. 'Particularly as you would have gone berserk if I had done the same thing.'

'This much is true,' he admitted, and his eyes were rueful as he touched the tips of her fingers to his lips. 'You think it unfair?' he questioned.

'I don't *think* it's unfair, I *know* it's unfair!' she retorted, knowing in her heart that it had not seemed that way to her. But then, she had never really wanted any other man in the way that she wanted her Sheikh.

He nodded. 'Yes. As in so much of life, sweet Jenna mine.' He looked down into her upturned face and saw the question in her beautiful eyes.

Say it, she thought, unable to look away from his glittering ebony gaze. Please just say it. Tell me that all these years I haven't cherished false hopes. Tell me what I felt on our honeymoon was real. Even if it is incomplete, tell me that there is something between us which could grow and grow.

'I love you, Jenna,' he said simply, but she heard the unfamiliar tremble of emotion in his voice.

Tears brightened her eyes and then his voice became urgent. 'Don't you know that, my own sweet love? Believe me when I tell you that I have always loved you. *Always*,' he breathed, but his face tightened with a fleeting look of regret. 'I thought I needed to find out what I was missing,' he sighed. 'Only now I realise that I wasn't missing anything at all.'

'But you let me go away to America,' she accused, though as accusations went it was pretty much on the gentle side.

'Don't you know why?' he demanded. 'I had just inherited

a country in turmoil—so how in heaven's name could I have taken on a wife at the same time?'

'And if I'd stayed then you couldn't have gone on having all your other women, could you?' she asked jealously.

'If you'd stayed I would have been unable to think or eat or sleep or breathe with the frustration of wanting you,' he admitted heatedly. 'Your beauty exploded into life like a flower, my sweet Jenna, and it so captured me with its sweet perfume that I was unable to think of anything else. And certainly not about Quador.' He bent his face close to hers. 'Oh, Jenna—can you still find it in your heart to love me, my wife?'

For the first time in her life she saw vulnerability written on the proud, cold face of a man whom she had always considered to be invulnerable.

But beneath the magnificent body and the heavy weight of his destiny he was reaching out for her in a way she had always dreamed of. Stripping away the proud and arrogant exterior to show her, and only her, the heart of the man which lay beneath.

'Can you?' he repeated huskily. 'Love me?'

She felt filled with a new and heady kind of power, and she curved her lips into a thoughtful smile.

'I can,' she agreed serenely.

He briefly closed his eyes and expelled a long, shuddering breath, unaware that he had been holding it. 'And I will spend the rest of my life showing you how much I love you,' he promised shakily.

It was time to test out her new power! 'I shall look forward to that,' she purred, but shook her head as he lowered his mouth to claim hers in a kiss. 'On two conditions, Rashid.'

'Conditions?' He frowned the frown of a man who was unused to making concessions of any kind. 'What kind of conditions?' he asked suspiciously. 'And how many?'

'Only two,' she answered demurely.

'Then name them!'

'Firstly, I want to use my law training to help negotiate the freedom of the Quador press.'

'A free press?' Rashid demanded. 'It is unheard of!'

'In the past, yes. But the internet has made news so accessible,' she argued. 'You know it has! So why must we be dragged kicking and screaming into the twenty-first century, my love? Why not embrace change willingly?'

He frowned, unable to fault her logic. 'And the second condition?' he growled.

'I want you to persuade my father to allow my sister to marry the man she loves.'

CHAPTER TEN

THE band was playing as Rashid smiled down into his wife's eyes. 'A very different wedding from our own,' he observed softly.

She smiled back at him. These days she never seemed to stop smiling! 'Outwardly, very different indeed,' she agreed, her voice low. 'But you were the one who once told me that a wedding is a wedding is a wedding. And the emotion is the same for everyone, surely?'

He shook his head. 'No man could love a woman as much as I love you, Jenna,' he declared.

Well, she certainly wasn't going to argue with *that*!

They were gathered at one of Long Island's most glittering hotels, waiting for the wedding of her sister Nadia to Brad Toulmin, a ceremony made possible by the intervention of her Sheikh.

Jenna had told Rashid all about Nadia and Brad's forbidden love affair, and his calm and accepting reaction had both surprised and delighted her.

'The ways of the heart are mysterious,' he had commented thoughtfully. 'What use will it serve if they are forced to part and Nadia comes home to marry a Quadorian if she is not happy? No use at all!' he had finished passionately.

It had been Rashid himself who had broken the news to her father.

'Two such different cultures!' her father had protested. 'It is rare for such a union to last!'

'But you married an American yourself, Bulent,' Rashid had pointed out softly. 'Why should your daughter not do the same?'

It was unarguable logic and the older man had caved in immediately.

And of course, as Jenna had gleefully told Nadia afterwards, how could their father possibly refuse Rashid anything? He *was* the Sheikh!

The wedding was to be held in the extravagant flower-laden gardens of the hotel, and Jenna was brimming over with excitement. And with love. It seemed scarcely credible that it was over a year since their own wedding. The last six months had whizzed by like six seconds, and they had been so very happy together. She looked up to find her husband watching her closely.

'What is it?' she questioned.

He smiled. Sometimes he felt as though she could read his mind! Come to think of it, she probably could! She could certainly twist him with great ease around her little finger. He had made many concessions to his fiery wife to improve the quality of their life together—and had actually discovered that he enjoyed making them, much to his surprise. He had begun to delegate more, and to trust her with his confidences. And every week they spent a whole day and night together which were set aside just for the two of them.

But Jenna was busy herself these days, helping to free the Quador Press—to the complete astonishment of the world at large.

'You know that such a move will boost your international standing, Rashid,' she had told her husband winningly.

And of course she had been right.

He sighed with a tender indulgence. When was she ever wrong?

'Do you grow more beautiful with each day that passes?' he questioned softly, thinking how radiant she looked today.

'Well, I certainly hope so,' she said demurely, and then looked up at him. 'Do you still want to give me a baby, darling?'

He nodded and traced the outline of her lip with the tip of his finger. 'Yes, I do—but I'm not sure that I can bear to share you with anyone just yet,' he admitted slowly. 'Imagine what my people would say if they knew that!'

She hid a smile. The Rashid of old would never have put his feelings on the line like that! But she had taught him that communication was vital in a happy marriage. And that love and showing your feelings never equalled weakness. 'Then we'll wait a little longer, shall we?'

'You don't mind?'

She shook her head. 'The only thing I would ever mind would be if I didn't have you,' she said seriously.

'Then only death shall part us, my sweet.' And he brushed his lips against hers, feeling her shiver beneath him, loving her instant responsiveness. 'I wish I could take you to bed right now,' he said huskily.

The band began to strike up the 'Wedding March', and Jenna slipped her hand into his.

'You'll have to wait for that too, my Sheikh.'

'Not for too long,' he growled, sizzling her a look of hungry intent which set her heart racing.

'N-no, not for too long,' she agreed unsteadily, and with a harmony of body language which reflected their closeness more than words ever could they both turned round to watch the marriage service begin.

CONTENTS

THE FIRST HUMANS
THE SEARCH FOR OUR ORIGINS

Herbert Thomas

THAMES AND HUDSON

Astrophysicists believe the sun will have burned all its hydrogen in six billion years. After that it will dilate and turn into a giant red star that will swallow up the earth. If human beings are still alive then, they will disappear, unless they have conquered another planet in our galaxy. In the face of these few billion years, humankind's history has only just begun.

CHAPTER 1

ANTEDILUVIAN PEOPLE

According to the Bible, God made the world from the primitive chaos and in six days created the heavens, the earth and the waters, the fish, the birds, all the animals and finally the first human couple, Adam (right) and Eve. It was only in the 20th century that humans were able to contemplate the earth from space (left).

On the sixth day, 'God created man in his own image'

With the emergence of monotheistic thought, in the Judaeo-Christian tradition, the biblical account of Genesis was for many years the sole explanation as to how the entire universe had been created. Humankind, like all the other animal species, formed part of a grand design, conceived by the creator. It was not until the 19th century that a different interpretation was outlined, drawn from the observation of nature. Following several 'revolutions' in the life and earth sciences, people were no longer considered to be the outcome of a unique and uniform creation, in which species were fixed, but rather the product of a history, in which species evolved through natural selection.

Humankind and the present-day great apes have a common ancestor: this was the shocking idea of more than a century ago. A decisive idea if ever

During the 16th and 17th centuries in Europe prehistoric archaeology was still in limbo, despite the fascination that megalithic monuments like Stonehenge held for scholars and 'antiquaries'.

In the Middle Ages the Bible provided the only explanation for the creation of the universe. This illumination shows the alpha and omega, the first and the last.

there was one, carrying with it the seed of the notion that modern biological science would from then on strive to demonstrate: humans and our cousins the apes share similar features, just as they shared the same ancestor. Today we know that almost ninety-nine per cent of human and chimpanzee genetic material is the same. From the remaining one per cent, which separates us from the chimpanzee, our closest relative, we can reconstruct the gigantic puzzle of the history of our origins.

Humans meet apes…

Around 460 BC Hanno, the Carthaginian navigator, sailed beyond the Pillars of Hercules, today's Straits of Gibraltar, at the head of sixty galleys with fifty rowers, in order to explore the west coast of Africa. Penetrating into the interior of these lands, the soldiers saw strange hairy beings with human heads. Three of these creatures, which they called gorillas – they were probably chimpanzees – were captured and their hides brought back to Carthage; at the time of the Roman conquest, in 146 BC, they could still be admired, as Pliny tells us, in the temple of the goddess Astarte.

This engraving, taken from the 1732 Bible of Canon Scheuchzer, evokes in allegorical fashion the traditional vision of the earthly paradise and the creation, a literal expression of the holy text of Genesis.

Whatever the truth in this tale, three centuries later Galen, a Greek physician and anatomist (AD 129–c. 199), carried out the first autopsy of monkeys – macaques and baboons – which he considered to be 'comical copies' of people. Thus, although barely known to humankind, these hairy creatures with a tail – except

for Hanno's 'gorillas' – were already a source of fascination and a reason for concern.

At the time people were not worried whether humans were descended from apes, despite this 'family likeness'; they wanted to know whether apes were a type of human. This idea persisted until the second half of the 18th century, when the French philosopher Jean-Jacques Rousseau was still devoting long commentaries to it; although denying it, he was uncertain about the orang-utan, discovered less than a century earlier, because, he wrote, 'perhaps after more precise research they will be found to be men'. In the same century Georges Buffon, the famous French naturalist (1707–88), finally put an end to these 'philosophers' daydreams' by contrasting the anatomy of the most human of the apes – the orang-utan – and that of the most apelike humans, represented, according to him, by the Hottentots.

The path leading to the theory of evolution

During the centuries before the discovery of the first human fossils in the early 19th century, theories about human origins developed in a chaotic way with no logical thread. Freethinkers, philosophers, naturalists, scholars and 'antiquaries' all introduced innovatory ideas, which, by necessity, went against biblical tradition, but they were always very speculative in nature.

According to the Irish Archbishop James Ussher (1581–1656), who based his

Jacob de Bondt, a Dutch doctor who had lived in Java, was the first person, in 1658, to describe the orang-utan: 'The Javanese give them the name of Orang Outang [*sic*], which means people of the woods, and claim that they are born of the lewdness of Indian women who copulate with monkeys without tails.'

St Jerome points a finger at a human skull, perhaps meditating on human nature or its destiny. This painting no doubt expresses the concerns of Renaissance thinkers rather than the preoccupations of the 4th-century saint who is known especially for his translations of the Bible and his exegetical treatises.

Before Buffon, the great anthropoid apes were considered by some to be degenerate children of Adam, like the Hottentot 'savages' of southern Africa. This Hottentot Venus with very marked steatopygia was exhibited in Paris in 1829.

calculations on biblical chronology, the world was created in 4004 BC. Others, such as Leonardo da Vinci, Cyrano de Bergerac, the German philosopher Gottfried Wilhelm Leibniz and, later, Georges Buffon, were already thinking in terms of much larger timespans and considering the possibility that the universe had been in existence for hundreds of thousands of years, even millions of years, without being capable of proving the fact.

In 1616 Lucilio Vanini, an Italian philosopher (1584–1619), suggested that humans originated from the ape, an idea for which he was burned alive three years later in Toulouse. In the following century the French physician and philosopher Julien Offroy de La Mettrie (1709–51) did his utmost to show that the differences between humans and the 'lower echelons' – including plants – are only a question of degree.

In fact, the fundamental idea that humans might be descended from apes did not really take shape until Charles Darwin (1809–82) published his theory of evolution in *The Origin of Species* (1859). Species evolved from other species through natural selection.

Homo diluvii testis

In the period when these theories were being developed, numerous fossil bones – which were then called 'petrifications' – were frequently unearthed in different parts of Europe. At the start of the Age of Enlightenment, Canon Johann Jakob Scheuchzer (1672–1733), a Zurich doctor and a zealous propagandist for the popular biblical Flood theory, made a remarkable discovery. He found the imprint of a 'human skeleton' on a slab of schist extracted from a quarry at Oeningen, near Lake Constance. Described as one of the 'rarest relics of the accursed race that must have been swallowed up by the waters', it appears under the name of *Homo diluvii testis* (witness of the Flood) in a very curious work by Scheuchzer on fossil fish, called *Piscium Querelae et Vindiciae*, published in Zurich in 1708.

The canon stuck to his opinion, and a few years later he made a further discovery – this time of some black, shiny fossil vertebrae from the foot of a gibbet close to Altdorf. Although more astute naturalists expressed doubts about how well-founded Scheuchzer's opinions were, almost a century was to pass before the true nature of these fossils was at last recognized. In 1811 Georges Cuvier, the illustrious French naturalist, father of vertebrate palaeontology (1769–1832), was passing through Haarlem where the famous Oeningen skeleton was kept. In front of witnesses Cuvier demonstrated conclusively that the bones from the supposed witness of the Flood in fact came from a giant salamander.

In his 1731 work *Physica Sacra* devoted to fossil fish, in which the discovery of a supposed human skeleton was announced, the 'witness of the Flood' (opposite), Scheuchzer depicted other human remains, like these two vertebrae (left) collected from the foot of a gibbet close to Altdorf, near Nuremberg.

It is hard to believe that Scheuchzer, being a doctor, could have confused a giant salamander skeleton with a human one! As for the vertebrae, Cuvier, who had seen similar specimens in the Grand Duke of Tuscany's cabinet of natural history, attributed them quite correctly to an extinct marine reptile, the ichthyosaurus, the existence of which had just been discovered by English scholars.

'There are no human fossils' (Cuvier)

In the first half of the 19th century, Cuvier's prestige was considerable. The revelation that strange animals, which Cuvier had reconstructed from the fossil bones exhumed in the gypsum quarries of Montmartre, once inhabited the site of Paris itself made him a kind of god in the eyes of the Parisian public and his contemporaries. Just before the illustrious scientist died, the novelist Honoré de Balzac

In Cuvier's day the hill of Montmartre was a major centre for the extraction of gypsum, a rock used for making plaster. The gypsum from the hill, deposited at the end of the Eocene period more than forty million years ago, contains numerous fossil bones that the workmen collected and Cuvier reconstructed.

From 1796 Cuvier studied the numerous remains of fossil vertebrates that were already known at the time. Basing his theory on one of the principal laws of comparative anatomy that he had discovered – the principle of the correlation of forms – Cuvier set about reconstructing the whole of the animal's skeleton on the basis of sometimes fragmentary evidence in his famous work *Recherches sur les ossements fossiles de quadrupèdes* (1812).

At the beginning of the 19th century no fossil primates had been found. It is to Cuvier that we owe the description in 1822 of the first one, from a small jawbone discovered in the gypsum quarries of Montmartre. It belonged not to an ape but to a form close to present-day lemurs.

captured the mood of the time and hailed Cuvier as the greatest poet of his century in a lyrical extract in 1831. Of course, the century was only thirty years old by then....

Despite his scientific clairvoyance, Cuvier clung to the biblical Flood theory and set about explaining the appearance of new species through his belief in catastrophic destruction and the immutability of species. He brought all his authority to bear on the delicate question of early human remains, whose existence he denied – 'at least in our countries', he added, however. It is true that Cuvier, at this time, relied on arguments that were believed to be a priori legitimate. Firstly, he based his theory on the fact that he did not find any bones of humans or indeed of apes among the skeletons of extinct animals recovered from the Montmartre gypsum quarries. Naturally he did not know that the hill's gypsum deposits imprisoning all these animals dated back more than forty million years – so these animals lived long before either humans or even apes appeared. Secondly, it seems that all of the supposedly human skeletons that were presented to Cuvier, and that some believed to be antediluvian people, belonged, in fact, to elephants, tortoises, salamanders, cetaceans or marine reptiles.

Linnaeus' daring idea: classifying humans close to the great apes

At the same time research was continuing into the classification of animals. In 1735 the Swedish botanist Carolus Linnaeus (1707-78) published his *Systema Naturae*. In this system, which is still in force today, every living form is designated by two names transcribed into Latin – a genus name followed by a species name. For example, in *Homo sapiens*,

In 1735, in his *Systema Naturae*, Linnaeus proposed a binary nomenclature for classifying living beings, which, according to him, accounted for the plan of the divine creation. In his *Fundamenta Fructificationis* of 1762, however, he admitted that there may be a common root for all the species in the same genus, if not in the same order. Thus, God's work supposedly stopped with the genera or orders, their diversification being linked later to crossbreeding or hybridizations.

which means wise human being, *Homo* is the name of the genus and *sapiens* the name of the species. All people belong to the same species because they can interbreed, the criterion that defines every animal species. Of course, this criterion cannot be applied to fossil species; other criteria have to be used to identify the fossils of human species that preceded *Homo sapiens*. Finally, the whole group of related species that share one or several derived characteristics will belong to the same genus. Thus the dog, wolf, fox and jackal belong to one and the same genus: *Canis*.

One of Linnaeus' daring ideas was to classify humans close to a few great apes, including the gibbon. He was not trying to express a family connection between humans and gibbons but to account for the divine creator's plan. The Swedish scholar therefore called this group the primates, because in his view they held the first rank in nature's hierarchy; the other mammals were accorded the second rank, and the reptiles were relegated to third position: hence the names of primates, secundates and tertiates.

Only the first name survives in modern taxonomy: the primates, which include prosimians (the tarsiers, lorises, lemurs) and anthropoids (all New World and Old World – depending on the geographical area from which they come – monkeys, apes and humans).

Classification: the history of connections between living beings

If we are to place humans within

In the tenth edition of his *Systema Naturae*, published in 1758, Carolus Linnaeus created the order of primates as well as the genus *Homo*, which, according to him, comprised two species: 'day man' and 'night man'. The latter includes 'nocturnal man', the 'man of the woods' and the orang-utan, distinctions that express the uncertainty and imprecision of the boundaries between apes and humans. Linnaeus himself admitted that he '[had] not up to now extracted from the principles of [his] science any characteristic that might make it possible to distinguish humans from apes'.

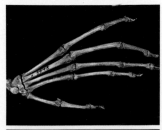

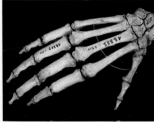

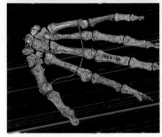

this order and to study our origins, it is essential to understand a few principles of the modern language of classification.

Based on organic similarities, classification tries to account for the relationships between the numerous living forms. However, these similarities do not all have the same meaning; indeed, some do not express any real relationship at all. For instance, the wings of a butterfly, a swallow and a bat are organs that have appeared independently in insects, birds and mammals as an adaptation for flight. Other similarities are due to characteristics that have remained unchanged since their initial state. These characteristics, known as primitive, are evidence only of a very distant connection. In the case of our five fingers and toes, it is a question of an initial state that goes back to the origin of the tetrapod vertebrates.

Other characteristics known as evolved or derived, as they are distant from their initial state, differentiate the primates, for example, from the other mammals: the growth of the brain leading to the reduction of the snout, the acquisition of three-dimensional vision, the possibility of pushing the thumb against the other fingers and the replacement of claws by flat nails.

As we move up the hierarchy of derived characteristics in primates, we inevitably encounter characteristics that

Since Aristotle it has been observed that the feet and hands of non-human primates resemble each other and these primates have been called quadrupeds or quadrumanes in turn. Whereas, among the non-human primates, hands have a double purpose for both locomotion and grasping, in humans only the latter function remains. What is particularly remarkable is that our thumb can swivel fifty-four degrees and so can push against all the other fingers. In the indri (top), a big lemur from Madagascar, the thumb has already separated from the other fingers; in the gorilla (centre), which is more like us, the thumb can rotate. This movement will attain its maximum range in humans (bottom).

are exclusively human, such as our mode of locomotion – bipedal (on two legs) – or the growth in certain parts of the brain such as Broca's area (the motor speech centre) that, together with the increase in volume of the pharynx and the lower position of the larynx, enabled us to acquire articulate speech and develop abstract thought.

It is clear that derived characteristics play an important role, as they show family connections; whereas primary characteristics are merely an expression of a distant kinship at best, and at worst of a vague similarity.

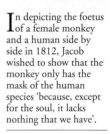

In depicting the foetus of a female monkey and a human side by side in 1812, Jacob wished to show that the monkey only has the mask of the human species 'because, except for the soul, it lacks nothing that we have'.

The 'Red Lady', the first specimen of a Cro-Magnon man

Until 1820 the rare discoveries of authentic human remains – such as those buried in the cave at Gailenreuth

in southern Germany, or the worked flint axe found by the English antiquary John Frere (1740–1807) in a Suffolk quarry with the remains of extinct animals – did not lead anywhere, either because they went unnoticed or because they were not really understood.

However, after 1820 the number of excavations in caves started to increase rapidly. In 1822 the Reverend William Buckland (1784–1856) was digging in a Paviland cave in Wales, and unearthed a skeleton covered in ochre. It was not until many years later that the so-called Red Lady was

William Buckland (left), professor of geology at Oxford, did not believe that humans and large extinct animals lived at the same time despite the countless discoveries he made, such as the skeleton of the 'Red Lady' of Paviland, which he considered was buried during the Roman period.

revealed to be the first specimen of a Cro-Magnon man.

Further discoveries soon followed. Excavations carried out by a pharmacist from Narbonne called Paul Tournal (1805–72) revealed that human bones had been mixed with the remains of extinct animals in several caves in southern France. In 1830 the Belgian naturalist Dr Philippe-Charles Schmerling (1791–1836) brought to light the first Neanderthal remains of a child's skull at Engis, near Liège.

Despite the real antiquity of all these human remains, unfortunately none of them presented any particular anatomical traits that distinguished them immediately from modern humans. Consequently their immense significance was overlooked. Although the fields of archaeology and geology were increasingly overlapping in their interpretations, and it seemed obvious that fossil humans were contemporaneous with extinct animals, very few people reached the inevitable conclusion about the period when humankind appeared.

It is true that Cuvier, who was still very influential, believed that humankind appeared at the same time as the ape. But no fossil apes had been found. Their discovery, which was to follow shortly, indirectly contributed to the theory of human origins.

Pliopithecus antiquus

One of the many people who attended public classes, especially those given by Cuvier at the Jardin des Plantes, in the Latin Quarter in Paris around 1820, was a young Gascon by the name of Édouard Lartet (1801–71). Although his father sent him to Paris to study law in order to take up a career as a

In 1833 Dr Schmerling of Liège published an important work entitled *Recherches sur les ossements fossiles découverts dans les cavernes de la province de Liège*. It featured bones from extinct animals as well as humans, including this child's skull (above), which would only be recognized as Neanderthal and of great antiquity in 1936.

Left: an engraving from Buckland's book, *Reliquiae Diluvianae*, published in 1823, in which he wrote about his excavations in England.

barrister, he was, in fact, to become one of the founders of human palaeontology.

Once his studies were finished, he returned to his native Gascony to settle down in the family home, the Château d'Ornezan. The windows of this ancient manor look out towards the hill of Sansan in the distance, and, by one of those quirks of fate that were so frequent in that century, this hill would become one of the key sites in French palaeontology.

In 1834 a shepherd brought Lartet a large tooth that he had found at the bottom of the slopes of Sansan hill. He was told that one could collect bones by the shovelful there. Having recognized that it was a tooth from an extinct animal species – a mastodon – Lartet carried out major excavations, armed with spades and picks, and brought to light countless remains of fossil mammals. Among them, one lower jaw particularly attracted his attention – it came from the first fossil anthropoid ape to be found. His discovery was announced in 1837.

Pliopithecus antiquus, as it would later be called, bore a strange resemblance to the modern gibbons of Southeast Asia. The eminent French naturalist Etienne Geoffroy St-Hilaire (1772–1844), who had been alerted by Lartet, did not overlook the significance of this find, which, he claimed, was destined to start a new

Ducrotay de Blainville, then professor of comparative anatomy at the Muséum d'Histoire Naturelle, compared the first fossil ape (lower jaw, below) discovered by Lartet with the modern gibbon.

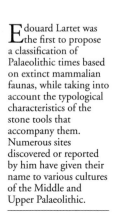

Edouard Lartet was the first to propose a classification of Palaeolithic times based on extinct mammalian faunas, while taking into account the typological characteristics of the stone tools that accompany them. Numerous sites discovered or reported by him have given their name to various cultures of the Middle and Upper Palaeolithic.

era in 'humanitarian' knowledge. Indeed, both Lartet and Geoffroy St-Hilaire argued that fossil humans must exist because fossil apes did.

Some twenty years later, in 1856, Lartet had another stroke of good fortune. An amateur naturalist presented to him the lower jaw of another ape found in a tile works on the outskirts of St Gaudens in the Haute Garonne. The teeth of this new fossil ape, which Lartet called *Dryopithecus*, or ape of the oaks, were similar to those of modern great apes and even of humans. The existence of such fossil apes turned the possibility of discovering fossil humans into a probability.

Several skeletons found in Guadeloupe in 1803 (engraving, left), near the port of Le Moule, which were taken to be antediluvian people were really, according to Cuvier, merely 'corpses who perished in a few shipwrecks'.

In a letter dated 1859 Boucher de Perthes (seen here in the uniform of director of customs) informed Isidore Geoffroy St-Hilaire, the son of the French naturalist, of the circumstances that led him to discover 'works by men in the Flood' from 1835.

From Celtic antiquities to antediluvian people

Whereas Tournal, Schmerling and a few others were certain that humans existed in prehistoric times, official scientific thought had not made much progress. Somewhat unexpectedly, it was thanks to the stubbornness of an amateur, Jacques Boucher de Crèvecoeur de Perthes (1788–1868) that – after many trials and tribulations – the academic

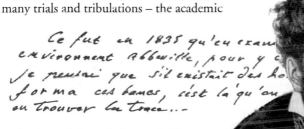

authorities of the period were finally convinced.

Boucher de Perthes, who came from a wealthy family, was the director of customs at Abbeville, and possessed literary talents that he used in very different genres. In addition, he was a

Coupes prises à Saint Acheul (Somme) le 13 Avril 1860. E. Collomb

Opposite: under the dome of the Institut de France, a meeting of the Académie des Sciences is in session. In 1846 Boucher de Perthes addressed his unfinished report, *Antiquités celtiques et antédiluviennes* to this institution. Unfortunately, one of the members of the commission appointed to examine it, Elie de Beaumont, completely rejected his philosophical convictions.

great lover of antiquities – this was the period of Romanticism. He never tired of wandering the vast chalky plateau of Picardy, cut by the valley of the Somme, in search of worked stone tools. In the course of nine years, from 1837 to 1846, he collected more than a thousand worked flints just from the ancient alluvia of the Somme's high terraces.

In 1847 he was finally in a position to publish the sum of his efforts in a monumental work, *Antiquités celtiques et antédiluviennes*, in which he demonstrated in particular that humans had been the contemporaries of the great antediluvian animals: the mammoth, southern

This biface found in the heart of the gravel quarries of St Acheul (watercolour above), near Amiens, no doubt led Dr Rigollot, president of the Société des Antiquaires of Picardy, to be the first to rally to the ideas of Boucher de Perthes.

and straight-tusked elephants, the Etruscan ox, the bison and the rhinoceros.

While retaining the traditional division of world history into two epochs separated by the universal catastrophe of the Flood, which he transposed into the domain of archaeology, Boucher de Perthes foreshadowed in the first volume of his great work the current subdivision of prehistoric times into Palaeolithic (flaked stone culture) and Neolithic (polished stone culture), terms that would only be created some twenty years later by Sir John Lubbock (1834–1913).

Unfortunately, Boucher de Perthes' book contained numerous flights of fancy in varying degrees of eccentricity, which were mingled with digressions on the origin of art. For instance, he claimed that some curiously shaped stones had been worked by people rather than – the actual case – by nature.

The work was greeted with virtually unanimous scepticism, and added to the extreme reluctance of the Académie des Sciences and the Académie des Inscriptions et Belles-Lettres to accept these new ideas.

In 1863 Boucher de Perthes unearthed the jaw of an alleged antediluvian human, five metres below the ground in the quarry of Moulin-Quignon, near Abbeville. It had in fact been placed there fraudulently. This discovery, which was the source of much debate among British and French scholars, would, paradoxically, bring him the fame to which he had aspired throughout his life.

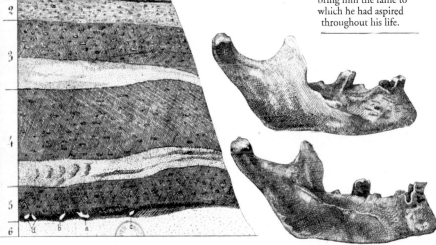

Far from being discouraged, Boucher de Perthes published the second volume of his *Antiquités celtiques et antédiluviennes* ten years later. In it he dealt with the objections raised by his first publication.

The idea that fossil humans were contemporaries of extinct species finally finds acceptance

Although many scientists were still inclined to wait and see, these new theories managed to win over some new supporters, and prestigious ones at that, such as Edouard Lartet and Etienne Geoffroy St-Hilaire.

From this time on events were to progress very quickly. In the year in which it was founded in 1859,

the Société d'Anthropologie in Paris devoted several of its sessions to the discoveries made by Boucher de Perthes.

In the same year British scientists, whose evidence played a large part in the establishment of the truth, gave their support to these new ideas. Neither the Scottish palaeontologist Hugh Falconer (1808–65), fellow of the Royal Society in London, nor the English archaeologist John Evans (1823–1908), still less the British geologists Joseph Prestwich (1812–96) nor even the illustrious Charles Lyell (1797–1875) had any doubts that flint tools were made by humans who lived at the same time as extinct species.

As for those with unshakeable beliefs, the last of those to hold Cuvier's view, their days were numbered.

These engravings from the second half of the 19th century portray primitive humans grappling with ferocious beasts in a hostile nature. The one on this page came from *L'Homme Primitif*, written by Louis Figuier. In his praiseworthy desire to instruct, Figuier denied the 'distressing doctrine' extolled, according to him, by the 'materialist sect', which imagined a link between apes and humans. But Sir Charles Lyell (below), the foremost British geologist, adopted Boucher de Perthes' ideas and would permanently secure the cause that the latter defended for twenty years.

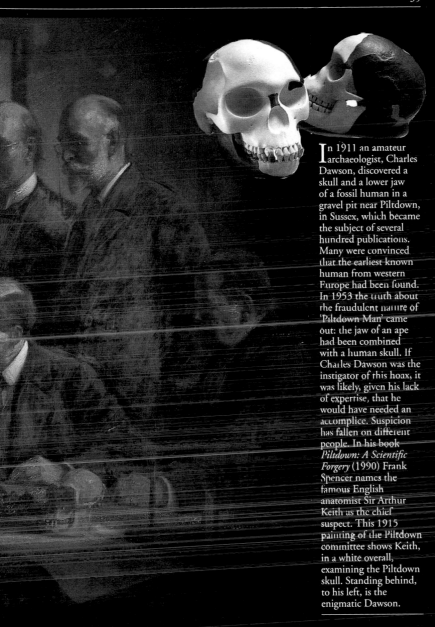

In 1911 an amateur
archaeologist, Charles
Dawson, discovered a
skull and a lower jaw
of a fossil human in a
gravel pit near Piltdown,
in Sussex, which became
the subject of several
hundred publications.
Many were convinced
that the earliest known
human from western
Europe had been found.
In 1953 the truth about
the fraudulent nature of
'Piltdown Man' came
out: the jaw of an ape
had been combined
with a human skull. If
Charles Dawson was the
instigator of this hoax, it
was likely, given his lack
of expertise, that he
would have needed an
accomplice. Suspicion
has fallen on different
people. In his book
*Piltdown: A Scientific
Forgery* (1990) Frank
Spencer names the
famous English
anatomist Sir Arthur
Keith as the chief
suspect. This 1915
painting of the Piltdown
committee shows Keith,
in a white overall,
examining the Piltdown
skull. Standing behind,
to his left, is the
enigmatic Dawson.

1. Mittelländer (Kaukasier). 2 Nubier. 3. Dravida. 4. Malaye. 5 Mongole. 6. Amerikaner. 7. Arktiker (Eskimo). 8 Australier. 9. Neger. 10. Kaffer. 11. Hottentotte. 12. Papua.

The remains of prehistoric people and their tools started to be interpreted in the 19th century because of the emergence of new ideas, such as Darwin's theory of evolution. It became apparent that humankind was closely related to the great apes.

CHAPTER 2

HUMANS: NAKED APES OR LITTLE GODS?

The diversity of the environments that humans have colonized during the last 100,000 years helps to explain their physical differences. Any division of humanity into races, as was so typical in the 19th century (opposite), is, in reality, quite arbitrary. Humanity is the fruit of a single history, the dawn of which was shared with the great apes more than five million years ago.

Right: *The Travelled Monkey*.

As the 19th century progressed, the belief in the biblical Flood theory gave way to a more scientific approach to our early origins. Whatever the legitimacy of the metaphysical view, it is more than three centuries since people were burnt for heresy, and the weakening of dogmas has contributed to a renewed craze and fascination for the prehistory of humanity. As the stakes are high, one inevitable consequence is that old, theologically based ideas surface again periodically.

In actual fact, the close kinship of humans and great apes does not mean that humans are based on the same model as animals. The family relationship is certainly clear from the way both are classified according to common traits. However, this classification simply reflects our genealogy.

In the course of their evolution, humans became capable of communicating and developed a most important attribute: cultural transmission. In the words of François Jacob, winner of the Nobel Prize for Medicine in 1965, humans gradually became 'programmed to learn', thus moving away from simple organic transformation, the programme for which consisted almost entirely of copying innate behaviour from one generation to another.

The different cultures – such as (above) ancient Egyptian and medieval European – that succeeded each other have helped to shape our belief in the advancement and adaptability of the human race. Today the racist philosophies of the past have largely given way to the view that our differences stem from cultural, not biological, variations. Thanks to human evolution and the passing on of knowledge from generation to generation, we may soon – in the 21st century – be in a position to harness the energy of thermonuclear fission and colonize part of our solar system.

Are humans part of the animal kingdom?

Under the Second Empire (1852–70), the question of whether humans belonged to the animal kingdom was still regularly agitating the stormy meetings of the Société d'Anthropologie. Together with other French naturalists, Jean-Louis Armand de Quatrefages (1810–92), professor of anthropology at the Muséum National d'Histoire Naturelle and director of the Société d'Anthropologie, defended the existence of a human kingdom distinct from the animal kingdom. He believed that this view was justified by the fact that only humans possess a notion of good and evil, and a belief in an afterlife and in superior beings.

Quatrefages was not a transformist – in the sense that he did not believe that one species could descend from another – and could not imagine that the classification of living beings might reflect their history. For him, classification was merely a convenient contrivance meant to smooth language and permit reasoning. The creation of a category for humans alone, separate from the animal kingdom, was inevitable. Johann Friedrich Blumenbach, the German anthropologist (1752–1840), shared the same anthropocentric view.

In the course of their history, humans have gradually been less influenced by the natural world around them and the changes in climate that were responsible for their organic evolution. This evolution, which only becomes apparent with the passing generations, takes place slowly because it obeys the laws of genetics. With the appearance of articulate language and then, much later, of writing, people reached a new evolutionary stage – a cultural one – in which every piece of acquired knowledge is rapidly transmitted within each generation. Then, as the African proverb has it, 'An old man who dies is a library burning down'.

Première espèce humaine supérieure:
Méditerranéens (12), *quatre races*:
12ᵃ *Semites*, 12ᵇ *Basques*,
12ᶜ *Caucasiens*, 12ᵈ *Indogermains*.

12	10	8
Méditerranéens	Dravidiens	Arctiques
11	9	7
Nubiens	Américains	Mongols	Au

The eminent German zoologist Ernst Haeckel (1834–1919) subdivided humanity in his *Natürliche Schöpfungsgeschichte* (1868) into twelve species on the basis of hair type, skull shape, skin colour and eye colour, perhaps using anthropological instruments like this board of artificial eyes (right) and this palette of skin colours (left). In Haeckel's opinion, the twelve human species had arisen from one single

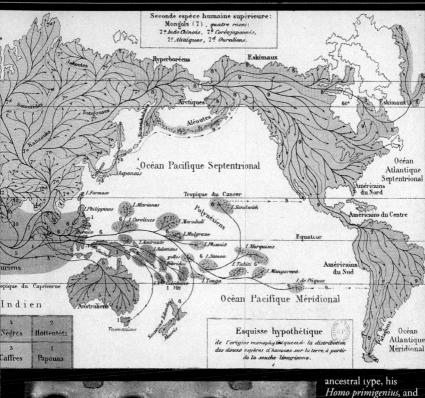

Seconde espèce humaine supérieure:
Mongols (7), quatre races:
7ª Indo-Chinois, 7ª Coréojaponais,
7ª Altaïques, 7ª Ouraliens.

Esquisse hypothétique
de l'origine monophylétique et de la distribution
des douze espèces d'hommes sur la terre, à partir
de la souche lémurienne.

| 4 Nègres | 2 Hottentots |
| 3 Caffres | 1 Papouas |

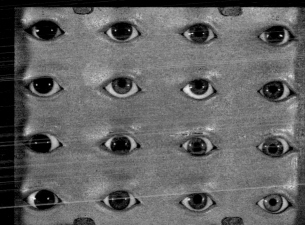

ancestral type, his *Homo primigenius*, and consequently originated in the same country, a continent which he imagined to be submerged beneath the present-day Indian Ocean, touching Madagascar and East Africa (in purple on the map).

In 1791 he had already contrasted bimanous beings (humans) with all the other animals, the quadrumanes. Others, such as the German zoologist Johann Karl Illiger (1775–1813), had already mentioned the *Erecta* (upright position), while the English palaeontologist Richard Owen (1804–92) was talking in terms of beings with superior brains. Today nobody seriously doubts that humans form part of the animal kingdom.

An unwanted ancestor

In 1809 the French scientist Jean-Baptiste de Monet de Lamarck (1744–1829) published his *Philosophie zoologique*, a prophetic book in which he expounded his theory of evolution and set out a system to explain the acquisition of new traits. However, his evolutionary

This typical early 19th-century anthropological instrument was used to measure human skulls whose parameters, it was believed, revealed racial characteristics.

Darwin avait raison

Roman Ciné par MAURICE AUBYN FOX-FILM

In the America of the 1920s, the Protestant traditionalists campaigned against the 'antibiblical' ideas then in vogue in school textbooks, which taught that humankind was descended from the ape. Not wishing his children or anybody else's children to be forced to study such books, John Washington Butler, the Tennessee legislator, managed to have a law passed in 1925 forbidding the teaching of the theory of evolution in public schools.

ideas, which he had toned down for fear of going too far, did not find acceptance at the time. It is true that, in this period, the emperor himself was using his despotic authority to uphold the highly popular creationist views championed by Cuvier.

Half a century later, in 1860, the English biologist Thomas Huxley (1825–95), nicknamed 'Darwin's bulldog', gave a brilliant lecture setting out his illustrious colleague's transformist ideas, and incurred the wrath of the bishop of Oxford, Bishop Wilberforce, who was present. When the bishop asked him whether he claimed descent from an ape through his grandfather or his grandmother, Huxley retorted scathingly that he would rather have an honest ape for his grandfather than a man of restless and versatile intellect who used skills of oratory to obscure scientific questions of which he knew nothing. Like the bishop of Oxford, most people still found the idea that they descended from apes profoundly humiliating.

'The most bestial of all known human skulls'

The year 1856 saw the discovery not only of the first

At the remarkable Scopes trial, held in the state of Tennessee in 1925, evolutionists clashed with the supporters of divine creation. Above: the headquarters of the Anti-Evolution League, which stood opposite the courthouse in which John Thomas Scopes, a science teacher, was sentenced to pay a $100 fine. He was found guilty of teaching that humans are descended from an inferior order of animals.

fossil apes but also of the first recognized fossil humans. In August workmen quarrying marble uncovered a little cave in a vertical cliff nearly twenty metres high, dominating the Neander Valley (Neandertal in German) near Düsseldorf. Beneath their feet the quarrymen were surprised to find a human skeleton in the thick layer of clay; it was stretched out, with its head turned towards the cave entrance.

Believing they had discovered the remains of a cave bear, which were often found in neighbouring caves, the quarrymen did not take much care of the bones and discarded them. Luckily, the quarry's director saw fit to notify one of his friends, Mr Fuhlrott, a natural history teacher, who taught a few kilometres from there in the village of Elberfeld. Fuhlrott immediately recognized that the remains came from a human being and not from a cave bear. He thus saved from complete destruction a skullcap, the femurs, humeri, ulnas, a clavicle, a shoulder-blade, half a pelvis and a few ribs.

Fuhlrott was struck by the skullcap's primitive appearance, with its very low vault, receding forehead, and, particularly, by the presence of enormous brow ridges. He was also intrigued by the unusual thickness of the bony walls, which led him to think that the individual to whom these remains belonged was extremely muscular.

Fuhlrott remembered that the presence of enormous brow ridges was a feature that the English scientist Owen had pointed out in the gorilla, in 1848, on the basis of two heads sent to him by a Protestant missionary from Gabon. He was now convinced that he had in his possession the remains of a remote ancestor, an intermediary between the great apes and humans.

The Neanderthal skullcap (above), which was discovered in 1856, provoked thirty years of memorable debates.

The German anatomist Schaaffhausen reconstructed the Neanderthals in 1888 from two skeletons discovered in a cave at Spy, in Belgium, two years earlier.

Neanderthal: a controversy lasting several decades

As the skull was found by workmen, some people thought they could dispute its authenticity. The question of the primitive Neanderthals was fiercely debated at the Kassel congress of 1857, where the most improbable flights of fancy were constructed. According to one scholar, the skull probably belonged to a stupid hermit. For the French scientist Franz Pruner-Bey it was without doubt a representative of the Celtic race. Others thought they were dealing with a Russian cossack who had died there in 1814; it was opportunely recalled that General Chernichev's cossack army had indeed camped nearby.

Only the anatomist Professor Hermann Schaaffhausen (1816–93) from Bonn shared Fuhlrott's point of view. The human skull that he held in his hands was by far the most interesting he had ever seen in his entire life. For him, the Neanderthal remains undeniably displayed apelike features. In fact, Schaaffhausen, who had long held evolutionist ideas, was convinced that these remains provided proof of humankind's animal origins.

Everyone waited for an opinion from the famous pathologist Rudolf Virchow (1821–1902), who was an undisputed authority in his field in Germany at the time. In his view, it was not a normal man but a malformed idiot, afflicted with rickets and arthritis.

Nowadays Neanderthals are considered to be very close to modern humans; indeed they were classified as *Homo sapiens neanderthalensis*. These stocky and very muscular people had a large flattened head with a prominent nose and receding cheekbones. Below: a late 19th-century reconstruction of a Neanderthal man.

In fact, the controversy raged on for almost thirty years, even though Charles Lyell himself, having carefully examined the remains as well as the cave, was in favour of a new species of human distinct from *Homo sapiens*. His assistant, William King, even named it *Homo neanderthalensis* in 1864. But it was not until the discovery of the Neanderthal jaw in La Naulette Cave near Dinant in Belgium, in 1866, that the hypothesis that this Neanderthal was a pathological case was seriously called into question. The absence of a chin – considered an apelike feature at the time – on the La Naulette jaw was immediately striking. For the French anthropologist Ernest T. Hamy, the people of La Naulette, Gibraltar and Neanderthal belonged to a single species, and even to a single race, which, according to him, was the first of the fossil human races.

After the discovery in 1886 at Spy in Belgium – of two skeletons, one of which was almost complete – that again displayed the same features, even the most hardened sceptics had to admit that the Neanderthals were not idiots or even a hoax, and that another kind of human had indeed walked the earth before us.

The site of La Ferrassie, in the Dordogne, was discovered towards the end of the last century. After ten years of methodical excavations, on 17 September 1909, Denis Peyrony uncovered the tibia and femur of the first of the eight Neanderthal skeletons buried in the great rock shelter some 40,000 years ago. Above: two Neanderthal skulls.

The so-called Cro-Magnon 'race'

Around the same time, the world recognized the existence of another type of human with the discovery in 1868 of five skeletons at the back of the rock shelter of Cro-Magnon, very close to the village of Les Eyzies in the Dordogne. According to Louis Lartet (1840–99), son of the palaeontologist Edouard Lartet, who was entrusted with the excavation of Cro-Magnon by the Ministry of Public Instruction, the position of the skeletons and the distribution of the remains accompanying them provided evidence that they were deliberately buried. Six years after their discovery, in 1874, these people with anatomically modern traits were considered the prototypes of a new race: the so-called Cro-Magnon 'race'. Although they were associated with Palaeolithic tools, the antiquity of these Cro-Magnon people – who succeeded Neanderthals in Europe – was called into question, in particular by the French prehistorian Gabriel de Mortillet (1821–98), who could not bring himself to admit that Palaeolithic people were already burying their dead. Some French people who bore a grudge against Germany after the Franco-Prussian War of 1870–1 were delighted that a human type with a well-developed physiognomy and fine and elegant features had been discovered in their country, while the uncivilized Neanderthals, who still gave the impression of being ape-men, had been found in Germany.

In 1868, during the construction of the railway between Agen and Limoges, workmen discovered a rock shelter at Cro-Magnon, filled with bones and worked tools. Louis Lartet undertook the first excavations. Several adult human skeletons, which became the type-specimens for the Cro-Magnon 'race', were found, including this skull nicknamed the 'Old Man'.

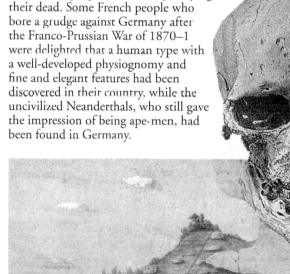

Section of the Cro-Magnon rock shelter.

The discovery of the Cro-Magnon people caught the imagination of the illustrators of popular educational works, who portrayed what they saw as the customs of these 'indigenous savages'. Yet the Cro-Magnon people had many of the features of modern humans, as is shown in both this recent reconstruction (below left) and the skull of the 'Old Man' of Cro-Magnon with its vertical brow and protruding chin. Below and opposite: the site of Les Eyzies in the Dordogne.

There still remained the task of discovering the makers of the oldest worked flints, collected most notably by Boucher de Perthes; no authentic vestiges of them had yet been found.

Did the 'missing link' live in Asia?

Those who were convinced that humankind was descended from apes began searching for the 'missing link', as it was known at the time, between the great apes and ourselves.

In 1868 the eminent German biologist and zoologist Ernst Haeckel did not hesitate to represent a Papuan at the end of his human family tree; he was convinced that the Papuans and Melanesians were closely related to the ancestral type, the hypothetical *Homo primigenius*, as some took pleasure in naming it. Struck by the resemblance between human embryos and those of gibbons, which live in Southeast Asia, Haeckel concluded that there had been 'Gardens of Paradise' in this part of the world, on a continent that was partly submerged beneath the present-day Indian Ocean, the 'Lemuria' of the English scholar Philip Lytley Sclater.

Thomas Huxley, the passionate advocate of Darwin's ideas, believed that there was no distinction between humans and other animals, especially apes. In his book *Evidence as to Man's Place in Nature*, he demonstrated particularly that there are more differences between the hand and foot of the gorilla and the orang-utan than between those of the gorilla and those of man. Humans were simply a family within the order of primates.

Below: skeletons of a gibbon, an orang-utan, a chimpanzee, a gorilla and a human.

Ernst Haeckel taught that our distant ancestors resembled gibbons. This photograph shows him holding the hand of a gibbon skeleton in a symbolic gesture. Behind him, on his right, is the skeleton of a child.

In contrast to Haeckel, Thomas Huxley and Charles Darwin respectively put forward the hypothesis – in two remarkable books published a few years apart, *Evidence as to Man's Place in Nature* (1863) and *The Descent of Man* (1871) – that our primitive ancestors must have lived in Africa rather than Asia, since chimpanzees and gorillas were, in their view, humankind's closest relatives. It was not long before the finds in Asia, in Java, were made, and for a while appeared to support Haeckel's point of view.

Anticipating the discoveries, Haeckel named the missing link – with his customary audacity – *Pithecanthropus alalus*, that is, silent ape-man.

Eugène Dubois sets off on the ape-man's trail

During this period a young Dutch anatomist by the name of Eugène Dubois (1858–1940), a keen reader and admirer of Haeckel, enlisted in the Dutch army medical corps, and in 1887 embarked for Sumatra and, later on, for Java, which were then Dutch colonies. Fired by the idea of

In reconstructing the genealogical tree of all living organisms, Haeckel relied on the embryogenic method. He adopted for his own ends one of the laws already observed by Geoffroy St-Hilaire, according to which an animal's embryogenic development is merely a brief and rapid 'recapitulation' of the successive stages of its evolution.

finding the relics of these ape-people, Dubois was thoroughly convinced that humankind's ancestor was descended from a primitive gibbon. The island of Sumatra, as Dubois was well aware, was indeed inhabited both by gibbons and by orang-utans. But only gibbons lived on Java.

It is astounding to think that, after months of relentless searching, Dubois was really able to discover the remains of a hominid (a neutral term for a human being that does not specify time or gender) on Java, when one considers how extremely rare they are. It is true that during these long months he amassed no less than 12,000 fossil bones.

In 1891, having already found a jaw fragment and an isolated tooth, he unearthed a skullcap of vaguely human appearance

B elow: the skullcap of *Pithecanthropus erectus,* so-called Java Man, and photographs of Eugène Dubois.

Eugène Dubois, the young Dutch military doctor, had just arrived in Sumatra when he learned that a human skull, which turned out to belong to *Homo sapiens,* had been discovered near Wajak, in Java (landscape left). He immediately set off to Java and shortly afterwards discovered the human remains at Trinil on the banks of the Solo River (below) at the foot of the Lawu-Kukusan volcano. Dubois was undeniably blessed with incredible luck, but he also had the good fortune to be helped by fifty workers that he had recruited on the Trinil dig alone. He wrote to Haeckel from Batavia to announce the happy news. The discovery of the missing link provided final confirmation of the zoologist's bold predictions. Presented at the third international congress of zoology in Leiden, Holland, in 1895, the remains of *Pithecanthropus erectus,* Java Man, were the subject of endless discussion for decades.

as well as an isolated tooth at the town of Trinil, under the alluvia of the Solo River

The skull had a very low, receding brow as well as prominent brow ridges. To Dubois' astonishment, when viewed from above there was marked narrowing behind the eye sockets. Curiously, he at first tried to establish a link between these remains and a chimpanzee; since this

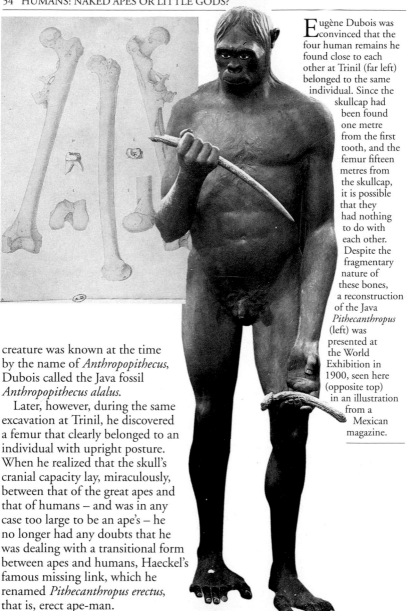

Eugène Dubois was convinced that the four human remains he found close to each other at Trinil (far left) belonged to the same individual. Since the skullcap had been found one metre from the first tooth, and the femur fifteen metres from the skullcap, it is possible that they had nothing to do with each other. Despite the fragmentary nature of these bones, a reconstruction of the Java *Pithecanthropus* (left) was presented at the World Exhibition in 1900, seen here (opposite top) in an illustration from a Mexican magazine.

creature was known at the time by the name of *Anthropopithecus*, Dubois called the Java fossil *Anthropopithecus alalus*.

Later, however, during the same excavation at Trinil, he discovered a femur that clearly belonged to an individual with upright posture. When he realized that the skull's cranial capacity lay, miraculously, between that of the great apes and that of humans – and was in any case too large to be an ape's – he no longer had any doubts that he was dealing with a transitional form between apes and humans, Haeckel's famous missing link, which he renamed *Pithecanthropus erectus*, that is, erect ape-man.

The discovery of Java Man marks the birth of human palaeontology

Although the importance of the find was hailed on all sides, and people paid tribute to the man who had discovered it, scepticism remained almost universal. For some, the Java fossil was a somewhat primitive native; for others, it was merely a large gibbon. In Virchow's view, the narrowing visible behind the eye sockets had never been found in humans: it was only seen in apes. However, Dubois carried on claiming that the enigmatic form from Java was clearly a transitional stage between apes and humans. Discouraged and bitter about the fierce opposition to his theory, he only permitted a few rare visitors to examine his finds.

At the turn of the century, new expeditions went to Java, but they did not make any new finds. The controversy dragged on interminably. Dubois grew weary of the struggle and of being misunderstood, and refused access to his fossils.

Meanwhile, a skull had been discovered in 1929 at Zhoukoudian in China. Known as Peking Man, it displayed undeniable affinities with the skull from the Java *Pithecanthropus*. In the 1930s Ralph von Koenigswald, a German palaeontologist (1902–82), brought to light more *Pithecanthropus* remains in Java, first not far from Trinil, and then at Sangiran. Studies showed that the Peking and Java remains came not from an ape-man but from a true human, who was then named *Homo erectus*. Today they are regarded as two subspecies – *Homo erectus erectus* (from Java) and *Homo erectus pekinesis* (from China). Human palaeontology had just been born.

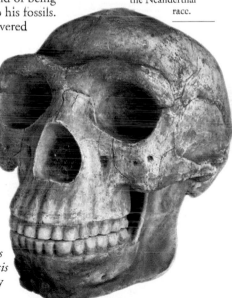

Dubois denied that there was any resemblance between the skulls found in Trinil and Peking (below), which he regarded as representing the Neanderthal race.

Humans cannot be descended from the apes because, in some ways, they are apes themselves. Really we should ask whether humans descend from 'an' ape. Naturally, people are not descended from a present-day ape, any more than we are descended from our cousins. But palaeontology and all the disciplines of the biological sciences have taught us that humans and modern great apes had common ancestors several million years ago.

CHAPTER 3

OUR ANCESTORS' ANCESTORS

This footprint (opposite), dating to 3.8 million years ago, proves that a bipedal, upright hominid existed long before the first humans. There is evidence of a big toe alongside the other toes and a double curve of the plantar arch.

Right: a chimpanzee.

The protein clock

In the early 1970s scientists studying modifications in the structure of blood proteins in the primates calculated how long ago the lineage leading to the great apes (chimpanzees and gorillas) in the family Pongidae diverged from the human lineage. This 'protein clock', as it would soon be called, was based on a constant rate of protein evolution during the history of the primates. Just as for the measurement of temperature, the date chosen for zero degrees is arbitrary, depending on whether one refers to the Kelvin, Celsius, Fahrenheit or Réaumur scale, so in the case of the protein clock, it was decided to make zero point the moment

The term 'ape' covers a wide category of primates. The suborder anthropoids, which includes all the monkeys, apes and humans, contains all the descendants of a common ancestral type. Although opinions differ on the antiquity of the common ancestors, there is no doubt that they were apes.

Numerous attempts have been made to teach the great apes a language. Today more emphasis is placed on the study of the abilities and mental processes brought into play by the use of a language based on symbols that are meaningless in themselves, which the animal has to combine and re-use.

when the Old World monkeys separated into the super-families hominoids (gibbons, gorillas, chimpanzees and humans), and cercopithecoids (macaques, colobuses, baboons, etc). At the time this date was thought to be well known, and was estimated to be thirty million years ago. Working from this date, it was calculated that the human line diverged from the African great apes about six million years ago.

Of the 23 pairs of chromosomes that are common to humans and chimpanzees, 13 are identical but the other 10 are arranged differently: some segments are completely reversed (diagram opposite).

Closer and closer cousins...

Although other dates were subsequently proposed, using data from genetics, cytogenetics, serology and immunology, it was later confirmed that humans and great apes had only recently diverged; indeed, further confirmation was provided by their extreme genetic similarity in that they shared almost ninety-nine per cent of their chromosomal material. Thus, only a one per cent difference in the genes of the common ancestor was sufficient to produce major effects in its descendants, in terms of both anatomy and behaviour, which finally resulted in humankind.

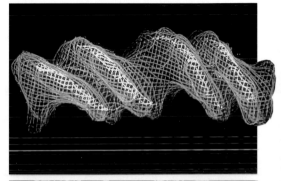

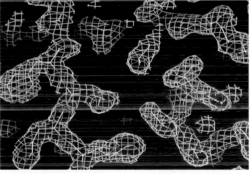

Some scientists believe that only five to seven million years separate us from this event, although at present neither palaeontologists nor molecular biologists agree about the actual date. Be that as it may, one of the most important points is that the great apes and humans are closely connected. After all, it has recently been noticed that chimpanzee communities share with us an incest taboo (mother–son), a cerebral

Much information can be gleaned from the study of chromosomes – made up of DNA molecules wound into a double helix (top) – and proteins (above).

capacity for elementary language, a developed social organization, an intolerance between males, and even a consciousness of their own identity.

Geographical distribution of early primates

The early history of humankind merges with the history of all the primates – tarsiers, lorises, lemurs, and, later, monkeys and apes. Sixty million years separate one of the last primates, humans, from the first known primate.

Although the oldest primate undoubtedly did not live at the same time as the last dinosaurs, it formed part of a whole procession of archaic primates that bore far more resemblance to rodents than to small lemurs, because of the peculiar shape of their incisors. In this period, at the start of the Tertiary, they colonized Europe and North America at the same time, because there was then a land bridge linking arctic Canada, Greenland and Europe, which thus formed a single continent.

Barely five million years later, two new groups of prosimians lived on this continent, this time prosimians of a far more modern appearance: the tarsiiforms and the adapiforms, the first of which was found in 1822 in the gypsum quarries of the hill of

The origin of the lemurs from Madagascar (below and opposite) is unknown because no fossil of the group has yet been found on the island or anywhere else. These lemurs constitute a very diverse group, with about thirty surviving species. Such diversification resulted from the fact that Madagascar became detached from Africa a very long time ago, forming a real Noah's Ark where lemurs could

thrive without competition. Certainly Madagascar became separated more than thirty-five million years ago, since it is then that the first apes appeared in Africa. They never existed on the island.

Montmartre. At the time
they were considered to be
the origin of the anthropoids,
the suborder that includes all the apes,
monkeys and humans, but the question over the
origin of the apes, although debated, was not resolved.

As for the sudden appearance of these two groups in
Europe and North America, an enigmatic phenomenon
in itself, it too would have remained the subject of bitter
controversy, if North Africa had not recently produced
fossils of prosimians that are older than those of the
northern continent, since they are more than sixty
million years old. This unexpected discovery
constitutes a serious argument in favour of an African
origin for not only the prosimians but also all the apes.

Whatever the validity of these new hypotheses, almost
all the prosimians – both adapiforms and tarsiiforms
– were to disappear suddenly around thirty five million
years ago. Their abrupt extinction
was certainly caused by a profound
deterioration in the climate.

The *Leptadapis*
(skull below) is
one of the best known
adapiform primates.
Like the rest of its genus
that lived forty million
years ago, it has
enormous eye sockets
on the front of its
skull which give it
stereoscopic vision,
a *sine qua non*
condition for jumping
and running from
branch to branch.

The key role of Africa and Arabia

From then on, the main theatre
of primate history was to shift, and
events would take place further south,

in the tropics of Africa and Arabia. It was here
that the oldest known apes appeared between
forty and thirty million years ago. Whereas almost all
African apes come from the Fayum region, to the
south-west of Cairo in Egypt, the remains of apes from
the Arabian peninsula were discovered recently in the
stony mountains of Dhofar, halfway between
the Persian Gulf and the Red Sea in
the sultanate of Oman.

Distant ancestors of the great apes and hominids, they were the first to possess, like us, a set of thirty-two teeth after the loss of a premolar in each half-jaw. Being tree-dwellers and good climbers, these quadrupeds, the size of a small macaque, probably inhabited the tropical forests that border the rivers and deltas.

It was perhaps in a landscape like this – a humid tropical mangrove forest stretching along a sea shore, the scene of occasional intense volcanic activity – that our most distant ancestors lived.

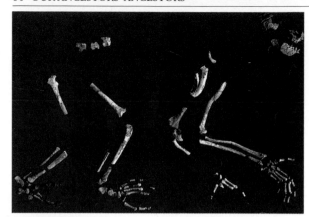

Although the first apes suddenly appeared in Africa around 30 to 35 million years ago, no fossil ape is known on that continent for the next 12 million years. With the appearance of the great fault in the East African Rift Valley, more than 20 million years ago, palaeontologists have discovered numerous remains of fossil apes, some of them very complete, like the famous *Proconsul africanus* skeleton (above left) found on Rusinga Island in Lake Victoria by Mary Leakey in 1948.

It is curious that no fossil apes have been found in the Old World from between thirty and twenty-two million years ago. After that period they suddenly reappear in East Africa.

From now on the Old World would be the theatre for a whole series of movements in the earth's crust, including the upthrust of the Alpine chain, the rise of the Himalayas, the beginning of a series of geological faults in the East African Rift Valley, the opening of the Red Sea, and, most importantly, the collision of the two great continents, Asia and Africa, which was to have such a profound effect on the relief of the continents.

From forest to savannah

Around fifteen million years ago major climatic changes on a global scale were to bring about the birth of a new type of landscape in East Africa: the savannah, into which many animals quickly moved. Leaving the relatively safe environment of the forest that they had occupied until then, some apes would spread throughout the Old World, in Europe and Asia, taking advantage of the existence of a land bridge between Africa and Asia after the collision of these two continents.

In Asia the changes in habitat resulted in some apes becoming orang-utans several million years later, while in Africa they found expression in a new diet and, most notably, in locomotion.

In these savannahs with few trees, tree-dwelling animals were forced to descend to the ground from time to time. As they started to spend more and more time on the ground, they gradually adapted their mode of locomotion. Around five million years ago bipedalism became the primary form of locomotion in the australopithecines, the early primitive hominids. The reason for this major change in behaviour was further severe drought to the east of the African Rift.

As for the gorillas and chimpanzees, being more conservative, they would take refuge in the more humid environments of West Africa.

Around five million years ago the mountains forming the roof of Africa created a barrier that dramatically reduced the amount of rainfall to the east of the rift. The result was these very open savannah landscapes (bottom) on the great plains of East Africa.

The Rift Valley, the enormous fault that cuts through East Africa, is clearly visible on this satellite image of the earth.

Opposite bottom: skull of *Aegyptopithecus*, an early quadruped.

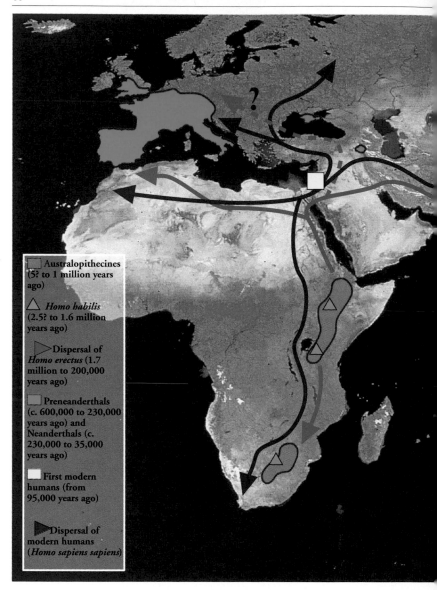

Australopithecines
(5? to 1 million years
ago)

△ *Homo habilis*
(2.5? to 1.6 million
years ago)

▷ Dispersal of
Homo erectus (1.7
million to 200,000
years ago)

Preneanderthals
(c. 600,000 to 230,000
years ago) and
Neanderthals (c.
230,000 to 35,000
years ago)

First modern
humans (from
95,000 years ago)

▶ Dispersal of
modern humans
(*Homo sapiens sapiens*)

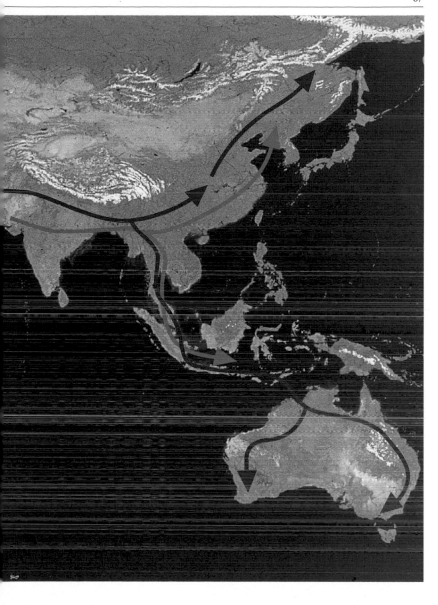

On 7 February 1925, Professor Raymond Dart, an Australian-born anatomist working in Johannesburg, published in the journal *Nature* the description of a fossilized skull that had been discovered at a limestone quarry at Taung in South Africa. He named it *Australopithecus africanus* (southern ape from Africa), the missing link, in his view, between apes and humans.

CHAPTER 4

FROM THE TAUNG CHILD TO LUCY

The reconstruction of a couple of australopithecines from Afar in Ethiopia, more than three million years ago (left), and the entrance to the famous Olduvai Gorge in Tanzania (right) symbolize the adventure of Africa, the place where our most distant ancestors lie buried and where palaeontologists try to piece together the puzzle of our evolution.

Australopithecus, **Africa and humans**

Dart's controversial theories were not accepted immediately. His missing-link theory proved to be a red herring, though he was correct in thinking that these were the remains of the oldest known human ancestor to be discovered in Africa. This continent, which until then had been silent on the problem of human origins, would from now on be the scene of the most tremendous palaeontological adventure: in fact, the earliest hominids, known as australopithecines, have turned up in Africa. As Charles Darwin had already predicted in *The Descent of Man*, this continent was undoubtedly the place where our first ancestors emerged. Known today to have existed five million years ago, and perhaps more, in East Africa, the australopithecines were small bipedal creatures that became extinct less than a million years ago, if the age (less than 900,000 years) of the deposits at Taung Cave in South Africa is confirmed.

In 1924, during a mining operation at a limestone quarry at Taung in South Africa, the fossil skull of a child was blasted out of the rock from a depth of fifteen metres. Having been used for a while as a paperweight by the mine's director, it finally came into the hands of Raymond Dart (left). In February of the following year he announced the discovery of an extinct ape intermediate between living anthropoids and humans, which he named *Australopithecus africanus* (reconstruction below), the first species, according to Dart, of a new family of primates – the *Homo-simiadae*.

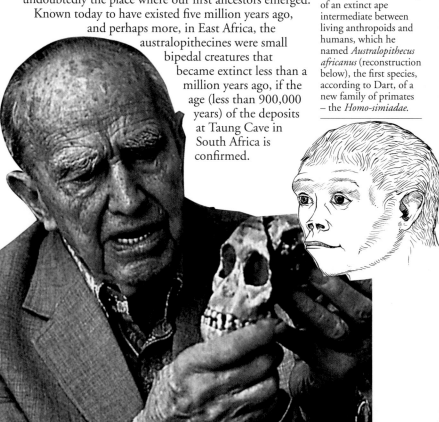

Discovered at the beginning of this century, the sites of Omo in Ethiopia (left) were explored in 1932 by the French palaeontologist Camille Arambourg. In 1967 Omo was the scene of an international expedition. Almost 100 tonnes of fossil bones were collected.

The eldorado of the East African rifts

Some thirty years later, it was the turn of the Rift Valley, an enormous fault running through more than 3000 kilometres of East Africa, to witness a tremendous deployment of equipment and researchers. In these rifts, marked by a string of great lakes and formed almost twenty million years ago, several thousand metres of lacustrine and fluviatile sediments have accumulated, making an ideal trap for fossilization. This exceptional phenomenon accounts for the fact that all the ancient sites containing fossil hominids in Africa – except for a few sites in South Africa – are located along this fault.

Due to the effect of the movements of the earth's crust, these sedimentary layers, at first piled on top of one another, often toppled over until they looked like the pages of an open book; the finest example

This view of the great Rift Valley shows the immensity of the scar that cuts through East Africa from north to south, caused by the slow separation – a few hundred metres per million years – of the African plate to the west and the Somalian plate to the east.

is provided by the famous sites in Ethiopia's Omo River Basin. Here the fossil remains of our ancestors and their numerous worked tools can often be found lying on the ground. Volcanic deposits interspersed with these geological layers make it possible, through the radioactive elements they contain, to date this evidence of our remote history.

All these sites in Africa have yielded two distinct groups of australopithecines. One comprises three small 'gracile' forms: the smallest, *Australopithecus ramidus*, which was the most apelike hominid ancestor, dating to around 4.4 million years ago, *Australopithecus afarensis* – best represented by Lucy (see p. 84) – and finally *Australopithecus africanus*. The other group comprises three 'robust' forms (*Australopithecus aethiopicus*, *Australopithecus robustus* and *Australopithecus boisei*).

They all had a concave and forward-jutting face, a poorly developed brow, a more or less pronounced ridge above the eyes, and molars and premolars that were generally enormous (except in the case of *Australopithecus ramidus*). None had a chin. Equipped with a brain that was still small (450 to

A group of African australopithecines (below) and hyenas fight over the carcass of an antelope.

550 cubic centimetres) compared with ours (1400 cubic centimetres on average), these hominids were already moving around upright on their two legs, but had not lost their ability to climb trees.

The robust australopithecines, who were distinguished from their gracile counterparts by the presence of a very marked crest on the top of their skull, were strange beings with enormous cheek teeth, operated by a powerful jaw. They had a cranial capacity of 550 cubic centimetres. Strictly vegetarian, living off a diet of roots, nuts and seeds, they disappeared, with no descendants, around one million years ago.

The gracile australopithecines, some of which left the forest environments along the rivers and gradually reached the savannahs, are considered by some to be the makers of the first worked tools. Hunters of small game, and occasional meat-eaters, they had a fairly omnivorous

Discovered in 1911 by a German entomologist, Olduvai Gorge (left) was to become one of the centrepieces of African prehistory. From the 1930s the famous British scholars Louis Leakey (1903–72) and his wife Mary (1913–) devoted themselves to exploring the site, where there were outcrops of major lacustrine deposits dating to the last two million years. Their extensive work in the area earned them great distinction. However, it was not until 17 July 1959 that Mary discovered one of the most famous australopithecine skulls (far left) which Louis called *Zinjanthropus boisei* – Zinj being an ancient East African name; in fact it was a robust australopithecine, the first to be found in this part of Africa.

diet. Contemporaries of the robust australopithecines, these far weaker beings – ranging in stature from 1 to 1.3 metres, and in weight from 30 to 40 kilos – had a slightly smaller brain, close to 450 cubic centimetres on average.

In the wake of *Homo habilis*

While some palaeontologists regard the australopithecines to be an evolutionary cul-de-sac, in the sense that they are not considered to be the direct ancestors of humankind, others believe that they may have given rise to the first humans, who differed from their predecessors the australopithecines in several respects – their larger size, a flattened face with no ridge above the eyes, smaller molars and premolars, and, most importantly, a much bigger brain, with a capacity up to 800 cubic centimetres. In 1964 Louis Leakey named this new type of hominid *Homo habilis*, that is skilful person, because the study of the phalanges of their hands revealed an ability to grip stone tools.

The fossilized remains of this new species, which came from the famous Olduvai Gorge in Tanzania, were dated to 1.8 million years ago. Leakey's announcement immediately provoked some very strong criticism concerning the attribution of these bones to a human species, and the inevitably arbitrary definition of humanity. In order to solve the problem, scientists enumerated a hundred anatomical features peculiar to the human genus. This list of characteristics, drawn up especially for palaeontologists – who only ever have disparate fragments of fossils at their disposal – left out, with good reason, all the other biological features, not to mention behavioural and cultural traits.

In 1961 Mary Leakey discovered in Olduvai Gorge a skull of a new human species, *Homo habilis*, the oldest representative of the genus *Homo*. Eleven years later her son Richard would in his turn reveal a far more complete skull of *Homo habilis*, better known by its catalogue number at the National Museum of Kenya, the famous ER-1470. The head has been reconstructed (below) by adding the missing parts and the tissues and muscles of the face. The imprint of the brain, whose size is up to forty-five per cent greater than that of the australopithecines, suggests that it might have possessed the neurological bases of speech. In any case, the discovery of circular structures provides evidence that *Homo habilis* had a relatively complex culture.

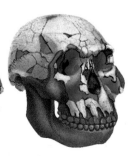

The significance of tools in defining humans

In the course of time, as the great East African sites were explored, a very ancient industry of pebbles that

Homo habilis (left) undeniably made an extensive toolkit, mostly made up of pebbles worked on one or both faces. The technique of striking flakes off a pebble is known as the Oldowan industry, after the site of Olduvai, where the first such tools were found.

The skull of *Homo habilis*, ER-1470, which was found at Koobi Fora near Lake Turkana, was originally made up of hundreds of bone fragments; fitting them together took several weeks of patience and skill. Below is a reconstruction of *Homo habilis*.

had barely been retouched and of broken quartz flakes was discovered. Dating back almost three million years and probably made by the australopithecines, the earliest tools used in the world provide irrefutable evidence of the development of thought – with all its cultural and even social implications – in beings which were not yet human.

Faced with the often contradictory interpretations of the fossil hominid remains, the prehistorian considers that a tool, that is, a deliberately modified natural object, speaks volumes about the degree of 'hominization' (or the process of becoming human) in the person who made it. However, it is very difficult to identify exactly who this person was,

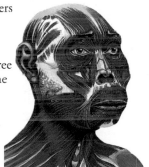

because, in the case of East Africa, we are more or less certain that two, or even three, types of hominid coexisted during this crucial period – around two million years ago. And this invention was made independently by at least two of them. In fact, we can no longer be sure that the use of tools is a factor in what makes us human. For this reason many palaeontologists continue to define humans in terms of biological rather than cultural behaviour. However, it is certain that the making of tools, even very primitive ones, requires a logical series of actions conceived by reflective thought.

While it is still very difficult to know whether the oldest hominids altered or retouched organic materials such as wood, bones or teeth, it is certain that the first objects to be made of stone date back almost three million years. Several sites in East Africa lay claim to this honour at present. Two of them are located in Ethiopia – at Afar and Omo.

At Afar, worked pebbles, cores and flakes have been found buried in volcanic ash dating to more than two and a half million years ago. The worked pebbles were obtained by striking flakes off a pebble. This task was not performed in an arbitrary manner; it affected one or both faces, or even truncated the whole thickness of the pebble.

The oldest stone tools known in the world come from three sites: Kada Gona in the Afar Triangle of Ethiopia; localities 71 and 123 at Omo; and Koobi Fora to the east of Lake Turkana in Kenya. Made of worked pebbles, in the case of Kada Gona (below), or small flakes of quartz as at Omo (left), these still rudimentary tools are dated to between 2.1 and 2.6 million years ago. In this photograph taken in the 1960s (opposite) Louis Leakey points out the very spot where, in 1929, he discovered countless tools of volcanic glass at Kariandusi in Kenya. From that moment on Leakey would become increasingly convinced that he would find similar remains in Olduvai Gorge.

These tools, which were still very crude, were no doubt used for cutting hides, scraping bark and skins, or crushing bones and shells. As for the core, it was a stone block, generally of volcanic rock, which had had flakes detached from it. Although the technique was identical to that of working pebbles, the intention was different because it involved obtaining flakes that were extremely sharp when fresh.

At Omo, there is just an industry of very numerous little flakes, obtained from pebbles or from quartz nodules. While for a long time it was thought that the upright stance in hominids freed the hands for making tools, it now seems increasingly clear that two to three million years, or even more, separate bipedalism (and consequently the freeing of hands) from the first worked tools. It therefore appears that the mental faculties had to be developed before pebbles could be fashioned almost three million years ago.

Bipedal locomotion

The increase in the size of the brain, the centre of thought, was one of the main factors in making humans unique.

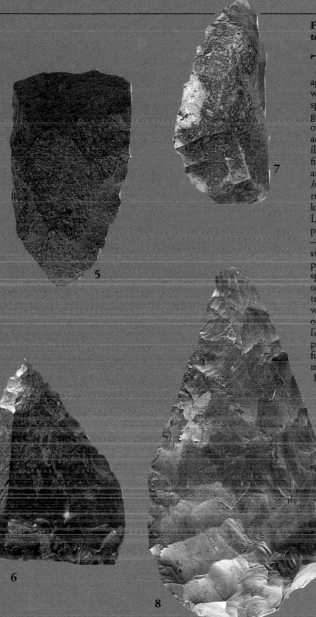

From worked pebbles to harpoon points...

The typical tool of 1.9 million years ago was the pebble that was worked without special preparation, generally flaked on only one side (2) and often accompanied by crude flakes (1). This toolkit, first found at Olduvai and made by *Homo habilis*, defined that still rudimentary industry known as the Oldowan. Later on, the way pebbles were worked – some over their whole surface, resulting in polyhedrons or spheroids – started to develop. Knapping techniques, which would gradually be organized around a function, evolved particularly slowly for several hundred millennia before humans – *Homo erectus* this time – managed to produce new tools in a wide variety of rocks (3, 4, 5). At first these were rather crude knives with a sinuous cutting edge, then, because of increasingly precise actions, beautiful almond-shaped flints with a regular cutting edge (8).

80

The invention of tools

The Acheulian bifaces or handaxes (3, 4, see pages 78–9) and cleavers, tools with a transverse cutting edge (5), were used for a very long time before other cultures started to employ tools made on flakes once again. These later cultures applied new pressure techniques (6, 7, 10, 11, 12), consisting of detaching flakes from the surface of a core (9) by means of pointed instruments. The fabrication of such tools sometimes required a long series of preparatory stages. It is only towards the end of the last glacial period that the nomadic hunters of the Upper Palaeolithic would learn to make tools that were increasingly sharp and pointed. With these tools bone and deer antler were worked to produce awls, eyed needles, harpoons or spearpoints (14, 18).

13

16

17

18

14

15

In other words, it made them different from other animals. Indeed, some scientists have even chosen the arbitrary figures of 700 to 800 cubic centimetres as the point at which apes become human. To attain a cranial capacity higher than this means crossing the 'cerebral Rubicon'. Of course, in a more or less continuous evolutionary process, a cut-off point like this has no meaning. Nevertheless, a number of scholars have always thought, albeit without proof, that an upright stance and bipedalism preceded the increase in the brain's size.

When, after the First World War, the skull of the Taung Child was presented to Professor Dart, he was convinced that the young individual to which it belonged usually stood upright. In fact, this theory was not based on any evidence, because the appropriate bones – the limb bones and the pelvis – which alone would have provided conclusive proof, were missing. Support for Dart was to come from a Scottish physician and part-time palaeontologist, Robert Broom (1866–1951), who, a few years after the Second World War, discovered several pelvic bones as well as a spinal column in two other sites in South Africa – at Sterkfontein and Swartkrans. These finds provided decisive evidence for the existence of an upright stance in australopithecines.

The use of sophisticated techniques, like these broken-down images of walking (below) employed in studies of the biomechanics of the locomotion of fossil humans, or those obtained by scanner that allow the inaccessible parts of a brain (bottom) to be seen, shows the specialized nature of palaeoanthropologists' work.

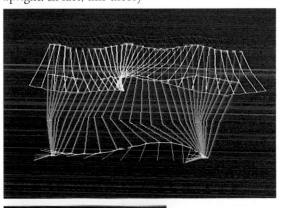

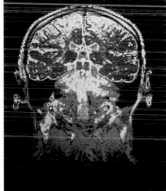

As the genus *Australopithecus* had been founded on the skull of a child (who was, therefore, not fully developed), further fossil evidence was needed to confirm Dart's hypothesis, Dr Robert Broom (opposite) became the first to find the skull of an adult australopithecine at Sterkfontein, near Johannesburg, in 1936.

The resounding confirmation of bipedalism
in remote prehistory came from the discovery by
Donald Johanson and his Franco-American team at
Hadar in Ethiopia in 1974 of an astonishingly complete
skeleton, known as Lucy.

Two years later humanlike footprints were found
at Laetoli in Tanzania in volcanic ash that has been
dated to 3.6 million years. For two seasons, none
of the palaeontologists working at Laetoli had
suspected their existence. It was only on a September
evening in 1976 that one of them, Andrew Hill,
a British scientist, noticed two prints that resembled
those made by human feet among numerous tracks
of birds, elephants, rhinoceros and other mammals.

In 1978 Mary Leakey uncovered a series of prints
with two parallel trails. Analysis of the footprints
showed that they had been made by two individuals,
perhaps walking side by side, one of whom was
140 centimetres tall, while the other was smaller
and measured 120 centimetres. Thanks to the
exceptional state of preservation of the footprints,
it is possible to prove that these individuals were
walking perfectly upright. It is clear from this
evidence that bipedalism is an extremely ancient
attribute and probably goes back well beyond
five million years.

Below: the palaeo-
anthropologists Yves
Coppens and Donald
Johanson (right).

It is in the sites in the Afar Triangle of Ethiopia that the Franco-American team of Maurice Taïeb, Donald Johanson and Yves Coppens unearthed the fifty-two bone fragments of an australopithecine known as Lucy, after the Beatles song 'Lucy in the Sky with Diamonds' that was popular at the time. Conclusive proof of bipedalism came from the fragile remains of this young female representative of *Australopithecus afarensis* – from her skeleton (opposite top), of which forty per cent has been found, and from these footprints (opposite far left) discovered at Laetoli in Tanzania, left by members of Lucy's genus a few hundred thousand years earlier.

Left: a reconstruction of Lucy.

While the species *Homo habilis* proved that the genus *Homo* had originated in Africa, several human fossils generally attributed to *Homo erectus* testify to its appearance there 1.7 million years ago. Setting out from the sub-Saharan regions where this hominid lived for several hundred thousand years, *Homo erectus* eventually inhabited North Africa, Asia and probably Europe.

CHAPTER 5
THE LONG MARCH OF 'HOMO ERECTUS'

A rational explanation for the origin of fire was given in the 1st century BC by the Roman poet Lucretius: 'It is lightning that brought the first flame down to earth for the use of mortals.' In the picture opposite *Homo erectus* discovers fire.

Right: bust of Peking Man.

We owe *Homo erectus* a lot

Homo erectus, those humans who are sometimes called pithecanthropes – a name that should really only be used for the Java *Homo erectus* – gradually spread throughout the temperate regions of the Old World. The oldest *Homo erectus* populations were certainly descendants of *Homo habilis* and showed features of a more evolved species. They appeared approximately 1.7 million years ago in the Lake Turkana region of Kenya.

Outside Africa, some would reach Asia, Java to be exact, around one million years ago. However, there is some evidence to show that they may have arrived in Asia and even Europe long before. Recent research on the child's skull of Modjokerto and the human fragments from Sangiran discovered in Java in 1936 and 1974 respectively point to ages as great as 1.8 and 1.6 million years.

Although they migrated over a vast geographical area, these hominids all shared the same physical features, a fact that suggests they belonged to a single species. However, some anthropologists believe that *Homo erectus* did not actually exist as a biological species, but has merely been conceived to explain human evolution. Others disagree – the debate continues.

As far as physical traits went, the stature of *Homo erectus* was close to our own – some individuals reached a height of 1.7 metres. However, their cranial capacity, which varied between 775 and 1250 cubic centimetres, was much smaller than ours today. While they had robust jaws, and teeth that were still enormous, their skull presented a number of peculiar bony super-structures, such as a keel on its vault, and a thick brow ridge above the eye-sockets, forming a kind of visor.

Two fossil skulls discovered on the eastern shore of Lake Turkana, Kenya (above), in the early 1970s, and a virtually complete skeleton found at Nariokotome on the west side of the lake in 1984 suggest that the species *Homo erectus* originated in Africa.

Occupying the stage of the Old World for almost 1.5 million years, they controlled fire for the first time. They gradually became skilful hunters and at the same time set up the first habitations. They also developed a more sophisticated toolkit – the biface (or handaxe), a core worked on both sides. The regular cutting edge of this tool was used for a variety of different tasks, such as scraping, digging and cutting. This industry formed part of the Acheulian tradition, named after the site where it was first found in St Acheul, France.

Conquering their fear: the control of fire

The first undeniable traces of the use of fire occurred around 450,000 years ago. However, the origin of fire-making may date back even further, to almost

In 1966, during salvage excavations carried out by Henry de Lumley near an alley named Terra Amata in Nice, several prehistoric levels of occupation were unearthed. Each layer corresponded to different seasonal camps made by hunters 380,000 years ago (above). Five years later, the French prehistorian discovered at Arago Cave near Tautavel, in the eastern Pyrenees, the oldest human skull in Europe, dating back some 450,000 years (left).

1.5 million years ago, as shown by the site of Swartkrans. Several anthropologists stress the fact that humans first had to overcome their fear of fire, a fear they shared with all animals. The control of fire involved a major change in behaviour. From that moment on, the capacity to create and use fire must have developed very rapidly. While we are more or less sure that *Homo erectus* repeatedly used embers produced by natural forest fires, we do not know how humans learned to make and maintain fire. Simple techniques, still in use today, using flint lighters or rubbing two sticks together, were undoubtedly discovered very quickly by *Homo erectus*.

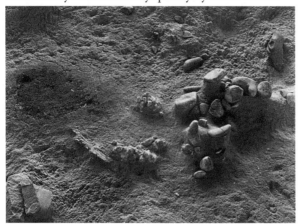

The hearth structures discovered on the occupation floors at Terra Amata in Nice (left) constitute, along with those at Vértesszöllös near Budapest in Hungary and at Torre in Pietra in Italy, the oldest evidence for the control of fire. At Terra Amata the prehistoric humans set up their fireplace in the very centre of the hut, in the form of a small hollow dug out of the sand, and protected from the prevailing winds by a little wall of pebbles.

Fire brings people together

Although fire-making in itself was not a basic need, it did help people to control their world. The use of fire had many consequences. Firstly, fire provided warmth, which may not have been very useful in this period. Secondly, as a source of light, fire enabled people to escape the rhythms of nature and, for example, to occupy the depths of caves. Thirdly, fire was also a powerful means of protecting themselves from wild animals. Finally, fire enabled food to be cooked, a phenomenon that seems to have appeared at the same time as the use of fire. Cooking implies that meals were eaten communally. Coming together to eat was an act

of strong social or family cohesion, just as it is today. So the control of fire played a major role in the evolution of human societies.

It does seem that *Homo erectus* was a peaceful hunter-gatherer, as not one fossil bone from this long period bears any trace of violence. The first evidence of it only appears during the Neolithic period, when cultures would become increasingly settled.

When did humans learn to speak?

Long before prehistorians ever looked into this puzzle, thinkers and philosophers have been passionately interested in the subject from the earliest times. While some wondered if thought could exist without speech, those who commented on the Bible affirmed that Adam and Eve spoke Hebrew. Even though we do not have all the answers to the problem, quite a few prehistorians are now convinced that *Homo erectus*

Evidence of the first *Homo erectus* in China was discovered near Peking (now Beijing) in Zhoukoudian Cave, which had been occupied for more than 200,000 years. After its roof collapsed, these hominids had to find shelter in the western part of the cave, which they finally abandoned after it filled up with sediment. They clearly knew how to use fire, as is shown by the existence of four ash layers, one of which was up to six metres thick in places.

communicated by speech with some degree of skill. The culture of these toolmakers who knew how to use fire and who lived from hunting and gathering was certainly so complex that they must necessarily have given names to objects, plants and animals, identified places and exchanged ideas.

The extent of their activities undoubtedly called for a highly developed means of communication that was far superior to that used by apes, though some people take issue with this point of view. Indeed, reconstructions of the vocal apparatus of a few fossil humans, albeit highly controversial, seem to indicate that the acquisition of language was a more recent phenomenon. Be that as it may, even if this language was rudimentary, comprising simple sentences pronounced slowly, it may have been accompanied by a large number of other acoustic or visual signals: cries, whistles, facial expressions. These humans were also able to resort to sign language like that used by deaf-mutes, or in some cases by New Guinea tribes or by Bushmen.

In humans, the larynx (in red) is located lower in the throat than in the chimpanzee. Above the larynx, the pharynx (in pink), which plays the role of an organ pipe, amplifies the sounds emitted by the vocal cords. In the course of human evolution, it was not until the larynx dropped, which in turn led to an increase in volume in the pharynx, that language could be acquired.

'Dragon bones', which were ground up in order to be sold in the form of a powder renowned for its medicinal properties, have been used by Chinese apothecaries, it is said, since the Sung dynasty (AD 960–1279). They are, in fact, the teeth of fossil animals.

The misadventures of Peking Man

The first clues to the existence of fossil humans in China go back to the beginning of the century. At this time Chinese pharmacies sold individual teeth, which, when ground into powder, were meant to be a treatment for everything. Then one of the teeth that came from the limestone quarries in the caves of the 'Dragon Bone Hill', not far from what was then Peking (now Beijing), turned out to belong to a primitive human. Methodical excavations were undertaken after the First World War in the biggest of these caves, and two teeth were extracted in 1926, followed by a third tooth the next year. Dr Davidson Black, professor of anatomy at Peking Medical College, studied

After three years' hard work at Zhoukoudian, in 1929, Dr W. C. Pei, the leader of the Chinese team, found the first almost complete skull of *Sinanthropus* (left); it was taken for analysis to the Canadian anatomist Dr Davidson Black, (below, with a pipe). On his left is G. B. Barbour, a renowned American geologist; on his right Father Teilhard de Chardin, a scientific adviser to the Geological Survey of China, C. C. Young, one of Teilhard's colleagues, and Dr W. C. Pei.

the teeth and named the remains of this primitive human *Sinanthropus pekinensis*, that is, the Chinese man from Peking. Today it is known as *Homo erectus pekinensis*.

This discovery marked the start of feverish activity at the site. Major excavations lasted until 1937, when the political situation in China, which was then at war with Japan, reached a crisis point. Just before the war, it was estimated that the remains of forty-five individuals had been unearthed.

In 1941, as Japanese troops drew threateningly close, China decided to send the remains of Peking Man to the United States. They were carefully packed and handed over to a detachment of American marines who were to embark for the United States a few days later. But the warship on which the American soldiers are said to have embarked was sunk. It is now generally believed that the *Sinanthropus* remains are lying somewhere in the Yellow Sea, at a depth of less than 200 metres, with the skeletons of the American marines.

Found in 1906 in a sand quarry near the village of Mauer close to Heidelberg (see section, left), the massive jaw (below) of a hominid with voluminous teeth lacks the protruding chin that characterizes modern humans.

The traces of the first people in Europe

The oldest human fossil in Europe, a lower jaw found at Mauer, not far from Heidelberg, is no more than 600,000 years old. Not so long ago it was thought that Europe was colonized from Africa much later than Asia. However, in the last few years, several discoveries, limited at present to a few worked pebbles and flake tools, have led us to reconsider this view.

For the time being, the site of Chilhac has provided the oldest evidence of a human presence in Europe. Located in the Auvergne, Chilhac has produced several stone tools found with fauna dating back almost 1.5 million years. A great number of sites, both open-air and caves, dating from about 900,000 years, are known in France (such as Blassac, Soleilhac, Wimmereux, Vallonnet Cave) as well as in other countries of western and central Europe.

It appears that Europe was rather sparsely populated during the long glacial period known as Mindel (450,000–300,000 years ago). Thanks to milder climatic conditions, during the Mindel-Riss interglacial (300,000–200,000 years ago), human settlement gradually became more dense. While it seems certain that Europe was populated at an early period, we still have much to learn about these hominids.

Overlooking the plain of Tautavel, Arago Cave made an ideal hunting camp for prehistoric people 450,000 years ago. On the steep slopes they hunted ancient forms of mouflon, tahr and chamois. Below the cave in the valley and on the plateau above there were grasslands, where herds of aurochs, bison and musk ox grazed.

Excavating 'Zinj'

L ouis Leakey and his wife Mary, pictured here with their son

Philip, began work at Olduvai Gorge in the 1930s. In 1959, after painstaking work on the geological beds, Mary Leakey discovered the *Zinjanthropus* skull in Bed I, the oldest at Olduvai. The excavations, carried out over an area of 330 square metres, revealed an ancient occupation level. The bone fragments and worked tools abandoned by a group of hominids who had camped there more than 1,750,000 years ago were rapidly buried beneath the clays left when the waters of the Olduvai lake rose.

Painstaking work at Olduvai Gorge

The excavation of the *Zinjanthropus* skull at Olduvai was a long and exacting task. For nineteen days, in overpowering heat, Mary and Louis Leakey worked intensely, fired by emotion, to collect the four hundred bone fragments that remained of the skull. After the excavation, Louis Leakey (opposite) points out the exact stratigraphic position of the 'Zinj' skull. The vertically dug walls show lacustrine deposits alternating with layers of volcanic ash.

The sites at Olduvai, like those at Lake Turkana in Kenya (overleaf), yielded many bones of a strange elephant, the *Deinotherium*, which had no tusks in its upper jaw, unlike modern elephants. Curiously, the lower jaw curved downwards and was continued by two backward-curving tusks (left).

A horizontal and vertical reading

Numerous prehistoric sites have yielded a high concentration of different remains, like this extraordinary tangle of mastodon bones (left), laid down in a random fashion nearly five million years ago. In cases like this it is essential to carry out meticulous excavations; every object is located on a horizontal plan using a grid of metre squares, before being removed and catalogued (pages 100–1). Detailed plans are used as the basis for analysing and interpreting the associations between objects. The way in which bone fragments, like those of this rhinoceros (opposite bottom) found in Saudi Arabia, are arranged provides evidence about the direction and strength of the currents when they were buried. Pieces discovered are recorded meticulously to give an overview of the site both horizontally and vertically through the superimposition of the different plans. In this way past events and human activities are placed in a chronological framework.

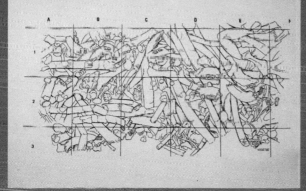

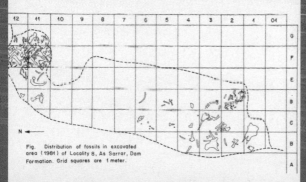

Fig. Distribution of fossils in excavated area (1981) of Locality 8, As Sarrar, Dam Formation. Grid squares are 1 meter.

N ←

I n the last 200,000 years, during which major climatic changes took place, the course of human evolution became more complex: technical innovations occurred, spiritual preoccupations emerged, societies became increasingly ritualized, and aesthetic feelings began to appear. Cultural evolution took precedence over biological evolution.

CHAPTER 6
FROM NEANDERTHAL TO LASCAUX

Some 15,000 years separate these two figurative paintings. The rhinoceros on the right symbolizes the preoccupations of the hunters during the last Ice Age (c. 110,000 –10,000 years ago). The genre scene on the left bears witness to the scientific and didactic spirit that was emerging in the 19th century, an age that tried to make sense of this vanished world.

Among the artists who have depicted the life of prehistoric people, the Czech Zdenek Burian (1905–81) is preeminent. Though he was the heir to the academic painters of the late 19th century in his realistic and picturesque reconstructions, Burian also distanced himself from them in his more scientific and more humane vision, as in this depiction of Mauer Man (left).

A difficult transition

When, how and where did *Homo erectus* give rise to *Homo sapiens*? The origin of *sapiens* is one of the hardest problems to solve in the whole of human palaeontology. The period between 600,000 and 200,000 years ago, during which Europe was twice covered by an ice sheet (the Mindel glaciation and Riss glaciation), is certainly one of the most obscure periods in the history of humanity. It is somewhat paradoxical that whereas our earliest ancestors, the australopithecines, are relatively well known – more than a thousand specimens and dozens of skulls have been found – the human remains from this later period are rather rare. Moreover, doubts have been expressed about the dates attributed to these finds. However, analysis of the fossil animals generally gives an approximate age based, in Europe, on the alternation of glaciations and milder periods, the interglacials.

Although most of the human remains have indeed been found in western Europe and a few in North Africa, it would be wrong to conclude that they did

not exist elsewhere. Not only do the fossil beds of immense areas of the globe remain unexplored, but the age of some sites is still uncertain (such as Broken Hill in Zambia, and Hopefield in South Africa). Many sites of this period, which range in area from the Maghreb to China, reveal, in their stone tool industries, the existence of these humans, the last *Homo erectus* populations.

In Europe, a dozen sites containing human fossils remain problematic for prehistorians. They include Bilzingsleben, Petralona, Mauer, Atapuerca, Boxgrove, Montmaurin, Vértesszöllös, Swanscombe, Steinheim and Arago. What do they tell us?

Two human populations

Because of the incomplete nature of these remains, palaeoanthropologists still disagree about the different stages in human evolution. Until recently it was thought that we were dealing with two populations evolving in parallel in Europe, one of them leading to the well-known Neanderthals, the other resulting in modern *Homo sapiens*, the real ancestor of modern people.

The Neanderthals acquired a degree of technological complexity that is reflected in the evolution of their toolkit. Increasingly sophisticated tools were used to perform various functions – cutting, piercing, scraping. At the same time social organization became more developed, as each new technique had to be passed on to the group. Tools then became 'social objects'.

This spontaneous drawing by the famous prehistorian Abbé Henri Breuil summarizes in naive fashion his vision of the social organization of Neanderthals.

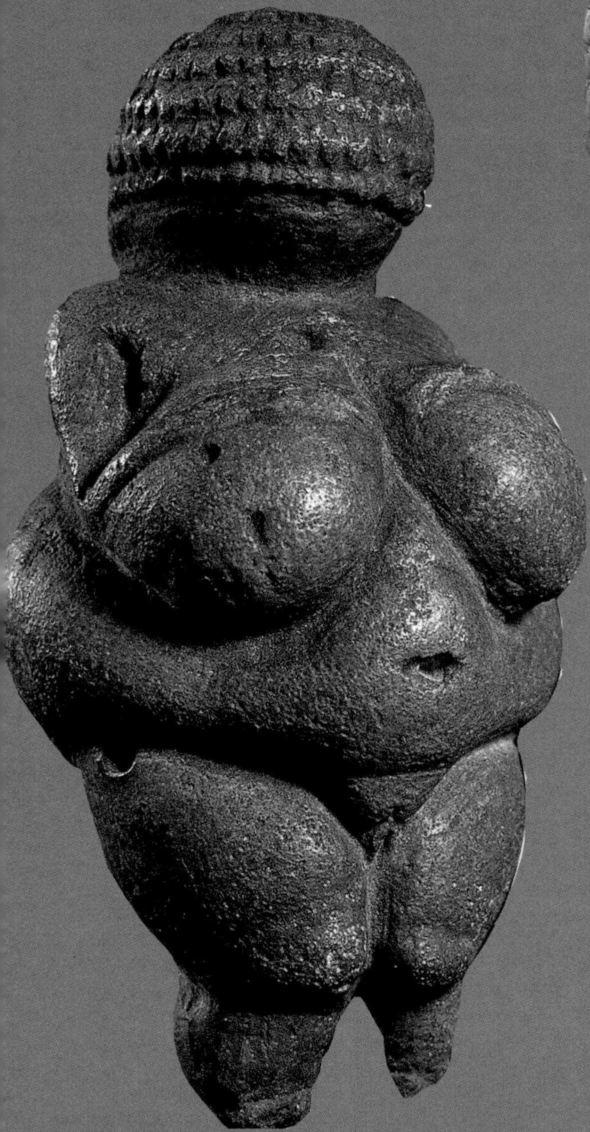

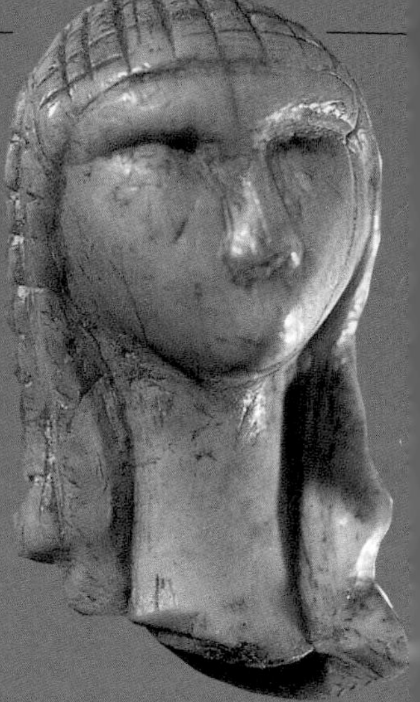

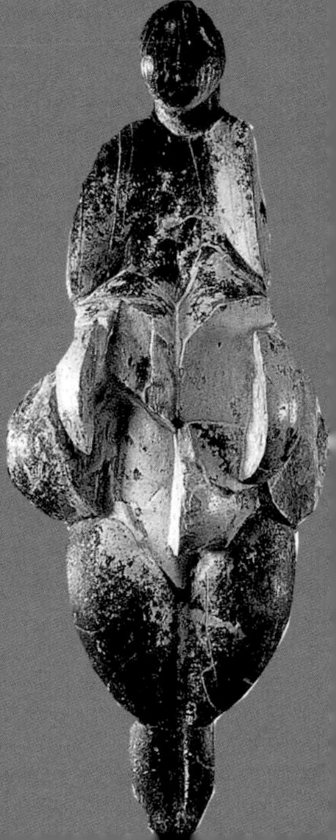

A great number of female statuettes known as Venuses, sculpted in stone or ivory, and sometimes engraved (like the Venus with a horn from Laussel, left), have been found in Upper Palaeolithic sites all over Europe and as far as Siberia. In Europe these Venuses often have exaggerated features – they are very fleshy, with marked steatopygia, enormous breasts, protruding stomachs and broad hips. Facial features, as in this figurine (opposite top right) found in the last century in a cave at Brassempouy in the Landes, are rare. It predates by a few millennia the great period of parietal cave art represented by Lascaux. Without any doubt these statuettes show how women were viewed in the Upper Palaeolithic culture: as a matriarch or as a woman-mother with a magical power linked to the fertility that ensured the group's survival.

The term 'modern' *Homo sapiens* is used because the Neanderthals also came from the species *Homo sapiens*, but were a sub-species; this is why they were given the scientific name of *Homo sapiens neanderthalensis*. Recent studies have shown that only the lineage leading to the Neanderthals was actually present in western Europe. The Neanderthals, whose peculiar anatomical characteristics gradually appeared around 230,000 years ago within European populations, colonized the whole of peninsular Europe around 70,000 and subsequently reached the Near East and Central Asia. They disappeared about 35,000 years ago.

The other lineage, leading to modern humans, has to be sought outside Europe, perhaps in Africa. According to this theory, anatomically modern *Homo sapiens* originated in Africa, reaching North Africa and the Near East around 100,000 years ago. And it is precisely in this last region of the world, in Qafzeh Cave, near Nazareth in Galilee, that the oldest skeletons of modern humans have been found.

This double grave (opposite) of a young woman with a six-year-old child at her feet dates back almost 100,000 years. It was discovered in Qafzeh Cave, near Nazareth in Israel, and is the oldest known burial. The excavations carried out at Qafzeh in 1933 led to five human skeletons being unearthed. Between 1965 and 1975 the French prehistorian Bernard Vandermeersch discovered more human bones. Six adults and seven children, many of whom – in particular a youth – had been deliberately buried. They displayed many similarities with the European Cro-Magnons, who appeared some 60,000 years later.

The techniques of reconstructing the Neanderthals have been considerably improved since the first portrait drawn by Schaaffhausen in 1888. Nevertheless, we have still not formed a clear image of many of their physical features, such as the shape of their noses and lips, the colour of their skin and the amount of hair on their faces and heads.

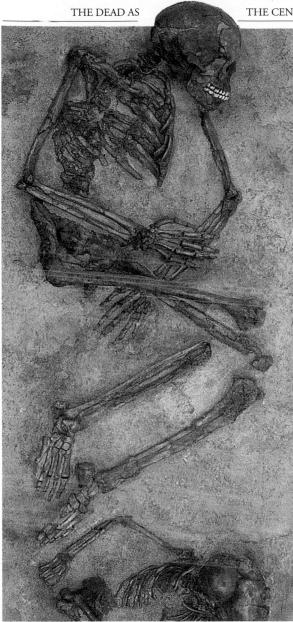

The use of natural objects from 40,000 years ago provides evidence for the first aesthetic or religious preoccupations. The first pieces of jewellery, pendants often made of animal teeth pierced with a circular hole or marked with a groove so that they could be hung, appear five thousand years later, with the start of the Châtelperronian culture (named after the site of Châtelperron). The choice of these teeth, often of carnivores

– foxes, bears, wolves, hyenas – suggests that the artisans hoped to benefit from the qualities that they thought lay in these animals. Moreover, wearing such ornamental objects was perhaps intended to denote differences in age or sex, or even in an individual's social status.

The time of the Würm glaciation

Whether there is any truth in this theory of recent human evolution, modern people like the Neanderthals emerged at the start of the last great glacial epoch, called the Würm after one of the Danube's tributaries. Several oceanic, atmospheric and astronomical phenomena produced a major cooling of the climate 110,000 years ago. This period ended barely 10,000 years ago. The cooling was caused by changes in the earth's orbit around the sun and in the tilt of the globe's axis of rotation, magnified by profound modifications in polar marine currents and in variations in the atmosphere's carbon dioxide content.

In the northern hemisphere, landscapes and the contours of land and sea were completely transformed by these phenomena. During the time of maximum cold, 18,000 years ago, when the ice reached a thickness of 3 kilometres in places, the increase in the ice sheets' extent caused the sea level to drop by 120 metres. As a result, a continental bridge of more than 1000 kilometres joined Alaska to Siberia.

Some 18,000 years ago an icecap covered the whole of Scandinavia, the Baltic Sea, part of the North Sea and the British Isles, as well as the plains of North Germany.

During this period, in western Europe, the Neanderthals experienced very varied living conditions. The climate was sometimes cold and dry, sometimes mild and humid. At times the extreme polar harshness caused the ground to be frozen all year round. These Neanderthals lived in very different environments, occupying open-air camps or rock shelters and caves. While some lived in the steppes or near the great glaciers, where the reindeer, mammoths and woolly rhinoceros grazed, others inhabited the tundra of northern Europe.

Several complete Neanderthal skeletons have made it possible for a very faithful profile to be drawn. Neanderthals were quite small and thickset with short legs. They had a large, receding head with a bun at the rear. Their face was marked by a prominent nose, receding cheekbones and a low brow with a strong bony ridge over the eye sockets.

Because of their powerful musculature, their strong build and, particularly, the size of their head, the Neanderthals have long personified the bestiality that people liked to imagine existed in our prehistoric

During the last great glaciation Europe was covered by a mosaic of steppes, tundras, grasslands and forests. Their extent varied with the fluctuations in the climate. The Neanderthals, who mostly inhabited these regions, often lived in the coldest areas, alongside mammoths, cave bears and woolly rhinoceroses or on the tundra with reindeer and musk oxen. Other Neanderthals were to be found in the steppes and grasslands with bison, aurochs and horses.

Without any doubt the mammoth is the prehistoric animal that has most caught our imagination and that of our ancestors, judging by their paintings and engravings. In its most recent form, *Mammuthus primigenius*, the woolly mammoth, was covered in a thick shaggy coat with hairs that could reach a metre in length. It appeared during the penultimate glaciation around 300,000 years ago and suddenly disappeared some 12,000 years ago. (However, some 'dwarf' mammoths survived on Wrangel Island, north of Siberia, until about 3000 years ago.) Having spread throughout Europe and Asia, in a fairly small form close to that of the present-day Asian elephant, it colonized North America by crossing the land bridge that joined Alaska to Siberia during the glacial maxima (the coldest phases of the Ice Age).

ancestors. However, their spiritual concerns, their highly worked tools (resulting from a technique that could not have been learned without the help of language) and their hunting methods have made people today reassess their image of them. Besides, their brain was so large that it sometimes exceeded the average cranial capacity of present-day humans. They are associated with a very developed industry of worked stones, known as Mousterian. They shaped tools from flakes to make points and scrapers, retouching them into various forms.

Ritual cannibalism?

Like the first modern humans, the Neanderthals have left behind in their burials evidence for their attitude towards death. They certainly were the first to bury their dead. Palaeontologists are always delighted to discover such burials because – apart from exceptional cases like Lucy, from Hadar in Ethiopia, of which forty per cent of the skeleton was found, and the recently discovered Preneanderthal of Altamura in Italy – only these put complete skeletons at their disposal. The remains are well preserved because they had been protected against scavenging animals on purpose.

Some bodies have been found in a semi-flexed position: for example, the rock shelter of La Ferrassie in the Dordogne contains a family burial of the presumed parents and six children, including a foetus and two newborn infants.

While traces of such burials are common in France, others are known in Italy, Palestine and further east in Central Asia. At the famous cave of Shanidar in Iraq nine individuals were found at different depths. The oldest dated back 70,000 years.

Tools and worked objects are sometimes buried with them. In the case of Shanidar flowers – including cornflowers, thistles and hollyhocks – known for their medicinal properties, were placed in the grave.

Burials made by Upper Palaeolithic people express their attitude towards death. Only a few individuals in the group were worthy of this special treatment and they were buried in a variety of ways. At the Magdalenian burial of St-Germain-la-Rivière in the Gironde the deceased's head was protected by stone slabs (below), whereas the bodies buried at Grimaldi in Italy (pages 116 and 117 top) were arranged very differently.

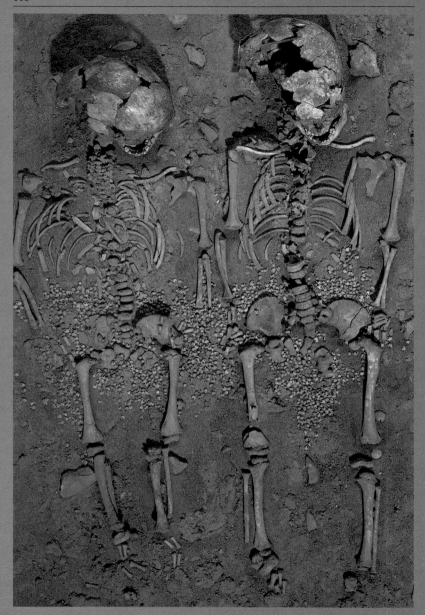

Evidence for deliberate burial came from La Ferrassie in the Dordogne, where a Neanderthal man lay buried with his knees drawn up to his chest (bottom left). The drawing (below), which reproduces the layout of the body as it was found, was made by Abbé Breuil (1877–1961) in 1909.

They may have been placed there either to honour the deceased for his or her healing powers, or, simply, to provide decoration.

All these burials show evidence of some sort of ritual taking place and a preoccupation with an afterlife.

Some of these burials may have been linked to cannibalistic practices. In the cave of Hortus in the Hérault in France, several human bones have been discovered mixed with food debris. Similarly, at Krapina in Croatia, many of the human bones bear traces of having been smashed and split.

Although the evidence has been disputed, it is possible that these two examples reveal the existence of ritual cannibalism, which is still found today among some peoples in Africa and Melanesia.

In any case, these burials provide proof that Neanderthals, in contrast to the crude, uncivilized image we have of them, had a concern for spiritual matters.

While the Magdalenian culture in Europe has left numerous traces of habitations in the open-air or in natural shelters, during the same period the hunters of central Europe and as far as Siberia erected huge settlements with mammoth bones and tusks. Mezhirich in the Ukraine, which was occupied about 15,000 years ago, is a particularly spectacular example. The lowest layer of each hut contained almost a hundred mammoth lower jaws stacked one on top of another.

Homo sapiens sapiens: the invader from the East

For reasons that still remain a mystery, the Neanderthals, whose last representatives are associated with the Châtelperronian industry, were to disappear suddenly around 35,000 years ago. They then gave way to anatomically modern humans, who no longer had any of the physical characteristics of the Neanderthals. Most palaeoanthropologists now accept that modern humans did not evolve from the Neanderthals in Europe. For their part, prehistorians have observed a clear break in the evolution of knapping techniques, between the Châtelperronian stone toolkits made by the last Neanderthals and the more recent toolkits from the Aurignacian culture.

Numerous decorated, engraved or sculpted objects, very often depicting animals, as in the case of these spearthrowers, express the rich artistic sense of the Magdalenian hunters. Weapons of this type, with a hook at one end, enabled finely worked spearpoints of reindeer antler to be thrown with a rapid movement of the arm and wrist.

Further evidence of a break is provided by the first manifestations of figurative art and by a more elaborate boneworking technology seen in the emergence of perforated batons and spearpoints.

These biological and cultural developments suggest that the Neanderthals were replaced by modern humans who invaded western Europe from the East. If this was the case, there can be no doubt that the two populations crossbred. But who were these invaders? To judge by their physical features – an elevated skull with a high brow, a face with prominent cheekbones and a protruding chin – they were the first modern humans, *Homo sapiens sapiens,* direct ancestors of the Cro-Magnons.

The Cro-Magnon people, hunter-gatherers who appeared in Europe 35,000 years ago, bear such a close resemblance to modern humans that, it has been said, if they walked around London in a suit, it is unlikely that anybody would comment on their appearance.

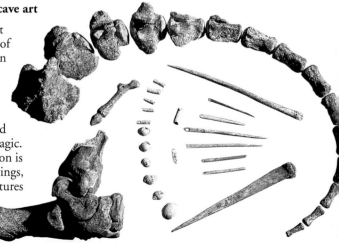

This pink sandstone lamp, carefully shaped and decorated with chevron signs, was found in the bottom of a shaft in the cave of Lascaux together with other lamps made of simple hollowed stones. Lumps of tallow and a wick of juniper were burnt in them, providing a source of light for about an hour.

Cro-Magnon: cave art

One of the most striking aspects of the Cro-Magnon age is the development of aesthetic feelings, which are closely linked to religion or magic. Artistic expression is found in engravings, paintings, sculptures and ornaments. Ochre, whose colour varied

On 12 September 1940 four youngsters from the village of Montignac on the Vézère in the Dordogne discovered the entrance to the cave of Lascaux, which was to become one of the centrepieces of prehistoric art. This cave, a monumental underground museum about 17,000 years old, contained more than six hundred rock paintings and almost fifteen hundred engravings. Abbé Henri Breuil, who was a talented draughtsman, was called in to the site to authenticate the paintings. He drew the first tracings (left) and devoted the whole of his life to depicting and studying Upper Palaeolithic cave art. In 1902 he made known the famous painted ceiling at Altamira in Spain (pages 124–5) to the world.

according to the mineral, was widely used. The Cro-Magnon people seem to have attached a religious meaning to red ochre, on which they sometimes laid their dead. It is also possible that they tinted animal hides and practised bodypainting. Certainly, bone, ivory and shells were worked into decorative objects, pendants and necklaces.

Their first drawings, mostly engravings, rarely painted, were still crude and generally clumsy. Figurative art in the shape of more elaborate engravings and paintings gradually emerged from the first scrawls. Throughout Europe this interest in art found expression in small female statuettes, known as Venuses – young girls with elegant features and fleshy matrons, often with extremely stylized features.

The people of the last Ice Age developed bone working to a high level. Examples of their craft include awls, which enabled them to sew skins, and necklaces made by stringing various objects on to tendons (opposite).

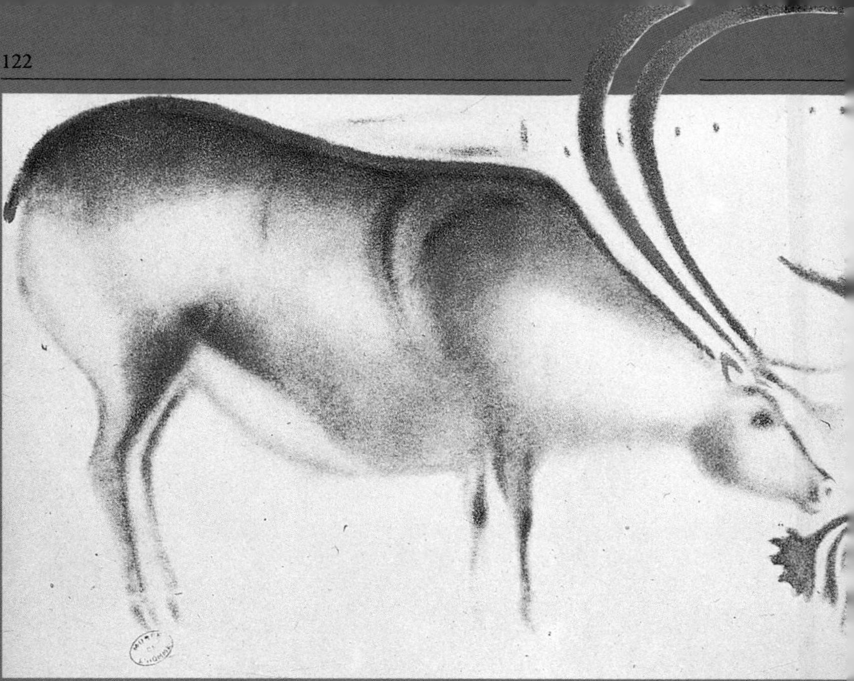

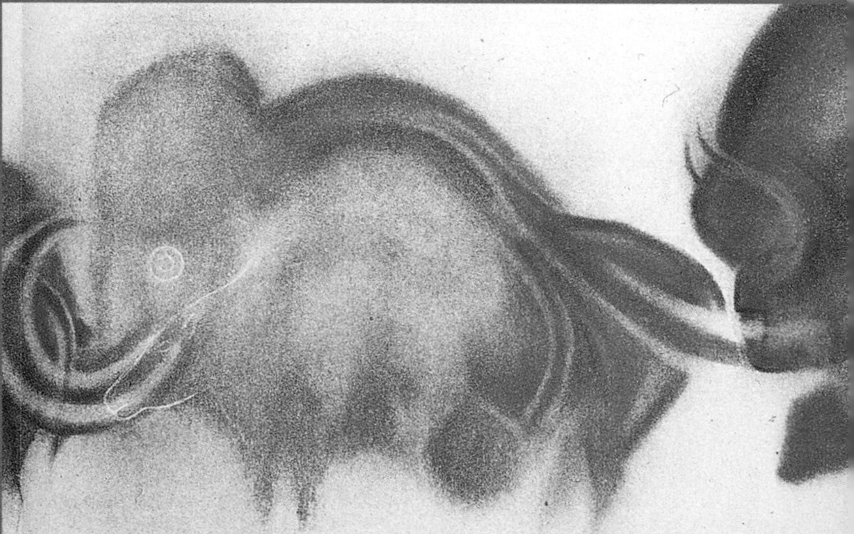

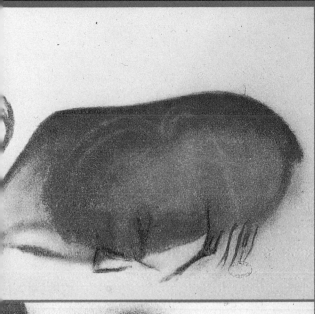

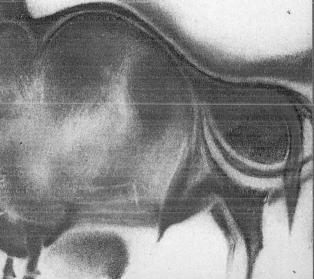

An underground art

It is true to say that the parietal depictions of the numerous underground sanctuaries of France – especially in Aquitaine and the Pyrenees – and of Spain – such as Altamira, where one of the very first decorated caves was discovered in 1879 – share a common theme. The countless depictions of animals – horses, aurochs, bison, reindeer and mammoths hunted at the time – are found during the last 15,000 years (from about 25,000 to 10,000 years ago) of the Upper Palaeolithic. This era produced art of extraordinary skill and achievement. There is evidence that the people of this period took part in cult ceremonies in the depths of these dark caves, in which they stayed only for a short time.

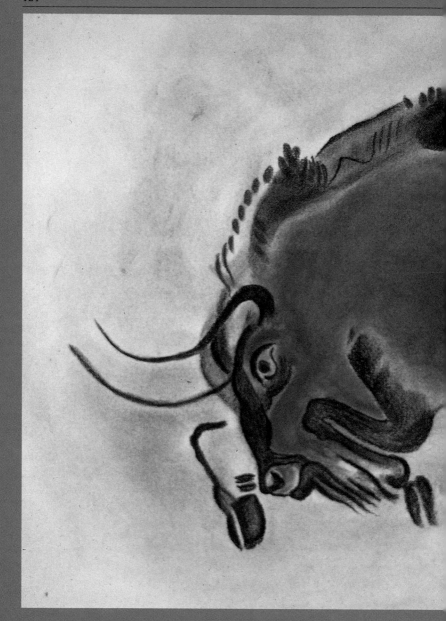

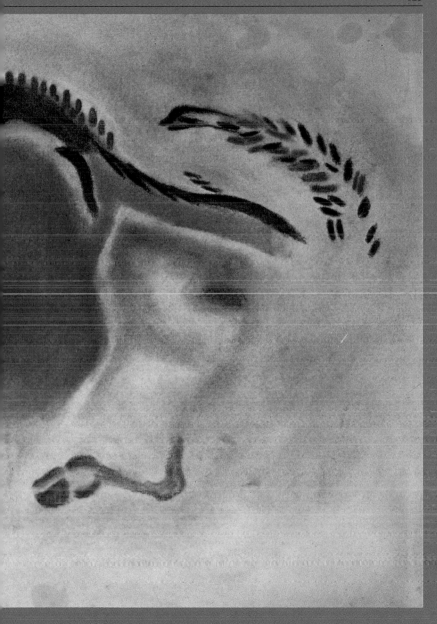

The people of this culture known as the last Ice Age, who lived exclusively from hunting, fishing and gathering, brought cave art to its zenith between 17,000 and 9000 years ago; one of the best examples of their art is provided by the cave of Lascaux. The artists tended to work in relatively accessible caves, though they sometimes ventured far underground, as at the cave of Niaux in the Ariège, which could only be reached after a long and sometimes perilous journey.

Apart from a few rare exceptions, these underground sanctuaries, where magical rites of sorcery and initiation linked to the world of hunting were performed, have only been found in France and Spain, on both sides of the Pyrenees. Cave art was to disappear abruptly nearly 10,000 years ago, just as the last great glacial epoch ended. It then took just a few millennia for humans to domesticate plants and animals, invent pottery and discover metallurgy.

And what does tomorrow hold? Dawn or twilight?

Theoretically, no plant or animal in the future will remain as it is now. Evolution is a permanent process that continues to take place. But humans are peculiar animals. For a few thousand years human biological evolution has slowed down considerably, while the pace of cultural evolution continues to speed up. A few hundred years from now it is likely that humanity will almost totally free itself from the biological laws that have governed its evolution.

The processes underlying biological evolution – those that led us from being apes to being humans – work extremely slowly in comparison with those underlying cultural evolution. Indeed, the mechanisms of natural selection (relying on the success of individuals) do not enable acquired characteristics to be passed from one generation to another. Biological transmission is essentially deferred and is carried out by small alterations that are barely perceptible over a short period.

With the emergence of consciousness – which sets us apart from other forms of life – humans started to question where they fitted into the divine mechanism. Whatever humankind's destiny might be in this universe – whether we become inhuman or superhuman – Albert Einstein (below) was continually amazed at our ability to understand the world around us.

Overleaf: Neanderthals.

In the case of cultural evolution (relying on the success of the group), change takes place very rapidly, because the transmission process is cumulative in the sense that each generation passes on – either through speech or through the written word -- its acquired knowledge to the next.

Thanks to our exceptional intelligence, which is linked to the constant increase in the size of our brains over tens of thousands of years, humans possess the capability to mould the future with complete awareness. In this respect humans are unique in the animal kingdom. However, at the same time, we are the only animals who have become a threat to ourselves.

It is impossible to foresee which of the two forces will prevail in the future: either the force of cultural evolution that would lead us towards a new form of *Homo sapiens* or the force of destruction that would eliminate us in order to restore the balance of nature before she herself is engulfed in a few billion years by a gigantic ball of fire.

DOCUMENTS

The Descent of Man

In 1859 Darwin published his ground-breaking Origin of Species, *in which he set out his theory of evolution based on natural selection. Twelve years later, in 1871, he applied his theory to human beings in* The Descent of Man.

This caricature of Darwin appeared the year he published *The Descent of Man*. People were still shocked by his ideas.

Natural selection

We have now seen that man is variable in body and mind; and that the variations are induced, either directly or indirectly, by the same general causes, and obey the same general laws, as with the lower animals. Man has spread widely over the face of the earth, and must have been exposed, during his incessant migrations, to the most diversified conditions.... The early progenitors of man must also have tended, like all other animals, to have increased beyond their means of subsistence; they must therefore occasionally have been exposed to a struggle for existence, and consequently to the rigid law of natural selection. Beneficial variations of all kinds will thus, either occasionally or habitually, have been preserved, and injurious ones eliminated. I do not refer to strongly-marked deviations of structure, which occur only at long intervals of time, but to mere individual differences....

Man in the rudest state in which he now exists is the most dominant animal that has ever appeared on the earth. He has spread more widely than any other highly organised form; and all others have yielded before him. He manifestly owes this immense superiority to his intellectual faculties, his social habits, which lead him to aid and defend his fellows, and to his corporeal structure. The supreme importance of these characters has been proved by the final arbitrament of the battle for life....

On the birthplace and antiquity of man

We are naturally led to enquire where was the birthplace of man at that stage of descent when our progenitors diverged from the Catarhine [monkey] stock. The fact that they belonged to this stock clearly shews that they inhabited the Old World; but not Australia nor any oceanic island, as we may infer from the laws of geographical distribution. In each great region of the world the living mammals are closely related to the extinct species of the same region. It is therefore probable that Africa was formerly inhabited by extinct apes closely allied to the gorilla and chimpanzee; and as these two species are now man's nearest allies, it is somewhat more probable that our earliest progenitors lived on the African continent than elsewhere....

The principle of evolution

The main conclusion arrived at in this work, and now held by many naturalists who are well competent to form a sound judgment, is that man is descended from some less highly organised form. The grounds upon which this conclusion rests will never be shaken, for the close similarity between man and the lower animals in embryonic development, as well as in innumerable points of structure and constitution, both of high and of the most trifling importance, -- the rudiments which he retains, and the abnormal reversions to which he is occasionally liable, – are facts which cannot be disputed. They have long been known, but until recently they told us nothing with respect to the origin of man. Now when viewed by the light of our knowledge of the whole organic world, their meaning is unmistakeable. The great principle of evolution stands up clear and firm, when these groups of facts are considered in connection with others, such as the mutual affinities of the members of the same group, their geographical distribution in past and

present times, and their geological succession. It is incredible that all these facts should speak falsely. He who is not content to look, like a savage, at the phenomena of nature as disconnected, cannot any longer believe that man is the work of a separate act of creation. He will be forced to admit that the close resemblance of the embryo of man to that, for instance, of a dog – the construction of his skull, limbs, and whole frame, independently of the uses to which the parts may be put, on the same plan with that of other mammals – the occasional reappearance of various structures, for instance of several distinct muscles, which man does not normally possess, but which are common to the Quadrumana -- and a crowd of analogous facts – all point in the plainest manner to the conclusion that man is the co-descendant with other mammals of a common progenitor.

Variation

We have seen that man incessantly presents individual differences in all parts of his body and in his mental faculties. These differences or variations seem to be induced by the same general causes, and to obey the same laws as with the lower animals. In both cases similar laws of inheritance prevail. Man tends to increase at a greater rate than his means of subsistence; consequently he is occasionally subjected to a severe struggle for existence, and natural selection will have effected whatever lies within its scope. A succession of strongly-marked variations of a similar nature are by no means requisite; slight fluctuating differences in the individual suffice for the work of natural selection. We may feel assured that the inherited effects of the long-continued use or disuse of parts will have done much in the same direction with natural selection. Modifications formerly of importance, though no longer of any special use, will be long inherited. When one part is modified, other parts will change through the principle of correlation, of which we have instances in many curious cases of correlated monstrosities. Something may be attributed to the direct and definite action of the surrounding conditions of life, such as abundant food, heat, or moisture; and lastly, many characters of slight physiological importance, some indeed of considerable importance, have been gained through sexual selection....

The origin of man

By considering the embryological structure of man, – the homologies which he presents with the lower animals, – the rudiments which he retains, – and the reversions to which he is liable, we can partly recall in imagination the former condition of our early progenitors; and can approximately place them in their proper position in the zoological series. We thus learn that man is descended from a hairy quadruped, furnished with a tail and pointed ears, probably arboreal in its habits, and an inhabitant of the Old World....

Intellectual ability

The greatest difficulty which presents itself, when we are driven to the above conclusion on the origin of man, is the high standard of intellectual power and of moral disposition which he has attained. But every one who admits the general principle of evolution, must see that the mental powers of the higher animals, which are the same in kind with those of mankind, though so different in degree, are capable of advancement. Thus the interval between the mental powers of one of the higher apes and of a fish, or between those of an ant and scale-insect, is immense. The development of these powers in animals does not offer any special difficulty; for with our domesticated animals, the mental faculties are certainly variable, and the variations are inherited. No one doubts that these faculties are of the utmost importance to animals in a state of nature. Therefore the conditions are favourable for their development through natural selection. The same conclusion may be extended to man; the intellect must have been all-important to him, even at a very remote period, enabling him to use language, to invent and make weapons, tools, traps, etc.; by which means, in combination with his social habits, he long ago became the most dominant of all living creatures.

A great stride in the development of the intellect will have followed, as soon as, through a previous considerable advance, the half-art and half-instinct of language came into use; for the continued use of language will have reacted on the brain, and produced an inherited effect; and this again will have reacted on the improvement of language....

Morality and religion

The belief in God has often been advanced as not only the greatest, but the most complete of all the distinctions between man and the lower animals. It is however impossible, as we have seen, to maintain that this belief is innate or instinctive in man. On the other hand a belief in all-pervading spiritual agencies seems to be universal; and apparently follows from a considerable advance in the reasoning powers of man, and from a still greater advance in his faculties of imagination, curiosity and wonder. I am aware that the assumed instinctive belief in God has been used by many persons as an argument for His existence. But this is a rash argument, as we should thus be compelled to believe in the existence of many cruel and malignant spirits, possessing only a little more power than man; for the belief in them is far more general than of a beneficent Deity. The idea of a universal and beneficent Creator of the universe does not seem to arise in the mind of man, until he has been elevated by long-continued culture.

He who believes in the advancement of man from some lowly-organised form, will naturally ask how does this bear on the belief in the immortality of the soul.... Few persons feel any anxiety from the impossibility of determining at what precise period in the development of the individual, from the first trace of the minute germinal vesicle to the child either before or after birth, becomes an immortal being; and there is no greater cause for anxiety because the period in the gradually ascending organic scale cannot possibly be determined.

I am aware that the conclusions arrived at in this work will be denounced by some as highly irreligious; but he who thus denounces them is bound to shew why it is more irreligious to explain the origin of man as a distinct species by descent from some lower form, through the laws of variation and natural selection, than to explain the birth of the individual through the laws of ordinary reproduction. The birth both of the species and of the individual are equally parts of the grand sequence of events, which our minds refuse to accept as the result of blind chance. The understanding revolts at such a conclusion, whether or not we are able to believe that every slight variation of structure, – the union of each pair in marriage, – the dissemination of each seed, – and other such events, have all been ordained for some special purpose.

Conclusion

The main conclusion arrived at in this work, namely that man is descended from some lowly-organised form will, I regret to think, be highly distasteful to many persons. But there can hardly be a doubt that we are descended from barbarians ...

Man may be excused for feeling some pride at having risen, though not through his own exertions, to the very summit of the organic scale; and the fact of his having thus risen, instead of having been aboriginally placed there, may give him hopes for a still higher destiny in the distant future. But we are not here concerned with hopes or fears, only with the truth as far as our reason allows us to discover it. I have given the evidence to the best of my ability; and we must acknowledge, as it seems to me, that man with all his noble qualities, with sympathy which feels for the most debased, with benevolence which extends not only to other men but to the humblest living creature, with his god-like intellect which has penetrated into the movements and constitution of the solar system – with all these exalted powers – Man still bears in his bodily frame the indelible stamp of his lowly origin.

Charles Darwin
The Descent of Man, 1871

The Scopes trial

In 1925 the whole of America found itself watching a spectacular confrontation between ancient and modern, between fundamentalists and evolutionists. The trial brought against John Thomas Scopes (below), a teacher from Tennessee, focused attention on whether humans were a product of a literal biblical creation or whether we had evolved from apes.

George W. Rappelyea [a mining engineer]...saw in a newspaper that Chattanooga had given up its plans to start a case to test the Butler Act. He got an idea, and he telephoned F. E. Robinson, local druggist and head of the county board of education, and Walter White, county superintendent of schools. He argued earnestly with them. The next day he was at them again. They gave in. Then Rappelyea sent for John Thomas Scopes and asked him to come down to Robinson's drugstore....

John Scopes was a guileless young man, with blue, contemplative eyes. Only 24 years old, he had graduated from the University of Kentucky the preceding year and had come to the high school at Dayton as science teacher and football coach. His local popularity was very great. Here was the man Rappelyea wanted. Scopes was drawn into the discussion, and found himself observing that nobody could teach biology without using the theory of evolution. Being the person he was, he was trapped. Rappelyea said, 'You have been violating the law.'

'So has every other teacher,' said Scopes. 'This is the official textbook.'...

On May 7 John Scopes was arrested.... It was charged that on April 24 he had taught the theory of evolution to his class....

If Governor Peay and others saw the Scopes trial partly as political speech and partly as pious gesture, such men as George Rappelyea, Sue Hicks [a male lawyer] and Dayton merchants viewed it as a civic promotion. This could really put Dayton in the headlines, on the map. It could bring a lot of business to local stores. But it needed celebrities. Who better than William Jennings Bryan, the one man of world reputation in the fundamentalist movement?...

Henry Fairfield Osborn [director of the American Museum of Natural History] said that the trial would do great good by clarifying the issues.... *The Real Question Is, Did God Use Evolution in his Plan?* Beside this question all of the others – 'such as personal rights, rights of opinion, rights of free speech, constitutional rights, education liberty' were insignificant....

Clarence Darrow [the chief defence lawyer] agreed. Although he thought the references to God were impertinent, he did regard the truth of evolution as the main issue. His whole approach to the trial was to establish this truth by means of scientific testimony....

It was not enough, said Malone [the defence lawyer] in presenting the defense theory, for the state to show that Scopes had taught the theory of evolution; the state must show in addition that Scopes had 'also, and at the same time, denied the theory of creation as set forth in the Bible'. In brief, what did the Butler Act forbid: Teaching that man had descended from a lower order of animals? Teaching a story of human origins that conflicted with Genesis? Or both? The state held to the first construction of the law; the defense, to the third. They wrangled about it throughout the trial – and beyond....

Darrow began quietly, asking if Bryan [prosecution counsel, here in the witness stand] had not 'given considerable study to the Bible'. Bryan admitted it. Then Darrow began his ruthless efforts to make Bryan admit that the Bible could not always be taken literally, that it was sometimes vague, that the Butler Act was fatally indefinite when it forbade the teachings of 'any theory that denies the story of the Divine Creation of man as taught in the Bible'....

Darrow kept worrying at the witness about the dates that Bishop Ussher, calculating from the ages of the various prophets, had assigned to Scriptural episodes. The Bishop had computed the date of Creation as 4004 BC. He had been even more specific: this happy event had occurred on October 23 at 9 AM....

Bryan wriggled and writhed, but Darrow kept pressing him. And eventually Bryan gave answers.

Did Bryan believe that all of the species on the earth had come into being in the 4200 years, by the Bishop's dating, since the Flood occurred? Yes, said Bryan finally, he did believe it.

Didn't Bryan know that many civilizations had existed for more than 5000 years? Said Bryan: 'I have never felt a great deal of interest in the effort that has been made to dispute the Bible by the speculations of men, or the investigations of men....'

By this time Bryan's self-esteem was suppurating, and his wits had entirely deserted him. Having discredited himself with everybody who did not believe in the literal truth of the Bible, he now destroyed himself with those who did. It took one deft question by Darrow, and a six-word reply.

Darrow asked: 'Do you think the earth was made in six days?'

Bryan: 'Not six days of twenty-four hours....'

Bryan said that the defense lawyers had 'no other purpose than ridiculing every Christian who believes in the Bible'.

Darrow said directly to Bryan: 'We have the purpose of preventing bigots and ignoramuses from controlling the education of the United States and you know it – and that is all.'

Ray Ginger, *Six Days or Forever?*, 1974

Australopithecus africanus: the southern ape from South Africa

In 1925 the Australian-born anatomist Professor Raymond Dart (opposite) published the results of his investigation into a fossil skull found at Taung (or Taungs) in South Africa. With great audacity he proposed a completely new view of human evolution based on this child's skull. He named the species to which this child belonged Australopithecus africanus *and saw it as the 'missing link' between apes and humans. His controversial theories met with a mixed reception. Until the discovery of Lucy in 1974, this species was thought to be the oldest known human ancestor.*

Towards the close of 1924, Miss Josephine Salmons, student demonstrator of anatomy in the University of the Witwatersrand, brought to me the fossilised skull of a cercopithecid monkey which, through her instrumentality, was very generously loaned to the Department for description by its owner, Mr E. G. Izod, of the Rand Mines Limited. I learned that this valuable fossil had been blasted out of the limestone cliff formation – at a vertical depth of 50 feet [15 metres] and a horizontal depth of 200 feet [60 metres] – at Taungs, which lies 80 miles [nearly 130 km] north of Kimberley on the main line to Rhodesia, in Bechuanaland, by operatives of the Northern Lime Company. Important stratigraphical evidence has been forthcoming recently from this district concerning the succession of stone ages in South Africa...and the feeling was entertained that this lime deposit, like that of Broken Hill in Rhodesia, might contain fossil remains of primitive man.

I immediately consulted Dr R. B. Young, professor of geology in the University of the Witwatersrand, about the discovery, and he, by a fortunate coincidence, was called down to Taungs almost synchronously to investigate geologically the lime deposits of an adjacent farm. During his visit to Taungs, Prof. Young was enabled, through the courtesy of Mr A. F. Campbell, general manager of the Northern Lime Company, to inspect the site of the discovery and to select further samples of fossil material for me from the same formation. These included a natural cercopithecid endocranial cast, a second and larger cast, and some rock fragments disclosing portions of bone. Finally, Dr Gordon D. Laing, senior lecturer in anatomy, obtained news,

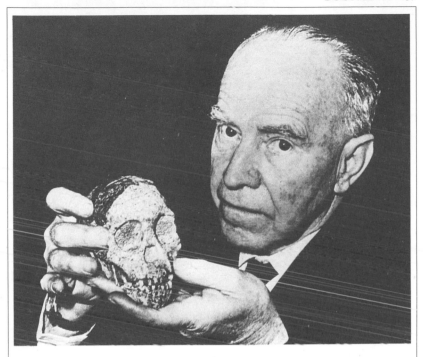

through his friend Mr Ridley Hendry, of another primate skull from the same cliff. This cercopithecid skull, the possession of Mr De Wet, of the Langlaagte Deep Mine, has also been liberally entrusted by him to the Department for scientific investigation....

In manipulating the pieces of rock brought back by Prof. Young, I found that the larger natural endocranial cast articulated exactly by its fractured frontal extremity with another piece of rock in which the broken lower and posterior margin of the left side of a mandible was visible. After cleaning the rock mass, the outline of the hinder and lower part of the facial skeleton came into view. Careful development

of the solid limestone in which it was embedded finally revealed the almost entire face....

It was apparent when the larger endocranial cast was first observed that it was specially important, for its size and sulcal pattern revealed sufficient similarity with those of the chimpanzee and gorilla to demonstrate that one was handling in this instance an anthropoid and not a cercopithecid ape. Fossil anthropoids have not hitherto been recorded south of the Fayum in Egypt, and living anthropoids have not been discovered in recent times south of Lake Kivu region in Belgian Congo, nearly 2000 miles [about 3220 km] to the north, as the crow flies.

All fossil anthropoids found hitherto

have been known only from mandibular or maxillary fragments, so far as crania are concerned, and so the general appearance of the types they represented has been unknown; consequently, a condition of affairs where virtually the whole face and lower jaw, replete with teeth, together with the major portion of the brain pattern, have been preserved, constitutes a specimen of unusual value in fossil anthropoid discovery. Here, as in *Homo rhodesiensis*, Southern Africa has provided documents of higher primate evolution that are amongst the most complete extant.

Apart from this evidential completeness, the specimen is of importance because it exhibits an extinct race of apes *intermediate between living anthropoids and man*....It is obvious, meanwhile, that it represents a fossil group distinctly advanced beyond living anthropoids in those two dominantly human characters of facial and dental recession on one hand, and improved quality of the brain on the other. Unlike Pithecanthropus, it does not represent an ape-like man, a caricature of precocious hominid failure, but a creature well advanced beyond modern anthropoids in just those characters, facial and cerebral, which are to be anticipated in an extinct link between man and his simian ancestor. At the same time, it is equally evident that a creature with anthropoid brain capacity, and lacking the distinctive, localised temporal expansions which appear to be concomitant with and necessary to articulate man, is no true man. It is therefore logically regarded as a man-like ape. I propose tentatively, then, that a new family of *Homo-simiadae* be created for the reception of the group of individuals which it represents, and that the first known species of the group be

designated *Australopithecus africanus*, in commemoration, first, of the extreme southern and unexpected horizon of its discovery, and, secondly, of the continent in which so many new and important discoveries connected with the early history of man have recently been made, thus vindicating the Darwinian claim that Africa would prove to be the cradle of mankind....

Professor Raymond A. Dart
Nature, 7 February 1925

The new missing link

Professor Raymond Dart, whose discovery of a 'missing link' in South Africa has fallen like a bombshell on anthropological Europe, is well known to British anatomists. He is one of the many young medical graduates of Sydney University whose minds were bent towards research in anatomy by Professor J. T. Wilson, before this distinguished anatomist left Australia for Cambridge. In post-graduate days Professor Dart worked at University College, London, with Professor Elliot Smith, at the Royal College of Surgeons, and in research laboratories of the United States. He went to Johannesburg some three years ago to occupy the chair of anatomy in the University of Witwatersrand. In South Africa he found an earnest band of investigators opening up unexpected chapters in the early history of man. Old river-beds were yielding a sequence of stone implements almost as ancient as those of Europe. The remains of a fossil man had been found at Boskop, and soon after Professor Dart's arrival other human remains were found deep in the floor of a rock shelter on the southern coast of Cape Colony. These were examined by Professor Dart, and found to be of the Boskop race. Then came the discovery of Rhodesian man in the bowels of a limestone kopje in Rhodesia – a much older and more primitive type than that of Boskop. And now comes an equally remarkable discovery which is largely due to the initiative and perspicuity of Professor Dart.

In November last a lady demonstrator brought him the fossil skull of a monkey – a baboon. It came from a limestone quarry situated at Taungs, eighty miles [nearly 130 km] to the north of Kimberley. There the quarrymen had worked their way 200 feet [60 metres] into a limestone bluff which rises 50 feet [15 metres] above the dry veldt of the surrounding country. The monkey's skull was blasted from the rock. Finding that his colleague, Dr R. B. Young, professor of geology, was going to Taungs, he asked him to inquire into the source of the fossil bones in the quarry. Dr Young arrived at the quarry in time to receive a mass of material just blasted from the base of the working face of the quarry. He gathered the fragments, and handed them to Professor Dart on his return.

In the mass of limestone Professor Dart found a cast which had formed within the brain cavity of a skull, and from the adjoining block he chiselled out the forehead and complete facial parts which went with the brain cast. The blasting had shivered and destroyed most of the cranial bones. From these fragments the discoverer reconstructed the being to which he has given the name *Australopithecus africanus*. So exact and clear are his drawings and his descriptions that those who have studied his preliminary account in *Nature*… have all the data placed at their disposal for coming to an independent opinion. Indeed, those who have charge of much larger collections of anthropoid and human skulls and brains than were at the disposal of Professor Dart have a somewhat unfair advantage over him. But with all these disadvantages against him his main conclusions are certain to stand.

He speaks of this new being as a 'man-ape', and as standing 'between living anthropoids and man'. These are his expressions, but when we examine his text we find him quite alive to the fact that the animal he has brought before the scientific world is a man-like ape or anthropoid. The size and convolutionary pattern of its brain leaves one in no doubt of this matter. Many fossil fragments of higher anthropoid apes have been found on previous occasions in Europe and India, but this is the first time we have seen the complete face of one of them. In this case the animal is young: the first permanent molar teeth have cut and are coming into place; this happens in the gorilla and chimpanzee towards the end of the fourth year – two years earlier than in human children. The face in all its lineaments is that of an anthropoid; there are blended in it some features of the chimpanzee, others of the gorilla, and some which belong to neither. But of humanity there is no trace save in one respect – its jaws are smaller and its supraorbital ridges less developed than in a chimpanzee of a corresponding age. There is a reduction in jaw development, and such a reduction has certainly taken place in the evolution of man. Further, the milk canines are less pointed than are those of the young chimpanzee, and the interdental space in front of the upper canine is less.

Sir Arthur Keith
The British Medical Journal
14 February 1925

Finding ER-1470, a *Homo habilis* skull

In 1972 Richard E. Leakey (below) brought world attention to focus on a skull discovered at Koobi Fora near Lake Turkana in Kenya. Known by its catalogue number at the National Museum of Kenya, ER-1470 was important because it was, at the time, the oldest, most complete representative of Homo habilis *to have been found.*

The year 1972 was an eventful one. Meave gave birth to our first daughter, Louise, on 21 March; the best known of all our discoveries from Koobi Fora, the skull '1470', was made in July; and in October my father died....

The skull '1470', the earliest evidence we had for *Homo* at Koobi Fora, was discovered by Bernard Ngeneo who, although he had only joined Kamoya's search team the previous year, quickly became an accomplished fossil hunter....

The 1972 discovery of '1470' has had tremendous publicity and is certainly the best-known fossil from Koobi Fora. When found, however, it caused no real excitement other than the usual good feeling that another hominid had been discovered. I was away in Nairobi at the time, but when I visited the site several days later on 27 July, everything was just as Bernard had found it, nothing had been disturbed. The specimen was badly broken and many fragments of light-coloured fossil bone were lying on the surface of a steep-sided ravine. None of the fragments was more than an inch long, but some were readily recognizable as being part of a hominid cranium. One good thing that was immediately apparent was that some were obviously from the back of the skull, others from the top, some from the sides, and there were even pieces of the very fragile facial bones. This indicated that there was a chance that we might eventually find enough pieces to reconstruct a fairly complete skull. It was clear, however, that a major sieving operation was required to recover other fragments that might be lying buried in the top few inches of soil or which had been washed down the steep slope. This sieving operation was not begun until a fortnight later and it continued over many weeks.

A number of fragments were collected in the first few days of sieving. On the fifth day, Meave, Bernard Wood (a friend who had been with me on several previous expeditions) and I flew to the site to help. At lunch time we returned to Koobi Fora with a number of fragments and after eating and a welcome swim we retired to the shady verandah of our house to examine the pieces. Meave carefully washed the fragments and laid them out on a wooden tray to dry in the sun and before long we were ready to begin to find which pieces could be joined to others. In no time at all, several of the bigger pieces fitted together and we realized that the fossil skull had been large, certainly larger than the small-brained *Australopithecus* such as we had found in 1969 and 1970. By the end of that exciting afternoon, we knew that we could go no further with the reconstruction without more pieces from the sieving.

Over the next few weeks more and more pieces were found in the sieving and Meave slowly put the fragments together. Gradually a skull began to take shape and we began to get a rough idea of its size. It was larger than any of the early fossil hominids that I had seen but the question was, how large was the brain? We decided to attempt a crude guess. Beginning by carefully filling the gaps in the vault with Plasticine and sticky tape, we then filled the vault with beach sand and measured the volume of sand in a rain gauge. By a most complicated conversion we came up with a volume of just under 800 cubic centimetres. The actual value for the brain size of '1470' has since been established by accurate methods as 775 cubic centimetres, so we were very close. This was fantastic new information.

We now had an early fossil human skull with a brain size considerably larger than anything that had been found before of similar antiquity. Also, we had found some limb bones. At the time we believed that the skull must be older than 2.6 million years – this being based upon the dating of the KBS tuff and the assurances that we had from John Miller [a British geophysicist at Cambridge] and Frank Fitch [a colleague] to the effect that this was a good date. It turned out that we were wrong by at least half a million years but this we only learned much later....

The whole question of whether a skull should be called *Homo* or something else is a matter of definition. None of the fossils that we find are labelled. We give them names for our own convenience. We have to judge whether 'X' looks more like 'Y' than 'Z' and this decision is often made more difficult because 'X', 'Y' and 'Z' are incomplete. I called this particular skull *Homo* because I believed it to be more like other fossils that had been called *Homo* than it was to those called *Australopithecus*. More importantly, '1470' has a brain size which is considerably bigger than any of the known fossils of *Australopithecus* and this is, in my opinion, very significant.

The intelligence we have, along with our technology and culture, all stems from some event way back in time when it was advantageous to be larger brained. My interest in early *Homo* is nothing more than a desire to determine exactly when the brain began to increase in size and there is no doubt, even after the revision of the dating, that '1470' is one of the earliest examples of a large-brained hominid.

One Life: Richard E. Leakey: An Autobiography, 1983

The discovery of Lucy

On 30 November 1974 in a gully at Hadar in Ethiopia Donald Johanson (below) made a unique find in the history of hominid fossil collecting. Here he recounts the actual discovery of Lucy, as she soon became known, and tells of the excitement he felt at finding a hominid dating back approximately 3.1 million years in such a good state of preservation.

As a paleoanthropologist – one who studies the fossils of human ancestors – I am superstitious. Many of us are, because the work we do depends a great deal on luck. The fossils we study are extremely rare, and quite a few distinguished paleoanthropologists have gone a lifetime without finding a single one. I am one of the more fortunate. This was only my third year in the field at Hadar, and I had already found several. I know I am lucky, and I don't try to hide it. That is why I wrote 'feel good' in my diary. When I got up that morning I felt it was one of those days when you should press your luck. One of those days when something terrific might happen....

At Hadar, which is a wasteland of bare rock, gravel and sand, the fossils that one finds are almost all exposed on the surface of the ground. Hadar is in the center of the Afar desert, an ancient lake bed now dry and filled with sediments that record the history of past geological events. You can trace volcanic-ash falls there, deposits of mud and silt washed down from distant mountains, episodes of volcanic dust, more mud, and so on. Those events reveal themselves like layers in a slice of cake in the gullies of new young rivers that recently have cut through the lake bed here and there. It seldom rains at Hadar, but when it does it comes in an overpowering gush – six months' worth overnight. The soil, which is bare of vegetation, cannot hold all that water. It roars down the gullies, cutting back their sides and bringing more fossils into view.

[Tom] Gray and I parked the Land-Rover on the slope of one of those gullies. We were careful to face it in such a way that the canvas water bag that was hanging from the side mirror was in the shade. Gray plotted the locality on the map. Then we got out and began doing what most members of the expedition spent a great deal of their time doing: we began surveying, walking slowly about, looking for exposed fossils....

Tom and I surveyed for a couple of hours. It was now close to noon, and the temperature was approaching 110. We hadn't found much: a few teeth of the small extinct horse *Hipparion*; part of the skull of an extinct pig; some antelope molars; a bit of a monkey jaw. We had large collections of all these things already, but Tom insisted on taking these also as added pieces in the overall jigsaw puzzle of what went where.

'I've had it,' said Tom. 'When do we head back to camp?'

'Right now. But let's go back this way and survey the bottom of that little gully over there.'

The gully in question was just over the crest of the rise where we had been working all morning. It had been thoroughly checked out at least twice before by other workers, who had found nothing interesting. Nevertheless, conscious of the 'lucky' feeling that had been with me since I woke, I decided to make that small final detour. There was virtually no bone in the gully. But as we turned to leave, I noticed something lying on the ground partway up the slope.

'That's a bit of a hominid arm,' I said.

'Can't be. It's too small. Has to be a monkey of some kind.'

We knelt to examine it.

'Much too small,' said Gray again. I shook my head. 'Hominid.'

'What makes you so sure?' he said.

'That piece right next to your hand. That's hominid too.'

'Jesus Christ,' said Gray. He picked it up. It was the back of a small skull.

A few feet away was part of a femur: a thighbone. 'Jesus Christ,' he said again. We stood up, and began to see other bits of bone on the slope: a couple of vertebrae, part of a pelvis – all of them hominid. An unbelievable, impermissible thought flickered through my mind. Suppose all these fitted together? Could they be parts of a single, extremely primitive skeleton? No such skeleton had ever been found anywhere.

'Look at that,' said Gray. 'Ribs.'

A single individual?...

That afternoon everyone in camp was at the gully, sectioning off the site and preparing for a massive collecting job that ultimately took three weeks. When it was done, we had recovered several hundred pieces of bone (many of them fragments) representing about forty percent of the skeleton of a single individual. Tom's and my original hunch had been right. There was no bone duplication.

But a single individual of what? On preliminary examination it was very hard to say, for nothing quite like it had ever been discovered. The camp was rocking with excitement. That first night we never went to bed at all. We talked and talked. We drank beer after beer. There was a tape recorder in the camp, and a tape of the Beatles song 'Lucy in the Sky with Diamonds' went belting out into the night sky, and was played at full volume over and over again out of sheer exuberance. At some point during that unforgettable evening – I no longer remember exactly when – the new fossil picked up the name of Lucy, and has been so known ever since, although its proper name – its acquisition number in the Hadar collection – is AL 288-1.

Donald Johanson and Maitland Edey
Lucy, 1981

Australopithecus ramidus

The oldest hominid found to date was discovered by a team led by Professor Tim White of the University of California at Aramis in Ethiopia in 1992. The seventeen fossils, which date back as far as 4.4 million years ago, are judged to belong to a new species – Australopithecus ramidus. *From the evidence currently available this species seems to represent the 'missing link' that brings together the family trees of apes and humans.*

The earliest known member of the human family has been discovered in Ethiopia. The hominid, who lived 4.4 million years ago, is the most ape-like human ancestor yet found, according to the scientists who found it.

Tim White of the University of California at Berkeley, Gen Suwa of the University of Tokyo and Berhane Asfaw of the Ethiopian government's Paleanthropology Laboratory, found fossils of the hominid in a barren part of northern Ethiopia called the Middle Awash in the Afar Depression.... They have named it *Australopithecus ramidus* after a word meaning 'root' in the language of the Afar people. The new species narrows the gap between the last common ancestor of African apes and humans and the earliest known hominids, or australopithecines.

White and his colleagues believe that the new Ethiopian species is distinct from the famous Lucy and her kin – the early hominids called *Australopithecus afarensis*. Until the latest discoveries, these were the most ancient human ancestors known. *A afarensis* dates from about 3.9 to 2.9 million years ago, Lucy herself having lived around 3.1 million years ago. In the winters of 1992 and 1993, White and his colleagues, searching near the village of Aramis a few kilometres west of the Awash River, found fragmentary fossil specimens of the new hominid representing about 17 individuals – pieces of skull, a child's lower jawbone, many teeth and broken arm bones, three of which were from the same limb. The site is about 75 kilometres to the southwest of Hadar, where Lucy and several other *A. afarensis* fossils were discovered.

No one is surprised at finding a hominid older than 4 million years, and fossil hunters have long searched for specimens in the Rift Valley of East Africa. The human and African ape lineages diverged between 8 million and 6 million years ago, but no one has ever found fossils of creatures resembling apes or humans from that period in Africa. The new fossils, together with molecular evidence, place the split near to 6 million years ago.

A few nondescript fossils from four sites in Kenya are between 5.5 and 4 million years old. They are probably from australopithecines but have not proved very helpful in clarifying when certain human features first appeared. In particular, it is not known whether these creatures walked on two legs. No hip or leg bones were found among the *A. ramidus* fossils, so it is not clear whether they were bipedal either. However, there is one clue. In *A. ramidus,* the foramen magnum, the opening at the base of the skull through which the brain connects to the spinal cord, is further forward than it is in apes. This suggests that the head was balanced on the backbone. White and his colleagues claim that this feature, together with several other characteristics, including the size and shape of the teeth, distinguish the Aramis hominid from extinct and living African apes.

Not much can be said about the general appearance or lifestyle of *A. ramidus.* Since no facial bones were found at the site, a skull cannot be reconstructed. The arm bones suggest that the hominids were taller than the diminutive Lucy, who was only 105 centimetres in height, but shorter than some other *A. afarensis* individuals, who stood around 150 centimetres tall.

More is known about the environment in which the Aramis hominids lived. It was a flat plain covered with woods and forest, and according to [scientists at] Los Alamos National Laboratory in New Mexico, *A. ramidus* lived among colobus monkeys, kudus and other treeloving animals.... The forested environment may have meant that the hominids spent a good deal of time climbing about in trees, just as *A. afarensis* may have done.

The suggestion that the Aramis hominids walked on two legs reinforces the idea that open grasslands were not necessary for the evolution of bipedalism, and lends support to a theory...that an upright posture evolved for the purpose of gathering fruit from trees in open forest and woodland....

Until more fossils of *A. ramidus* are found, and in particular more skull and lower limb bones, it is difficult to assess the relationship of this species to *A. afarensis* and to later humans. However, it is possible to speculate about two main hypotheses. One is that *A. ramidus* was the ancestor of *A. afarensis,* and that *A. afarensis* was the last common ancestor of the heavy-jawed 'robust' australopithecines, such as *Paranthropus* (or *Australopithecus*) *boisei,* and of a line that eventually led to our own genus, *Homo.*

Another possibility is that *A. ramidus* was the last common ancestor of the *Homo* lineage and of the robust australopithecines. In that scheme, *A. afarensis* would not be a direct human ancestor. The robust australopithecines became extinct a little before a million years ago. A third possibility, tentatively suggested by Bernard Wood of the University of Liverpool, is that *A. ramidus* was the ancestor only of the robust australopithecines.... This would make *A. afarensis* a direct human ancestor, but not *A. ramidus.*

Sarah Bunney, *New Scientist,*
1 October 1994

Out of Africa versus multiregional theories

Two rival camps hold diametrically opposed views on the origins of modern humans. The multiregional model, or theory of regional continuity, and the population replacement model put two different interpretations on the same fossil evidence.

Today there are two main competing scientific camps, each believing it holds the solution. Both accept that there was a migration out of Africa by *Homo erectus* populations beginning around 1 million years ago ('Out of Africa 1' as we shall call it). One camp, however, argues that there was at least one other major wave of migration ('Out of Africa 2') around 100,000 years ago, this time of anatomically modern humans – *Homo sapiens* – people who had evolved in Africa from *Homo erectus* stock and subsequently replaced all other populations in the world including the Neanderthals. Against this model of *population replacement*, the rival camp sets its model of *regional continuity*. For the followers of this latter school, there was no pronounced Out of Africa 2 migration. Instead, modern humans evolved semi-independently in different regions of the world from independent populations of Ancients (Neanderthals in Eurasia, *Homo erectus* in China and Java), with continual gene flow or interbreeding between geographically contiguous groups so that a single but racially diverse modern human species was the result.

It becomes clear that the Neanderthals – for whom we have a wealth of evidence greater than for any of our other fossil relatives – are central to this argument. Did they evolve into people like us, as the multiregionalists would have us believe, or were they an evolutionary dead end, as the proponents of population replacement would argue?...

According to current scientific thinking, speciation – the process by which new species are formed – is most commonly a product of the geographic isolation of an interbreeding group or population. Set out by Ernest Mayr, this geographical model of speciation is known as allopatry, and in the case of human evolution may draw on genetic, anatomical and archaeological evidence. Isolation can be produced either by geographical barriers, such as mountain formation or a rise in sea levels, or by new behavioural or morphological obstacles to interbreeding within a previously continuous population. The multiregional and replacement models for speciation disagree over the extent of isolation present in widely dispersed early human populations.

Multiregional evolution emphasizes continuity in both time and space. According to this model, isolation was never sufficient to allow allopatric speciation, since genes (the basic units of heredity) were circulated and exchanged between all the human populations of the Pleistocene. There could be no speciation because throughout the last 1 million years there was really only one species: *Homo sapiens*. This judgment implies that since the first dispersal of hominids out of Africa a million years or more ago, all the observable variation is within this one species. Multiregionalists argue that the mechanism of change was predominantly behavioural, with anatomy eventually evolving to accommodate progressive changes in behaviour that usually involved improvements in technology. These changes, like the genes, circulated around the inhabited world. The different regional lineages responded in similar ways to these universal forces, directing change globally towards modern-looking humans. Nevertheless, certain local differences were, at the same time, being maintained. Selection for specific features in particular environments kept them in local populations as they gradually became more modern, e.g. the large noses of Neanderthals were

maintained throughout the transition to modern Europeans, probably in response to the European climate, and the strong cheek bones of Javanese *Homo erectus* were maintained in the transition to modern native Australians, perhaps due to behavioural or dietary factors. The mechanism of interregional gene flow is all-important in multiregional evolution, to continually introduce new characteristics which can be worked on by local selection, and to counterbalance the tendency to local specializations which would increase divergence between geographically remote populations.

The population replacement camp has not so far produced a comparable theoretical dogma to account for evolutionary change.... The differences between the Neanderthals and modern humans...lay in their society and culture as well as in their anatomy.... The two communities were supported by different capacities for communication – verbal, visual and symbolic – and...this in turn affected their organization of camp-sites, their exploitation of the landscape, and their colonization of new habitats. But to conclude that the Neanderthals were different from us is not to condemn them in the same way that earlier popularizers and scientists did.... The Neanderthals were not ape-men, nor missing links – they were as human as us, but they represented a different brand of humanity, one with a distinctive blend of primitive and advanced characteristics. There was nothing inevitable about the triumph of the Moderns, and a twist of Pleistocene fate could have left the Neanderthals occupying Europe to this day. The 30,000 years by which we have missed them represent only a few ticks of the Ice Age clock.

C. Stringer and C. Gamble, *In Search of the Neanderthals*, 1993

GLOSSARY

Acheulian Cultural facies of the Lower Palaeolithic. It owes its name to a suburb of Amiens, St Acheul. The lithic industry comprises numerous tools worked on both sides, known as bifaces.

Aurignacian Upper Palaeolithic culture dating to between 33,000 and 26,000 BC.

Australopithecus A fossil hominid found in eastern and southern Africa about 5 to 1 million years ago. This small biped, which ranged in height from 1 to 1.5 metres, had a small brain (450 to 550 cc) and a massive face with projecting jaws. It comprised both 'gracile' (*ramidus, afarensis, africanus*) and 'robust' (*aethiopicus, robustus, boisei*) forms.

back This term is used in the typology of lithic traditions to designate an abrupt retouch that has removed the cutting edge of a blade (backed blade) or bladelet (backed bladelet).

backed tools Tools with a lateral surface that cuts more or less perpendicularly both sides of a flake, blade or bladelet in the direction of its greatest size.

biface Stone tool worked on both faces.

bifacial retouch Retouch on both sides of a flint tool.

bipedalism The ability to walk on two legs.

blade Elongated flake with two parallel edges, whose length is more than twice its width. Blades are particularly numerous in the Upper Palaeolithic industries. Unlike the earlier cultures, those of the Upper Palaeolithic systematically made blades. Bladelets are small blades less than 12 mm wide.

borer Tool of bone, ivory or antler, with a single bevelled base.

burin Worked stone tool that is very common in the Upper Palaeolithic. It has a bevelled edge formed by the junction of the scar made by removing a bladelet with another surface. This may be either the scar of the removal of another bladelet (in which case it is a dihedral burin) or a series of continuous retouches (in which case it is a burin on truncation).

Carbon 14 (C14 or 14C) The use of this radioactive isotope of carbon to date ancient materials was discovered in 1947 by the American chemist Willard Libby. All organic matter contains carbon, including a minuscule quantity of C14. When an organism dies, the C14 in it starts to decay at a very slow but consistent rate; its half-life is 5730 years. Measuring the radioactivity remaining in

a sample enables scientists to tell how long ago the organism died.

Ceraunia or thunderbolt-stone From the Greek *Keraunos* meaning lightning. Before the 19th century, this word was used to designate prehistoric tools of stone (especially polished stone), whose origin was then unknown.

Châtelperronian Culture that marks the transition between the Middle and Upper Palaeolithic: around 34,000 to 30,000 BC.

core Block of stone worked to produce the flakes, blades and bladelets needed to make tools and weapons.

Cro-Magnons See *Homo sapiens sapiens*.

dating (conventions) BP means 'before present', the present being 1950, the year considered to be zero in this dating system. BC means 'before Christ', while AD means *anno domini* (year of Our Lord), or after Christ. Dates BC are 1950 years less than dates BP.

end-scraper Worked stone tool, very common in the Upper Palaeolithic, characterized by a series of continuous retouches, forming a more or less rounded edge at the extremity of the piece.

Eocene The second part of the Tertiary period. It lasted about 20 million years.

Epipalaeolithic Group of cultures starting at the end of the last glaciation and ending in the Neolithic, around 3000 BC. This term is more especially used to designate the cultures of hunter-fisher-gatherers that emerged from the Palaeolithic tradition. The term Mesolithic designates cultures that were more inclined towards food production and settling, but that still derived a large part of their needs from hunting.

flake Fragment of rock, intentionally struck from a block of raw material or from a core, by percussion or pressure. A flake has an upper face, with the scars left by earlier removals, a lower face or struck face, with the bulb of percussion, and the heel, which is part of the striking platform carried away with the flake.

Gravette point Worked stone knife with a straight back and a sharp end. This tool characterizes the Gravettian and owes its name to the site of La Gravette in the Dordogne.

Gravettian The constant presence of Gravette points or microgravettes in all phases of the Upper Perigordian has led to this term being supplanted by 'Perigordian'.

hominid a term for an early form of human being that does not specify gender or time.

Homo erectus This human species, which appeared in East Africa 1.7 million years ago, eventually inhabited the Old World – North Africa, Asia and probably Europe – for almost 1.5 million years. In terms of height – they could reach 1.7 metres – these individuals were close to modern humans, though their cranial capacity was much smaller than ours today, varying from about 775 to 1250 cc. Their teeth were still enormous in comparison with those of *Homo sapiens*, but they were smaller than those of earlier hominids. These hunter-gatherers were the first humans to control fire and to set up habitations. They invented a new technique of working stone.

Homo habilis From the Latin term meaning skilful person (because of the ability to work tools), this species, the oldest representative – as far as we are currently aware – of the genus *Homo*, appeared in East Africa 1.8 million years ago. These individuals differed from their predecessors the australopithecines in several ways – they had a larger cranial capacity (650 to 800 cc), a more compact face and smaller teeth.

Homo sapiens From the Latin meaning intelligent or wise person, this final evolutionary form of humans developed from *Homo erectus*. These individuals show signs of evolutionary change in their increased brain size (1400 cc on average), developed frontal lobes, reduced face projection, decrease in the size of teeth and the appearance of a chin.

Homo sapiens neanderthalensis, an archaic sub-species of *Homo sapiens*, found mainly in Europe and parts of Asia, appeared about 230,000 years ago and disappeared about 35,000 years ago. The Neanderthals had to adapt to very varied climate conditions – sometimes cold and dry, sometimes mild and humid – and lived in open-air camps, rock shelters, the steppes or the tundra. Physically, they were small and muscular. They had a broad, receding head with a bun at the rear and a face distinguished by a prominent nose, receding cheekbones, a low brow and no chin. Their cranial capacity often exceeded the average of modern humans. The Neanderthals acquired a degree of sophistication, which is reflected in their tools, their spiritual preoccupations and their hunting methods.

Homo sapiens sapiens, a more evolved lineage, going back more than 100,000 years. These anatomically modern humans originated in Africa. They appear to have invaded western Europe from the East and replaced the Neanderthals. They differ from *Homo erectus* in having a larger skull with, on average, a cranial capacity of 1350 cc, a high brow, prominent cheekbones and a distinct chin. The best-known example of western *Homo sapiens sapiens* is the Cro-Magnon people, who appeared in Europe 35,000 years ago. One of the most striking features of these hunter-gatherers is the development of aesthetic feelings, closely linked to religion or magic, found in their cave art – paintings, engravings, sculptures and ornaments.

Levallois (technique) Method of knapping stone which enables one to obtain, through preparing the core, large flakes of predetermined shape. This block of raw material was first shaped by a series of removals made by blows almost perpendicular to its principal plane; a second series of removals, made by tangential blows on the ridges separating the flake-scars of the first series, gave the core an asymmetrical section and a tortoise-shell shape; a striking platform was then often produced at one of the core's narrow ends and made it possible to extract a single large flake. This thin, oval flake bears on one of its faces the convergent flake-scars of the second series of blows: it is a Levallois flake.

Magdalenian Culture of the end of the Upper Palaeolithic (about 17,000 to 10,000 BC) which owes its name to the site of La Madeleine. The lithic industry, based on blade production, became miniaturized towards the end of this period. The bone industry was developed, and was often decorated and became portable art objects, while deep caves saw the zenith of parietal art.

microlith Very small piece of worked stone, usually of flint, average length: 2 to 3 centimetres.

Mousterian Prehistoric culture that developed between about 100,000 and 35,000 years ago. It owes its name to the rock shelter of Le Moustier in the Dordogne. Neanderthals were associated with the so-called Mousterian industries. Tools were shaped from flakes that had been retouched into different forms, including side-scrapers.

Neanderthal Named after the site of Neanderthal, a valley close to Düsseldorf in Germany, where the remains of a fossil human were discovered in 1856.

Neanderthals See *Homo sapiens neanderthalensis*.

Neolithic Period of prehistory following the Palaeolithic around 8000 years ago. It is characterized by polished stone tools, the making and firing of ceramics, and especially by an important change in the way of life: people settled down; they became farmers and grouped their dwellings into villages.

Palaeolithic Period characterized by flaked stone tools during which primitive people emerged. The Old Stone Age or Palaeolithic is subdivided into three great parts: the Lower Palaeolithic which lasts until about 100,000 and corresponds to the development of the Acheulian industries; the Middle Palaeolithic, from about 100,000 to 35,000, the period during which the Neanderthals made the Mousterian industries; and the Upper Palaeolithic, from about 35,000 to 10,000, during which modern humans discovered art and made great use of blade production and boneworking.

palynology The study of pollen. The identification of fossil pollen contained in the sediments filling a site provides information on the plant environment at the time when these sediments were deposited. The variations in this environment reflect the evolution of the climate.

parietal From the Latin 'paries', wall. Designates engravings, drawings or paintings produced on the rocky walls of prehistoric caves.

perforated baton Object of reindeer antler perforated by one or, more rarely, several quite large holes. This instrument, sometimes called a commander's baton, is often decorated. They are found in all Upper Palaeolithic levels from the Aurignacian period onwards.

Perigordian Culture of the early Upper Palaeolithic subdivided into the Lower Perigordian (Châtelperronian) and Upper Perigordian (Gravettian).

Pithecanthropus From the Greek *pithekos* (ape) and *anthropos* (man). Fossil of the species *Homo erectus*, discovered in 1891 in Java.

side-scraper Lithic tool, generally made on a flake, with continuous retouch on one edge. The retouched edges of side-scrapers were most usually made on one of the long sides.

Sinanthropus Fossil of *Homo erectus* discovered in 1927 at Zhoukoudian near Peking (Beijing).

Solutrean Upper Palaeolithic culture dating to between 20,000 and 16,000 BC and which occupied a large part of western Europe. The lithic industry is characterized in particular by leaf-shaped points with parallel oblique retouches that sometimes affect both sides of the piece (laurel-leaf points).

spearthrower Instrument sculpted in a reindeer antler and with a hook at one end. These pieces, very characteristic of the Magdalenian, are often magnificent art objects. In comparison with analogous objects that are still used by Eskimos and Australian aborigines, they are thought to have been used for throwing projectiles by extending the hunter or warrior's arm.

steatopygia Major development of fatty tissue in the buttock area. This racial feature is much more marked in women than in men. It is often mentioned in relation to prehistoric 'Venuses'.

stratigraphy The study of the succession of sedimentary deposits that are generally grouped into layers, taking into account their nature and content.

Tertiary Period in the Cenozoic era – the most recent geological era – during which mammals became dominant. It comprises the Paleocene, Eocene, Oligocene, Miocene and Pliocene eras.

typology Study of the forms of the stone and bone tools found in archaeological layers. This study enables one to define types, classify the tools and produce a quantitative analysis of prehistoric industries.

Venus Name given to prehistoric statuettes, bas-reliefs and engravings representing women.

Würm Last Quaternary glaciation which lasted from 110,000 to 10,000 years ago. It owes its name to a tributary of the Danube. During the period of maximum cold 18,000 years ago, the ice was 3 km thick in places and the sea level dropped by 120 metres.

Glossary drawn from *Art et civilisation de la préhistoire*, 1984, and *Dossier d'archéologie*, January 1991

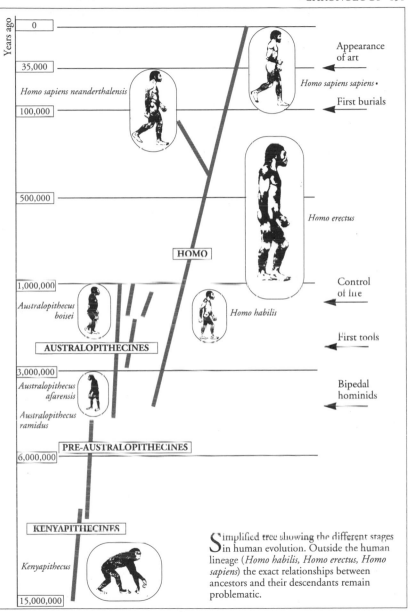

Years ago

0

35,000

Homo sapiens neanderthalensis

100,000

500,000

HOMO

1,000,000

Australopithecus boisei

AUSTRALOPITHECINES

3,000,000

Australopithecus afarensis

Australopithecus ramidus

PRE-AUSTRALOPITHECINES

6,000,000

KENYAPITHECINES

Kenyapithecus

15,000,000

Appearance of art

Homo sapiens sapiens •

First burials

Homo erectus

Control of fire

First tools

Bipedal hominids

Homo habilis

Simplified tree showing the different stages in human evolution. Outside the human lineage (*Homo habilis, Homo erectus, Homo sapiens*) the exact relationships between ancestors and their descendants remain problematic.

FURTHER READING

Aiello, Leslie, and Christopher Dean (eds.), *An Introduction to Human Evolutionary Anatomy*, 1990

Bahn, Paul G., and Jean Vertut, *Images of the Ice Age*, 1988

Burenhult, Göran (ed.), *The First Humans: Human Origins and History to 10,000 BC*, 1993

Cole, Sonia, *Leakey's Luck: The Life of Louis Leakey, 1903–72*, 1975

Eldredge, Niles, and Ian Tattersall, *The Myths of Human Evolution*, 1982

Fagan, Brian M., *The Journey from Eden: The Peopling of Our World*, 1991

Falk, Dean, *Braindance: New Discoveries about Human Brain Evolution*, 1992

Fleagle, John G., *Primate Adaptation and Evolution*, 1988

Grine, Frederick E. (ed.), *Evolutionary History of the 'Robust' Australopithecines*, 1988

Johanson, Donald C., and Maitland A. Edey, *Lucy: The Beginnings of Humankind*, 1981

Leakey, Mary D., *Olduvai Gorge: My Search for Early Man*, 1979

Leakey, Richard E., *The Making of Mankind*, 1981

Lewin, Roger, *Human Evolution: An Illustrated Introduction*, 1993

Lister, Adrian, and Paul Bahn, *Mammoths*, 1994

Reader, John, *Missing Links: The Hunt for Earliest Man*, 1981

Spencer, Frank, *Piltdown: A Scientific Forgery*, 1990

Stringer, Christopher, and Clive Gamble, *In Search of the Neanderthals*, 1993

Sutcliffe, Antony J., *On the Track of Ice Age Mammals*, 1985

Tattersall, Ian, Eric Delson and John Van Couvering (eds.), *Encyclopedia of Human Evolution and Prehistory*, 1988

Tobias, Philip V. (ed.), *Hominid Evolution, Past, Present and Future*, 1985

Turnbaugh, William A., Harry Nelson, Robert Jurmain and Lynn Kilgore (eds.), *Understanding Physical Anthropology and Archeology*, 1993

LIST OF ILLUSTRATIONS

The following abbreviations have been used: *a* above; *b* below; *c* centre; *l* left; *r* right; BN Bibliothèque Nationale; MNHN Muséum National d'Histoire Naturelle

COVER

Front *Australopithecus africanus* on the savannah. Painting by John Gurche. 1986
Spine *Australopithecus robustus*. Drawing by Mario Caselli
Back Cro-Magnon skull in Jean Louis Armand de Quatrefages and Ernest T. Hamy, *Crania Ethnica: Les Crânes des races humaines*, 1882. BN, Paris

OPENING

1 Apes. Drawing by Mario Caselli
2–3 Australopithecines. Drawing by Gilles Tosello
4–5 *Homo habilis*. Drawing by Gilles Tosello
6–7 *Homo erectus*. Drawing by Gilles Tosello
8–9 Neanderthals. Drawing by Gilles Tosello
10–1 *Homo sapiens sapiens*. Drawing by Gilles Tosello
13 *Australopithecus robustus*. Drawing by Mario Caselli

CHAPTER 1

14 The earth seen from space. NASA photograph

15 Adam. Miniature in H. von Bingen, *Livre des Oeuvres de Dieu*. 11th–12th century Latin codex. Bibliothèque Civique, Lucques
16a Herbert Pugh. Stonehenge. Watercolour. Early 19th century. City Art Galleries, Manchester
16b The alpha and the omega. Illumination by Beatus de Léon. c. 1047. Biblioteca Nacional, Madrid
17 The creation of man. Engraving in Canon Scheuchzer's 1732 Bible. BN, Paris
18 Orang-utan. Coloured engraving. 1778. Amsterdam
18–9 *St Jerome or the Thinker*. Painting by Marinus van Reymerswaele. c. 1493. Musée des Beaux-Arts, Orléans
19 The Hottentot Venus, who was exhibited in Paris in 1829. Watercolour
20 and 21 The supposed remains of the 'witness of the Flood' (detail). Engravings in Canon Scheuchzer, *Physica Sacra*, 1731
20–1 The quarries of Montmartre. Anonymous engraving. 19th century. BN, Paris
22a Cuvier gathers the evidence for his book on fossil bones. Fresco. 1823. Sorbonne, Paris
22b The first fossil primate discovered. Illustration from Georges Cuvier, *Recherches sur les ossements fossiles de quadrupèdes*, 1812
23l Classification of anthropomorphs in Carolus Linnaeus, *Systema Naturae*, 1756. BN, Paris

DOCUMENTS

INDEX

PHOTO CREDITS

A.F.P., Paris 85. All rights reserved 44, 129, 130, 137. Anthropological Museum, Institute of Human Palaeontology, Beijing 87. Archiv für Kunst und Geschichte, Berlin 32. Archives Gallimard 18, 32–3, 33r, 41, 46l, 60l, 78 (4), 117b. Bibliothèque Muséum National d'Histoire Naturelle, Paris 26a, 42a. Bibliothèque Nationale, Paris back cover, 17, 20–1, 23l, 24, 27a, 27b, 28a, 29a, 31b, 40–1, 47r, 48 inset, 48, 49a, 50–1, 51c. Bridgeman Art Library, London 34–5, 37. Bulloz, Paris/Musée Carnavalet, Paris 31a. Mario Caselli, Florence spine, 1, 13, 75a, 90–1, 112–3. Charmet, Paris 19, 20, 21, 30a, 36, 43, 134. City Art Galleries, Manchester 16a. Centre National de la Recherche Scientifique (C.N.R.S.) 83a, 83b. C.N.R.S.-S.M.C. 58r. C.N.R.S.-L.M.C. 59a. Cosmos, Paris 110. Cosmos, Paris/S.P.L. 56, 59b, 65, 66–7, 72l, 84a, 84l, 92b. Cosmos, Paris/Earth Satellite Corporation/S.P.L. 127. Cosmos, Paris/E. Ferobelli 58l. Cosmos, Paris/L. Pesek/S.P.L. 62–3. Cosmos, Paris/J. Reader/S.P.L. 35, 46r, 52, 100–1. Dagli Orti, Paris 15, 23r, 38, 38–9, 44–5. DITE, Paris 82. Edimédia, Paris 104. Explorer, Paris/A. Bertrand 72a, S. Cordier 64–5, Fiore 71r, Lorne 112. Frisano, Paris 72–3. John Gurche front cover. Claus Hausman, Munich 109a. Institut de Paléontologie, Paris/Serette 61b. Jacana, Vanves/J.M. Labat 57, 60r. David Keith Jones, Lichfield 71l, 88. Courtesy Michael Joseph Ltd, London 140. Hubert Josse, Paris 22a, 106–7. Kharbine Tapabor, Paris 42b. Keystone, Paris 126. Lauros-Giraudon, Vanves 18–9. Collection Prof. Henry de Lumley, Laboratoire de Préhistoire, Institut de Paléontologie Humaine, Paris 79 (7, 8), 88–9, 90, 94–5. Magnum, Paris/E. Lessing 93a, 115. Daniel Moignot, Paris 74–5, 92a. Musée Boucher de Perthes, Abbeville 29b. Musée de l'Homme, Paris 28b, 52–3, 70r, 80 (12), 81 (15), 94a, 94b, 117a, 117r, 121, 122–3, 151, D. Destable 40, 108br, M. Delaplanche 45, 49bl, J. Oster 76a, 80 (9, 10), 89, 105, 108l, 109bl, 109br, 111r, 124–5, D. Ponsard 80 (11). Muséum National d'Histoire Naturelle, Paris/D. Serette 22b, B. Fayes 25. N.A.S.A. 14, 39. National Geographic Society, Washington, D.C. 78 (1, 2), David Brill 64b, 70l, Joseph J. Scherschel 69, Melville Bell Grosvenor 77, Robert F. Sisson 96–7, 97, David S. Boyer 98, Des Bartlett 99a, 99b. Natural History Museum, London 55b. Nationaal Natuurhistorisch Museum, Leiden 55a. Novosti, Paris 118b. Oronoz, Madrid 16b. Pavillion/Institut Anthropos, Moravské Muzeum, Brno, Czech Republic 86, 106, 114, 128. Musée du Périgord, Périgueux 49br. Réunion des Musées Nationaux, Paris 30r, 116, 119a, 120a. Rijksmuseum voor Volkenkunde, Leiden 53. H. Roche, Laboratoire de Paléontologie 76b. Roger Viollet, Paris 54r. Société Historique et Archéologique du Périgord 47l. Christopher Stringer 146. Fondation Teilhard de Chardin, Paris 93b. Herbert Thomas, Paris 78 (3), 79 (5), 81 (18), 84br, 102a, 102b, 103a, 103c, 103b, 142. Gilles Tosello, Paris 2–3, 4–5, 6–7, 8–9, 10–1, 68. Ullstein, Berlin 51a. B. Vandermeersch, Bordeaux 111l. N.K Vereshchagin 118a. J. Vertut, Issy-les-Moulineaux 79 (6), 81 (13, 14, 16, 17), 108ar, 109bc, 119b, 120b. J. Vigne, Gennevilliers 54a, 61a. The Dean and Chapter of Westminster 26b.

TEXT CREDITS

Grateful acknowledgment is made for use of material from the following works: (pp. 144–5) Sarah Bunney, *New Scientist*, 1 October 1994; reprinted by permission of *New Scientist*, London. (pp. 136–8) Professor Raymond A. Dart, *Nature*, 7 February 1925; reprinted by permission from *Nature*, Vol. 115, pp. 195–9, copyright © 1925 Macmillan Magazines Ltd. (pp. 134–5) Ray Ginger, *Six Days or Forever?*, Oxford University Press, 1974; reprinted by permission of Victoria Brandon. (pp. 142–3) Donald C. Johanson and Maitland A. Edey, *Lucy: The Beginnings of Humankind*, Granada Publishing, 1981; reprinted by permission of the Peters Fraser & Dunlop Group Ltd, London. (pp. 138–9) Sir Arthur Keith, *The British Medical Journal*, 14 February 1925; reprinted by permission of BMJ Publishing Group, London. (pp. 140–1) Richard E. Leakey, *One Life: Richard E. Leakey: An Autobiography*, Michael Joseph Ltd, London, 1983, pp. 147, 148–9, 153–4, copyright © Sherma BV 1983; reproduced by permission of Penguin Books Ltd. (pp. 146–7) Christopher Stringer and Clive Gamble, *In Search of the Neanderthals*, Thames and Hudson Ltd, 1993; reprinted by permission of the authors.

Herbert Thomas,
deputy director of the
Laboratoire de Paléoanthropologie et Préhistoire
at the Collège de France, has directed
numerous excavations in Africa and Asia.
He was given an award by the Fondation de la Vocation
and the Tchihatchef prize by the Académie des Sciences.
A member of the Explorers' Club, he is the author
of more than one hundred scientific and popular works.
In 1974 he took part in the Franco-American expedition to Afar,
in Ethiopia, which led to the discovery of Lucy.
Since 1987 he has been leader of the Franco-Omani
palaeontological expedition, on which the oldest
anthropoid primates have been discovered.
Among other major projects, he is to lead
an expedition to Vietnam
under the aegis of the Ushuaïa Foundation,
in search of further evidence of
a new, living, large mammal – the saola –
which was discovered in 1992.

For Alexandre

© Gallimard 1994

English translation © Thames and Hudson Ltd,
London, 1995

Translated by Paul G. Bahn

All Rights Reserved. No part of this publication may
be reproduced without prior permission in writing
from the publisher.

British Library Cataloguing-in-Publication Data

A catalogue record for this book is available
from the British Library

ISBN 0–500–30056–9

Printed and bound in Italy
by Editoriale Libraria, Trieste

tightrope

Gillian Cross

PUFFIN BOOKS

SAO13040 CRO
3 WKS

PUFFIN BOOKS

Published by the Penguin Group
Penguin Books Ltd, 27 Wrights Lane, London W8 5TZ, England
Penguin Putnam Inc., 375 Hudson Street, New York, New York 10014, USA
Penguin Books Australia Ltd, Ringwood, Victoria, Australia
Penguin Books Canada Ltd, 10 Alcorn Avenue, Toronto, Ontario, Canada M4V 3B2
Penguin Books (NZ) Ltd, Private Bag 102902, NSMC, Auckland, New Zealand

On the World Wide Web at: www.penguin.com

Penguin Books Ltd, Registered Offices: Harmondsworth, Middlesex, England

First published by Oxford University Press 1999
Published in Puffin Books 2000
3

Copyright © Gillian Cross, 1999
All rights reserved

The moral right of the author has been asserted

Made and printed in England by Clays Ltd, St Ives plc

Except in the United States of America, this book is sold subject to the condition
that it shall not, by way of trade or otherwise, be lent, re-sold, hired out, or otherwise
circulated without the publisher's prior consent in any form of binding or cover
other than that in which it is published and without a similar condition including this
condition being imposed on the subsequent purchaser.

British Library Cataloguing in Publication Data
A CIP catalogue record for this book is available from the British Library

ISBN 0–141–30535–5

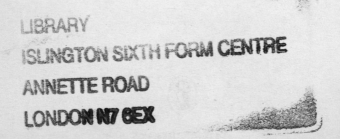
LIBRARY
ISLINGTON SIXTH FORM CENTRE
ANNETTE ROAD
LONDON N7 6EX

To Kaby

One

Ashley stopped at the traffic lights on the Row, looked across the road—and saw the best wall in the world.

And it had been there all her life.

Jabbing her elbow into Vikki's ribs, she raised her eyebrows and nodded over the road, towards Fat Annie's and the chippie. Vikki followed where she was looking, and her eyebrows almost disappeared into her hair.

'Ash! You *can't*!'

'Sssh!' Ashley hissed. 'Shut up.' They were on their way home from school, and there were other people all round them.

Vikki shut up, but her eyes were like marbles as the lights changed and they crossed the Row. She couldn't stop looking up at the wall.

It was a big, blank space, where Fat Annie's rose a whole storey higher than the chippie next door. The top of the side wall was exposed, and there was nothing on it at all. Not a mark. It was just waiting for someone to get up there and tag it. And all you'd have to do was climb on to the roof of the chippie and walk along.

Twenty feet up in the air, in full view of the Row. With nothing to stop you if you fell.

'You can't!' Vikki whispered again, when they reached the other side of the road. 'Ash, you're mad. You'll kill yourself.'

'Be quiet!' Ashley growled, looking over her shoulder. She didn't want anyone else getting there first.

But it wasn't that easy to make Vikki give up. She grabbed Ashley's arm and shook it. 'Listen to me—'

'There's nothing to say.' Stubbornly Ashley ignored her, heading sideways, into Fat Annie's. 'Got to pick up some cheese.'

She had to push her way in. The place was full of kids scrabbling round the counter with chocolate and chewing gum, trying to barge in front of each other. Fat Annie's eyes were everywhere—on the shop door, flicking up at the security camera, and checking every coin she was offered—and as her fingers banged away at the till, she was bellowing at the queue-jumpers.

'Get back and wait your turn, Dean Fox! And you, Shorty! And watch your language, or I'll be round to talk to your mother.'

Ashley pushed through the crowd, heading for the cheese counter and trying to lose Vikki in the scrum. But Vikki was right on her heels, still banging on about the wall.

'Ash, you've got to listen! You'd be crazy to—'

Ashley ignored her and began burrowing in the cheese cabinet, hunting for a bit of cheap Cheddar. Vikki leaned closer, to whisper in her ear.

'You'll fall! You'll break your legs! And even if you don't, someone's going to catch you. It'll be a disaster.'

'I can handle it,' Ashley said. 'Now be quiet. I don't want everyone to—'

Out of the corner of her eye, she caught a movement. She glanced up and stopped dead. The Hyena was marching across the shop towards them, like the US Cavalry riding over the horizon.

That wasn't typical. Usually, he was the opposite of his mother. Where Annie yelled and bullied the customers, the Hyena crept around, turning his soft pasty face away from people's eyes. He slunk round the shop like a hyena with its tail between its legs—if a hyena can be going bald on top.

He wasn't slinking today, though. He was heading straight for Vikki, looking fierce and determined. But she hadn't realized yet. Ashley struggled not to laugh.

2

'You'd better let me alone,' she murmured. 'It looks as if I'm going to be rescued.' Then she fluttered her eyelids pathetically and whimpered, 'Please leave me alone.'

At first, Vikki thought it was a joke and she bared her teeth, pretending to snarl. Then she realized that Ashley was serious and she whipped round.

By then, the Hyena was just behind her. He looked at Ashley. 'Is she bothering you?'

Vikki didn't give Ashley a chance to reply. She leaned back against the cheese counter and looked at the Hyena with bold, bright eyes. 'How could I bother anyone?' she drawled.

Then she hitched up her skirt—the last possible centimetre—and took a step towards him. The Hyena stepped backwards, nervously, and she grinned and strolled past him, to the magazine shelves. Standing on tiptoe, she reached down a copy of *Penthouse* and began to flick through the pages.

The Hyena's pale face turned pink.

He was hesitating on the brink of saying something, but Annie got there first. She screamed at him, all the way across the shop.

'Geoffreeee! Don't let the children at the men's magazines!'

Immediately, everyone in the queue turned to look. Vikki grinned again and raised the magazine higher, and Ashley bent over the cheese, trying not to laugh.

The Hyena couldn't bring himself to look directly at Vikki, but he reached out a long arm to take the magazine away. His bony hands were shaking faintly, the way they always did. Vikki pretended not to notice. Whisking the magazine out of his reach, she turned her back and went on looking through it.

Fat Annie yelled at the top of her voice, as she rang in a couple more Mars Bars and three bags of crisps. 'Geoffreeee! Come on the till!'

Even from the far end of the shop, Ashley could feel the Hyena's relief. He turned away from Vikki and scuttled to the counter to take his mother's place, and Annie lumbered out, heading for the magazine rack.

Vikki wasn't stupid. By the time Annie got there, she was reading *Smash Hits*, and her skirt had dropped to its full length. But that didn't make any difference to Annie. She tweaked the magazine away and jerked her head at the door.

'Outside, madam.'

Vikki was beaten, but not squashed. She sauntered to the door, saying 'Hi,' to everyone in the queue and rolling her eyes at the Hyena. Ashley grinned to herself and went on with her cheese hunt.

When she finally decided which piece she could afford, the queue had vanished. Fat Annie was still by the magazine rack, tidying it up with brisk, angry fingers, and the Hyena was alone at the counter. He took Ashley's cheese and looked sideways at her, flicking his tongue over his lips.

'How's your mother coming along, then?'

Why did people always ask that? She gave him her standard plastic smile.

'She's fine, thanks.'

Flick, went the Hyena's tongue again. Flick, flick. He made Ashley feel clammy all over. She dropped her money on to the counter, avoiding his hand, and got out of the shop as fast as she could.

Vikki was waiting outside, ready to start up about the wall again, but Ashley didn't give her a chance.

'*No!*' she said. 'OK?'

'But—'

'Look, Vik, you don't really think you're going to change my mind, do you?'

Vikki thought about it for a moment and then shrugged. 'OK, so you're pig-headed. But you *are* going to fall, you know. One day.'

'That's my lookout.' Ashley dropped the cheese into her

4

pocket and swung her bag on to her shoulder. 'You just wait until tomorrow, and see what that wall's like.'

Vikki put her head on one side. 'There's other ways of getting kicks, you know. You could come to the party tonight, instead. With me and Matt.'

'I'm a bit busy tonight,' Ashley muttered. 'But—thanks.'

It was what she always said, but she was pleased to be asked. Vikki always asked her, even though she got the same answer every time. Ashley smiled at her.

'Hope it's a good party, though. Be nice to Matt.'

'I'll be so nice he'll think it's his birthday.' Vikki closed her eyes dreamily. 'Wait and see what *he's* like tomorrow. He'll be dancing on air.'

She waved a hand and floated away down the Row. *As if,* Ashley thought. Things were never straightforward with those two. Matt was twice Vikki's size, but she'd got him on a lead, and she could never resist wrapping it round his neck. There was bound to be some drama or other to sort out at school tomorrow.

The wall was a whole lot simpler than all that stuff.

Ashley walked round the corner, into Railway Street, where she lived, but she wasn't heading home. Not yet. She was going to spy out the ground.

Immediately behind the shops there was a little service road, running parallel to the Row. She glanced round and then strolled into it. To work out how to get on to the roof of the chippie.

GEOFFREY

You always have a favourite, don't you? In any crowd of people, there's one who catches your eye. There must be hundreds of schoolchildren who come into the shop, but Ashley's my special one. She's neat and tidy, for a start. And quiet. And she looks so— It's that fair hair and those big blue eyes, I suppose. She's always stood out from the others. Even before I knew about her.

5

But when you know about her life—well, it's like a fairy tale, isn't it? The other children come in pushing and shoving, grabbing for chewing gum and Cokes, and they've got more money than they know what to do with. Ashley always buys real food. Eggs and cheese. Milk and flour and margarine. And you can see her checking the prices.

I didn't understand at first. I thought she was just doing the shopping to help her mother out. I didn't know that she does a lot more than the shopping. Not until Mrs Macdonald told me.

I don't like to gossip, of course. It gets the shop a bad name. But once I knew about Ashley I kept my ears open and it's wonderful what you pick up if you stay quiet and listen. Little bits here and there. Things she says to the other children, and odd remarks people make. I know all about her now. Where she lives. The date of her birthday. Where she goes to school. Lots of things.

I get really angry when I see other children pestering her. Like that girl today. You can see what *she's* like, with that short skirt and dyed hair. She's a— Well, I don't like to say it, but it's obvious, isn't it? It makes me feel sick just seeing her talking to Ashley.

And Ashley's so good about it. You could tell she was being bullied, but she didn't fuss. When I saw her looking up, I thought—I know it was silly, but I couldn't help it—I thought *I wish I could protect her.*

It's not fair, the sort of life she has to live. Not when you think about someone like Eddie Beale. He never does a stroke of work, and he has it all. When Ashley comes in looking tired and worried, I wish I could scoop up an armful of luxury items and drop them into her basket. 'Take these, my dear,' I'd say, 'for being such a good customer.'

I'd give her frozen rump steak, and petit pois. Fruits of the forest cheesecake and extra thick double cream. She deserves the very best. Sometimes, when I see her with her baked beans and pork luncheon meat, my hands actually ache with wanting to snatch extra things off the shelves.

But it wouldn't do, of course. Mother would have a fit, to begin with. And the other customers wouldn't like it. So I have to make do with giving her that extra bit of attention, to help her feel good.

I always smile and ask how her mother's doing. She never says much, but I know she appreciates it. This is a rough, difficult neighbourhood, and everyone's in a hurry. There aren't many sensitive people around. I like to think

6

that she looks on this as a special place, where she has a true friend. Someone quiet and gentle and considerate, who understands her and what she has to put up with.

I hope she'd come to me if she was ever in trouble. I'd look after her.

Two

Ashley stood in the alley behind Fat Annie's and looked up at her wall. It wasn't going to be easy. But she could manage it. She *knew* she could.

First, she had to get into the yard behind the chippie. All the shops had yards at the back, surrounded by brick walls topped with broken glass or barbed wire. The chippie's had broken glass, and it didn't look too threatening. Her bit of blanket would take care of that.

Inside the yard, the real climbing began. The chippie had a single-storey extension, sticking out at the back. She reckoned she could shin up the drainpipe at the corner of that. The real problem was getting on to the main roof. That was going to be fingertip stuff. She'd have to use the window ledges and put a foot on the guttering.

If it was strong enough.

She narrowed her eyes, trying to see how good the brackets were. They looked pretty solid, and the gutter was cast iron. She reckoned she could make it. Then she could crawl up the slope of the roof.

After that, it was a tightrope walk. Four or five metres along the ridge of the roof. If she kept her balance, she'd be fine. If not—curtains. She'd go pitching down into the yard, or into the Row on the far side. It wouldn't take much. Just a loose tile, or a slip in her concentration.

She looked up at the ridge and felt her whole body come to life.

And now, the beautiful Miss Cindy will risk her life to bring you a daredevil display of balance and courage! Watch her climb to the roof, without a safety net!! Thrill to her death-defying ridge walk!!!

8

Marvel at her calmness as she leaves her signature on this IMPOSSIBLE WALL!!!!

She was going to do it all right. She knew it, in her bones.

A second later, she was strolling out of the alley again, thinking about time. Three in the morning ought to be safe enough. There was no one around then except people like Spider Mo. Deadheads. She could get away with anything then, as long as she planned it right.

As she went home, she worked out all the details. That was how she'd done so many great walls without being spotted. Planning. She was hardly aware of how slowly she was going. Not until she reached the front door, and realized that she was half an hour later than usual.

Her mother was already shouting as she walked in.

'What time do you call this? You've been out of school for an hour! You know I won't have you hanging around like that. You'll get into all sorts of trouble.'

Here we go. Ashley hung her bag on the end of the banisters and walked into the front room letting the shouting wash over her. Pauline was sitting on the bed, and she was white and shaking with fury.

'You knew I was all on my own here! You're just taking advantage. If you don't get in on time, I'll have to come and look for you . . . ' Her breathing was already getting rougher. 'What do you think it's like for me? Sitting here and waiting? You don't care, do you? You're stupid and lazy and self-centred . . . '

The only thing to do was think of it as a storm. Ashley had worked that out long, long ago. Sit it out and then see if there's any real damage. She thought about rocks and lighthouses. Strong things that could take a battering.

Pauline thumped her fist on to the bed. It was a sad, soft sound, muffled by the blankets.

'Just because I'm not too good at the moment, you think . . . '

Ashley bent her head and let the words wash over her.

9

'You wait until I'm a bit better! Then you'll see . . . '

Her mother's face was hectic pink now. The words she was shouting were as fragile as smoke. If she panted any harder, her gasps would blow them away.

'Answer me!' Pauline shouted. 'Why don't you ever answer? I hate it when you go blank like that! You're so . . . so . . . so . . . '

That was it. The pink flush on her face drained away and the words dissolved in a fit of coughing. Ashley went across the room and sat down on the bed.

'It's all right,' she said. She put her arm round Pauline's shoulders and began to chant. 'Don't panic. Just breathe and breathe and breathe. And breathe. And breathe . . . '

She kept it up until her mother's body took over the rhythm, and the dreadful juddering breaths slowed down. And down. And down. Until, for one calm moment, they sat together, breathing at the same speed. Perfectly still.

Then Pauline pulled away and put her hands over her face.

'I'm sorry. Oh, I'm sorry, Ash.'

'It's all right,' Ashley said. 'I was only getting some cheese, you know.' She stood up quickly, but she couldn't get away before Pauline started.

'No, it's not all right. I'm a lousy mother. It's no life for you. You should be out with your friends. You ought to be having a good time—'

Ashley hated that. It was worse than the shouting.

'I'll make some tea,' she said. And she went through to the kitchen.

Normally Pauline was in bed by ten o'clock. But it took her a long time to calm down after one of her storms. It was nearly midnight before Ashley finished helping her on with her nightdress. Pauline was very thin and everything had to be done carefully, in case she bruised. She had taken two hours

10

to eat her share of the cauliflower cheese, and then she'd brought half of it up again. Ashley had said, *It doesn't matter* and *It's all right* so often that she thought her tongue would drop out.

By the time they shuffled across the front room to the bed, it was ten to twelve. On good days, Pauline could walk with just an arm to lean on, but that night Ashley was half carrying her.

Pulling the covers back, she lowered her mother carefully, to sit on the bed. Then she picked up the hairbrush and began to brush Pauline's long, brown hair, teasing out the tangles with her fingers.

'I ought to have it all cut off!' Pauline said suddenly. Viciously. 'It's just another job for you to do, isn't it?'

Ashley's fingers didn't falter. 'It's all right. I don't mind. You look nice with it long.'

Pauline took a strand between her fingers. 'I'll manage it myself tomorrow. Really I will. It's just . . . I'm so tired tonight.'

'It's all right,' Ashley said again, plaiting the hair with quick, practised fingers. 'I'll send you a bill tomorrow. Slave driver.'

Pauline relaxed and let her finish the plait. Then she lay back in bed and let Ashley pull up the duvet round her shoulders. Ashley gave her plait a tweak.

'Sleep well.'

'And you. Don't sit up.'

'I won't,' Ashley said.

She didn't. She went upstairs and changed into her leggings and her black sweatshirt. Then she lay flat on her bed and started to think about what she was going to put on Fat Annie's wall.

Pauline started snoring at twenty-five past one. In a couple of minutes, the sounds were steady and regular. Ashley waited another hour, to let the streets clear, and then slipped off the bed and took her spray-cans out of the chest of drawers. Four of them this time. Black, red, orange, and yellow.

She wrapped them in rags, to stop them clinking, and pushed them into her rucksack, with a piece of old blanket bundled on top. Then she crept downstairs and into the kitchen. Very carefully, she opened the back door.

She had done it so often she could manage in the pitch dark. One step down into the garden. Close the door. Then six steps to the fence.

She felt her way down to the loose board and slipped through into Mrs Macdonald's garden. That was safe enough. Mrs Macdonald was always in bed by eleven. The dangerous part came on the other side, when she let herself out into the alley. It was a narrow, arched space between Mrs Macdonald's and the rest of the terrace. A good place for drunks.

She was in luck today. There was no one there except a very old man, flat out on his back. She stepped over him and edged out of the alley into the street. It was completely empty. Like a shadow, she slipped up the road in her old trainers.

Behind the shops, the service road was very dark, but that was good. She could be invisible. Padding along to the chippie's yard, she took out her bit of blanket and folded it into a thick pad. Then she reached up and settled it on top of the broken glass. In a couple of seconds, she was up and over, tugging the blanket after her.

If she made a sound, she was dead meat. The Cavalieris lived over the chippie and next door were Geoffrey and Fat Annie. She had to be totally, absolutely silent. Tightening the straps of her rucksack, she dried her hands on her leggings. Then she began to pull herself up the drainpipe.

It was like being in a dark, private world, locked into her own concentration. Up the drainpipe on to the extension.

Along the extension to the main building. Up on to the windowsill . . .

The drainpipe was fine, just as she'd expected, but when she put her foot on to the windowsill she felt the edge crack. The wood was old and crumbling, and she had to lean sideways and run her fingers over it to find a safe part.

Trusting her weight to the right hand edge of the sill, she reached up for the gutter. Thinking, *It's got to be OK*. Everything depended on that and its brackets.

The first bracket she tried felt risky, but the second was as solid as a rock. Putting one foot on the lintel at the top of the window, she pulled herself up and planted the other on the bracket. Then she was up, leaning into the slope of the roof, crawling over the tiles and up towards the ridge.

She heard a burst of sound from the other side of the building as two cars roared down the Row together. *Joyriders*, she thought. With any luck, they would circle round behind the Newenthal flats and come back down the Row a second time.

She waited for them. As the scream of brakes and the noise of their engines filled the Row again, she crawled on to the ridge, letting them camouflage the faint sounds she made.

Then they went for good, racing off towards the industrial estate, and she was on her own. Exposed. Anyone who looked up could see her. Drunks out late. People from the flats opposite. Police cars patrolling the Row. From the moment her head came over the top, she was in the front line.

Gathering her feet under her, she stood up, and saw the Row spread out below her. On the side she'd come from, there was a web of old, terraced streets. She could pick out her own house by the street light outside Mrs Macdonald's.

Opposite, facing her across the Row, were the five huge blocks of the Newenthal flats. Toronto House and Canberra House. Marshall and Livingstone and Nightingale. They dwarfed the cinema and the single storey shops in front of them.

For a second, she stood looking down at it all. The place where she lived, spread out for her to see. Then her concentration sharpened and she focused on the wall. Steadily she walked along the ridge towards it.

It looked ten times as big as it did from ground level. She ran her hands over the rough, dirty surface and slid her rucksack round to the front, so that she could reach the spray-cans without taking it off.

She knew exactly what she was going to do. No fancy pictures. Those were fine in the right place—she had a brilliant Mickey Mouse on the side of Nightingale House— but this was the sort of wall where you had to write your tag or nothing. And she was going to do it full size in four colours. With shadows, to show she'd taken her time.

She pulled out the black can and stood there, feeling the adrenalin come. It would only take one wrong line to blow the whole thing—but she wasn't going to blow it.

Her finger pushed down on the button.

She laid out the letters as if she were dancing. Five lovely shapes, in a level straight line, all exactly the same size. Perfectly spaced to fill the whole width of the wall. When she reached the end, she went back and doubled up the black on the shadow side, to make the whole thing solid.

That would have done, of course. She'd written enough to amaze people. But she wanted something better this time, and she glanced up and down the Row, to check it was still empty, and then swapped the black can for the yellow.

Yellow at the top of every letter, shading down through orange to red. That was how she'd planned it.

The paint went on like a dream. She couldn't see the real colours in the faint, false light of the street lamps, but she could sense the weight of them. Airy yellow at the top, gathering down through orange, to the heavy, heavy red. It felt so good that she let the red spill out at the bottom in

14

drops of blood, one under each letter. Big, swelling drops, with a highlight on each one.

If she outlined those drops in black, it would be the best tag she'd ever seen. She dropped the red can into the rucksack and felt for the black, grinning like an idiot.

Then she heard the joyriders coming back. She glanced sideways—and saw a movement in the shadows across the road.

There was a figure standing on the pathway at the side of the cinema. She couldn't make out much, but she could see a face turned towards the roof of the chippie.

Someone was down there, watching her.

Don't panic, she thought. *Keep calm.* She dropped the can back into her rucksack and started to move back along the ridge, keeping half an eye on the watcher.

The figure was still motionless by the time she slid down the roof and lost sight of it. For a moment she wondered whether she would be safer hiding in the yard, but she didn't fancy being trapped. Better to get home, if she could.

As she let herself down on to the windowsill, feeling for a secure foothold, she was listening all the time. Trying to catch the sound of a footstep among the other night noises. Twice, she was convinced that she heard a sound in the service road, but when she reached the ground everything was silent outside the yard.

She threw up her blanket pad and heaved herself on to the wall. There was no one in sight. The watcher—whoever it was—hadn't come round to catch her.

She jumped down, pulled the blanket after her and crept out into the street. No one there, either.

She didn't see anyone, all the way home. Even the old drunk in the alley had disappeared. As she slid through the fence, she was feeling triumphant.

I managed it! I tagged that wall without getting caught!

She went through the back door, pulled it shut after her and locked it. With a click.

It was the first careless thing she'd done. For a second she froze, waiting for her mother to shout. But there was nothing. No sound.

She was safe. And she'd done it. Grinning in the dark, she crept up the stairs to her bed.

PAULINE

Does she think I'm unconscious? Or deaf? Does she really think I can't hear the door?

I've tried talking to her, but she just gives me that blank, blue-eyed stare. *Why would I go out at three in the morning? Honestly, Mum! You must have dreamt it.* She won't admit anything.

If I felt better, I'd try and catch her, but at the moment—it's hopeless. By the time I've struggled out of bed, she's away. I tried sitting up once, right by the door, but she didn't go out that night. And next day I could hardly move.

It's not every night, you see. And never two nights in a row. She'll go weeks and weeks—months, even—without stirring out of bed. And then, when I think it's all over, I'll hear that little creak at the top of the stairs that always wakes me up. And I'll lie there sweating. *No, God, please God. Don't let it be that. Let me be imagining it.*

Sometimes He answers me, and there's no more sound, so I know the stair must have creaked on its own. But sometimes the second creak comes, halfway down, and then I know it's real. It's no use calling out, because she won't answer. I just lie there with my fists screwed up and the prayer going on and on in my head. *Don't let her go out. Please, God, don't let her go out.* And then—after I've heard the door click—*Don't let anything happen to her. Please, God, don't let anything happen. Keep her safe out there.*

She doesn't understand. I've tried talking to her, and telling her about the gangs and the drugs and the joyriding. She knows that terrible things happen round here, like that fight when Tony Cavalieri was crippled. But she thinks she can handle anything.

You can't blame her, I suppose. She does handle a lot of things at the moment. Helping me out. She cooks and cleans and shops. And does the washing. *And* she manages all right at school. *And* she's not anorexic and she's not on drugs and she doesn't go out with boys . . .

16

I lie there in the dark, telling myself all those things. Telling them over like beads in a rosary. She's strong and sensible and she's never got into trouble so far . . .

But none of it's any use. It would only take one drunk. One junkie. One man with a knife. Whatever she's doing, she can't be safe out there in the street. In the dark. On her own.

And suppose she's not on her own . . . ?

Sometimes I think I ought to tell Janet. But she'd make such a *fuss*. She might even try and take Ashley to live with her, like Karen and Louise. And it's not as if—

It's only till I'm feeling better. Then I'll sort everything out. And Ashley won't have to work so hard then. It's just that I need a bit of help at the moment . . .

Three

The next morning, Vikki was there on the doorstep at half-past eight.

Ashley was still making her mother's lunchtime sandwich, chewing a piece of bread while she did it. When the door bell rang, she guessed who it was and she darted down the hall.

'You're OK!' Vikki said, before the door was properly open.

Ashley put a hand over her mouth and nodded towards the front room. 'Sssh!'

Vikki jerked her head free. 'I couldn't sleep a wink!' She'd dropped her voice, but her whisper was just as dramatic. 'I felt sick all night!'

'Must have been some party,' Ashley said.

'I hardly *noticed* the party! Honestly, Ash, I couldn't dance, or . . . or do anything. I just kept worrying about you. Matt thought I was being silly, and we had the most terrible row—'

'You didn't tell him?' Ashley said quickly.

'Of course not!' But Vikki's eyes flickered, and she looked away.

Ashley wondered whether to push it. Then she let it go. It was too late now, anyway.

'Well, everything's OK,' she said. 'Look at me. I'm all in one piece.'

'That's good. Because I need you to talk to Matt when we get to school. He's really annoyed with me. D'you think you can—?'

'I suppose so.' Just then, Ashley was more interested in the tag. 'Have you seen the wall? What d'you think?'

Vikki's eyes opened wide. 'It's absolutely—'

That was as far as she got, because Pauline called from the front room. 'Ashie? Who's that? You'll be late for school if you don't hurry.'

'You mustn't be late!' Vikki hissed. 'If you get lunchtime detention, you won't be able to talk to Matt—'

'OK, OK.' Ashley looked at her watch. 'Why don't you go on ahead?' She had no chance of getting through everything with Vikki hanging around. 'I'll catch you up.'

Vikki nodded and whirled away, and Ashley looked into the front room. 'Sorry. Mum. That was Vikki. I'll just get your breakfast and then I'll come and help you get dressed.'

Pauline heaved herself up on one elbow. 'Don't be silly. You haven't got time.'

'I can't just leave you. I haven't even brushed your hair.'

'I'll probably be able to manage myself. In a bit. You go to school.'

'But—' Ashley knew she ought to insist, but she could see the clock over her mother's shoulder. She let herself pretend. 'Well, if you're sure. I'll just get your breakfast.'

She ran into the kitchen and tipped some cereal into a bowl. Then she added milk and poured out a glass of orange juice.

'Is that enough?' she said, as she carried them into the front room.

'Of course.' Pauline struggled up in bed and leaned forward to let Ashley put a pillow behind her back. 'You get off to school!'

Ashley kissed her on the nose and snatched up her school bag. 'Be good, then. See you later!'

She raced up the road at top speed. It wasn't just to avoid being late. She was dying to see her wall.

When she reached the end of the road and swung round the corner, it shouted down at her. Yellow like the sun. Screeching orange. Red as a pillarbox. The best thing she'd ever done. CINDY.

It sang in her head all day, and she found herself grinning at people and humming under her breath. None of them knew who Cindy was—no one knew except Vikki—but when they saw the tag they would envy her. Because she'd dared to climb up there.

All day, she looked forward to the end of the afternoon. To walking back with Vikki and seeing the wall again.

But when that moment came, it was like a slap round the face.

She and Vikki walked through the Newenthal flats and up the side of the cinema, to come out by the traffic lights on the Row. Facing the wall.

And the wall was bright white. All over.

Fat Annie must have phoned a painter the moment she saw the tag. It hadn't even lasted twenty-four hours. *The mean, miserable . . .*

'The cow,' Vikki said.

Ashley was too stunned to reply. She didn't even notice when the lights changed. She was left behind, staring up at the white paint while everyone else surged across the road. By the time Vikki noticed, and started yelling at her from the other side of the road, it was too late to move. The cars had surged forward and she was cut off. Looking at a blank wall.

She hadn't left any mark on it. She was nothing.

'Makes you sick, doesn't it?' said a voice from beside her.

She jumped and looked round.

There was a boy leaning against the traffic lights, lounging back with one long leg crossed over the other. He was chewing gum, working it round and round in his mouth.

He nodded across the road, towards the wall. 'It was a great bit of writing. A real gob in the eye for Annie.'

It sounded funny the way he said it. *A real gob in the eye.* As if he was using someone else's voice. Ashley looked cautiously at him. He was older than she was, a thin,

20

gangling boy with big hands and feet and a white, bony face, like a clown's. Wisps of curly hair poked out from under his old striped bobble hat.

'You don't want to fall out with Annie,' he said. 'If you touch her property, she stamps on your fingers.'

'Maybe someone ought to stamp back.' Ashley was still feeling sore and disappointed.

The boy shifted his chewing gum to the other cheek. 'Great idea. How are you going to do it?'

Ashley felt herself go cold. Cold and very still inside. 'Do what?' she said.

He didn't answer. He just looked up at the white wall and then back at her face.

He knew.

'Do what?' Ashley said again, trying to sound bewildered.

The boy pulled a long string of chewing gum out of his mouth. 'OK. *If* you'd done that,' he nodded towards the wall, 'how would you get back at her for painting it over?'

'I'd tag the wall again,' Ashley said. '*If* it was me.'

The boy's mouth stopped moving and he looked her straight in the eyes. The lights changed above his head and the people round them began to cross the road, but he ignored that. He was staring at Ashley, and the stare kept her there too.

'You're going up again tonight?' he murmured.

Oh no, you don't. 'That's what I would do,' Ashley said tartly. '*If* it was me.'

She could have saved her breath. 'You want to watch out,' the boy said solemnly. 'Annie's going to have Geoffrey on guard.' He pushed his face forward suddenly and barked at her. 'You get out there, Geoffrey! Get out and watch. Don't you let those kids at my wall!'

It was Annie. Annie to the life. His whole body even seemed to thicken. Ashley choked on a giggle.

But while she was still giggling, the boy's face changed.

21

He was someone else now. He lowered his eyes shiftily, peering under the lids, and his tongue moved over his lips. Flick, flick.

'Maybe . . . um . . . it's a girl,' he muttered. 'I . . . I might catch . . . um . . . a girl . . . ' And his hand snaked out, heading for Ashley's arm.

For a moment it *was* the Hyena's hand, reaching out for her, and she jumped back, feeling clammy and revolted.

The boy's tongue flicked over his lips again. 'Maybe . . . um . . . you're not so tough?'

'I'm fine,' Ashley said defiantly. She spotted a gap in the cars and launched herself over the road, without waiting for the lights to change.

But the boy was right behind. As she hit the opposite pavement, he drew level, whispering in her ear.

'Pity about those drops of blood.'

'Don't know what you mean,' Ashley muttered.

He laughed at her, under his breath. 'You should have gone round them. In black.'

That was it! She could take all the other stuff, but art criticism was the last straw. Ashley stopped dead and scowled at him.

'OK!' she snapped. 'Take a look tomorrow then! And see if you could do better!'

His face was transformed. As if that was what he'd been waiting for, he gave her a grin and vanished into the crowd. Ashley tried to see where he went, but there was no chance to watch, because Vikki was there, at her elbow, hissing eagerly into her ear.

'Why was he talking to you? What did he say?'

'What? Who?' Ashley blinked and turned round. 'What was who talking about?'

'That boy,' Vikki frowned. 'Honestly, Ash, don't you know who he is?'

Ashley couldn't see what all the fuss was about. 'Just some boy.'

22

'Don't be daft. Haven't you seen him? He goes round with *Eddie Beale.*'

It still wasn't making sense. 'Who's Eddie Beale?'

The moment the words were out, Ashley knew she'd said something stupid. Vikki's eyes opened wide and she gave a squeal. 'You're kidding! Come on, Ash, you *are* kidding?'

Ashley shook her head. 'I've never heard of Eddie Beale.'

VIKKI

I couldn't believe it. *Who's Eddie Beale?* she said, and I could see she wasn't joking. I didn't think you could live on the Row, or anywhere near it, and not know about Eddie.

But then, this is Ashley we're talking about. Every mother's dream daughter. I've never heard her swear. Never seen her smoke. She doesn't stay out late or hang around in the street—except when she's doing that crazy writing—and she never, never, *never* gets into trouble at school. She hasn't even had her ears pierced.

Don't get me wrong. She's my best friend, and I always go to her when I'm in trouble, because she can keep secrets and she's really sensible. She doesn't just nod and agree with you, either. When I had that row with Matt, and he cut my purple jacket to bits, she really let me have it.

'It's all your own fault. You shouldn't have stood him up.'

'It was only a joke —'

'Some joke. You should have guessed the other kids would laugh at him. And you know what his temper's like.'

She was certainly right about that. He's got a real red-head's temper. Like all his family. You should see him and his sister Ginger when they get going.

Ash grabbed my arm and marched me across the playground, then and there, and made me apologize to Matt. Then she went off and left us alone. That's another good thing about her. She doesn't try to own you. She's great about people.

But she doesn't know about . . . things. Outside school, she's like a baby. Doesn't know who the dealers are, or where the party's going to be, or who's

23

out to get who. She's straight home and into that house and you don't see her again until school the next day.

I thought I was used to all that. I wasn't even surprised she didn't recognize that kid at the traffic lights. But then she comes out with it.

Who's Eddie Beale? And I'm, like—where do I start?

Hasn't she seen Eddie walking up the Row, as if he owned the place? With Dougie Barrett and Shaun James behind him acting really heavy. Hasn't she even looked through her window and seen the flash cars go past, with all the kids cheering and waving? Eddie wired a BMW last week and drove it right past the police station, cool as a cucumber.

People are always talking about him. Last winter, he suddenly turned up on Mrs Barrett's doorstep, when they were going to cut her electricity off. He said, 'There you are, Ma. Present from me and Doug.' But from the way Doug went round singing his praises, you could see he didn't know anything about it beforehand. Eddie's like that. If he fancies doing something, he just does it.

I tell you, if that boy had spoken to *me* at the traffic lights, I'd have been so-o-o-o cool and funny, to try and get him to tell Eddie about me. I'd want him to say, 'I saw this really amazing girl yesterday.' So Eddie would fancy meeting me.

That would be brilliant, wouldn't it? Just imagine. Eddie Beale hears about me, and he comes down the Row at ten to four, just to catch me on the way home from school. He wouldn't be looking out, of course. That's not his style. He'd be on the corner, with that kid and two or three friends. Shaun and Doug and Phil Carson maybe.

So I come across at the lights and all the other girls are, like—*WOW! That's EDDIE BEALE!* And they're all eyeing him up and talking extra loud to each other, to get him to notice them.

But I'm being really cool, just chatting to Ashley—no, maybe Ashley's had to go home early. Maybe I'm on my own and looking really great and a bit dreamy. With this little smile—like that—as if I'm standing back and watching the others acting like idiots. And I don't even notice Eddie because I'm so busy thinking about Matt . . .

No, I think I'm deciding to give Matt up. For his own good, of course, because he's so dependent on me. That means I'm really sad, and I don't even notice Eddie. I'm going right by him when he sticks his hand out and touches my arm and it's, like . . . like fire.

The moment he touches me, I just know that this is *it*. So he's ten years older than me. Who cares about that? I look round real slow, waiting for the wisecrack, and there's complete silence because for a moment—just for a moment—he actually can't speak because he's felt it too, and . . . and we're in this bubble together . . . and everything's very slow . . . and we're staring at each other . . . and then he says . . .

Eddie Beale says . . .

He says to me . . .

Oh, wouldn't it be great?

Four

When Vikki had got over being amazed, she tried to explain about Eddie Beale, but Ashley hardly listened. Who cared about some man with a gang? She'd got much more important problems than that.

What had got into her at the traffic lights? She'd given herself away to that boy in the bobble hat. *Take a look tomorrow!* she'd said. What had possessed her? Now he knew for sure that she was Cindy.

She'd only been boasting, anyway. She couldn't really go out again tonight, not with the Hyena watching out for her. It would be crazy.

Maybe that was a good thing. The boy would come past tomorrow and see a wall that was still blank. Maybe he'd decide that he'd picked on the wrong person after all.

Ashley tried to look on the bright side, but it didn't help much. She said goodbye to Vikki and trailed home, feeling sour and sick. By the time she reached home, she was at rock bottom—or so she thought.

But when she slid her key into the lock, there was a voice from the kitchen.

'There she is, Pauline! I'll put the kettle on.'

Suddenly, everything was ten times as bad. Janet was there.

Ashley had no time to gather her wits. The moment she opened the door, the twins came bouncing out of the front room.

'Look, Ashley, we've got our hair different! Don't you think mine's great?' Karen grabbed her hand and swung on it, gabbling at top speed.

Louise didn't say a word, but she threw herself at

Ashley's other side, like a chimpanzee, hugging her round the waist.

'Hi,' Ashley said.

Janet's head came poking round the front room door. 'Surprise, surprise! It's your horrible aunt and your beastly little sisters!'

That was supposed to be a joke, but it was clumsy and lumbering, like everything about Janet, and it was too near the truth. Ashley smiled politely and pretended that she was glad to see them.

'Hi,' she said again.

Karen was giggling and dragging her into the room, but Louise let go suddenly and stepped back, plaiting her fingers together. She picked up a lot more than Karen did. Ashley felt like a rat. She smiled and put a hand on Louise's head.

'It's nice to see you, Lou.'

She was only seven. She couldn't help what Janet was like.

They couldn't have been there very long, but the whole house reeked of Janet, already. Furniture polish and hot ironing. Ashley was barely through the door before Janet's arm slid round her shoulders.

'How are you, darling? Tired?'

'I'm fine,' Ashley said. Meaning, *No, I'm not tired. I can cope. All right?* She went across the room to kiss her mother. 'Hallo. Did you have a good day?'

Her mother's eyes flickered at her, sending unspoken messages. Ashley could read them horribly well. Pauline was out of bed, sitting in a chair and dressed in clothes she would never have chosen herself. Janet had picked out a thick jumper and trousers. She'd brushed Pauline's hair until it gleamed as well—and Ashley knew how long that took—and tied it back with a ribbon.

Ashley could imagine the whole scene. The key in the front door. Janet's head peering round. *Hallo, Pauline! I've brought the girls to see you!* And then the frown, as she saw

27

her sister's nightdress. *Why don't you two girls go and play in the garden while I sort things out a bit?*

Janet's arm tightened, pulling Ashley towards the kitchen. 'Let's go and have a cup of tea, shall we? Give the girls a bit of time alone with their mum.'

She shut the door behind them and patted a stool, as if it were her own home and Ashley was the visitor. 'Sit down and have a rest.'

'I'm fine,' Ashley said again.

Janet didn't answer straight away. She just smiled and made a complicated business out of pouring the hot water into the teapot and finding the cups. But when the tea was poured, she sat down next to Ashley and patted her hand.

'Look, you don't have to pretend. It might do you good to have a moan.'

Prod, prod, prod. Ashley felt like a mouse in a hole, with a sharp stick poking at her. She edged away and picked up her teacup.

'I'm fine. Everything's fine.'

Janet sighed. 'You're managing really well, darling, but— things aren't really fine, are they? Pauline's getting worse. Don't you think we ought to try and find you some help?'

Ashley's fingers tightened round the cup. 'I can manage. Mum's just going through a bit of a bad patch.'

'You wouldn't like to come and stay with us for a bit? For a rest?'

'No,' Ashley said. It was too fast to be polite. She said it again, more carefully. 'No thank you. We like it here.'

Janet sighed again and bit her lip. *Any minute now,* Ashley thought, *she's going to put her arm round my shoulders again.*

She did.

'I know what Pauline's like,' she said. 'She's a fighter. But it's your life too. If we got on to the doctor and the Social Services—'

'That's ridiculous! She just needs a bit of help at the moment, that's all. And I can cope.'

28

Janet's arm fell away. This time her voice was colder. 'So that's why she was sitting round in bed in her nightdress? At half-past three?'

'She's not usually in her nightdress,' Ashley said stubbornly. 'I was a bit late today, that's all.'

'Just today?' Janet raised her eyebrows.

'Yes!'

'You really are loyal, aren't you?' Janet's fat, ringed hand patted Ashley's shoulder.

Ashley resisted the longing to twist her head sideways and bite it.

From the front room, she could hear the sound of the twins' voices, getting more and more excited. Karen kept giving whoops of wild laughter, and even Louise was giggling. Janet nodded towards the door.

'They need their mother, you see. If she came to live with us, they could be like that all the time.'

That's all you know, Ashley thought sourly. Pauline always put on a good show for the twins, but by the time they went she would be exhausted. She'd probably cry before she went to bed, and it would take her hours to relax enough to fall asleep.

But once she is asleep, she'll be out for hours . . .

The thought came by itself. Ashley really hadn't meant to think about the wall again, but suddenly, with the picture of her mother fast asleep, she saw herself moving through the night. Sliding out into the darkness with her spray-cans.

Who would know if she did go? No one. Not if she didn't get caught. Surely she could outwit the Hyena?

The idea danced in her head. Suddenly, she found herself smiling at Janet. *You'd faint if you knew what's in my mind You'd die*. She reached for the big cake tin and took the lid off.

'Have some chocolate cake,' she said.

It was all right now. She was on top again, and Janet couldn't touch her. No one could touch her.

LOUISE

Janet's always strange after we've been to see Mum. She keeps asking us questions. *Mummy was looking all right today, wasn't she? And Ashley looked very happy, didn't she?* The sort of questions that make you say the answer she wants.

Mummy was fine. She laughed all the time. But Janet wasn't happy. Going to see Mum always makes her miserable. I could feel it all the way home. I wanted to snuggle up to her on the bus, so she could hug me, but Karen sat in the middle and I couldn't get near.

Karen kept on and on talking. 'Ashley's road isn't as nice as ours, is it, Janet? Why haven't the houses got front gardens? Gardens are much nicer. Why don't Mummy and Ashley live in our road? Why don't they come and live with *us*?'

She's so silly. Anyone can see that Frank wouldn't like it. He likes pretending that we're *his* little girls. So does Janet. That's why they've got all those photos in the lounge, looking like Mummy and Daddy with their children. It fits really nicely.

As long as you don't think about Mummy and Ashley, living in that dirty place.

There's such a lot of broken things there. Cars with all the wheels missing. Houses with wood over the windows. Big, coloured scribbles on the walls. *Tiger. Super-Cindy.* Silly words that don't make sense.

Mummy said, 'Why don't you stay a bit longer? Ashley can go out and get some pizzas.' But Janet said we had to get back before it was dark. She never says that when we go to see Frank's family. We always walk home late, and she tells us the stars.

Perhaps they don't have stars here.

I think I'd be scared here, in the dark. There's some places that feel horrible, like that alley behind the shops. And the chip shop, where the fat man looks through the upstairs window.

I'm glad I don't have to live here.

Five

After Janet took the twins away, the house was quiet and empty. Ashley spread her homework out on the table in the front room and tried to cheer Pauline up by asking her questions about History and French. Sometimes it worked, but that night neither of them was interested.

Pauline lay back in the lumpy, uncomfortable chair and shook her head. 'I'm sorry, but I can't. I just can't. I think I'll go to bed after tea.'

'You can go now if you like.'

Pauline shook her head again. 'Not before tea.'

Why not? Ashley was going to say. But she bit her tongue. She knew the answer. Only invalids had their meals in bed.

She took out her books and tried to start on her homework, but it was impossible to concentrate. Every time she looked up, she saw Pauline's grey, exhausted face. After twenty minutes, she hadn't written a word, and she knew she wasn't going to. Standing up, she swept the books into her bag.

'What do you want for tea?'

Pauline closed her eyes. 'I think—Ashie, I'm really not very hungry. Maybe I'll go to bed now.'

'Do you want me to bring you some scrambled egg when you're lying down?'

'I said I'm not hungry!'

Pauline's voice was sharp. It was a waste of time to argue. Ashley helped her wash and change into her nightdress, and then she left her to go to sleep.

The house was even quieter then. Ashley found she didn't want more than scrambled egg herself. She ate it in the kitchen and went upstairs without giving her homework another thought. She was just waiting until it was late enough to go out.

When she did, it was quiet outside, as well. There was no one sleeping in Mrs Macdonald's alley. There were no joyriders up on the Row. The whole place was eerily still, and Ashley went up the road in something like a trance, sliding from shadow to shadow.

When she reached the entrance of the service road, she stopped for ten minutes, standing motionless and listening. There was nothing. No sound. No sign of anyone about. She padded along to the yard behind the chippie and threw her blanket over the broken glass at the top of the wall.

Even the flap of the blanket seemed loud in the stillness. Every second of the way up to the roof, she was tense and nervous, expecting someone—Fat Annie or the Hyena—to come charging out of the shop next door, yelling about the police.

There was nothing.

Like someone in a dream, she padded along the rooftop to her wall. It was twice as beautiful now that it was painted white. A perfect surface, waiting to show up her tag. This time, it was going to look stupendous.

She focused on that, forgetting everything else. Pulling out the black spray-can, she swung her arm down in a great semi-circle, making the shape of the first letter.

And then the second.

And then the third . . .

The whole thing was almost finished, and she was just shading the last drop of blood, when she heard the sound of the gate opening, down in the chip shop yard. A faint, rusty scrape. Her head jerked round abruptly, and she saw a shifting shadow slide in through the gate.

Someone was standing in the yard, waiting for her to come down.

If she hadn't heard, she would have walked straight into the trap. And then— A split-second horror movie played itself out in her head. She saw herself finishing off that last drop of blood, sliding down triumphantly off the roof, and—GOTCHA!

She would have slithered straight into the Hyena's arms. She imagined him hanging on to her legs and yelling for the police. And all the social workers and Auntie Janets in the world racing up to wag their fingers at her.

Bad girl! You're out of control! You can't cope!

Well, they were out of luck. She'd spotted him down there and she was going to work out a way to escape. Even though she was twenty feet above ground with no way down but the drainpipe.

But first she was going to finish her tag. Her hand tightened round the spray-can and she finished that last drop of blood, filling the black outline with crimson, except for the little highlight. Then she put the can away and slipped her rucksack round, on to her back. So. Now she needed a plan.

And that was when the Row erupted.

Half a dozen cars roared round the corner and squealed to a stop outside Fat Annie's, screeching their brakes and burning rubber. People jumped out and started banging on Annie's front door, yelling and swearing and kicking at the paintwork.

Ashley froze, trying to work out what to do. The gang down there sounded crazy enough to take the whole house to bits. If Annie phoned the police, they might not stop at the gang. They might look up on the roof as well. And then—

At the back of the shop, a window rattled down. Annie's voice bellowed into the night.

'Geoffrey! Don't bother about the roof. Go and stop that lot! You hear me?'

Ashley couldn't believe her ears. The Hyena had trouble

tackling Vikki about a copy of *Penthouse*. What was he supposed to do with a gang of twenty rowdies? He'd be petrified.

Petrified or not, he didn't hesitate. Ashley saw his dark shape move again, pushing the yard gate open. A moment later, he appeared at the end of the alley, caught in the glow of the street lamp. He edged round the corner of the buildings, towards the Row.

For a minute, Ashley couldn't believe he was so stupid. Then she came to her senses and seized the chance he'd given her. Running along the ridge, she slithered down to the guttering. By now, she knew the footholds exactly, and in a couple of seconds she was on the extension roof. There was no need to be careful. The noise at the front of the shop masked any sounds she made.

She slid down the drainpipe so fast that she scorched her hands. When her feet hit the ground, they were already running, and she crossed the yard in three strides. There was no need to climb the wall, because the Hyena had left the gate open. She raced through it at top speed.

And someone grabbed her arm, holding on tightly.

No!

No, no *no*! It wasn't fair!

She flung herself sideways, trying to break free, but whoever was holding her was very strong. His hands clamped her arm so hard that she wanted to scream. She actually opened her mouth—

'Don't blow it,' whispered someone on the other side of her.

Slowly her mouth closed. She recognized the voice. And now she could see the shape of his silly bobble hat, outlined against the light at the end of the service road. It was Eddie Beale's boy.

'She's OK now, Doug,' he said. 'Let's go.'

The hands gripping Ashley's arm loosened suddenly, and the boy caught hold of her hand.

34

'Hurry up. Before the Hyena gets back.'

He shot off, pulling Ashley after him. Doug raced on ahead. By the time they came out into Railway Street, he was already twenty metres down it, heading away from the Row.

He stopped beside a parked car and hauled the door open. The boy sprinted towards it, still dragging Ashley, and pushed her into the back, ahead of him.

She tried to struggle against him, but he hissed in her ear. 'Don't be stupid. You'll never make it home without the Hyena seeing you. Get down on the floor!'

Ashley gave in and slid into the car with him, and Doug piled in after them, crouching low as well. 'Let's get going, Joe,' he grunted.

'Not yet.' The boy was kneeling on the seat with his head down, peering through the back window. 'He's not in sight yet.'

Ashley was wedged on to the floor, with no idea what was happening. She started to feel the door next to her, hunting for the handle, but before she found it the boy hissed triumphantly.

'Yes! They're on their way. Sock it to them, Sam!'

Ashley had thought there were only three of them in the car, but suddenly someone shot up in the front seat, reaching for the controls. The engine started with a cough and they screamed away from the kerb, with a jerk that flung Ashley back against the seat.

The boy was bouncing up and down like a maniac. 'Look at them, Doug! They're going crazy! They're *demented.*'

He went into a frenzied version of his Hyena voice, stuttering and stammering so much that he almost choked.

'I . . . um . . . you can't . . . but that's our—'

A woman's voice yelled from the driving seat. 'Sit down, Joe, or you'll go through the windscreen.'

He slithered down into a sitting position, just as she flung the car round a corner, and he and Doug started to laugh helplessly, throwing themselves around. Ashley hauled herself off the floor and squeezed on to the seat.

'What's going on?' she said. 'What's so funny?'

The car lurched the other way, round another corner, and Joe fell against her, gasping for breath.

'The car . . . it's . . . it's . . . '

He couldn't get the words out. It was Doug who told her.

'We've got the Hyena's car. And he and Annie are going loony.'

SAM

Yes! Oh, yesss! I've really got to her this time!

That's one of our games, Eddie's and mine. Getting to Annie. She pretends to ignore us most of the time. Won't even speak to us if we go into the shop. Looks down her nose at us, as if we were rubbish.

No one treats me like rubbish.

So we get our own back. It's not always like this, though. Usually, it's more . . . subtle.

Like last week. I caught the Hyena outside, straightening that vegetable stand they have in front of the shop and I went right up to him. Really close, so we were almost touching.

'Hi there,' I said. 'What's the matter? Someone been playing with your apples?'

And I reached across (just being helpful) and moved one of the apples to a better position, brushing my arm against his chest. Accidentally, *of* course. Then I fluttered my eyelashes at him and he went pink. Stammered so hard he couldn't get the words out.

'Th-thank you, b-b-but . . . '

I could see Eddie out of the corner of my eye. He was watching us with that twisty smile of his, and I knew I'd amused him. That was good enough for me, really, but just then Annie came lumbering out of the shop. Like a rhino rushing to protect its cub. And I thought, *Aha!*

She looked down her nose at me with her *you are garbage* expression. 'That will do, thank you very much. We don't need any help from people like you.'

36

And she reached across and tugged at my arm, to get me out of range of the Hyena.

Oh, fantastic! Another five points at least. But I couldn't leave it like that. I could feel Eddie watching to see how far I'd go. If I could come out on top now she'd started pushing me around.

No problem. I didn't even need to think. I just went where she pushed me, until she started pulling the Hyena back into the shop. Then I called. Very suddenly, so they wouldn't be able to stop themselves reacting.

'Hey!'

Their heads snapped round, and I gave the Hyena a long, long stare—*you* know the kind of stare—and ran my tongue over my top lip. He went beetroot. It was the funniest thing I've ever seen in my life. He was sweating with embarrassment.

Annie grabbed his shoulder and shouted, 'Tart!' at me. Then she threw him into the shop in front of her. But it was too late by then. There must have been fifty people in the Row and they were all in fits.

Eddie held out his arm to me, as if I was coming off a stage, and then paraded me right down to Shepherds Corner. And people were cheering all the way.

Eddie and me, we understand each other. We knew it the moment we met. I've got to have a strong man, that I don't need to make excuses for, and Eddie is *the* strong man. The King. Walking down the Row with him is like being in a procession. Everyone's watching, and he always gives them a show for their money.

There's nobody like him.

We're equals, and we respect each other.

Six

Ashley sat bolt upright. 'You mean—we've stolen this car?'

That just made it worse. It sent Joe hysterical, and Sam started falling about too. She shrieked with laughter, flinging herself from side to side in the seat as she drove.

Doug leaned over from the back and thumped her shoulder. 'Knock it off. You want to mince us all?' He tried to hold her steady, but that only made her laugh even more. She shrieked like a lunatic and the car swerved right across the road.

Joe stopped laughing too, and banged on the back of the seat. 'You're out of your tree, Sam. Calm down. We've got to ditch the car. Annie's bound to have the police on our tails. Pull in by those garages.'

Whatever Sam was on, it was happy stuff. She didn't argue. Humming loudly, she spun the wheel, throwing Ashley against Joe, and they roared across the tarmac in front of the garages. She jammed on the brakes and it looked as if they were going to stop just in time, before they hit the far wall.

But, just at the last moment, she swung the wheel and sent the car crashing into the nearest garage. There was a loud clank, and a crunch, and then the engine died.

'You *maniac*!' Joe said. 'Let's get out of here!'

They hadn't travelled very far. They were round the other side of the Newenthal flats, close to the school. Joe slithered out and reached back to pull Ashley after him.

'Quick!' he said.

Ashley dithered, untangling her rucksack from the seatbelts, and he tugged at her arm.

'What are you doing? Waiting for the police? *Out!*'

38

Doug was pushing her from behind, and Sam was out already, running past the garages, towards the flats, and the three of them raced after her.

Ashley could see that she knew the estate. A stranger would have stayed on the main paths, between the tower blocks, but Sam struck out across the grass, doubling unpredictably round corners. Two or three times they would have lost her, except for the fluttering end of the long scarf she was wearing.

By the time she ran out of breath, she was round the back of Toronto House, in the dark patch where the winos hid out. There was no one there that night except Spider Mo, tucked up snoring among her carrier bags. Sam stopped next to her, leaned against the wall and slid slowly down it. When the others caught up, she was sitting on the ground with her legs out straight in front of her.

'You sad cow,' Doug said. 'What were you doing? Trying to kill us all?'

Sam looked up at him and smiled, as if he'd paid her a compliment. Even sitting on the ground, completely out of it, she was shining. She had the kind of face you see on magazine covers. Maybe not more beautiful than everyone else—she had jagged blonde hair and gaps between her teeth—but twice as real.

Doug caught hold of her hands and hauled her up. 'Time you were home,' he said. 'It's been a long night.'

Sam nodded sleepily. 'Cold,' she said. Bending over, she unwrapped her long scarf and wound it solemnly round Spider Mo's shoulders. Mo stirred for a moment, growling in her sleep. Then she settled back into the middle of her bags.

Doug pulled at Sam's arm. 'Let's go,' he said firmly.

The two of them turned and began to walk away.

'Hey—' Ashley took a step after them, but Joe caught at her arm, holding her back.

'What's the matter?'

'They're just leaving us here. And it's the middle of the night.'

'So?' Joe looked scornful. 'Who's going to touch us? Everyone knows Eddie looks after me.'

Spider Mo stirred at their feet. She wasn't awake, but her long arms were groping around, feeling for her belongings. Joe stepped back as one of her hands brushed his ankle.

'Let's go. She'll make a racket if she wakes up. I'll walk along with you if you like.'

Ashley fell into step beside him as they headed for the Row, going up to Shepherds Corner to avoid passing Fat Annie's.

'You'll be safe on your own soon,' Joe said cheerfully. 'When people see you hanging round with Eddie, they'll lay off you.'

'What are you talking about?' Ashley said. She hadn't hung around with anyone since she was seven. 'I've never even met Eddie Beale.'

Joe grinned. 'You will. Now he's taking an interest in you.'

'How can he be taking an interest in me? He's never even heard of me.'

'Oh, come *on*. You think we were there by accident tonight?'

Ashley hadn't thought about it. Things had been moving too fast for her to work out what was going on. Now she started to work it out.

'You mean—you were there on purpose? To help me out?'

Joe nodded, still grinning. 'I told Eddie you were going to paint that wall again. And he said, ''She'll need a bit of back-up then. Annie won't get caught twice. Maybe you ought to hang around with a few of the others.'' We were watching out for you for hours before you turned up, but he was right, wasn't he?'

'But why would he bother? He doesn't know me at all.'

'I bet he knows about you. There aren't many things he

misses round here. And he's . . . ' Joe hesitated and looked sideways at Ashley. 'You'll be OK. Like I said, he looks after people.'

So how does he look after you? Ashley thought. But she didn't ask, and Joe didn't volunteer anything else. He just padded beside her, all the way home.

Normally, she would have sneaked in round the back way, as usual. But some sort of caution stopped her. She didn't want Joe to see her secret route. Stopping at the front door, she pulled out her key.

'Nice house,' Joe muttered. 'Maybe I'll come round some time.'

Ashley nodded and smiled, putting a finger to her lips. He got the message. With a wave of his hand, he took off into the darkness. Ashley opened the door, very softly, and stepped inside.

Something rustled under her foot.

Pulling the door shut, she bent down and felt the corner of an envelope and she picked it up, peering at the front. But she couldn't see a name, so she pushed it into the pocket of her jeans and began to climb the stairs, slowly and silently. She was desperate to get to bed and sleep, but if she hurried all the boards would creak.

By the time she reached the top, she had almost forgotten about the envelope in her pocket, but it slipped out when she began to undress and she picked it off the floor and opened it.

Inside was a single sheet of paper, folded in four. She unfolded it, and words shouted up at her, written in ugly bubble writing.

CINDY—I KNOW YOU.

JOE

Eddie never explains when he takes up someone new. He just says 'Do this,' or 'Go there' and we find there's another person around.

His mind moves so fast you can't keep up with him. You've got to watch his eyes all the time, the way you'd watch a snake, or a tiger. He's dangerous if he gets bored.

Some of the others don't understand that. They just hang around him because he makes things happen. He gets them living, and doing things they couldn't get together on their own.

I started out like that too. There's always three or four younger kids tagging on to the crowd, and I was one of those. Eddie let me stick around because my imitations made him laugh. That was the only reason—until that day he decided we were all going to the seaside.

It was very hot. He got a few cars and had us all pile in, and we set off for Margate or somewhere. It was a real laugh, lounging round on the beach and eating ice cream and candy floss.

But then some of them decided to go in the sea in their underwear. They were fooling about and yelling that the water was cold and I could see Eddie looking at me. I knew he wanted some imitations. It was really funny the way those big blokes suddenly shrank when the water hit them.

I knew just how I'd do it, but there was no way I was going to strip down, so I put it off as long as I could. And then I saw that look in his eyes. Annoyed. I thought, *Maybe I'd better go along with it,* so I went down and played at being Doug, shivering on the waterline. It had them all in fits.

But I kept my T-shirt on.

Eddie didn't say a word. Not then. He just laughed like the others and barracked Doug. But when we were going back, he nodded at me to go in the car with him and Sam. And as soon as we got going he turned round and looked at me.

'Take off that shirt,' he said.

I would have argued, but I knew he'd make me do it in the end, so I stripped off my T-shirt and sat there shivering while he looked at the bruises. That was the time I had a cracked rib as well, and I was purple all down one side.

Sam was watching in the mirror, and I heard her catch her breath, but Eddie didn't say anything for a minute. Then he nodded. 'Put your shirt on again.'

I pulled it over my head, and I was shivering worse now. And not just because the T-shirt was damp.

'He'll hit my mother . . . ' I said.

If you make a fuss. That's what I meant. Eddie just shook his head.

'I'll see to him. He won't lay a finger on her. But you're not going back there.'

I didn't know what he meant, but I had this sudden, wonderful feeling. Like I'd had my fists clenched tight for years and years and all at once I could straighten them. *You're not going back there*. I never even asked him where I was going instead. Just sat back in a daze and knew it was all right.

Eddie turned back to Sam. 'How about if he goes to your mum?'

Sam didn't look too sure, but Eddie's never wrong about things like that. He always knows what he can ask people. When we turned up at Tricia's house and I saw her blonde hair and her high heels, I thought, *He's crazy. She's not the sort of woman that wants a kid around*.

But all he had to do was strip off my shirt. Tricia took one look at the bruises and gave him a long, straight look.

'I'll do whatever you want,' she said.

And that was it. I've been there ever since. The next day, Eddie sent his mate Rick round to photograph my bruises and they posted the pictures to Vince with an anonymous letter.

As long as you treat Gayle right, the police won't get these.

That was all it took. Vince hasn't laid a finger on Mum, from that day to this, and I know I'm safe at Tricia's.

The only thing is—I've got to keep in with Eddie. I've got to make sure he doesn't get bored with me.

Seven

Ashley didn't fall asleep until it was nearly light. After what seemed like less than an hour's sleep, she was woken by the sound of banging on the front door. 'Ash! Are you there? *Ash!*'

As she opened her eyes, she could hear Pauline, too. Shouting and knocking on the radiator.

'Ashley! Ashie!'

It was half-past eight.

She wasted one more second staring at her watch, and then she shot out of bed, wrenched the curtains apart and opened the window. Down in the street, Vikki stepped backwards to look at her.

'What's the matter?' she called up. 'Are you ill?'

Ashley groaned and shook her head. 'I overslept!'

'But you never oversleep!'

'Well, I did today!' Ashley snapped. 'Don't wait for me.'

She slammed the window shut. And thought, *Vikki doesn't know about the wall. She hasn't been up to the Row yet*. Her mind filled with pictures from the night before. In horrible, clear detail. She saw herself prancing about on the roof of the chippie. Spraying Fat Annie's new white paint. Jumping into a stolen car.

Being in the car when it was wrecked.

She couldn't believe she'd been so crazy. In the mirror, she saw her face, smudged with dirt, and her tumbled, tangled hair. She snatched up the hairbrush and brushed savagely until her scalp tingled. Then she wrenched the whole bunch of hair back into an elastic band.

Pauline was still shouting, in a tired, ragged voice. 'Ashley! What's the matter? I've been calling for hours.'

Wearily, Ashley opened the door and shouted back. 'It's OK. I won't be long.'

It took her three minutes to scrub at her face with a flannel and throw on her school uniform. When she went downstairs, she found Pauline sitting on the end of the bed.

'I was coming up,' she said.

'Oh, sure!' Ashley whisked past and went into the kitchen. She couldn't bear to pretend anything just then. There was enough to cope with. Noisily, she filled the kettle and plugged it in. Then she called down the hall.

'Toast?'

'You haven't got time,' Pauline said. 'You'll be late unless you go straight away, and then—'

'Well, I'm not going yet!' Ashley jammed two slices of bread into the toaster and stuck her head out of the kitchen. 'I'm going to have some breakfast, so you might as well have some too.'

'But there'll be trouble—'

'So? Why not?' Ashley marched down to the front room door and stood there with her hands on her hips, glaring down at her mother. 'Come on. Tell me. Why have *I* got to be so perfect?'

Pauline wavered. 'I'm not asking you to be perfect.'

'Yes you are! You're making a fuss, just because I've overslept. Teenagers oversleep all the time. It's called *adolescence*. Some of the people in my class are only there three days a week. And Lisa rolls in at eleven o'clock sometimes. Why have I got to be different, just because you're ill?'

'It's not that.'

'Oh, *isn't* it?' Ashley said nastily.

The toast popped up, and she marched back to the kitchen, to make the tea with one hand while she buttered the toast with the other. *Just an ordinary morning,* she thought, in a rage. *Get the breakfast. Make a sandwich for Mum's lunch. Wash her. Put her clothes on. That's enough for one person. Why do I have to be better than everyone else as well?*

She was still in a temper as she put the tea and toast on the tray and took it through. Sweeping her mother's magazines away, she banged the tray down on to the bedside table.

'We'll have this and then I'll get you dressed.'

Pauline winced and struggled on to the bed. 'You don't need to—'

'Yes I do. I'm going to make sure you're dressed absolutely perfectly. And I'm going to brush your hair till it's like silk. Just in case Janet comes again.' Ashley sliced the toast into fingers and posted one into her mother's mouth, to stop her talking. 'Or do you want her catching you in your nightie two days running?'

Pauline took the toast out. 'She only wants to help. You're not being fair.'

'What's so great about being fair?' Ashley pushed in another piece of toast, while Pauline's mouth was open. Then she gulped down her own tea and went to sort out some clothes. No point in breaking her neck to get to school now. Mrs Prosser would only give her one detention, however late she was.

She was wrong. Mrs Prosser gave her two detentions. One at lunchtime, for being late, and one after school, for forgetting to do her homework. The only good thing about them was that they kept her away from Vikki. By the time Ashley got to school, she'd seen the wall, and heard the rumours, and she kept nagging about it, all day.

'Ash, you're a lunatic. Annie had the police round first thing, and there's going to be terrible trouble. She thinks the person who painted her wall stole the Hyena's car too, and wrote it off.'

Every time they were on their own, she started up again. If

46

it hadn't been for the detentions, Ashley would have gone mad. She actually enjoyed sitting on her own at lunchtime and coming out after school to find the road deserted.

Though it was odd to find it so very deserted.

It was even odder when she walked past the flats and found nobody there, either. People usually hung around by the benches, chatting and eating chips. Where was everyone?

She found out when she reached the Row. Outside Fat Annie's, there was a huge crowd, laughing and shouting. They were all staring up at the roof of the chippie.

The Hyena was up there, with a pot of white paint. He was trying to ignore all the noise, but it wasn't easy. Every time he moved, someone yelled.

'Mind you don't fall!'

'Look out behind you!'

'WHOOPS!'

Vikki was near the back of the crowd. She looked round and beckoned, and Ashley wriggled through to her, scowling.

'Hope he slips off,' she muttered. 'Why couldn't he leave it alone?'

Vikki grinned. 'It's Annie, of course. She made him go up there. Don't you think it's cruel? He's petrified.'

The Hyena's pasty face was stiff with the effort of ignoring all the shouts. He had looped the handle of the paintpot over his arm, so that he could keep a hand against the wall, and he was dipping his brush in and dabbing at the coloured letters with jerky, irregular movements. The 'C' and the 'I' were already blotted out and he was halfway across the 'N'.

Someone at the front began to sing.

One hyena, hanging on the wall,

One hyena, hanging on the wall.

The song swept back through the crowd as everyone else picked it up. *And if one hyena should accidentally FALL—*

They bellowed the word, catching him by surprise, and he

47

tottered and clutched at the wall for support. The paintpot swung wildly, slopping white paint over his trousers and there was a great wave of laughter from below.

Ashley shook her head. 'He's an idiot! Why didn't he do it while we were all in school?'

'I think he was out,' Vikki said. 'He was only just back when I got here, because I heard Annie bawl him out.'

'But she didn't have to make him go straight up there. She's a maniac.'

'She certainly is.' Vikki grinned again and pointed across the road.

Fat Annie was standing in the shop doorway, waving the window pole at the crowd. 'You can stop that!' she bellowed. 'I've had the police round once already, and I'll fetch them round again if you don't clear off! Let Mr Galt get on with his work!'

There was a shriek of laughter from the front. 'Hey, *Mr Galt*! Let's see you fall off the roof!'

One of the boys started a slow handclap. 'Off! Off! Off!'

All around them, people started to pick up the chant, and Vikki nudged Ashley. 'It's getting nasty,' she muttered. 'Let's go.'

Ashley nodded, and they began to work their way through the crush, to the traffic lights. They were almost there when someone pulled at Ashley's sleeve.

'Hi.' It was Joe, with his hands in his pockets and his white clown's face lolling sideways. 'I was looking for you.'

'*Hi!*' said Vikki.

Joe ignored her. He was watching Ashley. 'There's a party tonight.'

'So?' Ashley shrugged.

Vikki nudged her, but she didn't take any notice. She was watching Joe as hard as he was watching her. There were dark hollows under his eyes and his cheekbones were sharp angles. He raised one eyebrow.

'Eddie said I had to bring you.'

48

'Did he?' Ashley shook her head. 'Well, I don't go to parties.'

Vikki almost exploded with impatience. 'Oh, go on! I'll come with you. It'll be a laugh.'

'You can't come,' Joe said evenly, still looking at Ashley. 'Eddie didn't ask you.'

'And I'm not—' Ashley began.

Joe didn't give her a chance to finish. Without any warning, his face crinkled into a simper and he edged closer and nudged her. 'Go *on*, Ash!'

Ashley stopped, catching her breath, and Joe nudged her again, leering sideways at her. 'Go on. It'll be fantastic!' he said shrilly.

Ashley laughed. She couldn't help herself. Vikki scowled and went bright red.

'Oh, great! You're a real friend, aren't you?'

'I didn't mean—' Ashley said.

But it was too late. Vikki flounced off in a temper, swinging her bag as she went and catching Ashley round the back of the legs.

Joe copied her, swinging his shoulders pettishly.

'Don't,' Ashley said.

'You like it,' Joe said. He was solemn now, staring at her disconcertingly.

'I *don't* like it. Vikki's my friend.'

'So why did you laugh?'

'Because . . . '

Because what? She didn't know. The words shrivelled away and she was left staring at Joe's big, hollow eyes.

Suddenly he smiled. A lop-sided grin that showed his irregular yellow teeth. 'I'll call for you then. Around nine o'clock.'

'But I'm not coming—'

It was too late to argue. Before Ashley could say a word, he had loped off, and she was on her own. Except for the crowd of people shouting up at the roof.

The Hyena had been painting, desperately, all the time she and Joe were talking. He was nearly at the end now, just laying the first streaky white stroke over the 'Y'. His clothes were splashed and stained and his shoulders hunched forward. Ashley couldn't bear to watch him.

She glanced away, towards the chippie. And for a moment she saw a face at an upstairs window. A pale, fat face peering out between the curtains to see what was going on.

Tony Cavalieri.

It was only a glimpse. When he saw Ashley looking up at him, he spun away, vanishing into the darkness of the room behind. That was all anyone ever saw of him now. Since the fight. He peered out at the Row from behind those net curtains, ducking back when anyone noticed him. Briefly, Ashley wondered how much he knew about what went on. Then the lights changed, and she crossed the road and forgot about him.

When she got home, there was another envelope lying on the mat. The same sort of envelope as yesterday's, with nothing written on the front. She scooped it up quickly, weighing it in her hand.

'Ashley?' her mother called. She sounded nervous and tentative.

'I'll be there in a minute,' Ashley called back. 'Wait till you hear what's going on up at the shop!'

As she spoke, she was opening the envelope. It was the same as the last one, with bubble writing in spidery blue biro. But there were more words.

CINDY, they said. I KNOW YOU. YOU THINK YOU'RE SUCH A GYMNAST, DON'T YOU? BUT ONE DAY YOU'RE GOING TO FALL.

ANNIE GALT

I don't know who that CINDY is, but if I get hold of her I'll wring her neck.

This used to be a decent neighbourhood. When Barry was alive, the

50

customers were our friends. They respected us. Now they're all out for themselves. I can't relax for a minute.

The children are terrors for shoplifting. Whatever I'm up to, I have to keep an eye on that video screen, and even then we lose about twenty pounds' worth of stuff a week.

The women are almost as bad. They don't shoplift—not most of them—but they're always moaning about the prices. And then there's the lads who want to smash the place up in the evenings. And the winos who'd fall asleep in the doorway if you let them.

Spider Mo camped out here for a week one winter. The police were useless. However much I complained, she was there again the next night. I had to act quite nasty before she got the message.

'Eddie told me it was a good place,' she kept muttering. She can't cope with more than one idea a day. 'Eddie said I'd be safe here. Better than on the estate. Said it was warmer.'

If Eddie Beale wants to keep her warm, he can buy her a sleeping bag. I knew what he was up to, and I wasn't going to let him get away with it. If my shop gets associated with people like her, I'll start losing customers.

I tried helping her along with my foot, but she just shifted a bit and crept back while I wasn't looking. So in the end I sent Geoff down, with a bucket of water.

He needed nagging, of course. When I looked out of the front window, he was standing there dithering. Looking down at the bundle of rags and old newspapers as if he didn't know there was a person in the middle.

I leaned out of the window and yelled at him. 'Just do it. Or you'll be spending the night out there with her.'

Even then he didn't do it on purpose. But he stepped back to look up at me, and the water slopped out of the bucket, all over Mo's bedding.

It worked like a charm. She sat up and swore at him, and then started gathering the whole lot up, just the way I'd meant her to. If I'd been down there, I would have given her another dose, to help her on her way, but Geoffrey just stood there like a dummy.

He's always let people push him around, ever since he was a little boy. The way he watched Mo shuffling across the road, you'd have thought he wanted our doorstep cluttered up with rubbish like that.

I was going to give him an earful when he came in, but he went straight past the living room and locked himself in his bedroom, so I couldn't get at him.

He doesn't realize how much the place has gone downhill. He was just a little boy when this was a nice respectable neighbourhood, and he's got used to the vandalism and the gangs and the terrible language. He hasn't got any idea of how to hit back. When he saw his car last night, he just cried.

Sometimes I feel so lonely I could scream. But it's no good giving in to that. If Geoffrey won't fight back, I'll have to do it myself. And the first person I'm going to get is that Cindy. She's the last straw. I wish she'd fallen off the roof.

Eight

Ashley stared down at the paper in her hand and tried to stay calm. Who could have sent it? And how did he know about her?

Pauline called again. 'Ash?'

Roughly, Ashley screwed up the paper, pushing it into her pocket, out of sight. Then she arranged a cheerful smile on her face and went into the front room.

'Hi. Sorry I'm late. I got a detention because of oversleeping, but it was OK. How about you?'

Her mother hesitated.

Ashley sat down on the end of the bed. 'I'm sorry I was a pig this morning.'

'It's not your fault.' Pauline looked down at her hands. 'I'm not being fair, am I? You've got too much to do.'

Ashley knew what that meant. 'You've been talking to Janet, haven't you? What did she do? Phone? Come round?'

'She did phone, but that's not why—'

'Oh no?' Ashley pulled a face. 'I bet I can guess what she said. She talked about me, didn't she? Said I'm looking peaky. And she's *horribly afraid* that I'm missing out on things. Not leading a normal life.'

'Well, it's true, isn't it?' Pauline said. 'You are missing out. Louise and Karen are always going to parties and having fun and—'

'You think I want to go to parties like that? To eat jelly and play Pass the Parcel?'

That raised a grin, but only for a moment. Then Pauline was frowning again. 'You know what I mean. You don't do anything any more. You've even stopped going to gymnastics. You ought to be mixing with people. Building up your confidence—'

'There's nothing wrong with my confidence. Or my friends. In fact—' (Ashley had an inspiration.) '—I was asked to a party tonight.'

'Tonight?' Pauline blinked. 'Well, that's a bit sudden, but—'

'Don't worry. I'm not going.'

The moment the words were out, Ashley knew she'd blundered. Pauline sat up sharply and two bright pink spots flamed on her cheeks.

'You see? That's how it always is! You say no to everything, just because of me.'

'It's not because of you. Don't be a moron.'

'I'm not a moron! And I'm not a baby, either. I don't need minding. You're going to that party, or I'll phone Janet up and tell her she's right, and we can't manage on our own.'

'Mum—'

'Shut up! I don't want to hear it. Go and do your homework and then sort yourself out some nice clothes.'

Ashley considered arguing, took another look at her mother's face and ditched the idea. It wasn't worth the hassle. Pauline wasn't going to give in, whatever she said. She'd just have to go to the party and put up with it.

If Joe turned up.

He turned up all right. Bang on the dot of nine. When Ashley opened the front door, he was lolling against the wall, and he stepped inside and into the front room without being asked.

'Hi,' he said.

'Hallo.' Pauline sat up straighter in her armchair and gave him a bright, determined smile. Then she looked at Ashley and frowned. 'Couldn't you find anything better than those old jeans? What about your blue dress?'

'Jeans,' Joe said. 'That's what she ought to wear.'

Ashley wondered why, but she didn't waste time asking. She picked up her jacket. 'Bye, Mum. I won't be very late—'

'You be as late as you want to be!' Pauline said fiercely. 'I'll be really angry if you get back too early!'

'What a great mother!' Joe grinned at Ashley. 'Think she'd adopt me?'

'No chance!' Ashley said. 'If I want a brother, I'll knit one.' She pushed him out of the room and opened the front door. 'Which way are we going?'

Joe stepped past her and set off down the road, away from the Row. 'Industrial estate.'

'For a party?' Ashley had to jog to catch him up. 'What are you talking about?'

'There's a great warehouse. No one goes down there at night. Only the winos, and we can handle them.'

'What sort of party is this?'

'You'll see.'

Ashley wasn't sure she wanted to see, but she knew her mother would go crazy if she went home. So she trailed after Joe, imagining noise and drugs in an echoing forest of steel shelving.

There was plenty of noise when they got there—they could hear the music halfway across the estate—but there was no shelving. Only a big, empty space, with a stack of boxes at one end and dozens of people standing around drinking and talking.

Not dancing.

Ashley wondered why for a moment, and then she realized that most of the people were men.

'Where's the girls?' she said.

Joe half-closed his eyes. 'Not that sort of party, mate,' he grunted. His voice rumbled in his chest. 'Eddie's parties are different. OK? No hangers on.' He flexed his shoulders, as if he had huge muscles, and stuck his thumbs into the pockets of his jeans.

Ashley looked round, wondering who he was being.

Across the warehouse she saw Doug, with his shoulders flexed and one thumb in his pocket.

Joe grunted again. 'Eddie does things his way, mate. You don't get asked to his parties unless you're on the firm.'

Ashley looked round again. 'So which one's Eddie, then?'

Joe stopped being Doug and stared at her. 'What do you mean? He's not here yet.'

'How was I supposed to know? I've never seen him.'

Joe stared again, and then shrugged. 'You will. When he turns up, you'll know all right.'

It was eleven o'clock before that happened. By then, Ashley was bored rigid. Some of the men had been out and bought chips, but no one had offered her any, and she didn't fancy the beer Joe had brought her. She was sitting all on her own in a corner, playing with a little dog who'd popped up from nowhere. Wondering if it was late enough to go home.

Suddenly, there was a blast of cold air. She looked up and saw a couple of men pushing the big warehouse door open. Outside there were blazing headlights and the sound of a car revving impatiently.

As the door swung open, the car edged forward, right into the warehouse. People fell away on each side and it came to a stop in the middle of them. No one said a word. The only noise was the music which was still blaring away, sounding thin and cheap in the glare of the headlights.

Is it him? Ashley wanted to say. *Is it Eddie?* But Joe wasn't near, and she was afraid to ask anyone else.

Doug walked over to the passenger's door, still holding his paper of chips. 'Hallo, mate!' he said. 'Thought you'd decided to give it a miss.'

Ashley couldn't hear the answer from inside, but she found herself holding her breath as Doug gripped the door handle with one huge hand and swung the door open. And she had a curious feeling that all the others were holding their breath as well. Waiting for someone (for Eddie—it had to be Eddie) to get out of the car.

Then he did, and the first thing Ashley thought was, *He's so small!*

She'd been expecting someone huge. Bigger than Doug, and rippling with tattoos. But he was no more than average height. A wiry man in jeans and a T-shirt, with an ugly, uneven face.

He walked round to the other side of the car and opened the door. Sam was leaning back in the driver's seat and she swivelled sideways, sticking out one long leg. Then she stood up, in a single, fluid movement. She was wearing something short and glittering, and very high heels.

For a party in a warehouse?

Ashley thought it was weird, but everyone else started to cheer, parting to make way for her. Sam walked between them, like a model on a catwalk, following the wide beam of light thrown by the car's headlamps.

At the far end she stopped, without turning, and the cheering voices stopped too. Again, Ashley sensed that curious, breathless feeling. As though all the men were expecting something to happen. She could see Joe opposite, with his eyes fixed on the back of Sam's glittering dress.

'Hey,' said Eddie.

His voice was not loud, but the word was an order. Ashley could hear that. An order from someone who doesn't expect to be disobeyed. Sam turned. Her face was very pale in the headlights and the front of her dress rippled and glittered as she breathed, quickly and nervously.

'What do you want?' she said. The words were sharp.

Eddie raised one hand, holding out a glass bottle, full of some colourless liquid. With her eyes on the bottle, Sam came down the beam of light again to face him. He gave her the bottle and she pulled out the cork with her teeth. Someone switched off the music and the silence was abrupt.

Eddie bent sideways, lifting something out of the car. It

was a heavy stick, with one end wrapped in cloth. Still staring at Sam, he pulled a lighter out of his pocket and flicked it on. The little flame licked at the wrapped cloth and it flared alight, burning with a smell of paraffin.

Eddie snapped the lighter off and dropped it into his pocket. Then he handed the stick to Sam and stepped back. She stood for a moment, studying the flames as all the men edged away too, leaving her alone in the centre of the warehouse.

Even then, Ashley hadn't realized what was going to happen. She moved back with the rest, watching Sam and the flame and the bottle. Beyond, she could see Joe. He was staring hard, with his mouth open and beads of sweat around his nostrils.

Lifting the bottle, Sam took a long swig, holding the liquid in her mouth. Then she raised the blazing stick high into the air. In that instant, Ashley guessed.

She can't—

Tilting her head back, Sam brought the stick slowly down towards her face. The flames flickered as her hand shook, but she didn't stop. Until, suddenly, she opened her mouth and breathed out a stream of fire.

It roared like dragon's breath, right across the warehouse, with men leaping away on each side. Ashley could feel the heat from where she was standing.

Sam raised the bottle again. No one made a sound. Joe had closed his eyes and Ashley could see him inhaling, very slowly, like someone afraid to disturb the air.

Sam poured the rest of the liquid into her mouth, raised the burning torch and tilted her head back again. Then she breathed again. This time, the fire shot out in a great tongue, up towards the roof. Its light glinted on the sequins of her dress and turned her hair scarlet. For a split second, she seemed to be all fire.

Then she laughed and tossed the empty bottle high into the air.

Eddie caught it. He weighed it in his hands for a second then threw it on, straight at Joe.

'Here! Catch!'

DOUG

Everyone does tricks for Eddie. Don't know how he does it, but he's always one step ahead.

We go back a long way, me and him. Been best mates since we were kids. He may not be as big as me, but don't let that fool you. He's hard. And he's got brains, too. I've never seen him put down, and we've been in some tight corners together.

Like that job we did a couple of years ago. Tony Cavalieri was still on his feet then, and his gang lifted a load of videos and stashed them away in a lock-up garage. I don't know how Eddie got the tip-off, but he comes up behind me in the pub at lunchtime and mutters in my ear.

'What would you say to a hundred brand new videos? Been lifted already, so they can't squeal. All we've got to do is wire a van and load them up.'

'We taking Phil?' I say. Like—we usually did. But Eddie wasn't having any of that.

'Just you and me. OK? And don't tell a soul.'

So that night we go out looking for a likely van and pick up one around Nettles Hill. Nice and anonymous, and a full petrol tank. And when we get to the garage, it looks a dream. End of a blind alley, with blank walls on both sides. No reason for anyone to come by. All we've got to do is back up and load the videos in.

I start on that and while I'm hauling the boxes, Eddie's poking round the back of the garage. Then suddenly—we hear the cars. Two of them.

They turn down the alley and line up side by side, blocking the way out. Blinding us with their lights. We hear the doors go, and a lot of feet. I had a blade in my pocket—you've got to have something—but Eddie smacked my hand away from it.

'Cut that out. Get into the van and put the headlights on.'

So I crawl round and knock the door open. When I turn on the headlights, I can see there's half a dozen blokes coming towards us. Big and ugly.

They didn't like the headlights and one of them starts yelling at me to turn them off, but Eddie's down by my feet hissing about the radio. To turn the radio on really loud.

Sounds stupid, but I do what he says and then he's pulling at my ankle to get me out again. When I land up beside him, I can see he's got his mobile phone out.

He's calling the police.

I thought he'd really cracked up, but he comes off the phone and he's humming to himself. *I've fixed them. I've fixed the bastards* . . . And I want to say, *Yes, but you've fixed us too*, but there's no time because we can hear the sirens already.

Three police cars screech across the end of the road, blocking the whole lot of us in. It looks like the end, and I'm sweating cobs, but Eddie doesn't turn a hair. Suddenly he's on his feet, throwing stones. One, two, three, four. And not a single miss. He knocked out all the Cavalieris' headlights, and suddenly *we're* the ones behind the light. The ones nobody can see.

'Come on!' Eddie goes.

He drags me back into the garage and suddenly I see there's a roof panel missing. And Phil's leaning through the hole, waiting to pull us up.

He had a van in the yard on the other side. In thirty seconds we were away, and the police never had a chance of catching us.

And the real joke was that Phil and Shaun had been lifting videos all the time we were having that stand-off with the Cavalieris. We got away with twenty of them and made half a grand. I was just a decoy.

Like I said, everyone does tricks for Eddie.

Nine

'Catch!' said Eddie. And he threw the bottle straight at Joe.

Joe reacted like lightning, stretching into the air, and catching the bottle one-handed.

The moment his fingers touched it, Eddie picked a beer can off the ground and slid that at him. And then another one. Ashley couldn't believe Joe was going to catch them, but he did more than catch.

Before the first can reached him, he sent the bottle spinning into the air. That left him free to catch the beer cans. And when the bottle came down, the cans went up.

He was juggling.

He moved forward, into the circle of people that had formed round Eddie and Sam. When he was standing in front of Eddie, he let the first can spin out of the dance and dropped it neatly at Eddie's feet. Then he did the same with the second one.

Giving the bottle a final, dizzying throw, he caught it by the neck and held it out to Sam.

'Pretty good,' Eddie said. He leaned over to Doug and grabbed the sausage out of his chip paper. 'Here.'

It looked like a reward and Ashley thought the show was over. But suddenly the little dog from nowhere bounded forward into the circle, rearing on to its hind legs and strutting towards the sausage. It whined on a long, pitiful note.

Eddie looked down at it and a long, slow grin spread across his face. Then he looked back at Joe.

'Nice sausage,' Sam said quickly. She reached out to snatch it away, but she wasn't fast enough. Eddie jerked it out of her reach, without taking his eyes off Joe's face.

There was a split second's pause and then Joe stepped forward, holding his arms high on his chest and letting his hands droop. Like a dog begging. Slowly, on stiff legs, he edged up to Eddie.

'Sausage?' he said.

He was mimicking the dog, holding his head on one side, with an eager, Jack Russell look. Doug started laughing.

But Eddie didn't laugh. He held the sausage higher, waving it from side to side.

'Dance for it.'

Joe began to totter round clumsily, with his mouth open and his tongue hanging out sideways. Everyone was laughing now. Eddie jerked the sausage upwards, and Joe leaped awkwardly after it, whining just like the dog.

It was horrible. Ashley didn't know why, but she screwed up her fists, so hard that the nails dug into her palms.

Eddie kept Joe jumping on and on, until all the men were roaring with laughter and Joe was completely out of breath. It looked as if he would have to give in and collapse, but, at the very last moment, Eddie nodded sharply.

'Die for the Queen!'

Flopping to the ground, Joe rolled over like a dog, arms and legs bent and red mouth open wide. With a casual, scornful gesture, Eddie flipped the sausage into his open mouth, and Joe scrambled up, chewing as he walked back towards Ashley.

Avoiding her eyes.

Behind him, the circle began to shrink, but the movement was reluctant. The men were looking about, as if they wanted something else to happen.

'What about the girl?' one of them said. 'Does she do anything?'

Ashley didn't realize that he meant her until Eddie turned towards her. Suddenly, she caught the full force of his stare. He didn't say a word, but she found herself stepping into the middle of the circle.

It was ridiculous. There was no point in making a fool of herself. What could she possibly do that wouldn't be an anti-climax, after the juggling and the fire-eating?

She almost stepped back again. And then Eddie raised one eyebrow, enquiringly. *So?* said his look. *What's your speciality?*

Suddenly, doing nothing wasn't an option. It wasn't the men standing round who made the decision for her. It was Eddie. He was staring at her, waiting for some kind of show. If she didn't come up with a performance, she didn't count.

And there *was* something she could do. Of course there was.

'I do this!' she said loudly. Purposely dramatic. Without giving anyone time to react, she launched herself forward into a chain of cartwheels. Head-over-feet-over-head-over-feet-over-head-over-feet-over-head—

She took the gamble that the circle would part for her, and so it did, just in time, with men shoving each other out of the way to avoid being knocked by her flying legs. She cartwheeled all the way up to the far end of the warehouse in an unbroken, spinning sequence.

As she turned to come back, she was working out the timing in her head. If she aimed slightly more to the left, she thought she could end up standing to attention, right in front of Eddie. She glanced at him once and then flung herself forward.

Each time she flipped over, her eyes found his face. He stood there waiting for her, with the same attentive, half-amused look as he'd had while he watched Sam and Joe.

Until the final cartwheel. Suddenly, just before she went into that, he tilted his head and stepped sideways. Ashley found herself facing the long, gleaming car. And instantly, as though it had leapt from his mind into hers, she had a vision of herself sailing right over the top of the car.

63

It was a dare. He had dared her to do it.

She had no idea whether it was possible, and there was no time to work it out. If she got the timing wrong, she would crash straight into the windscreen and break it. And probably injure herself, as well.

But—

Going into the last cartwheel, she saw Eddie staring at her, and she knew she was going to do it.

She went over and her feet came down (right, left) exactly in front of the car. Without hesitating, her hands smacked on to the bonnet (left, right) and up she went, on to the roof. Her feet touched down again (right, left) pushing her up and over into a last flip that took her clear of the back of the car. She landed neatly, with her feet almost together, and the warehouse exploded into cheers.

It was more than she'd ever dreamt she could do. She was speechless with the excitement of it. It was better than painting the best wall she'd ever imagined, in her wildest dreams. She stood in the middle of the cheers with triumph singing in her head.

Eddie didn't say a word. He didn't even smile. He just picked a handful of chips out of Doug's paper and walked round the car, holding them out to her like a bouquet. But she couldn't take one. She couldn't even speak.

It was well after midnight when she got back home. As she walked into the house, the phone started ringing.

She ran into the front room.

'I wouldn't answer it,' Pauline said. 'Not at this time of night.'

But Ashley had already snatched up the receiver. 'Yes? Who's that?'

There was an odd kind of mutter at the other end of the line. A man's voice, not a woman's.

'Hallo?' Ashley said. 'Who is it?'

There was another mutter. Then the voice whispered down the line, faint and distorted.

' Cindeee . . . '

'What?' Ashley heard her own voice rise.

There was a rustling, crackling noise, like someone crumpling paper, and the voice whispered again.

' . . . Cindee . . . you'll never keep it up . . . you'll lose your balance . . . '

'*What?*' Ashley's hand began to shake.

' . . . you know I'm right . . . there's going to be trouble . . . '

Sharply, Ashley put the receiver down. Her right hand was shaking so much that she had to put the left one over it, to steady it.

'Who was it?' Pauline said.

'I don't—I couldn't hear properly.' Ashley's voice came out sounding normal, but she didn't dare turn round for a moment. 'I'll just check the number.'

She tapped in the call-tracing code, but the message she expected came back.

'*You were called . . . today . . . at . . . one twenty-five. The caller withheld their number . Please hang up . . . please hang up . . .*'

Slowly she lowered the receiver, trying to be calm. It didn't matter. It was only a phone call.

But the words came spinning back at her . . . *you'll get into trouble* . . . Someone was trying to scare her.

Well, she wasn't going to be scared. Snapping the receiver down into its cradle, she turned to her mother.

'OK, Mum? Had a good evening? You must be really tired.'

'I'm fine,' Pauline said. 'What was the phone call?'

'Wrong number,' Ashley said briskly. 'Want me to make you a drink before we go to bed?'

But she was still shaking as she went into the kitchen. The same questions kept running round and round in her head. *Who is it? And how does he know about me?*

MRS MACDONALD

Phone calls! At this time of night!

It woke me up, and I'm sure it woke them up, as well. You'd think people would be more considerate. There's Pauline in the state she's in, and that poor wee girl with school to go to. They need their sleep.

Especially Ashley. I don't know how she does it. She goes up the road to do her shopping like a proper little housewife. Not like the rest of the young people around here. There are some wild ones, I can tell you. You've only got to look at the graffiti. And the vandalism. I've heard them joyriding up and down the Row at three o'clock in the morning, keeping decent people from their sleep.

They ought to take a leaf out of wee Ashley's book. She's like a little angel, with that fair hair and those lovely manners. *Good morning, Mrs Macdonald* she says when she sees me. *How's the arthritis?* And she waits for an answer, too. Not like some people.

I'm not saying it's right, mind. A girl like her, having to look after her mother, all on her own. What's the rest of the family thinking about? Even the Cavalieris do better than that. They've really rallied round to look after poor Tony, since he had that terrible accident. When I see Ashley struggling up the road with three bags of shopping, I want to give that aunt of hers a piece of my mind.

People just won't accept their responsibilities, these days.

Ten

'Vik,' Ashley said. 'What would you do if you got an anonymous letter?'

They were standing in the lunch queue on Monday. Ashley made the question sound as offhand as she could, but Vikki turned round sharply.

'Someone's sending you anonymous letters?'

Thanks, Vik. Now there were half a dozen people staring at them. Ashley tried to pass it off as a joke.

'It's a nightmare! There's this little fat man with glasses and green spots. Keeps writing love letters in shaving foam on my front door.'

Vikki gave her a long look, but she got the message. She let out a loud, delighted shriek. 'You're so *lucky*! Love letters *and* free shaving foam. What're you complaining about? He's probably a millionaire.'

Ashley picked up a tray. 'Don't care if he's a zillionaire three times over. He can't spell. He keeps calling me his "little purple pinnapple".'

'That's gross!' Vikki pulled a face and held out her plate for chips. 'Shall I sort him out? Does he like brunettes too?'

She kept the joke running, but Ashley knew that wouldn't be the end. Vikki would make sure she found out what was going on.

She did. When they came out of school, she dawdled on purpose, to give Lisa the slip, and she sent Matt away, even though he'd waited twenty minutes for her.

'I'll come round later, OK? I need to talk to Ashley just now.'

'Aw, Vikki!'

Matt was annoyed. Ashley saw the back of his neck turn

bright red. But Vikki didn't take any notice of that. She prodded him in the chest and looked up at him sternly.

'You don't own me, you know. Go home and ask Ginger to cut your hair. I'll see you at seven.'

Even though Matt was twice her size, she always got her own way. He muttered a bit, but he went off obediently, saying, 'Mind you're not late.'

Vikki sighed and picked up her bag. 'Boys!'

'Matt's OK,' Ashley said. 'That was pretty mean, you know.'

'Rubbish! If he had things his way, he'd never let me talk to anyone else.' Vikki started off down the road. 'Now what's all this about anonymous letters? How many have you had?'

Ashley felt stupid. 'It's not really worth fussing about.'

'Don't give me that. It's bugging you. You know I can always tell.'

It was true. That was why they were friends. They always knew about each other.

Ashley looked down at her feet. 'I've had two letters. And yesterday there was a phone call. But none of them said anything really. Only—'

'Only?'

'Only he called me Cindy.'

Vikki stopped. 'But you said no one knew except me.'

'That's right.' Ashley hesitated. But she had to ask it. 'You haven't told anyone, have you?'

'Of course I haven't!' Vikki said. Then she went pink. 'Well . . . only Matt.'

'But you promised!'

'Matt doesn't count. I said I'd never speak to him again if he told anyone. He won't say anything.'

'I suppose not,' Ashley said. But it took an effort.

'I reckon you ought to phone the police.'

'Are you mad?' Ashley rolled her eyes. 'What do I say? *It's like this, officer. I was just standing on the roof of the chippie, spraying my name on a wall . . . ?*'

'They wouldn't worry about that.'

'You want to bet? And what about that car crash? You said Annie was out for someone's blood for that.'

'Oh. Yes.' Vikki pulled a face. 'I told you you were crazy to get mixed up in that.'

'Well, I did,' Ashley said. Meaning, *And shut up about it*. 'So I can't go near the police. Anyway, there's nothing to show them. Just a couple of little notes.'

'Maybe there'll be something else today. Something in the post.' Vikki started getting excited. 'I'll come home with you and see, shall I?'

It was no good saying no. That sort of thing never put her off. Ashley looked wary. 'You're not to tell my mum . . . '

' 'Course I won't. What d'you think I am?' Vikki could hardly wait. She darted across the Row when the lights changed, and she was almost running when they reached Ashley's house.

Ashley unlocked the door and Vikki pushed her forward, leaning over her shoulder to see if there was anything on the doormat. The moment she was inside, she swooped forward, snatching up the envelopes.

Then she read them, and her face fell. 'It's all junk mail. Except this postcard. Here.'

Ashley took the postcard and called to Pauline. 'Hi! Have you had a good day?' It couldn't have been very good. Not if Pauline hadn't even fetched the post. But at least Janet hadn't been. 'There's a postcard from Karen and Louise!'

They sent one at least once a week, and this one was typical. A photo of a red London bus. Ashley could just imagine Janet choosing it. *Let's have something cheerful for Mummy, shall we? Time we sent her some news.*

Karen and Louise didn't manage much in the way of news. Just one stiff little sentence each. *Dear Mum, I went to my dancing lesson and my teacher says I'm really good, love Karen.* And *We've got a new hamster, his name is George, love Louise.* Ashley took the card into the front room and Vikki trailed

69

behind her, leafing through the junk mail to double-check that there was nothing exciting mixed up with it.

'Hallo, Vikki,' Pauline said. 'How was school?'

Vikki groaned dramatically. 'It was horrendous! You can't imagine! Mrs Burton had us reading poetry out loud. *O wild West Wind, thou breath of Autumn's being!*' She rolled her eyes and clutched her forehead.

Ashley left them to it, and went to put the kettle on. Vikki didn't come round very often, but she was good value when she did. In thirty seconds, there were giggles coming from the front room, and before the kettle boiled she could hear her mother laughing out loud. Vikki was declaiming at the top of her voice.

'Wild Spirit, which art moving everywhere;
'Destroyer and preserver; hear, O hear!'

That was when the doorbell rang.

Vikki leapt to answer it, before Ashley was even out of the kitchen. 'Hallo?' they heard her say. And then, 'You've got what?'

She put her head back inside and called down the hall. 'There's a van here, Ash. And someone with a video.'

'What?' Ashley put the teapot down and went along the hall. A middle-aged woman was standing there with a folded piece of paper in one hand. She had a short skirt and very bleached hair, but she looked friendly.

'Ashley?' she said. 'Message from Eddie.'

'I . . . um . . . ' Ashley didn't know what to say. 'Do you want to come in?'

'Thanks. Here.' The woman pushed the paper into Ashley's hand and stepped inside. 'I'd like to meet your mum. Joe says she's good fun.'

Ashley blinked. 'Joe?'

'He lives with me. I'm Tricia, Sam's mother.' The woman walked past her, into the front room, grinning at Pauline. 'Hi,' she said.

Vikki nudged Ashley. 'What does the note say?'

It was quite short, scrawled in heavy, energetic capitals.

YOU WOULDN'T TAKE THE CHIPS, SO I'VE SENT A VIDEO
INSTEAD. I ALWAYS PAY FOR GOOD PERFORMANCES.

EDDIE.

'Wah-hey!' Vikki said. 'Must have been *some* performance!'

'Don't be stupid.' Ashley snatched the note away. 'I just
did some cartwheels when I went to that party. It wasn't
anything much.'

Vikki snorted. 'I thought you'd given up gymnastics.
Except on people's roofs.'

'Shut up!' Ashley hissed.

She looked over Vikki's shoulder. Doug was lifting a
black video machine out of the van. And, in the front room,
Tricia was talking to her mother.

' . . . it's only an old thing, but Joe said you hadn't got
one, and we thought you might be able to use it . . . '

TRICIA

Eddie loves giving people presents. If you do something for him, there's
always a little knock on the door next day. After I took Joe in, he sent me
flowers for a week.

I knew he was right for Sam, from the moment she met him. Until then, I
was really worried about her. She was so *wild*.

I may not be your conventional mother, with a husband in the house and
dinner on the table every night, but I do have some standards. It was getting
so I didn't know where Sam was, from one day to the next. And she lost that
nice little job she had, in the florist's, because she couldn't be bothered to turn
up for work. It was getting so every time I saw her we had a screaming match,
with me saying, 'If you carry on like this, you'll be living on the street before
you're thirty!'

And she'd just yell back at me. 'Better than being like you, you old cow!
Think I want to land up like you, with everyone laughing at me for dressing
twenty years too young? And all the women locking their husbands up when I
walk past?'

71

She's always known how to hurt me. At least I've stuck to one man at a time. Until she met Eddie, she was running three or four at once, and I could hear her telling lies to them down the phone. 'No, I can't make it tomorrow. I've got to work late.' Or see my grandmother. Or visit my best friend who's got cancer. She'd say anything. She just didn't care.

And then Eddie brought her home that night and she came in through the door looking as if she'd dropped off a star. Stunned. Glowing. Didn't say a word. Just made herself a cup of coffee and made me one too (and she hadn't done that since she was ten). After that, she finished with everyone else. She was in every night, waiting for the phone to ring, or the knock on the door.

Eddie even got her back to work. They were sitting in the flat one evening, and I heard him say, 'You ought to get yourself some modelling or something. To keep you busy when I don't need you around. Want me to look out for something?'

And the next thing you know, she's working with that friend of Eddie's. Rick. And she's buying great clothes and treating me too.

Of course, I don't see her as much as I used to. Sometimes she's off for days at a time, but I never worry, because she's with Eddie.

And anyway, I've got Joe to look after now. Poor boy. He's not really much more than a child and that man had been knocking him about for years. I don't understand how people can do that to children, do you? If Eddie hadn't rescued him, I reckon he'd be dead by now. He's a real scream. Keeps you in fits of laughter, taking people off. (He's great at doing Sam, actually, but we never let anyone else see that. It's our little secret.)

'Course, it's made a difference to my life, having him around. It's not cheap, keeping a boy that age. But Eddie slips me a bit of money now and again, so that's all right. It's not as much as I'd get if I was fostering Joe properly, but, as Eddie says, we don't want the Social Services poking their noses in.

There's a lot of cooking to do. Joe needs feeding properly, to build him up, and I can never tell when Eddie's going to drop him home. It doesn't hurt a kid to stay off school once in a while, but sometimes they're really late.

Still, he's with Eddie, so I don't make a fuss. And I never mind running errands for Eddie, either. Like delivering that video. He said not to tell Pauline it came from him, in case the girl hadn't told her about the party, so I kept my mouth shut. I don't like secrets, but I always keep Eddie's.

I'll do anything for him, as long as he treats Sam right.

Eleven

It was almost an hour before Tricia left. By the time she had finished chatting, they knew all about Sam's modelling triumphs. *I'm so grateful to Eddie for getting her interested. And Rick, as well. Rick's absolutely made Sam's career. You should see some of the pictures he's taken . . .*

Doug had obviously heard it all before. He spent the time setting up the video and tuning it in.

The moment they left, Vikki started nagging at Ashley to go out and hire a video.

'You might as well test it out properly.'

Ashley wasn't convinced. 'We don't have to do it today.'

'Oh, come on! What's the point of having a video if you never watch anything?'

'But we've only just got it—'

'That's when you ought to try it out,' Vikki had said firmly. 'Isn't that right, Pauline? Think of all those great films Ashley's missed. It's time she started catching up, isn't it?'

Ashley expected her mother to say no. But she didn't. She was looking remarkably lively and cheerful.

'Go on, Ashie,' she said. 'It would be fun. You could go and get one from that shop next to Annie's.'

'That's right.' Vikki jumped up. 'Ravinder said the new ones were coming in today. Let's go and look them over.'

Ashley gave in. She stood up too. 'All right. But only one.'

Vikki grabbed her arm and almost dragged her out of the house. Ashley couldn't understand what was so great about borrowing some old video. It wasn't until they were out in the street that she realized that the video was only an excuse. What Vikki really wanted was a chance to talk about Eddie Beale.

'You're *so lucky*!' she said. 'If he's looking after you, you'll never need to worry about anything. Ever again.'

'He's not "looking after" me,' Ashley said crossly. She still wasn't sure how she felt about the video. 'He just—'

'Of course he's looking after you!' Vikki was too impatient and excited to listen. 'You know what you ought to do? You ought to tell him about those anonymous letters.'

Ashley wasn't having any of that. 'Don't be silly. They're not that important.'

'Of course they're important. You never know what he might do next.'

'How d'you know it's a he?'

Vikki snorted. 'Not going to be a woman, is it? It's some weird old man. He'll get nastier and nastier, and then he'll start threatening you, and you won't be able to go out on your own in case you meet him, and—'

'Come on!' Ashley began to laugh. Vikki was always launching into stories like that. 'This is real life, you know, not a horror film. And there's nothing I can do, anyway. If I go to the police, *I'm* the one who's likely to get into trouble. They aren't going to take any notice of those notes.'

'No,' said Vikki. 'That's why you ought to go to Eddie.'

Ashley shook her head, stubbornly. 'I couldn't.'

'Why not? If he likes you enough to give you a video, he'll help you. That's how he is. He looks after his friends.'

'But I'm not his friend.'

Vikki scowled. 'Oh, all right! *Don't* listen to me!'

She started walking again, fast and fiercely. Ashley could see that she was upset, and she jogged a little, to catch up.

'Look. I'm not being difficult. Honestly. It's just . . . well . . . there's not enough to bother him with.'

'And if something else happens?' Vikki said quickly.

'Well, then, I might—'

'Ask Eddie?'

'If you really think he'd do something.'

'I don't think he would. I *know*.' Vikki relaxed and

grinned at Ashley. 'So that's settled, then. If anything else happens, we'll go round to Eddie's together and tell him all about it.'

That wasn't quite what Ashley had meant, but they had reached the shops and she didn't want anyone to overhear them. She let it go, and pulled her purse out of her pocket.

'How much is this video going to be?'

'I'll treat you,' Vikki said grandly.

She swept into the shop and began to work her way along the shelves, pulling boxes down as she went.

'This is a good one. Really scary. And this is good, too. It made Lisa scream. Oh, and how about this . . . ?'

She collected half a dozen and held them out. Ashley pulled a face.

'How can I choose? I don't know about any of them.'

'It's only like picking a book. Go on. Look at the front of the box.'

Ashley studied the pictures, but before she could settle on anything, Vikki gave a shriek and darted across the shop.

'No! *This* is the one you ought to have! Look!'

She pulled out a box which showed a beautiful blonde walking down the street. Her eyes were big and scared and behind her, ostentatiously lurking, was a man in an overcoat. His shadow fell forwards, on to the path in front of her, and scarlet letters screamed over his head. *Street Stalker*. Vikki put back all the other videos and took that one to the counter, pulling Ashley along with her.

'Hi, Rav. We'll take this.'

Behind them, one of the other customers looked up. Ashley heard him draw in his breath sharply. Then a familiar voice said, 'I don't think— '

It was the Hyena. He came up to the counter and peered at the box in Vikki's hand, checking the video. His face crumpled into an expression of distaste.

'What's the matter?' Vikki said belligerently. 'Have you got a problem?'

The Hyena went pink. 'I . . . I don't think . . . ' he said awkwardly. 'I mean . . . um . . . it's not a very pleasant subject, is it? Stalking?' He looked at Ashley. 'Your mother might not like—'

'Pauline's OK,' Vikki said tartly. '*She* knows what teenagers watch. Not like some people.' She snatched the video box away from him and put it down on the counter. 'Hey! Rav! Aren't you going to serve us?'

Ashley had a feeling he'd been trying to ignore them, but Vikki obviously knew him, and she wasn't going to let him get away with it. She reached over the counter and pulled at his sleeve. '*Rav!*'

He looked up and sighed. 'Come on, Vikki. You know I can't give you that. You're not eighteen.'

The Hyena nodded. 'That's right.' He looked at Ashley. 'You're better off without . . . without things like that.'

Vikki turned round and gave him a long, hostile stare. He grew even pinker, but he didn't back away. Instead, he looked straight past her, over the counter.

'You've . . . um . . . I know this sort of thing is awkward, Ravinder. Don't worry. I'll back you up.'

'Thank you, Mr Galt,' Ravinder said politely. But he didn't look overjoyed. 'I'll ask these young ladies to choose something else, shall I?'

The Hyena nodded and turned back to the racks. Vikki leaned on the counter and gave Ravinder a long, smouldering look. 'OK,' she murmured. 'I'll choose another one. I'll have . . . um . . . *this* one.'

Picking *Street Stalker* off the counter again, she held it out to him.

Ravinder pulled a face. 'Give us a break, Vik,' he muttered. He nodded towards the Hyena. 'You know what his mother's like. If she thinks we're not doing things right, there'll be all sorts of trouble.'

'What's the problem?' Vikki murmured. 'We're with an adult, aren't we? Why don't you issue it to him?'

77

She glanced over her shoulder, at the Hyena's back, and Ravinder pinched his mouth shut, so that he wouldn't laugh.

'I can't do that.'

''Course you can.' Vikki picked up the pen. 'Look.' Reaching across the counter, she wrote the details herself, booking *Street Stalker* out to the Hyena. It was the last entry on the sheet, and she flipped the page over and held out her money. 'There you are. All done and dusted.'

Ravinder hesitated for a second. Then he gave in and found the video. As he slipped it into the box, he put a finger to his lips and Vikki grinned and wiggled her fingers in a little wave.

'Bye, Rav.' She tapped Ashley on the shoulder. 'Come on. Let's phone my mum and say I'm staying. If we get some pizzas, I can watch the video too.'

She bounded out of the shop, full of her new idea. Ashley was a little slower and, as she turned to follow, the Hyena moved away from the racks to stand in her way.

'I . . . um . . . ' He was very pink now, and breathing hard as he spoke. The words were causing him trouble. 'That young lady you're with . . . she's . . . um . . . I wouldn't like to see you get into trouble.'

Ashley stiffened. 'Why should I get into trouble?'

The Hyena took a breath. 'I mean she's a bit . . . if I were your father—'

'You're not my father,' Ashley said. 'My father's dead. And, for your information, Vikki is my best friend and she's really great. Excuse me, please.'

Pushing past him, she strode out of the shop. Vikki was on the pavement outside, grinning all over her face.

'I didn't know you'd got it in you.'

Ashley scowled. 'People keep treating me as if I haven't got a brain. Just because my mother's ill, it doesn't mean I'm a complete idiot. Let's go home and phone your mum.'

She stamped off down the road, without waiting for Vikki.

78

RAVINDER

That Vikki. She's a spoilt brat.

The business with the video was typical. She knew she was out of order, but she wasn't going to give in. Once Mr Galt interfered, that was it. She was determined to beat him.

She's the same with everyone. Even her boyfriend, Matt. Matt's sister, Ginger, is a mate of mine—ever since we were at school—and you ought to hear what *she's* got to say about Vikki. She hates her guts. Matt and Ginger are really close and he tells her everything. She goes ballistic about the way Vikki walks all over him.

That's Matt's lookout, I reckon, if he's stupid enough to go out with someone like that. But Vikki shouldn't pick on Mr Galt. He hasn't got a clue how to deal with a number like her.

He may be the original fogey, but he's got a good heart. When Kulvinder cut her leg, he shut up their shop so he could drive her to the hospital. And he didn't say a word about the blood on the upholstery, even though that car was his pride and joy.

That argument with Vikki must have shaken him up. When she went, he just stood and stared after her and her friend. Stared and stared, like an old man, for a good couple of minutes.

Next time Ginger comes in, I'm going to see if she can do something about it. If anyone can get Vikki to lay off Mr Galt, it'll be Ginger. She's great at handling people.

She'd be wonderful in the shop.

Pity she's going out with Phil Carson.

Twelve

After all the fuss, *Street Stalker* turned out to be a really dreadful film. Even Vikki had to admit it. For most of the second half, she kept up a running commentary.

'And there's a dark corner! Is he going to jump out of there? Is he? Isn't he? AAAARGH! It's a cat. So now she's a nervous wreck. And of course he's going to come when she *doesn't* expect it. Maybe when she puts the key in the lock and opens the door. Or maybe in the kitchen—yes, it's going to be the kitchen—'

A face pressed itself flat against the kitchen window on the screen, and Vikki shrieked and buried her head in the cushions on the couch.

'Oh, I can't bear it! It's so dreadful! Rewind it, Ash, so we can see that bit again.'

Pauline was laughing too. Snatching the remote control out of Ashley's hand, she rewound the video and Vikki started again, in the same bright voice.

'And there's a dark corner! Is he going to jump out of there? Is he? Isn't he—?'

It was half-past nine by the time they finished the film and the pizzas. Vikki's father knocked on the door and she pulled a face.

'Aw, *Dad*! I could've walked home on my own.'

Her father was large and calm. He patted her on the head. 'Think I'm worried about *you*? It's the lads I'm thinking of. They don't stand much chance if they run into you on a dark night.'

'They'd be quite safe,' Vikki said demurely. 'Unless it was Eddie Beale, of course. Now if I was to meet him . . . ' She fluttered her eyelids like Minnie Mouse and looked meaningly at Ashley.

Her father hauled her out of the chair. 'If you met Eddie Beale, he'd stare straight over your head. He doesn't have anything to do with little girls. Now let's be having you. Some of us have to go to work in the morning.'

Vikki went, with a loud moan, and Pauline leaned back against her cushions, giggling weakly.

'She's a real hoot, isn't she? That's the best evening I've had for ages. It was really kind of Tricia to think of lending us the video.'

Ashley opened her mouth. And shut it again.

'Homework?' Pauline said.

'I haven't got any. I did it in break.'

'That's good. Why don't we have some cocoa and do the crossword then?'

'You're not too tired?' Ashley said.

'I'm fine.' Pauline smiled. 'You know, I really think I'm getting a bit better.'

Ashley thought so too. She was humming as she went to make the cocoa.

It was Ashley who was tired. By the time they'd finished the crossword, she was so sleepy that she had to keep jerking herself awake.

'Help me on with my nightie,' Pauline said. 'Then you can go to bed.'

'But what about you?'

'I'll manage. I can sit up in bed and read. Go on. You're no use to me if you fall asleep down here.'

Ashley yawned. 'I'll just wash up the cups.'

'You will not. Why don't you stop working! I'll wash the cups tomorrow. It'll give me something to do.'

'OK,' Ashley said weakly.

She nearly said, *If I put your nightie on, can you brush your own hair?* But she knew the answer to that. It wasn't fair to ask. She went to fetch the hairbrush and the nightdress.

By the time she crawled up the stairs, she was utterly exhausted. She expected to fall fast asleep the moment her head hit the pillow, and she did.

But some time after midnight she woke up abruptly from her first, heavy sleep. Pauline was snoring downstairs, and the cistern in the bathroom was playing its usual monotonous tune, against a background of dull roaring from the traffic in the Row. Ashley twisted restlessly under her duvet, with every sound echoing in her head. The more she tried to ignore the little noises, the louder they sounded.

And then she heard a noise she couldn't place.

Scratch.

Her eyes flickered open.

Scratch-scratch.

It seemed to be coming from the back of the house. A harsh, scraping noise, like something sharp being drawn along a metal surface. Without switching the light on, Ashley climbed out of bed and padded into the bathroom.

Scratch.

The noise was coming from below, from somewhere close to the wall outside. For a moment, Ashley imagined silly things, like giant rats gnawing old saucepans. Then she pulled herself together and tried to visualize the things outside. What was made of metal?

Scratch-scratch-scratch.

Not the window-frame. That was wooden. And the walls were brick, covered with pebble-dash, and the windows were glass. There was nothing metal. The only other thing out there was the clothes-line which stretched from the pole in the garden right up to the house. Right up to—

Suddenly, she remembered. The clothes-line was tied on to the downpipe from the gutter. That was metal. Whatever was out there was scraping away at the downpipe.

Creeping over to the window, she peered down. Immediately, she saw that she was right about the downpipe. Someone was hunched at the bottom of it. A man.

Got you!

It was the man who'd sent the letters. It had to be! Ashley gave a small, triumphant grin in the dark. Then she crept back into her bedroom and found the torch in her chest of drawers.

When she went back into the bathroom, the scratching noise was still going on. She crouched by the window, working out exactly what she was going to do. When she was sure, she switched the torch on, jumped to her feet and flung the window open.

The man moved the moment the light hit him, covering his face with one arm and twisting away from her. She had a confused impression of a dark tracksuit with a hood pulled up to hide his face. Then he was scrambling over the fence, into Mrs Mac's garden.

He'll smash her pots, Ashley thought, as she followed him with the torch. *Mrs Mac'll be furious.*

But there was no sound of breaking. Whoever he was, he knew how to move. Even though she leaned right out of the window, shining the torch across the back of the houses, she couldn't catch him again. He must be sneaking round the side of Mrs Mac's, heading for the street.

She wanted to race down the stairs and fling herself through the back door, so that she could follow him through the midnight streets and see where he went to ground. But she had enough sense not to start that. She didn't even go down to see what he had been doing with the downpipe. If she woke Pauline up, there would be questions.

She'd check it out in the morning.

SPIDER MO

Did I see him? 'Course I seen him. Fell over my head, didn't he?

Wasn't hurting no one. Just lying in that alley round the side of the house, to get out of the wind. And then—POW! A boot in the ear.

(I'm used to that. People don't notice me, see. When you sleep outside, you get to be Mrs Invisible.)

This one noticed me, though. He stopped beside me and I opened my eyes and saw—

Ha! Thought I was going to tell, didn't you?

I'm not stupid. The minute I clocked his face, I got the message. *See me— and you'll be sorry.* So I started rolling my eyes, as if I was right out of it. Then I slid over sideways, on top of all my bags.

(Got to take care of the bags. Some people'll steal anything. Had a scarf pinched right off my neck the other night.)

I lay on my bags, pretending I'd passed out. Hoping he was in too much of a hurry to kick my head in. He hung around for a couple of seconds, but I wasn't dumb enough to open my eyes. I stayed curled round the bags, like a dead hedgehog, and at last he took himself off.

So I didn't see anything. OK? Not a whisker. That's how I've lasted so long. I don't see things.

Nothing.

Thirteen

It was him. The same man.

The moment Ashley looked at the downpipe next morning, and saw the scratches, she knew for sure. There was a single word gouged on to the downpipe, in letters that went right through the black paint.

CINDY.

Underneath it there was a shape, a perfect drop. Like a drop of blood.

He'd crouched under her window and scratched it, right outside the kitchen door. Ashley could see his footprints in the loose earth. The ground was churned and trampled round the pipe, but there were two or three clear prints further along, the marks of heavy shoes, with a deep tread. They were in the flowerbed beside the fence, where he'd come through from Mrs Mac's.

He'd come through and crouched there in the cold, under her window. Scratching the five letters that meant, *I know who you are. I can give you away.*

What else would he have done if she hadn't disturbed him? What did the drop of blood mean?

For the first time, she began to feel afraid

'What did he scratch?' Vikki said.

They were sitting in the library, pretending to work on the CD-Roms. Ashley reached over and tapped out the word on the keyboard, to avoid saying it out loud. It appeared in the *Search* box.

Cindy.

Vikki bit her lip. 'He knew? It must be the same person, mustn't it?'

'Suppose so.' Ashley frowned. 'But why? What's the point?'

'He's trying to scare you,' Vikki said. She ran the mouse backwards and forwards on the mat, not looking at Ashley. '*Are* you scared?'

'What of?' Ashley said lightly. 'A few scratches on the paint?'

'It's not what he did,' Vikki muttered. 'It's what he *might* do.'

Ashley wasn't going to admit that she'd thought of that as well. 'Oh, wow!' she said sarcastically. 'You mean—he might scratch on the back door next? That *would* be scary.'

Vikki kicked her under the table. 'Don't pretend you're not worried. You know I can tell. D'you want me to send Matt round tonight? To keep an eye open?'

'And make more footprints in the flowerbeds?'

'Footprints?' Vikki sat bolt upright and her fingers tapped the word on to the keyboard. *Footprints.* 'You didn't say that before. If there's footprints, you've got him! All you've got to do is go home and take a plaster cast. Then we can go to see Eddie.'

That was just like Vikki. Listening was never enough for her. She always had to be doing something. Ashley sighed.

'Eddie's not going to care about scratches on a drainpipe.'

'Of course he is. It was a *midnight intruder*!' Vikki was sitting on the very edge of her chair now. 'You've got to find out who it was. I'll come round straight after school and we'll do a plaster cast—'

'Don't be silly. We haven't got any plaster.'

Vikki waved the objection away. 'We'll measure the footprints and do a drawing, then. And take it round to Eddie and—'

Ashley saw Mrs Hunt coming into the library, and she

nudged Vikki hard. Without hesitation, Vikki clicked on *Search*, smiling cherubically.

But the computer was too quick for her. By the time Mrs Hunt reached them, the answer was on the screen.

No match for Cindy Footprints

'Working hard?' Mrs Hunt said. She looked at the screen and smiled acidly. 'It looks as though you need a bit more practice.' The smile snapped off her face. 'I think you'd better stay after school and memorize the rules for working on the computers.'

Vikki went pink. 'But, Mrs Hunt! We've got something really important to do this afternoon. And anyway, Ash has to get home and look after her mother—'

'Then she shouldn't have been wasting her time in school. These computers aren't toys.' Mrs Hunt's face was spiteful now. 'I'm sure Ashley's mother won't fade away just because she's half an hour later coming home.'

Vikki was all set to argue. 'But you don't understand! Ashley's mother is—'

Ashley kicked her under the table and she stopped, but she was still furious. The moment Mrs Hunt disappeared, she typed *Smelly Hunt* into the computer.

'I bet there are hundreds of matches for that,' she said.

When they came out of school at last, Joe was by the gate. He grinned at Ashley and fell into step.

'What are you doing here?' Vikki scowled at him. She wasn't one for forgiving and forgetting.

Joe ignored her, and answered as though Ashley had asked the question. 'Eddie asked what you were up to. I didn't know, so I came to find out.'

'I've been doing a detention,' Ashley said. She went on walking briskly down the road. She wasn't sure she could cope with Joe at the moment.

Vikki ran after her. 'Don't be stupid! This is your chance. You can send Eddie a message!'

Joe came up on the other side. 'You want me to tell Eddie something?'

'No I don't,' Ashley said crossly.

Joe's eyes were glittering like chips of coal in his pale face. 'Something's happened, hasn't it?'

'Of course not!' Ashley hoisted her bag higher on one shoulder, like a barrier, and walked away, but Vikki trotted along beside her, refusing to be shaken off.

'You idiot!' she hissed. 'What's the matter? Do you *like* being stalked?'

'I'm not being stalked!'

'Yes you are. That's what it is. *Stalking.* You've got to get Eddie to help.'

'But I don't even know him.'

'Of course you do. He sent you that video.' Vikki caught hold of Ashley's sleeve, dragging her to a standstill as Joe came up behind them.

He wasn't hurrying. He was slouching along, mumbling under his breath. As he came closer, Ashley could hear the words and he wasn't saying them in his own voice.

' . . . don't need any help,' he was muttering. ' . . . just got to concentrate . . . I'll be fine . . . I can manage . . . '

One of his shoulders was lifted higher than the other, and his face was closed and inaccessible. Frowning.

' . . . can't ask for help . . . got to keep going . . . '

Vikki suddenly gave a loud giggle.

'What's up with you?' Ashley said. She was annoyed that she couldn't see the joke.

Vikki started laughing, but Joe didn't even glance at her. He just went on muttering.

' . . . perfectly all right . . . got to be perfect . . . I can cope . . . '

'I don't see—' Ashley began.

And then, suddenly, horribly, she did see. It was like the sort of trick picture that shifts from nonsense to sense as you stare at it. One moment Joe looked completely mad, and the next she saw—herself. Scurrying along with her face turned away from everyone else. Fooling herself that she could manage.

She went bright red. 'Stop it!'

' . . . can't let anyone help . . . ' Joe mumbled.

'Stop it!' Ashley shouted.

She began to run away, racing between the blocks of flats and round Toronto House into the cinema car park. When she came out on to the Row, the traffic lights were in her favour and she went straight across.

She thought she'd shaken the others off, but as she turned to walk along the Row, Joe appeared at her elbow.

'Hi,' he said.

'Go away,' Ashley growled. She looked behind, expecting to see Vikki.

'It's all right,' Joe said. 'I told her to beat it. I said Eddie wouldn't listen to you unless you were on your own.'

I'm not going to tell Eddie! Ashley wanted to say. *I can handle it.* But she remembered how Joe had looked. How he'd said those words. *I can manage.* Shabby and scuttling. Pathetic.

'My . . . mum doesn't know,' she said slowly. 'About any of this.'

'So?' Joe shrugged. 'Who's going to tell her?' He looked sideways at Ashley. 'Come on. Spit it out.'

They were outside Fat Annie's when Ashley knew she was going to tell him. She was on the verge of speaking when she felt someone watching her. Glancing round, she saw Mrs Hunt inside the shop, staring through the window. Behind her was the Hyena.

He was staring too.

Ashley began to walk faster. 'Let's get round the corner. Then I'll tell you.'

'OK,' Joe said again. 'Hang on a minute, though.'

He stopped and turned to face the window. Pulling a face, he stuck his tongue out at Mrs Hunt, as far as it would go.

Then he followed Ashley into Railway Street.

89

Well!

Other teachers tell me that they are often subjected to that type of insolence, but I will not tolerate rude behaviour, so when the boy stuck his tongue out, I was speechless for a moment.

Then I pulled myself together and rapped on the counter. Mr Galt was goggling out of the window like a man struck deaf and dumb.

'*If* you don't mind!' I said.

He dragged his eyes back to my shopping. But even while he was weighing my tomatoes I saw him sneaking glances through the window.

'Something wrong?' I said sharply.

He coloured. 'I . . . er . . . I'm sorry, Mrs Hunt. I was taken aback. Seeing Ashley with that boy—'

I couldn't help feeling sorry for him. He's just the sort of man who would be taken in by Ashley. Those big blue eyes of hers, and that oh-so-innocent look.

'You would be surprised,' I said, 'by some of the company Ashley Putnam keeps. Her best friend is a most undesirable girl. *Most* undesirable. That boy is respectable by comparison, even if his manners are atrocious. Maybe he's her brother.'

'Oh no!' For some reason, Mr Galt looked ridiculously shocked. 'There's no brother. She . . . um . . . she hasn't got anyone. She . . . she lives with her mother, and that's why—'

'Thank you.' I cut him off. It's not my habit to gossip about my pupils.

Ashley Putnam used to be a promising girl. Very bright and hardworking, and a good gymnast, too. But it's obviously the usual story. She's discovered boys and work's gone out of the window.

Children today are so lazy.

Fourteen

Ashley slid her key into the lock. 'Remember,' she said. 'You mustn't tell my mum. Not a word.'

'No worries,' Joe said as he walked in after her.

There was a faint, unfamiliar scent in the hall. Like bluebells, or hyacinths. Ashley frowned, trying to work out what it was, but Joe knew straight away.

'Tricia's been.' He grinned and walked into the front room. 'Hi, Pauline,' he said. And then, 'You're looking good. I like the hair.'

'What hair?' Ashley hurried after him.

Pauline was sitting at the table peeling sprouts. She looked cheerful and excited—and different. Her great mass of hair had vanished. Someone had cut it into smart wisps at the front and chopped it as short as Joe's at the back. The bones of her face looked stronger and more solid as she grinned up at them both.

'Do you like it? Tricia did it.'

'I—' Ashley felt so strange that she had to sit down.

Pauline's smile faltered. 'You don't like it?'

'It's not that—'

'Of course it's not.' Joe said firmly. 'It's great. Come on, Ash. You've got to admit it.'

He was right. It looked wonderful. Ashley couldn't understand why she felt angry. She forced a smile on to her face.

'It's beautiful. It was just a shock, that's all. You look about ten years younger.'

Pauline grinned. 'Only ten? Tricia said fifteen. She was round for coffee, and suddenly she said, *Honestly, Paul, you'd look fifteen years younger with all that hair off. And it would be*

91

much more practical, too. Why don't I go home and get my scissors?
And she did. Just like that. Didn't she do it well?'

'It's brilliant,' Ashley said, fighting the ugly, angry lump
in her throat.

Joe grinned. 'Tricia's a genius with scissors. She even
does Sam's hair, and you've got to be good to make
something look as ragged as that.'

'Sam?' Pauline leaned forward. 'Has she got ragged hair?
I thought she was a model?'

'I'm not A Model!' Joe flung himself on to a chair,
straddling it backwards with his legs stretched out. His voice
was shrill and he tilted his chin aggressively. 'I do some
modelling, but that's not all I'm good for. Why do you want
to put me in a box?' He ran his fingers through his hair,
leaving it standing on end, and for a moment Ashley could
have sworn it was blonde.

Pauline was giggling. Joe jumped to his feet and glared at
her.

'You think that's funny?' He tossed his head. 'You're
pathetic!'

Still being Sam, he strutted out to the kitchen as though
his legs were twice as long, and Pauline laughed out loud,
shaking her head at Ashley. 'How does he do it?'

Ashley didn't answer. She heard a rattle as Joe picked up
the matchbox in the kitchen, and she remembered Sam, in
the warehouse.

Fire.

'I— Hang on, Mum. I'll make a drink.'

She shot down the hall. Joe was standing in the kitchen
with a lighted match in his hand and his head tilted back.
He was lowering the flame towards his open mouth and for
one crazy moment Ashley saw him lit up red and gold.
Playing with danger. She froze, waiting for a tongue of fire
to shoot across the kitchen.

Then Joe laughed and blew out the match.

'You lunatic!' Ashley said. 'You could've—'

'Don't be silly.' Joe grinned at her, mockingly. 'It was only a match. Are we going in the garden?'

Ashley blinked, and the world shrank back to normal. He was right, of course. The little match flame had been real, but all the rest—the fire and the danger and the drama—were imaginary. He'd tricked her into seeing them. A match was only a match.

And a scratch was only a scratch.

She pushed the back door open, abruptly. 'Come on then.'

Joe didn't waste time on the winter grass and the spindly bushes. Slipping through the door, he crouched beside the downpipe, examining the letters. With one forefinger, he traced out their shapes in the air. C.I.N.D.Y.

'Why that name?' he said.

'He's gloating. Letting me know he's found out—'

'I know *that*. I mean—why do you use that tag?'

Ashley looked down at her feet. 'No reason,' she said gruffly.

Joe raised one eyebrow, but he didn't push it. Turning sideways, he studied the footprints in the flowerbed. 'I think I'll draw these. Have you got a bit of paper?'

Ashley fetched him a pencil and paper from the kitchen. Then she went inside to make the tea, in case Pauline wondered what they were doing.

When she came out again, Joe had drawn two footprints, and he was checking the pattern, to make sure he'd got it exactly right.

'Want me to take this to Eddie?' he said.

Ashley frowned down at the pattern of waves and dots he had drawn. Three curves to each wave. Four waves on the sole and two on the heel. Six dots in between the front waves, and four nearer the back. Size ten or eleven at least. 'What can Eddie do?' she said.

Joe looked. 'You don't understand about him, do you?'

'No I don't.' Ashley was starting to find it rather annoying. 'Why does everyone keep going on about him?'

'Because he's the boss. He knows everyone, and people do what he says.'

'So why would he take any notice of me?'

Joe shrugged. 'Dunno, but he seems to. Maybe he's got a soft spot for cartwheels. He likes a show.'

'But he sent me a video for that. We're all square.'

'A video?' Joe looked amused. 'You think that's all he's done? Given you a video?'

Ashley frowned, not understanding. 'What else?'

'Oh, come on!' Joe jerked his head towards the house. 'Why d'you think Tricia came round? She's very nice, but she'd never do something like that on her own.'

'You mean—Eddie sent her? Why would he do that?'

Joe squatted back on his heels. 'Because he wants to help you. He asked about you, after the party. *What's she like, that girl? What kind of life does she have?*'

'And you . . . said . . . ?' Ashley could hardly get the words out.

Joe shrugged. 'I said you spend your life looking after your mum. And she's really nice—but she's bored out of her mind. Needs a bit of company. *I reckon her mother could do with a friend*, I said.'

'So it's all fake?'

'Don't be so stupid!' Joe stood up. 'Tricia really likes her. Tricia likes everyone. But she'd never have thought of coming round if Eddie hadn't suggested—'

Ashley clenched her fists. 'He didn't have to.'

'Of course he didn't have to! He did it to help. But you won't let anyone help, will you?' Suddenly, Joe was angry. He stood up and pushed his drawing of the footprint into Ashley's hand. 'Do what you want! No one's going to force you!'

He stamped into the house. Ashley heard him say goodbye to her mother and a moment later the front door slammed. Slowly, she unfolded the paper and looked down at it. Was Joe right? Should she ask Eddie for help?

No, it was ridiculous!

Pushing the paper into her pocket, she opened the kitchen door. She was about to step through when she heard her mother's voice.

'You won't know me next time you come!'

She was on the telephone. Ashley walked down the hall and looked into the front room. Pauline was perched on the end of the bed, with the phone to her ear, and she was talking excitedly. Her whole face seemed to have come alive, in a way that Ashley had never seen before.

KAREN

I couldn't believe it when I picked up the phone and it was MUM! She hardly ever telephones us.

Janet thinks that's really mean, but I don't see what all the fuss is about. It's great when we go and see Mum—she's a real laugh—but there's nothing much to talk about on the phone.

So when she said, 'Hallo. That's Karen, isn't it?' I just said, 'Hi, Mum, I'll get Janet.'

I could see Louise frowning at me, because she wanted to talk to Mum, but she's always trying to make out Mum likes her best, so I was going to yell for Janet when Mum said, 'Hey, not so fast, I've got a surprise.'

She sounded quite different from usual—sort of bouncy. And then she told me, and I was so surprised that I yelled right in her ear.

'YOU'VE HAD YOUR HAIR CUT OFF??!!!'

That did it, of course. Louise crowded in, squeaking, 'Oh, you haven't spoilt it, have you?' and 'Did you keep the hair for us?' And Janet came rattling down the stairs because she'd heard something was up. And all the time, I'm yelling into the phone, 'Does it look good? When can we come and see it? Can we come and see you this weekend?' And Mum's laughing and laughing—

I can't wait to see her on Saturday.

Fifteen

The haircut was only the beginning. After that, Tricia seemed to be there every day.

On Wednesday, Ashley came home from school, worrying about what the stalker might have left, and discovered Pauline and Tricia playing Scrabble. They were giggling hysterically. Tricia grinned at her and waved a hand.

'I did a bit of shopping for you. While I had the car out.'

There was enough food for the rest of the week, and she laughed out loud when Ashley tried to pay for it.

'Don't be daft. It's only a few bits.'

There was nothing from the stalker on Thursday, either. But Pauline and Tricia were in the kitchen, with a chocolate cake cooling on the table.

'I thought I might as well do something useful,' Pauline said. 'While we were talking.'

Ashley stared at the cake and tried to remember the last one her mother had made. Four years ago? Five?

On Friday, Tricia was there again, with a bag of clothes and a message from Sam. (*She's finished with these, and would they fit Ashley?*) On Saturday she brought some leggings for Pauline, and on Sunday she walked in with a new sink plug, because the old one was leaking.

On Monday morning, Ashley opened the bathroom window while she was cleaning her teeth, and saw the autumn colours in the back garden. She went downstairs humming to herself. She felt wonderful.

'Hi, Mum. What do you fancy wearing today?'

Pauline was sitting on the edge of the bed, wriggling her feet into a pair of slippers. She grinned. 'How about those new black leggings? And my big orange jumper?'

'Great! You'll match the autumn leaves. They're amazing this year. You should see the trees round the school field. I'll just make the tea, and then I'll get your jumper.'

Still humming, Ashley went out to the kitchen. She put the kettle on, took the bread out of the bread bin, opened the curtains and—

No.

She froze. Her fingers clenched on the curtain, screwing the material tight.

From the other side of the window, a skull leered back with ugly, open eye sockets. Not a human skull, but a long, grotesque head, with twisting horns, jammed sideways on to the sill. Two long bones were propped at the sides, meeting over the top in an arch, and someone had scrawled ugly, irregular letters across the white dome of the skull.

CINDY . . . TROUBLE . . .

The words were written in felt pen, in staring purple capitals. Above them, the ends of the bones lay round and smooth against the glass. Someone had fixed them on to the windowsill with big clots of Blu-Tack.

It took Ashley a moment to realize that she was looking at a sheep's skull, and even recognizing it didn't dull the shock. Because it wasn't the skull itself that was horrible. It was the thought of *him*. His thick, pale fingers scrabbling about in the dark, crawling over the kitchen window and squashing the Blu-Tack into place. She didn't know what he looked like, but she could imagine those fingers, as clearly as she could see the bones.

I can't, she thought. *I can't touch them*.

Then her mother called from the front room. 'Ash? You'll be late if you don't keep moving.'

And she knew that she could do it after all. She had to do it, before Pauline saw. Grabbing a wet rag from under the sink, she called back.

'There's some . . . er . . . bird's mess on the window. I'm just going out to wipe it off.'

'You haven't got time—'

'Of course I have. Anyway, I can't leave it. It's disgusting.'

Ashley slipped out of the back door. The moment she was outside, she saw that there were more footprints in the damp earth. They were even clearer than yesterday's. A pattern of waves and dots, with three curves to each wave. Four waves on the sole and two on the heel. Six dots in between the front waves, and four nearer the back.

That was his tag. As recognizable as her own. It was the same man all the time.

Reaching across the flowerbed, to avoid smudging the footprints, she pulled the skull free and laid it down on the path. Then she pulled off the long bones and the Blu-Tack, and looked round for a place to hide them.

'Ashley! Hurry up!' Pauline was getting anxious.

Quickly, Ashley tucked the bones and the skull behind the dustbin. Then, with a last look at the footprints, she whisked back into the kitchen.

'You didn't have to do that,' Pauline called. 'I could have managed.'

'Oh sure. It would only have taken you all day.' Ashley rubbed both hands fiercely under the hot tap, getting rid of the feel of the bones. 'It's all right. Don't fuss.'

'But you haven't got much time left. Let me do something.'

Ashley heard the shuffle of sticks as her mother started walking across the room. It looked as though she was having another good day. Lucky the bones were out of sight.

Pauline appeared in the kitchen and collapsed on to a chair. She was out of breath, but she was grinning.

'I can get dressed myself if you'll bring the clothes down,' she said.

'Are you sure?'

'I think so. You have some breakfast.'

Ashley had never felt less like eating, but she gulped down a couple of Weetabix and raced upstairs for the leggings and the jumper.

She was struggling not to think about the bones. They were safely tucked away behind the dustbin. What was the point of worrying about them? A match was only a match. A scratch was only a scratch. And a bone was only a bone.

She was still trying to convince herself as she walked up the road to school. Nothing serious had happened. *A letter is only a piece of paper. A word on a drainpipe is only a scratch. A sheep's skull is just a piece of bone.* Nothing to get hung up on.

As long as her mother didn't decide to look behind the dustbin.

That danger nagged away at her, all day. She couldn't wait to get home, and the last lesson in the afternoon seemed to drag on for ever. Mr Neale was dictating History notes and when the bell rang he hadn't quite finished. Some people stood up and he banged on his desk.

'How about some manners?'

'Aw, sir!' There were moans from the people who had buses to catch, but he wouldn't relent. So when he finally did let them go, they all charged for the door at once. Ashley and Vikki had to wait to get out of the classroom.

'Silly idiots.' Vikki took out her nail varnish. 'What's the big hurry? It's only another two or three minutes.' She started painting her left thumbnail black. 'What d'you reckon, Ash? Would it look nice with those little gold stars stuck on it?'

Ashley tried to focus her mind on thumbnails. 'Maybe. Only one, though. Off centre.'

Vikki started on the right hand nail. She didn't look up, but she said, 'You OK, Ash? You look a bit hassled '

'I'm fine,' Ashley said quickly. 'Just want to get home, that's all.'

'Has something else happened?' Vikki did look up then. Sharply, to catch her off guard. But Ashley was ready. Her face and her voice were both perfectly calm.

'Everything's fine.'

At that moment, the doorway cleared. Vikki began to screw the lid back on to her nail varnish bottle, but Ashley didn't wait for her. She headed straight for home.

When she arrived, there were no lights on. That was unusual. It wasn't completely dark, but it must be pretty dim in there, and her mother never sat in the dark unless she fell asleep. Or unless—

Ashley unlocked the door quickly and threw it open. 'Mum?'

There was no answer.

Her heart gave an enormous leap. That was what she always dreaded. She ran into the front room and switched on the light. But she didn't see what she was afraid of. Her mother wasn't lying there, sprawled helpless on the floor. She wasn't there at all.

The room was empty.

That was so extraordinary that for a second Ashley's mind went blank. Then she saw the note lying on the table.

> *Dear Ashie, Tricia and her friend Phil came in a car. We've gone to the country to see the autumn leaves. Back soon. Love, Mum.*

Pauline had gone out in a car? That hadn't happened since the twins grew so big that they couldn't all fit into Frank and Janet's Metro. Ashley had begun to think she'd never go out again.

But she had—and it was brilliant timing. The perfect opportunity to get rid of the skull.

Going through the kitchen, Ashley snatched a couple of plastic carrier bags out of the drawer. Then she went outside and crouched down beside the dustbin, feeling round the back for the skull.

Her fingers met the jagged edges of broken bone.

She snatched her hand back and pulled the dustbin away. The skull lay exactly where she left it, but someone had smashed the top in. With a boot maybe, or a hammer.

Behind it, lying across the bones, was a brown envelope, with a word written across it in the same purple felt pen that had scrawled on the skull.

CINDY.

Ashley bent down and picked it up. She felt completely unemotional. Icy-calm. But when she looked down at her arm, she saw that it was shaking. *How strange. I must be afraid after all.* Slowly, she opened the top of the envelope.

It was full of photographs. There were half a dozen of them and they were all pictures of her.

There she was, walking past the chippie. Standing by the video shop. Waiting to cross at the traffic lights. Talking to Vikki on the corner of Railway Street. The angles were different, but the pictures were all variations on a theme. In every one, she was somewhere in the Row, not looking straight at the camera but busy with her own life. And there was another thing that they had in common as well.

Someone had drawn on each one, in felt pen. A jagged black line running from top to bottom.

Right through her head.

With a huge effort, Ashley turned the pictures over. Five of them were blank on the back. The sixth said, *You're going to get into trouble . . .*

Just as she thought she was going to scream, she heard the car draw up outside.

PHIL

When Eddie asks you to do something, you don't exactly argue. I mean—he's the boss, isn't he? Like, there was ten or eleven of us in the pub on Thursday night, and he comes in and says, 'I need a driver for tomorrow. Got to be someone with a clean licence. I don't want any hassle.'

That knocked three of them out straight away, of course, but there were plenty of other blokes. I didn't even look up from my beer.

But Eddie seems to have taken to me recently. He clapped me on the back. 'Tricia wants to go out for a drive, with a friend of hers. Fancy being the chauffeur?'

I don't like to tell you what the others said. But they were wrong. When I turn up at Tricia's, it turns out we're doing a good deed. It's Ashley Putnam's mum who's going for a ride. Pauline, from Railway Street.

It looked like a dull day, especially when we picked up Pauline and she and Tricia piled into the back together. I thought, *Eddie wasn't joking when he said I was going to be a chauffeur.*

How wrong can you be?

We went out into the country, to look at the autumn leaves, and we were in fits, all the way. The two of them seemed to set each other off, and as for jokes—well, I'm not going to repeat the jokes they told, but I had to stop the car twice, I was laughing so much. Ginger's told me lots about that family, but she never told me Ashley's mum was so funny.

She was pretty wiped out by the time we got back, though. Even Tricia stopped talking and let her alone. 'We'll just drop Pauline off,' she said. 'OK, Phil? We won't go in.'

That was the plan. But the moment the car pulls up, Ashley—Pauline's daughter—shoots out of the house, like a bomb. And it's not her mum she wants to talk to. It's Tricia. She knocked on the window and beckoned, and when Tricia got out she pulled her away from the car and started whispering.

'What's that?' Pauline says. 'What's going on?'

But she's not asking very hard, because she's so tired. And I wasn't going to ask either. I've only been with Eddie a year or so, but that's one thing I've learnt. Keep your nose out of things.

After five minutes or so, Tricia came over and asked me to carry Pauline inside. I picked her up—there's no weight to her at all—took her inside and put her down on the bed. She looked ready to sleep for a week.

Tricia was right behind me. 'Take care of yourself,' she said, and she patted Pauline's hand. 'I'll be round soon.'

Then we took ourselves off. I thought Tricia might have explained the whispering, but she didn't say a word.

All she said was, 'Come back to my place. We haven't got long. I need the car here again at midnight.'

I gave her a funny look. Like, *Who d'you think you are, giving me orders?* But she didn't turn a hair.

'Eddie's business,' she said. 'Ashley wants to see him. We're picking her up as soon as Pauline's asleep.'

Sixteen

Ashley lay on her bed, waiting for midnight and going over what Tricia had said, again and again.

Eddie might help you. But it's not automatic. People are always after him for things. You'll have to get his attention.

How was she going to do that? Go in and yell at him? Wear something dramatic? (That was a laugh, given her wardrobe.) Set fire to his hair?

Round and round went her mind, growing wilder and wilder. And all the time, she knew that there was only one thing she could really try. Only one thing she could do well enough.

Her turn. Her trick.

Tricia and Phil were there at midnight, exactly as Tricia had promised. Ashley crept out of the alley, stepping over Spider Mo, and slid into the car.

'Here we go, then,' Tricia said, as the car pulled away. 'It's not easy, tracking Eddie down, but we'll give it a whirl. He and Sam have got a thing about this new club at the moment. Nighttrap. They're usually there a couple of times a week, so we'll try that. Have you brought the things?'

Ashley passed the bag forward for her to see the shattered skull and the letters and the photographs. Tricia rummaged through them, holding the photographs up to the window to catch the light. When she saw the jagged, scrawled lines, she shuddered.

'He's a nasty piece of work, isn't he? Deserves a good long talk with Eddie.'

'You think there's a chance Eddie's going to be interested?'

'Maybe.' Tricia shrugged and passed the bag back. 'It's worth a go. Depends if something else has cropped up. If not, he might be looking for an entertainment.'

Ashley twisted the top of the bag tightly, trying to think of it all like that. An entertainment. A show. What she had to do was put on a better show than anyone else. She could feel her blood flowing faster as her body prepared for it.

'Suppose they won't let me into the club?'

Tricia shook her head. 'No problem.'

Ashley didn't really believe it, but she hadn't seen Eddie's name in action. When the doorman raised his eyebrows at her, Tricia just muttered at him.

'Come to see Eddie.'

That was enough. He winked and waved them through to the stairs.

They went down into smoky darkness, hearing feet thud over their heads as they walked under the balcony. The disco lights lit up crowds of people on the main dance floor, and more people above them, all dancing fast and frantically. There was a circular balcony, running all the way round the club and everywhere—in front, behind, left and right and above—there were moving bodies, pulsing in time to the music. It was like stepping into a cauldron boiling with energy.

Ashley couldn't imagine how they were going to find anyone, but Tricia leaned closer, bellowing into her ear.

'See Eddie? Up on the balcony.'

Ashley looked across the club, to the steps that led up to the balcony. And the one still point At the top of the steps, just to one side, was a table with people sitting round it.

Ashley could see why Eddie chose to be there. The table was half hidden, but it dominated the whole place. From there, he could see everything that was going on.

Sam was leaning over the wrought-iron balustrade,

looking at the dancers. Her dress caught the lights, glittering red, then purple, then silver. Beside her, perched on the broad rail, was Doug, talking to a couple of other men.

Eddie was slightly further back than the others, with his chair tilted and a glass in his hand. It was impossible to make out his expression, but he was watching what was going on below.

Tricia put her mouth right against Ashley's ear. 'We can't fight our way through this lot. Better wait for a break in the music.'

Ashley nodded. She didn't attempt to shout back. She was busy looking round the club, working out how to do what she wanted. There would only be a few seconds to get it right. No time to hesitate. The plan had to be clear in her head.

It was like getting ready to do a wall. She could feel her adrenalin level rising as she waited for the moment when the music stopped. That split second of almost-quiet before the voices rose. Pushing her carrier bag at Tricia, she cupped her hands round her mouth, to be ready.

And when the moment came, she yelled at the top of her voice.

'Stand back!'

It was the risk she'd taken at the party, but magnified a hundred times. She hardly believed the floor would clear for her. But it was as though people had been expecting something to happen. When she flung herself into the first cartwheel, they scattered in front of her, squeezing back from the centre of the floor.

She spun between them, over and over, right to the bottom of the stairs. Then she flipped over into a handstand and began to climb the stairs. She knew she could probably manage six steps, but she played safe and let her legs drop over after five, climbing the rest of the flight in a backbend.

As she went, the lights came up gradually. The whole club

was silent, and she could feel the eyes on her back, but she wouldn't let herself think about them. She concentrated on climbing, and all she could see was the blue carpet on the stairs, inches away from her eyes.

Then, suddenly, there were no more stairs. She was at the top, and instead of staring at carpet, she was staring down at a pair of heavy black toecaps. They were polished to such a shine that she could see her face in them, and she knew, without being told, whose boots they were.

Sidling round them, she flipped the right way up, and turned towards Eddie. Very slowly, he tapped three fingers against the palm of his other hand, applauding. Mockingly. Watching her face.

Was that good or bad? What was she supposed to do? Ashley looked round at the others—Sam and Doug, two heavies, and a couple of girls dressed to kill. Was it time for her to speak now? They were all listening, but she wasn't sure.

Then a voice came from under the table. A shrill, whining noise, like the voice of a bored child.

'That's *nothing*. I could do that when I was *seven*. She's not expecting us to *clap*, is she?'

It was Joe.

Eddie's fingers stopped tapping and lay still in the palm of his hand. Everyone was quiet, waiting to see what would happen. She hadn't done enough yet. That was what Joe had been telling her.

So . . . what?

She glanced quickly over her shoulder, wondering whether she could make it down the stairs again. When she looked back, Eddie was staring. Cool and amused.

'Dull!' he said.

His eyes went sideways to the balcony rail, and her stomach clenched abruptly, as she understood what he wanted. She looked along the rail and thought of the danger. Then she looked back at him.

107

Quickly, before she could think, she spread her arms to the audience below, bowing left and right. Then—ignoring the half-hearted applause—she took three quick steps up. On to a chair. On to the table. And up on to the rail round the balcony. As fast as she could, not giving herself time to think, she went over into a handstand.

And she heard everyone gasp.

GINGER

You could have pushed me over with a banana.

It was Ashley Putnam.

(She's a friend of Vikki's and Matt reckons she does those fantastic graffitis. I used to reckon Vikki was kidding him about that, but now—well, see what you think.)

I was down on the floor, all on my own, in a flaming temper. Phil had promised to take me to Nightrap. Been promising for weeks. And then, at the last moment, there was a phone call: *We'll have to meet there. And I can't make it till after twelve.*

Was I pleased? You know the answer to that! I was just waiting for him to turn up so I could spit in his face and punch his nose sideways. And I knew just what I was going to yell while I did it.

It was a good night for a bit of drama. Eddie Beale was sitting up on the balcony, and the whole club had that feel you get when he's around. Like, *something's going to happen.* And I tell you, I thought *I* was going to be the show. Me and Phil.

But then Ashley turned up, out of nowhere.

She went cartwheeling across the floor, and strutting up the steps on her hands and suddenly I found I was one of the audience, after all. I was standing there gawping with everyone else.

Feeling the danger in the air.

When Ashley went up on the balcony rail, everyone edged into the middle of the floor. Partly to see better and partly to stay out of trouble. We all thought she was going to run round the rail, and we didn't want to be underneath if she fell off.

But she didn't run. She went over into a handstand.

108

Holy soap! You could have heard an ant sneeze. None of us could believe it. And when she started moving, I grabbed at the person next to me, like we were drowning. I was terrified to *think*—in case my brain made too much noise.

Left.

Right.

Left.

Right.

Every time Ashley moved an arm, I nearly died. But I couldn't have looked away. Not for a million pounds. I had to watch it all. Every lurch as she shifted her weight forward. Every wobble of her legs. And all the time, there's this voice going on in my head. *She's nearly done a quarter . . . now it's a third of the way round . . . now it's almost half . . .*

And then, when she was halfway round, she missed her grip. Her fingers slipped on the rail and I thought she was going right over.

I gasped. We all gasped. You just can't help yourself when it's like that. Phil appeared out of nowhere and put his arm round me, but I hardly even noticed him. I was watching Ashley struggle to keep her balance. And my fingernails were digging into the palms of my hands.

Phil was the same. I could feel him holding his breath as she steadied herself and started off again. It's step by step, and you can't think of anything, except how can she go on, how can she have the strength? But she keeps going on. And on and on, until it's only another two or three hand-steps. Another one.

And then she's there.

She flipped off the rail and landed on the balcony, on her feet, and the place exploded. But she wasn't the one who needed the clapping. We needed it, to let the tension go. We needed to stamp and cheer and clap our hands raw to let out the energy and the fear and the frenzy of it.

Ashley didn't take any notice of the clapping. She just stood in front of Eddie, looking him straight in the eye. As if she was saying, *OK, now what are you going to do about it?*

Seventeen

It was as if there was nobody else in the club. Only Eddie. Ashley stood in front of him, shaking slightly, and met his eyes square on.

'I need help,' she said. 'And you told me you always pay for good performances.'

Eddie nodded once, but he didn't smile. 'So what kind of help do you want?'

Ashley hadn't planned what she was going to say. And before she could think, Tricia came running across the club with the carrier bag in her hand. As the lights went down again, she came up the balcony steps.

Ashley grabbed the bag from her and turned it upside down over the table. 'Look!' she said fiercely. Bones fell helter skelter, mixed with photographs and pieces of paper. 'Look at those! How would you like to get messages like that?'

They were in a circle round the table now. Eddie and Sam, Tricia and Doug. Sam picked up the skull and ran her finger round the jagged hole in the top.

'Someone sent you *this*?'

Her face twisted in disgust. She dropped the skull back on to the table and rubbed at her hands.

'Doesn't look too good, does it?' said Doug. 'Whoever sent these, I wouldn't talk to him on your own, love.'

'But *why* send them?' Tricia spread out the photographs and looked down at them, wonderingly. 'Who hates you that much, Ashley?'

'Maybe he doesn't hate her,' Eddie said softly. 'Maybe he loves her.'

That's rubbish! Ashley wanted to say. *Don't talk rubbish!* But she could feel the others shifting uncomfortably around her. The skull leered up, threatening her in a different way, and the letters trembled on the table as the dancers round them stirred the air.

'Haven't you got any idea who sent them?' Tricia said.

'What about the shoes?' said a dark, sepulchral voice from Joe, still under the table.

Ashley remembered the drawings and took them out of her pocket. 'These are his shoes. I know they are. If we could only find out who wears shoes like this—'

'Then you'd know who shopped at Marks and Spencer,' Eddie said scornfully. 'There must be dozens of people round here who wear those. Is that the only clue you've got?'

'I—' Ashley scanned the heap of things on the table, looking for something distinctive. But there was nothing else. The letters were on ordinary paper, sent in ordinary envelopes. Written in cheap blue biro. The writing on the sheep's skull had been done in purple felt pen. And a sheep's skull might have come from anywhere. The only distinctive things were the photographs.

And how did you trace a photograph?

'There must be something else,' Sam said. 'There *has* to be.'

Eddie shrugged. 'There will be. All she's got to do is wait. He'll make a mistake in the end.'

'If he doesn't knock her off first,' Doug said heavily.

Ashley felt her throat tighten. She couldn't say a word.

'He won't try anything violent yet,' Eddie said easily. 'He hasn't worked himself up to it.' Lightly, he brushed a hand across the things on the table. 'These aren't vicious enough. Not yet.'

Sam made an odd little noise and put her hand on his arm, but he ignored her. He was looking at Ashley.

'You need one more thing,' he said softly. 'One more clue. If we follow that and then the footprints fit as well—then we'll know for sure.'

111

'So what do I do?' Ashley said. 'Wait? Like a human sacrifice?'

'Like a goat,' said Joe. He came out from under the table on all fours, bleating and butting at Eddie's hand with his head. But for once his imitation didn't work. Eddie pushed him away impatiently.

He was concentrating on Ashley. 'You need another clue.'

Ashley swept the things back into her carrier bag and picked it up. 'And if I get one—you'll help me?'

Eddie put out his hand. 'I promise.'

It was like a contract. 'Thank you,' Ashley said, and shook the hand.

Eddie grinned for a second and then snapped his fingers in the air. 'Who's got a car? Sam? You going to run Ashley home?'

Sam pulled a face at him, but she didn't argue. Uncoiling her long legs, she stood up. 'Come on, kid.'

'Be quick,' Eddie murmured. 'And don't let her mother see you. We don't want her asking questions. Can you go in quietly?'

Ashley nodded. 'There's a back way.'

'Fine. Don't let Sam drive like a maniac.'

Sam thumbed her nose at him and ran down the steps and across the floor. The dancers parted to let her through and Ashley followed, hearing the buzz of talking that started up behind her.

Sam didn't drive her own car as wildly as she'd driven the Hyena's, but she went much faster than Phil. Ashley looked out anxiously for police cars, but the streets were emptier than usual.

The only person they saw was Spider Mo, trailing up Railway Street, with her hands full of bags. Sam nodded at her.

'What's Mo up to? You don't often see her out this late. She's usually bedded down somewhere by the time it's dark.'

'Maybe she got moved on,' Ashley said.

'Maybe.' Sam turned off the engine and let the car glide the last few yards down the road. 'You all right, then? Sure you can get in without waking your mother?'

'I'm fine.' Ashley picked up her bag and opened the door. 'I'll go in the back way.'

Sam nodded and lifted a hand to wave goodbye. Then she started the engine again and she was off. It sounded as though one of the parked cars had pulled away from the kerb.

Every house in the street was dark except number fourteen, where the students lived. Ashley slipped down the side of Mrs Mac's house, treading soundlessly past the shed. Opening the garden gate, she slid through like a shadow and turned to fasten the gate behind her.

As it closed, she heard a step on the other side, in the alley.

It was only one, but it was unmistakable. Someone in heavy shoes had stepped out from behind the shed. If she opened the gate again, she would see who it was.

But that would be crazy.

Instead of looking through the gate, she ran lightly across the grass, to the broken piece of fence. She was just sliding it to one side when she heard the sound of the latch. And the creak of the gate, opening again.

Her heart gave a single, huge thud, and then she was icy calm. The only sensible thing was to get inside, as quickly as possible. She squeezed through the fence with her hand in her coat pocket, feeling for the back door key. By the time she reached the door, the key was ready in her hand.

It slid into the lock —but it wouldn't turn.

Not now. Don't stick now, Ashley thought, struggling to force it round. She could hear someone feeling his way along the fence, looking for the way through.

Turn! Dropping her carrier bag, she gripped the key with both hands, leaning all her weight into the effort. It turned at last, just as the loose fence board scraped sideways. Not bothering about her bag, she wrenched the door open and fell into the kitchen, slamming the door behind her. Then she shot the bolt and sat down abruptly on the floor. Her legs were shaking too much to hold her up.

There was a long, long silence. She listened until her ears hurt, but she couldn't hear anyone coming closer. No feet crunched on the path. No hand fumbled round the lock or scraped across the door. Whoever it was, he seemed to have given up.

After ten minutes, she decided that it was ridiculous to wait any longer. Slowly and cautiously she stood up, still feeling exposed and vulnerable. The kitchen curtains hadn't been pulled right over the window, and she reached forward to tug them into place before she turned on the light.

But as she leaned across the sink, something shot upwards, suddenly, from below the window. A face—a grotesque, squashed, swollen face—jammed itself up against the glass, leering horribly at her.

There was a split second of stark, paralysed terror. Then she thought, *No! I won't! I won't be terrorized!* Grabbing up the nearest weapon she could find—the heavy rubber torch that hung by the door—she turned the key again and threw the door open.

She hadn't got anything as definite as a plan. She was just furiously, uncontrollably angry. If the face had still been there, she would have smashed the torch into it, as hard as she could.

But the man didn't wait. Even before she had the door open, he was running away, as fast as he could. She charged after him, but he made straight for the fence and crashed through it.

Common sense stopped Ashley there. Instead of following, she switched on the torch, trying to catch a glimpse of him.

All she saw was a dark anorak, but as she turned to go back inside the torch fell on a patch of colour, lying beside her abandoned carrier bag. It was a scarf. Bending down, she picked it up with the bag and took them both inside, locking the door and pulling the curtains together tightly before she put the light on.

She put the scarf down on the table, to look at it. It was a long, knitted scarf, with an odd design. Yellow and black stripes, with little black horses galloping across all the yellow stripes except the first three. They were irregular, lumpy horses, as though the person who knitted the scarf hadn't known quite how to make them look real. Certainly, there couldn't be another scarf like it in the world.

Not from Marks and Spencer, Ashley thought. And her fear dissolved into triumph. The stalker hadn't caught her. He'd given himself away and she'd got the extra piece of evidence she needed.

Now Eddie would help her!

GRANDMA

That was a joke, that scarf. His grandad knitted it for him. He was a great knitter, was Fred. Made me some lovely jumpers. One with pink roses all over it, because my name's Rose. And one with silver lurex in, for our silver wedding.

He liked jokes about names. The scarf was just to use up a load of old wool, really, but he suddenly got the idea of a joke for that as well. He'd already knitted the first few stripes, and he couldn't be bothered to unpick them, but he knitted the rest with the horses and wrapped it up as a Christmas present.

I never thought the boy would wear it, but he did. That's the funny thing about boys. When they're fourteen or fifteen, they won't touch anything that's not fashionable, but when they get a bit older there's no saying what'll take their fancy. And he loves that scarf, or he seems to. Always has it on when he comes to see me.

But then again, maybe he does it to please me. To remind me of Fred. It's the sort of thing he would do, bless him.

He's a funny boy.

115

Eighteen

Eddie'll fix it! Ashley thought, exultantly.

And then, from down the hall, Pauline's voice punctured her triumph.

'What's going on?'

Ashley groaned. She pushed the scarf in with the other things and hid the carrier bag behind the bread bin. Then she arranged her face into a smooth, blank mask and went along to the front room.

'Sorry, Mum. I thought I could get a drink without waking you.'

'I didn't hear you come down.'

'You were asleep,' Ashley said firmly.

That was how those conversations always went. As long as she didn't waver, Pauline would believe her. Or pretend she did, anyway.

There was a silence. Then Pauline said, 'Was I snoring, then?'

'Like a lion,' Ashley said cheerfully. 'I thought it would be quite safe if I slipped down and—'

'No you didn't!'

'What?' Ashley was so startled that she nearly let her mouth drop open. But she managed to keep up the mask. 'Sorry?' she said again. Politely puzzled, this time.

'You're lying,' Pauline said. 'Put the light on. I want to see your face.'

'But you need to sleep—'

'No I don't. I need to talk.'

Reluctantly, Ashley flicked the light switch. She saw her mother look her up and down, taking in what she was wearing.

'I was just getting a drink,' she said quickly, before Pauline could comment. And she gave her the blank, open-eyed stare that usually fixed things.

'So why are you dressed?' Pauline said. 'And what were you doing out in the garden?'

There was a longer silence. This time, Ashley took in her mother's fierce, determined expression. Something had changed. She wasn't sure she could stare her down any more.

Pauline patted the bed beside her. 'Come and sit here.'

'I really ought to go back to sleep—'

'If you don't come here now,' Pauline said evenly, 'I'll phone Janet up. This minute. At two o'clock in the morning. I'll say I can't cope any more and you'll have to go and live with her.'

'You wouldn't!'

'Oh yes, I would. It's only the truth. You're always going out at night and pretending that you haven't. You could be getting into all sorts of trouble. Meeting boys, and taking drugs, and—'

'Oh, for goodness' sake!' Ashley's calm finally broke. 'Do you think I'm that stupid? I wouldn't—'

'How do I know?'

They had both spoken more loudly than they meant to, and Mrs Macdonald hammered on her bedroom floor. But they hardly heard her. They were facing each other like enemies.

And all the time, Ashley was thinking frantically, *I can't tell her! I can't, I can't, I can't!*

'Well?' Pauline said.

Ashley never remembered hearing her voice sound so strong. So confident. But that only made it worse. If she knew everything, that might all collapse into ruins. They'd be back where they were before.

Ashley sat down on the bed. 'I wasn't going to tell you,' she said slowly.

'No kidding?' Pauline's voice was bitter and sarcastic. 'Do you ever tell me anything?'

'I'm only trying not to upset you!' Suddenly, Ashley saw a way of managing. A way of telling the truth—or some of it—without risking too much. She leaned forward. 'I suppose you ought to know, though. The last few evenings there's been . . . well, there's been someone in the garden. At night.'

'What sort of someone?' Pauline said cautiously.

'I don't know who he is, but—' Ashley jumped up. Now she'd worked out what to do, it was hard to keep herself from gabbling. 'Wait a minute, and I'll show you.'

She ran into the kitchen and pulled out the scarf, and the drawing of the footprint. Then she ran back and dropped them on to the bed.

'Look. These are the footprints he left. Joe drew the pattern so we could show Eddie Beale. That's where I went tonight. To see Eddie and ask if he would help. When I came back someone was lurking in the alley, and he dropped this scarf.'

She was talking deliberately fast, to shut out any questions. Pauline picked up the scarf, looking bewildered.

'Who's Eddie Beale? And what's he got to do with all this?'

'He's . . . ' Ashley faltered for a moment. 'He's a friend of Tricia's. And he knows everyone. He knows everything that's going on.'

'But why ask him? Why not phone the police?'

'The police?' Ashley made herself sound incredulous. 'What's the point? They never found out who burgled the chip shop last year, did they? They couldn't even catch the people who put Tony Cavalieri into a wheelchair. They're useless.'

Pauline ran the scarf through her hands. 'And you think this Eddie Beale can do better?'

'That's what Joe says. And Vikki does too. They say Eddie knows everyone, and he can always find out what's going on.'

Pauline frowned. 'And this scarf's going to help?' She turned it over, examining the other side. 'It looks rather familiar.'

'You've seen it?' Ashley was startled.

'I think so. Or maybe I've heard someone talking about it. There's some kind of story . . . ' Pauline frowned harder, trying to remember. 'It's no use. It's gone. Maybe Eddie can find out. But I still wish you'd phone the police.'

'Let's try this first. Please.' Ashley caught at her mother's arm. 'If Eddie finds out who it is, he'll just warn him off. And I won't have to go to court or anything. It'll save such a lot of fuss.'

Pauline wavered for a moment, and then she nodded. 'I suppose it won't do any harm. As long as there's no more trouble. But you'd better make sure the back door's locked and bolted.'

Ashley hadn't worked out how to contact Eddie. On the way back from school that afternoon, she watched out for Joe, but there was no sign of him. As she came along the Row, she was wondering whether her mother knew Tricia's telephone number.

Then she turned the corner into Railway Street and she knew she didn't have to bother about any of that. Eddie was at her house, waiting for her. She could tell, from the far end of the street.

It wasn't just the big car double-parked outside. It wasn't even the noise of the radio, coming from the front room. She guessed that he was there when she saw the children hanging around in little groups.

They were pretending to kick a ball about, or do a bit of skate-boarding, but it was all half-hearted. Really, they wanted to know what was going on, and why Eddie Beale had come to visit. As she pushed her way through, to get to the front door, she could hear them whispering his name.

The door wasn't even closed properly. She pushed it open and marched into the house. Even above the noise of the radio, she could hear Tricia and her mother giggling. And there was another woman's voice as well.

It was Sam. She was draped over the end of the bed, gulping with laughter as she pretended to pose. Joe was leaping around in front of her, with an imaginary camera, pulling intense, ridiculous faces.

'That's *fabulous*, sweetheart. *Really* sexy. But we need a bigger pout. And some more glare. Give it all your *glare*, Sammy. And the chin. The chin needs to be a *teensy* bit higher—'

They didn't even realize that Ashley had come in, but Eddie saw her. He was sitting at the table, watching everything with a detached, ironic stare. As Ashley came through the door, he moved one hand sharply, signalling to the others. *Stop.*

Joe broke off in mid-word and Tricia and Sam stopped laughing instantly. Only Pauline looked puzzled for a second. Then she saw Ashley in the doorway and she smiled.

'Hallo, Ash,' she said. 'Guess what? Tricia dropped in for a cup of tea, so I told her you wanted to see Eddie. And she phoned him straight away.'

'Hi.' Ashley raised a hand, feeling suddenly shy of Eddie now that he was in her house.

If he noticed, he ignored it. He didn't even waste time saying hallo. He picked up the black and yellow scarf from the table in front of him and ran it through his hands.

'Your mother says you've had someone round the back of the house again,' he said carefully. His eyes were bright and sharp, and Ashley understood what he meant. *We haven't told your mother the rest.*

Ashley nodded, cautiously. 'He chased me in last night. And he dropped that scarf when he ran away.'

'Did you see his face?' Eddie said sharply.

'I . . . sort of. He jammed it against the kitchen window, but it was all swollen and squashed up.'

'Stocking over his head,' said Sam. 'Probably an improvement on his real face.'

Eddie turned the scarf over in his hands. 'You're probably right. If this scarf belongs to the person I think it does.'

Ashley's fists clenched, and Pauline leaned forward.

'You know who it is?'

'Maybe.'

'Who?' Ashley said. 'Tell me!'

Eddie shook his head. 'Not yet. I want to be sure. I want *you* to be sure. I think we'll do a little test. Here!' He screwed the scarf into a ball and tossed it across the room to Joe. 'Put that on.'

Joe draped the scarf round his neck, tucking it inside his jacket. Eddie made an impatient movement.

'Not like that. Spread it out. So people can see the pattern.'

When it was rearranged, Joe had black horses galloping lumpily all the way across his chest. Eddie gave an approving nod.

'Go on then. Up to the Row and into all the shops. See what reaction you get. And take Ashley with you.'

They went, obediently. Ashley had forgotten the children round the door and she almost fell over one of the little ones, Dean Fox, from across the road. But he didn't fuss. He was much too interested in what was going on.

DEAN

'Course we wanted to know what was up. I mean—you don't expect to see Eddie Beale hanging round here in the daytime, do you? And you certainly don't expect to see him in Super-Ashley's house. Super oh-how-all-the-old-ladies-love-her Ashley. When Steve said Eddie was *there*, I thought he was conning me. But I hung around to see, anyway, in case he was right. When Eddie's around, something always happens.

121

The first thing that happened was Ashley coming home from school. She went straight in the house, but she didn't stay long. A couple of minutes later she was out again, with that kid who hangs round with Eddie. The kid whose mother lives with Vince Rowlands. He was wearing a huge great striped scarf.

'Hey, Waspy!' I said, without thinking. 'Off to sting someone?'

Steve nudged me, to tell me not to be so thick. Whatever the kid was doing, it was probably something for Eddie, and Eddie doesn't like people snooping. But it was OK. The kid looked round and pointed a finger to zap me, but he didn't look annoyed. He just went on up the road, with Ashley.

And we all followed him, of course.

They walked up to the Row and started mooching in and out of the shops. It was weird. They didn't buy anything, but they weren't pinching things either. (That would have been a laugh. Super-Ashley on the lift. I wish.) And they didn't seem to mind being followed.

Just as well, really. The further they went, the more kids they collected. There must have been fifteen or twenty of us by the time they walked into Fat Annie's.

And that was where it happened. Straight away, the minute they walked in. Annie looked up from the till and saw the scarf the kid was wearing and she went berserk. Turned bright purple and bellowed across the shop.

'Hey! You! What are you doing with my son's scarf?'

Nineteen

Ashley was three or four steps behind Joe, and Annie obviously thought she was just one of the crowd. Ignoring Ashley, she concentrated all her fury on Joe. She came marching across the shop and wrenched the scarf off his neck, tugging so hard she nearly choked him.

'Thieving little—can't leave things around for a moment without someone grabbing them. Greed, that's what's wrong with the world today. Greed and no morals. Now get out of my shop. And don't come back!'

Tossing the scarf down behind the counter, she seized Joe's collar and began to haul him towards the door, through the crowds of people who had edged in behind him.

Ashley would have followed but, as Joe went past, he turned his head towards her, away from Annie. He was mouthing a single word.

Shoes.

For a moment, Ashley couldn't work out what he meant Then, when he reached the door, he lifted his foot and shook it at her, exposing the sole. He was telling her to check out the footprints.

For the first time, Ashley took in what they had discovered. It was the Hyena's scarf.

But it can't be. It can't be the Hyena who did all those things.

It was his scarf.

She stood quite still and watched Annie struggling to get Joe over the threshold. All the kids outside were jostling her and jeering.

'What's the matter, Mrs Galt?'

'Did he steal the scarf, then?'

123

'Lovely scarf, innit? Wish I had one with dear little gee-gees all over it.'

'Want me to bash him for you, missus?'

Dear little gee-gees, Ashley thought. *G.G.s*

She felt someone staring at her. Turning to look back into the shop, she saw the Hyena coming out of the stockroom. Before she could react, he was smiling at her.

She stepped sideways, trying to get out of his line of sight, and her elbow caught a shelf full of chocolate bars. She knocked the first one out of place and the rest of them began to rain down on the floor, in an avalanche of red and brown wrappings.

'Oh, I'm sorry!' She bent down and started to scoop them up, frantically.

'It's all right. Please don't— Let me—' The Hyena knelt down beside her and grabbed at the bars, to stop her picking them up. She jumped away from him and stood up.

And there were the soles that had made the footprints in her garden.

There was no mistake. She knew the pattern by heart now. Three curves to each wave. Four waves on the sole and two on the heel. Six dots in between the front waves, and four nearer the back. Size ten or eleven at least.

It didn't seem real. But when she looked again, the pattern was still there. There was no doubt about it. The Hyena's shoes had left the footprints. The Hyena's scarf had been dropped in her garden.

He must be the stalker. The man who had sneaked into her garden and bashed at the sheep's skull until it splintered and broke. The one who had crouched under her bedroom window, by the drainpipe. The one who took those photos, and then drew on them . . .

The person who knew who she was.

She had to get out of the shop. Fast. Dropping the chocolate bars she was holding, she started for the door.

124

He bleated after her. 'Wait a moment! Wasn't there . . . um . . . wasn't there something—?'

'Nothing, thanks.' She shouted it without turning round. The idea of looking at him was unbearable. 'I've changed my mind.'

There were even more people hanging around outside now. Kids from the flats, who'd come down when they saw the crowd. Ashley pushed her way through them and ran down the road to where Joe was standing.

'You were great!' he called, before she reached him. 'That was a brilliant idea with the Mars Bars. Did he have the right shoes?'

Ashley didn't want to answer with all the kids standing round. But her head was whirling, and she had to speak. To share it with someone. 'He . . . he . . . I saw—'

She could tell, from the way people were staring at her, that she looked peculiar, and she tried to calm down. But Joe wouldn't leave her alone.

'It was him,' he said. 'Wasn't it?'

There were strange kids everywhere, pressing in on her. Crowding nearer, with their mouths open and their ears flapping, trying to hear what her answer would be. She had just enough sense left to realize that she mustn't say any more. Pushing past Joe, she began to hurry home. Not quite running, but marching fast, with her hands in her pockets and her head down. She must get home. That was all she could think. She had to get home and see Eddie.

But Eddie hadn't hung around there. She was only halfway down the road when his car came gliding up towards her. Sam waved and pulled into the kerb. Eddie was in the back, with a can of beer, and he leaned across and pushed the door open.

'Get in,' he said.

Ashley hesitated and Joe pushed at her shoulder. 'Go on!' he said. 'It's better than talking with your mother there.'

They slid in and Eddie flicked at Joe's shoulders, where the scarf had been.

'Well?'

'We found the owner,' Joe said. 'He—'

'It *can't* be him!' Ashley said fiercely. 'It's nonsense.'

Eddie raised his eyebrows. 'No? What about the shoes? Did you check those?'

'Yes I did, but—'

'So what's your problem?'

She didn't know. She looked down at her fingers, plaiting them together in her lap.

There was a straggle of kids coming down the road now, looking curiously at Eddie's car. He leaned forward and tapped Sam on the shoulder.

'Drive round the block a couple of times. Then we'll take Ashley home.'

Sam nodded, put the car into gear and drove off. As they reached the Row, Ashley turned her head away, to avoid seeing Fat Annie's. She met Eddie's eyes.

'I'll tell you why you won't believe it,' he said silkily. 'It's because you know him, isn't it? You can't cope with it being someone you know.'

That was part of it. But there was more than that. 'It's not just because I know him. It's . . . how can *he* be the one who knows me? Like that? It's unbelievable. If I hadn't seen—'

'But you did see.' Eddie's voice was still silky, but it was relentless. 'He's the one who's been stalking you all right.'

'But . . . what am I going to do? Even if he stops, I'll see him every day. I'll know he said those things.'

'He hasn't got to be there,' Eddie said softly.

For a moment, Ashley didn't know what he meant. Her mouth fell open, and she imagined nightmares.

Death.

'Don't be silly,' Eddie said impatiently, so that she knew he had read her mind. 'There's no need for anything heavy. You've got him over a barrel. He's a shopkeeper.'

'So?' Ashley hadn't got a clue what he was talking about.

'Spell it out for her, Joe.'

Joe tossed his head, shaking imaginary curls. 'You've only got to tell people, you know.' His voice rose an octave. 'I'm not going *there* again! Not if he's been stalking that poor little girl. I mean—you could get *murdered*, couldn't you? And I'm certainly not sending my children! We'll do our shopping somewhere else from now on!'

'You see?' Eddie said softly. 'That's all it takes. The shop will go bust, and he and Annie will have to sell it and move.'

'But that's—' Ashley swallowed. 'That's not fair. Why should Annie suffer?'

There was a sniff from the front of the car. '*Poor* Annie.' Sam's voice was like vinegar. 'And she's so gentle and kind, too.'

'Yeah,' Joe said. 'Leave her alone, Ash. What does it matter if the Hyena bashes your head in? You can't be mean to Annie, can you?'

Eddie didn't say anything. He just waited.

Ashley plaited her fingers harder. 'But . . . he wouldn't really *hurt* me.'

'No?' Eddie shrugged. 'Well, you can believe that if you like. But stalkers do hurt people. Quite often.'

Ashley tried to imagine the Hyena hurting her. Putting his hands round her neck. Sticking a knife between her ribs. Her brain wouldn't make the pictures.

'So what are you going to do?' Eddie said. He dropped his beer can on to the floor and crunched it suddenly under his foot. The metal twisted into sharp, ugly creases. 'All you have to do is say yes, and I'll do the rest. I can put the word about, as long as you don't deny it. Do you want that?'

Ashley looked at the beer can. In her head, she saw the Hyena's heavy foot coming down like that, on top of the sheep's skull. She saw the bone splinter. And she thought, *That could be my skull.*

'Yes,' she said. It took an effort, but she didn't see what else she could say. 'Yes. Tell everyone.'

There was no time to think again. Eddie nodded briskly and Sam whipped round the final corner and pulled up outside Ashley's house.

'Tell Tricia and Doug we're going,' Eddie said.

Ashley nodded and dived out of the car. There were kids outside her house again, but she ignored them all, even the ones she knew. She wanted to be inside, away from everyone.

NADINE

She just dived into the house, without saying a word. And that made it even more mysterious. I couldn't work out what was going on.

I thought it was a fight at first, when I saw the crowd outside Fat Annie's. I was up in Diane's flat, minding her kids, and Kimberley called out from the window.

'Look! Look!'

Then she made for the door. She's only six, and there's nothing she likes better than watching a punch-up.

She was out of the flat and into the lift before I could stop her. I picked up Carl and chased after her, but I didn't catch up until we reached the cinema. And even then I couldn't persuade her to go back. She dragged me over the road to Fat Annie's.

Annie was throwing a boy out of the shop. Everyone was yelling and screaming and Kimberley started laughing like a maniac. The minute Annie went back inside, the boy darted over to the shop window and peered in.

That's when I noticed the girl.

It was that girl from Railway Street. She was in the shop, and she was bending over, picking something up. Mr Galt was there too, helping her, and when the boy saw that, he grinned—you've never seen such a huge grin— and punched the air, like, YESS!

A second later, the girl came running out, and he was on to her in a flash.

'Great idea with the Mars Bars! What about his shoes?'

Shoes? There must have been twenty or thirty kids there, and we all stopped yelling, because we wanted to know what shoes had got to do with anything. But the girl didn't say a word. She charged off towards her house and the boy ran after her.

And so did Kimberley.

That child's a menace. The minute I let go of her hand, she was away. I dodged after her, with Carl kicking my ribs to bits, but I didn't catch her until halfway down Railway Street. And there was the girl, getting into a car.

Eddie Beale's car.

If Eddie Beale's involved, there must be a story somewhere. But we didn't find out what it was, even though we all went and waited outside the girl's house. Like I said, she swept in like a film star. With *no comment* written all over her face. I felt like kicking the front door down.

You know how it is with a story. You've *got* to hear the end. She can *no comment* all she likes, but I'm going to find out what's going on. I'll go mad if I don't.

There were loads of kids outside the shop. They saw everything, and they feel just the same as me. Someone's going to get the story, sooner or later . . .

Twenty

Tell everyone, Ashley had said. But she'd never thought it could happen so fast. The next morning, when she was on her way to school, Lisa came bouncing up to her.

'Is that right? The Hyena's been stalking you?'

Ashley was caught off balance, and she just muttered something. But when the second person asked—and the third, and the fourth—she gathered her wits.

'I don't want any trouble,' she whispered. 'I can't say—'

That was all it took. No lies. Not even any need to tell the truth. Dozens of people had seen the business with the scarf and they were all desperate to know what was going on. By lunchtime, pretty well everyone in the school knew that Ashley was being stalked by the man from Fat Annie's. And that she wouldn't talk about it.

'They think you're scared silly,' Vikki said.

All through break, she hovered round, protecting Ashley, and at lunchtime she called in reinforcements. Matt. From the moment they left class, he was just behind Ashley, ready to sort out anyone who tried to speak to her.

If it hadn't been so irritating, it would have been funny. Matt was six foot two and very tough, but Vikki was determined to make him run round after Ashley. She stood there and stamped her foot, until he agreed.

'You're not to let people annoy her!' she said fiercely. 'She's got enough to put up with, without people going on at her. If anyone wants to know about the stalking, *I'll* tell them.'

And that was how it was. When the bell went, Matt ushered Ashley into lunch and stood beside her, like a sentry. If people tried to talk, he glared at them and once or twice he even took a threatening step forward. That was as far as it went, though. No one wanted to tangle with Matt.

Meanwhile, Vikki was having the time of her life, spreading the story to everyone who hadn't got the details. 'Yes!' Ashley heard her saying. Over and over again. 'There was a smashed skull. And photographs with *horrible* things scrawled on them. And he peered in at the kitchen window!'

Everyone was getting the message. And Vikki made sure they remembered it when they went home.

'Matt'll walk you back,' she said to Ashley. 'Won't you, Matt?'

'It's OK,' Ashley said faintly. 'Really. I don't need—'

'Of course you do!' Vikki was determined. 'Suppose you met the Hyena? You've got to be careful, Ash.'

After school, she and Matt both marched Ashley through the estate and past the cinema.

'Keep on the outside,' Vikki said. 'While we're going past the shop. You don't want him staring at you.'

But by the time they reached the traffic lights, they could see there wasn't a problem. The pavement outside Fat Annie's was crowded.

'What are they doing?' Ashley said.

Vikki pulled a face. 'They're ghouls, aren't they? Come to take a look at the Monster.'

'You mean—all those people know about the stalking?'

'Of course they do,' Matt said. 'Come on, Ashley. *Everyone* knows.'

'That's why there's no one *inside* the shop!' Vikki said triumphantly.

She was peering through the window as they passed. The Hyena was at the till and as she spoke he glanced up at the crowd outside, obviously puzzled. He caught Vikki's eye and she pulled a face and looked away.

'Yuck! Did you see him?' She put an arm round Ashley's shoulders, hustling her away. 'I'd like to go in there and tell him just what I think!'

131

She half-turned, as if she meant it, and Matt looked anguished.

'Victoria! You mustn't! If he starts noticing you—'

The sentence broke off, as if it was too frightening to finish. Matt began to hurry both of them, slipping slightly behind, as if he wanted to block the Hyena's view.

'It's OK,' Ashley said feebly. 'I'm sure he won't do anything.'

Matt took no notice. Once he made up his mind he was impossible to shift. 'It'll be better if you don't walk home this way,' he said. 'It's not much further if you go round the top of the estate. And Ashley can go into the Spar up there. Can't you, Ash?'

'I . . . suppose so.' It was the first time Ashley had thought about shopping. The Spar was another ten minutes walk away, but it was the only choice she had.

Vikki was already organizing her.

'If you bring your list into school, we can come with you. And Matt can carry the shopping.'

Matt nodded vigorously. 'We can go home together every day, if you like.'

'I really don't think you need to.'

'Of course we do!' Vikki's arm tightened. 'We're your friends, aren't we?'

She wasn't taking any chances. She and Matt marched stoutly down the road, all the way to Ashley's front door. One on each side.

'We'll leave you when you're safe,' Vikki said. 'When we've checked there's nothing . . . *unusual* going on.'

But when they reached the house, a cheerful voice called out as Ashley opened the front door.

'Come *in*, sweetheart! Pauline and I are playing Scrabble, and I'm *destroying* her!'

'What the—' Matt's eyes opened very wide. Then he stuck his head round the front room door and laughed. 'Oh, it's you. Hi, Joe.'

As they went into the room, Pauline looked up and grinned. 'Hallo, Vikki. Hallo, Matt. You know Joe, do you? He's a terrible cheat!'

Vikki just laughed, but Matt obviously knew Joe properly, because he went to read the words on the board. '*Inax*? *Klooga*? *Mzaarg*? What's the matter, pie-face? Can't you read?'

'You just don't understand the creative mind!' Joe threw himself back in the chair, spreading his arms flamboyantly. 'I like to expand the language!'

'I think my mind's expanded enough.' Pauline pushed her letter rack aside. 'My waist wants a turn now. Nip up to the shop and get some crumpets will you, Ashie?'

There was an instant of utter stillness.

Then Vikki reacted. 'Matt can go.'

'No, it's OK—' Ashley said.

But Vikki had already taken the money Pauline was holding out, and she was packing Matt off through the front door.

'If you run, you can go to the Spar instead, and she'll never know. You'll be back before we've made the tea.'

She slammed the door behind him and then followed Ashley down the hall, into the kitchen. But she wasn't really interested in helping with the tea. She opened the back door.

'Shall I take a look in the garden? In case there's . . . you know. In case he's been there.'

'You don't need to,' Ashley said quickly.

But it was too late already. They had both seen the envelope, just outside the back door.

'Don't touch it,' Ashley muttered.

But Vikki couldn't resist it. She bent down and picked up the envelope. 'Hey, it's *heavy*.'

'Don't—' Ashley said again, uselessly.

Vikki ignored her and ripped the flap open. Ashley saw a quick flash of red, and then Vikki sucked in a huge, terrified breath and opened her mouth to scream.

Ashley got there just in time. She jammed her hand over Vikki's mouth and hissed in her ear. 'Be quiet! Be *quiet*! Or my mum will hear.'

Shuddering, Vikki pushed the envelope at her, wriggling free and backing away. There was a polythene bag in it, with a red mess sealed inside. As Ashley took it, the polythene bag tipped out on to the table, falling flat so that they could see the crimson shape inside. Perfectly sculpted. Oozing blood round the edges.

It was cut into a neat heart shape, like something from a Valentine card, but without the prettiness. Raw and ugly. Vikki was staring at it with her eyes wide.

'What is it?' she whispered.

Ashley forced herself to look. Forced herself to stretch out and prod at the polythene. The package squashed under her finger in a soft, familiar way.

'It's OK,' she said. 'It's only raw liver. Look.'

'Only!' Vikki pulled a face. 'It's disgusting.'

Ashley picked up the polythene bag by one edge.

'Yuck!' Vikki whispered. 'Oh *yuck*! Get rid of it!'

It went straight into the dustbin outside. And Ashley made them both strong cups of tea, laced with sugar.

MATT

Victoria hasn't got a clue how serious all this is. It's a game to her. She likes a bit of drama, but she doesn't know how tough things are, out in the streets. She's just playing at looking after Ash.

I wish she hadn't got mixed up in it.

Who's to say he'll stick to stalking Ashley? I mean, Ash is OK, but next to Victoria—there's no comparison, is there? If he starts turning his snoopy eyes on Vikki, I'll . . . I'll—

I went past Annie's on my way to the Spar. The crowds had gone and it looked pretty empty in there. *He* was standing at the counter, looking as if he didn't know what to do with himself.

I really wanted to go in there and punch him. I wanted to get him by the throat and say: What d'you mean by it? Why don't you knock it off?

The Spar was full of people when I got there, and I had to queue to pay, but I didn't care about that. I'm not going into Annie's again.

And I'll tell my mates to lay off it too. Maybe Ginger can spread the word about a bit. She knows lots of people, especially now she's going out with Phil. And she's always asking me about Ashley, too. She ought to take an interest in what's happening to her.

It shows us up, having something like that happening round here. If we don't get rid of him, it'll look as if anyone can push us around.

We've got to get him out.

Twenty-One

'You can't stay in this house,' Vikki said. 'You can't!' She curled her hands round the cup of tea and Ashley could see the surface of the liquid shivering.

'So what do we do?' she said. 'Book a room at the Ritz? We haven't got anywhere else to go, Vik.'

'But it's not safe!'

'Keep your voice down.' Ashley poured her own tea, and some for Pauline and Joe. 'It was only a bit of liver, you know. Just a cheap trick.'

'It was *horrible*!' Vikki shuddered.

'I told you not to touch it.' Ashley sat down at the table beside her. 'Look, I'm sorry you had a shock, but it's nearly over. Now we know who it is, he's not going to be around for long. If Eddie's right.'

'Of course he's right!' Vikki said. 'You wait till I start telling people about the liver. No one's going to go near that shop!'

'You can't tell every single person.'

'I don't need to. People are all telling each other. It's spreading like a forest fire.'

There was a loud knock on the door. Vikki jumped up, eager with relief.

'That's Matt! I'll go and let him in!'

Ashley sat and thought about forest fires. And the way they spread.

Vikki hadn't been exaggerating. By Saturday morning, the story had reached Janet.

Ashley knew she'd heard, the moment she saw her. She

136

arrived with the twins, as they'd arranged, at half-past ten and when Ashley opened the door, Karen and Louise were on the doorstep, bouncing up and down as usual. Janet was beside them, with a bunch of flowers in her hand as if she'd come to visit someone in hospital. And behind her was Frank, who almost never came.

Janet erupted over the doorstep.

'Oh, *Ashley*! Why didn't you—?'

Frank prodded her arm—*not in front of the twins*—and she stopped elaborately, clapping a hand over her mouth. Then she put on her brightest smile.

'In you go then, girls! I bet Mummy's dying to show you her new hairstyle!'

That worked straight away for Karen. She gave a loud whoop and threw herself over the doorstep and across the hall. Louise didn't move so fast. She looked up at Ashley.

'It's OK,' Ashley said. 'Come in, Lou. Mum's been waiting for you.'

She would have liked to keep Louise there, as a shield against Frank and Janet, but that wasn't fair. And anyway, if Janet wanted to talk to her she would make sure she did, sooner or later. Better to get it over.

But Janet wasn't going to start until she'd been through the whole greetings ceremony. She swooped into the front room, stopped dead and let out a delighted shriek.

'Paulie, you look fabulous! Absolutely elegant, and so *well*! You should have had your hair cut years ago!'

Pauline reached for her sticks, but Janet wouldn't let her stand up.

'Don't move. The girls will tell you what they've been up to. Frank and I are going to take a look at the garden. With Ashley. She can tell us *all your news*.'

It was obvious what she meant. And just in case Pauline had missed the point, she finished with a long, sympathetic stare. Ashley was terrified that she was going to go on, but the twins interrupted her, bouncing across the room.

'You look great, Mummy!' Karen said. 'You look brilliant! Let's have our hair cut like that, Lou!'

Louise didn't answer. She was staring, and stretching out one finger to touch the short curls at the back of her mother's neck.

'Don't you like it?' Pauline said.

Louise looked at her, without smiling. 'What did they do with your hair? After they cut it off?'

'I kept it for you!' Pauline said. 'One for you, and one for Karen. Look!'

She pulled open the drawer beside the table and lifted out two long plaits. Ashley had a pang of such jealousy that she could hardly speak. *That's mine!* she wanted to say. She'd brushed that hair and teased out the tangles and plaited it, for years and years and years. But her mother wasn't going to give *her* a plait. She hadn't even told her they were there.

'Oh, how sweet!' Janet was cooing.

Louise reached for a plait and a huge smile spread across her face, showing the gap between her front teeth. And Ashley thought, *I wasn't much older than that when Mum started being ill.*

Turning away abruptly, she headed into the kitchen, to give Janet an excuse to follow and talk to her. Janet seized the opportunity.

'Let's go and look at the garden now, Frank. Ashley can show us if there's anything that needs doing.'

She swept them both in front of her, down the hall. As Frank stepped into the kitchen, Ashley saw him wince at the broken shelves and the worn-out floor. He hated shabbiness. Hurriedly he pushed the back door open and went out into the garden.

It was obvious, immediately, that there was nothing that needed doing. The grass had stopped growing for the winter, and Ashley had pruned the roses a month ago. But they all knew that the garden was only an excuse. They were going to have A Talk.

Janet closed the back door with dramatic care. Then she turned and flung her arms round Ashley, knocking the breath out of her.

'Oh, you poor little *thing*! Why didn't you ring us? Why didn't you *say*? You must have been having a dreadful time.'

Over her shoulder, Ashley could see Frank's face puckering, as though he felt slightly sick.

'I . . . it's all *right*,' she gasped. 'I'm fine, honestly.'

'But you must have been so terrified!' Janet loosened her grip and stood back, looking earnestly into Ashley's eyes. 'Ever since Mrs Macdonald rang me up last night, I haven't been able to rest, thinking of it. I didn't close my eyes for a moment last night, did I, Frank?'

Frank shook his head stiffly and turned away to walk round the garden. Looking for evidence, Ashley thought. Janet glanced at him and then leaned closer, whispering.

'Don't you take any notice of that. He's just as upset as I am, but—you know how men are. He's very keen to help, though.'

'There's nothing to *do*,' Ashley said. 'Honestly. It's just a silly thing—'

'Have you been to the police?'

'I—' Ashley thought fast. She didn't want Janet latching on to that. 'I *can't* go to the police. I don't want to worry Mum.'

Janet stared. 'What do you mean? You haven't told her?'

'Only a bit. She knows someone's been lurking round the back of the house, but that's all. It's not good for her to worry.' That was true, but it was a cheap excuse. Ashley looked down at her feet, hating herself for it.

It worked, though. Janet patted her arm with a hand that trembled slightly. 'You're a good, brave girl. But you must be careful.'

'I am.' Ashley went on looking at her feet. 'There hasn't been anything dangerous, really. He just followed me home one night—'

139

'That's your own fault,' Frank said sourly, coming back down the garden. 'It's asking for trouble, going out after dark.'

It's dark when I walk home from school, Ashley wanted to say. But it would be silly to annoy him. She smiled meekly.

'No, Uncle Frank.'

'And you ought to keep away from that man. And the shop. Get your groceries somewhere else.'

'Yes, Uncle Frank.'

'And you must *talk to us*,' Janet squeezed Ashley's arm. 'Learning something like that from an outsider was—well, it was hurtful. You *must* phone up and keep us in touch, Ashie. And if things get worse, *we'll* go to the police.'

Ashley nodded, but she didn't mean it. There was no way of explaining things to Janet. She hadn't got a clue what it was like, living by the Row.

'It sounds as if Ashley's going to be quite safe. As long as she's sensible.' Frank's voice was clipped and chilly. 'No point in making unnecessary fuss. Now how about some coffee? I don't want to hang about too long.'

They only stayed an hour. And when they went, there was a long brown plait, left lying on the couch.

'That's Karen's,' Ashley said. 'Do you want me to—?'

'Oh, leave it!' Pauline said, irritably. 'It can go in the bin if she doesn't want it.'

She was tired and petulant. When she wasn't looking, Ashley coiled up the plait and pushed it into her pocket. Then she fetched a dustpan and started to brush the crumbs off the carpet, before she forgot and trod them in.

'Leave that, Ash. I want to talk to you.'

'It won't take a minute—'

'LEAVE IT!'

Ashley dropped the dustpan and sat back on her heels. 'What's the matter?'

Pauline put a hand into her cardigan pocket. 'This came through the door. Karen picked it up while you were in the garden with Frank and Janet.'

Even before she pulled out the envelope, Ashley knew what it would look like. Long and brown. *But not liver*, she thought frantically. *Please not liver*.

It wasn't liver. Just another piece of paper. Pauline pulled it out.

'I thought it was a circular or something,' she said. 'That's why I opened it.'

Ashley held out a hand, but her mother didn't pass the paper over. She spread it out and held it up for Ashley to see. The message had been cut out of newspaper and stuck on, in whole words and single letters.

CinDY

You've gOt such tHin BONEs. You'VE got suCH Red BLOOD. YOU CAN't cARry On Like thaT. YouLL Fall.

FRANK

I reckon Ashley's made the whole thing up.

I've always had a feeling about that girl. She's too good to be true. Whatever you say, she smiles and agrees with you, but you can't tell what's going on in that head of hers. Give me our Karrie, any day, I say. She may be a bit of a madam, but you know where you are with her. Even Lulu will climb up on your knee and tell you what's the matter with her. But Ashley—she's devious. And she's itching for attention. You can see it in her face.

Janet won't hear a word against her, of course. She's always going on at me to talk to Pauline and tell her it's not fair to make Ashley work so hard. Janet reckons she ought to come and live with us. But I'm not having any of that.

'You don't know when you're well off,' I say. 'We've got our girls—isn't that enough for you?'

Because Karrie and Lulu are our girls really. We've had them since they were born, or very nearly. I don't know why Janet keeps up this nonsense of taking them to see Pauline. They haven't got the link with her. Not any more.

And it doesn't do them any good to drag them to a place like that. The house is bad enough, and the neighbourhood's worse. All that filth and graffiti. And the way people stare. We stopped off at the shops, and there was a man staring down at us from one of the windows upstairs. I don't want Karen and Louise dragged into all that, and there's no need. We've got the twins, and Pauline's got Ashley, and it all works fine.

It's true Pauline's hard up, but she can't really expect us to do any more. And we're certainly not taking on Little Miss Ashley Ice Cream.

She's the sort that puts on a good performance, but you never know what's going on inside her head. If you really want to know, I'm sorry for that chap in the shop. He's probably smiled at her a couple of times, and she's built up the whole thing in her imagination. He's in for trouble, if you ask me.

And the shop's suffering already. We stopped off there because Janet wanted to take a look at the man, so I said why not buy some flowers for Pauline. But there was no man there. Just a fat woman. And the flowers were rubbish. Jan had a job finding a bunch that wasn't wilting. The fruit and vegetables were past their best as well.

If you ask me, that shop's in a bad way.

Twenty-Two

CinDY

You've gOt such tHin BONEs. You'VE got suCH Red
BLOOD. YOU CAN't cARry on Like thaT. YouLL Fall.

For a split second—just the faintest flicker of time—Ashley
looked at the pasted newspaper letters and thought she was
going to tell her mother the whole thing.

Then common sense took over.

'It must be a mistake,' she said quickly. 'Look, it's not for
me at all. It says Cindy.'

Pauline gave her a long look. 'Who's that?'

'Cindy? She's—' Ashley knew it was boasting, but she
couldn't resist the temptation. 'She's a climber. No one knows
who she is, but she gets into the most extraordinary places—
really high—and writes her name there, to show she's been.'

Pauline frowned. 'You mean—graffiti?'

'Sort of. Only with lots of colours and shading and stuff.'

Ashley felt her face going pink. Quickly she turned away
and picked up the dustpan again.

'Shall I get the lunch?'

She could feel Pauline's brain working. Adding things up.
Maybe it was best to be out of the way. Scooping the last few
crumbs into the pan, she headed for the door, but she didn't
quite make it in time.

'Ashley?'

'Mmm?' Ashley didn't look round.

'What's going on?'

It wasn't an ordinary question. Ashley knew Pauline was
watching her and she answered smoothly, without turning
round.

143

'Some kid's obviously decided I'm Cindy. Maybe they've seen me climbing in gym. I'm pretty good at it. Or maybe it's not only me who's got a letter like that. Perhaps someone's delivered lots, to all sorts of people. To see who reacts. Shall I ask Vikki if she's got one too?'

Pauline hesitated. Then she folded the letter up and slipped it back into the envelope. 'That might be a good idea. Take it and show her. Here.'

She held the letter out, and Ashley was forced to turn round, to take it. But by then she had her face under control.

Until Pauline said, 'Ashie—'

It wasn't the word. It was the way she said it, as if she were talking to someone really small. A four year old. For a moment, Ashley had the most terrible, overwhelming longing for that to be true. She wanted to say, *Oh, Mum, I'm in such trouble.*

Then she looked at her mother's swollen, twisted fingers on the envelope and knew she couldn't do it.

'Oh, Mum, why do you *fret* so much?' Taking the envelope, she pushed it into her pocket. 'I'll go and talk to Vikki after lunch, if you like.'

She picked up the dustpan and brush and went out of the room, just in time. If she hadn't left then, she would have started screaming. It was like balancing on a rope of twisted lies. She kept having to wind in another strand, and another, to keep herself from crashing to the ground.

She opened the larder cupboard and chose a tin of soup for lunch, wondering how long it would all go on. How long would she have to play at being normal, while she waited for more and more horrible messages?

She upended the tin, and the soup flooded out. Tomato soup. Bright scarlet. And the words of the letter flooded into her mind.

You'VE got suCH Red BLOOD . . .

And in that instant, she knew she couldn't just sit around and wait. She couldn't cope if she had to be a victim,

144

looking over her shoulder and inventing excuses to stop her mother finding out. Maybe Eddie's plan would work in the end, but that wasn't enough. She had to do something herself. She had to be in charge.

As she put the soup saucepan on to the gas ring, she saw how to do it. Only one thing made sense. She imagined herself into the scene, as clearly as if she were watching a film. The same little pictures played themselves over and over again. She would take the bones and the letters and the photos, she would go up the road, she would push that door open, and then—

And then—

But it wasn't quite like a film. It was more like a clip that cut out exactly when it had you hooked. If she wanted to know the whole story, she had to step into it and make it real.

By the time she poured the soup into the bowls, her mind was made up. She took the soup into the front room and shared it with Pauline, chatting cheerfully about Janet and Frank and the twins. And about how she was going to visit Vikki after lunch.

But she hadn't got the faintest intention of visiting Vikki. When she'd done the washing up, she went upstairs and piled everything into her school backpack. She was sorry that she couldn't take the scratched drainpipe, or the liver heart, but she had enough for what she wanted to do.

Rattling down the stairs, she stuck her head round the front room door, without going right in, so that her mother wouldn't see the backpack.

'OK, Mum. I'm going round to Vikki's now. If she doesn't know anything about this Cindy stuff, she soon will. You know what she's like. Bye.'

Pauline's mouth opened, but Ashley didn't wait to hear

what she was going to say. Waving briskly, she went out and closed the front door firmly behind her.

It was a crisp, cold day. As she went up the road, she was busy pulling her coat round her and pushing her hands into her pockets. The busyness kept her mind full and she didn't need to think at all about the mad, inconceivable thing she was planning. All she had to do was keep walking, until she saw the shop. And all the people inside.

Her audience.

On she went, round the corner and along the Row until she reached Fat Annie's. Then she stopped and looked in at the window.

And her heart dropped like a broken lift.

In her imaginary clip, the shop had been crowded with people, with Fat Annie at the till and the Hyena skulking somewhere near the magazine rack. She had planned to march straight up to Annie and say, *I've got something here that belongs to your son.* Then she was going to tip out everything in the bag, all over the counter.

But Annie wasn't there. There was no one in the shop at all, except the Hyena. He was standing at the till, reading the newspaper. Ashley stared at his doughy face and the way the newspaper shivered in his hands, and she wanted to be a giant, so that she could step on the shop and squash him flat, the way children squash slugs. Her skin shrank round her in revulsion.

He was the one. He'd sent her those horrible messages and the disgusting liver heart. He'd chased her in the dark, and breathed down the phone, into her ear. *Cindy . . . thin bones . . .* He was—

Then he looked up, straight at her. The shock of it was like a blow in the ribs. All he did was smile, but it knocked the breath out of her, so that she couldn't do anything clever or subtle. All she could do was run away or go in to face him. And she'd had enough of running away. That was why she was there.

Taking a deep breath, she pushed the door open.

JANET

We went into McDonald's after we left Pauline, as a treat for the girls. And we'd hardly got home before the phone rang. When Frank answered it, he sighed, the way he does if it's Pauline or Ashley, and passed the phone straight to me. *Can't they ever leave you alone?* he was mouthing.

I thought it was Ashley, of course. I thought something else had happened. I grabbed the phone out of his hand.

'Ashie?' I said. 'Is that you? Is everything all right?'

Only it wasn't Ashley. It was Pauline. And she sounded desperate.

Maybe you can't see what's startling in that. Lots of people would sound desperate all the time, if they had Pauline's life. But she's always been the strong one. She's never given in. Not even when Ben died. Not even when the arthritis got so bad she could hardly stand up, and she had to move into that horrible house, with hardly any money. Frank and I have helped her a lot, of course, but she's never asked us to. Even when we took the girls, it was as if she was doing us a favour and giving us her twins because we couldn't have any children of our own.

There's times I've longed for her to give in. I've seen her so tense, so uptight, that I've said, *Go on, Paul. Shout and scream.* Moan *a bit.* But she never let go, not once. She's always the big sister, being wonderful. And I'm always the little sister who's not quite good enough.

But that day, it was quite different. *Oh, Jan,* she said, *I don't know what to do. I'm so scared. There's something wrong with Ashley and she won't tell me and I don't know what to do about it.*

She sounded as if she was going to collapse into tears. I wanted to reach down the phone and hug her.

Oh, Jan, please help me . . .

That was when I knew I had to tell her.

147

Twenty-Three

As Ashley walked into the shop, the Hyena looked up, eagerly, and smiled again. It was like watching a wolf smile at her, like watching a tiger. But there was no going back. She was in the shop, and she had to go through with what she'd planned, or things would only get worse.

Do it now, she thought. *Before there's time to be afraid. Now!*

She didn't dare to hesitate. Pulling the pack off her back, she walked straight up to the till and tipped the whole lot out, on to the counter. Letters. Skull. Photographs. They spilled over the grey surface, and the Hyena's hands went out, instinctively, to stop them sliding off.

'Look at them!' Ashley said fiercely. Shouting. 'Do you like them? Are you proud of them?' Her voice rose, but she didn't try to control it. She wanted it to batter him, like a cudgel. 'I'm sick of it! D'you hear? I'm sick of being chased and phoned and persecuted. Why don't you leave me alone?'

The Hyena didn't say anything. He was staring at her, white-faced, with his tongue flicking nervously over his lips.

'Everything you send me, I'm going to show people!' Ashley yelled. 'What d'you think about that? What do you think people will make of this—?'

She pushed the skull at him.

'—or *this*—?'

She splayed the photographs roughly in her fingers and slammed them down on top of his newspaper.

'—or THIS?'

With both hands, she wrenched the latest note open so that it lay accusingly in front of them both. The newspaper letters danced in front of her eyes.

148

... such tHin BONEs ...

... Red BLOOD ...

... suCH Red BLOOD ... YOU CAN't cARry On Like thaT ... YouLL Fall

... YouLL Fall ...

... YouLL Fall

Youll Fall ... CinDY ... CinDY ... CinDY

The Hyena was utterly stunned, but that only made her angrier. And she could feel her voice giving out, catching in her sore, raw throat. Before it gave way entirely, she picked up the newspaper note and pushed it at him, almost into his face.

'Look!' she shouted. 'LOOK! Are you proud of sending that to me? Did you—?'

She didn't go on, because the Hyena's face changed suddenly. It began to tremble, and he looked desolate. Distraught. *Got you!* thought Ashley. She let the note fall.

'Well?' she said.

When the Hyena spoke, his voice was a whisper. 'No,' he said. 'Oh, no. Please—'

She thought he was going to beg, to ask her not to give him away, and she stood there waiting for him to plead. So that she could refuse.

He was staring down at the note. When his eyes lifted and found her face, they were full of tears.

'Please,' he said. 'I . . . oh please—'

Ashley was flooded with triumph. There was no faking an expression like that. She'd beaten him!

'Please,' he said again. 'It's not true. Say it's not true.'

'What?' The triumph wavered. 'What are you talking about?'

'You're not . . . you're not really Cindy, are you? Please say you're not. You mustn't be Cindy!'

Some things don't make any sense. Some things are too unexpected to take in. All you can do is fix on a tiny part.

Ashley looked down at the grey letters and the Hyena's words rattled round her like the clatter of a marching band.

You mustn't be Cindy!

'Why not?' she said, half croaking. 'Why can't I be Cindy?'

'Because . . . because . . . '

He shrank backwards, but she couldn't bear not to know. Leaning over the counter, she hissed at him.

'What are you talking about? *Why* can't I be Cindy?'

'Because . . . because . . . '

Flick, flick went his tongue over his lips. He was choking with embarrassment and effort, but Ashley wasn't going to give up.

'*Why* can't I be Cindy?'

The words wrenched themselves out of him. Furiously. So that he was suddenly shouting them into her face.

'Because you're different from the others. Because you're good!'

'What?' Ashley's hands dropped away. She felt numb. 'What are you talking about?'

Behind her, the doorbell clanged and she heard someone walk into the shop. A man's shoes clumped heavily and somehow she managed to step back from the counter to let him buy his cigarettes. As he asked for them, he glanced sideways at her, but she didn't look back and after a moment he went away.

'I thought you weren't like the others,' the Hyena said, when the door closed again. He was talking in a low, painful mutter now. 'They come in from school and steal things and . . . um . . . make fun of me and treat me—'

He couldn't say it. Ashley didn't want him to say it. She nodded, quickly, to show she knew, and the low, stumbling voice went on.

'I always have to be looking out for shoplifters, and when I catch them, they don't care, they laugh in my face. And mother gets—she hates it. She's full of hate. That's the worst thing, you know. Living with that hate.'

He stopped for a moment. Ashley couldn't move. She couldn't speak. All she could do was wait for him to go on.

When he did, his voice was a little stronger. 'When the graffiti started, up on the wall, and there was this name—'

'Cindy?' Ashley whispered.

The Hyena nodded. 'Mother picked on that. Everything was Cindy. Not just the graffiti. Or the car. Everything. All the time she goes on and on about it, and how awful things are, and how people hate us, and it's always Cindy, Cindy, Cindy. And the only thing that's kept me going—'

Ashley knew what he was going to say. She wished she could stop him, but she couldn't say a word.

'—the only thing that's kept me going was you. Knowing that there was someone who was good and unselfish and . . . and . . . '

Ashley felt as if she'd thrown a brick at Spider Mo. Or jeered at Thick Ed in Special Needs. Or left her mother lying on the floor. She hadn't known, but that was no excuse. And there was no way to explain that his horrible Cindy was just as false as his idea of her as good and unselfish.

'Is that why you've been stalking me?' she said softly. 'Because you thought I was good?'

'What?'

The Hyena looked up at her like a sleepwalker suddenly coming to. And it was only then that Ashley realized what a mistake she'd made.

'You haven't got a clue what I'm talking about, have you?' she said. 'You're not the stalker.'

'What?' he said. 'What do you mean?'

'You can't be the stalker. Because you didn't know I was Cindy. *You don't really know me at all.*'

DENNIS

I always go into Annie's shop for cigarettes on a Saturday. I'd heard the gossip, of course, but I didn't see why I should stop, just because of that.

151

So what? I said, when Penny told me. *Even if it's true, it doesn't make his cigarettes any worse, does it?*

But that was before I went in and saw the girl there.

I'd never seen her before, but she can only have been about fourteen. Just like that girl they say he's been stalking. And the moment I walked in I could feel the vibes. There was something going on.

But what could I do? It's so tricky, isn't it? I wanted to say, *Does your mother know you're in here?* Or maybe just give her a look, so she knew she ought to get out of the place. But when I tried to catch her eye she wouldn't lift her head, and I was—

Well, to be honest, I was scared. You can't be too careful these days, if you're a man. Especially when there's gossip like that flying around. If I'd taken an interest in her—the way I knew I should—the next thing you know there might have been people whispering about *me* on street corners. Crossing the road to keep their children away.

So I went straight out of the shop.

But all the way home I was sick with myself for being a coward. If anything happens, I kept thinking, I'll know it was my fault. If they find that girl's body, I'll know I could have stopped it.

And that's what it's going to come to in the end, isn't it? If they let him go on stalking girls, something terrible's going to happen. I ought to have taken that girl out of the shop and walked her home. And talked a bit of sense into her.

When I got home, I told Penny, and she tried to make me feel better, of course. 'He can't do anything,' she said. 'Not in the shop, with everyone looking on. And if that girl you saw didn't know what people are saying, she'll find out soon enough. Everyone's talking about it. You don't need to worry, Den. It'll be OK.'

She's right, of course. But it keeps coming back to me. And I get a horrible, sick feeling every time I pick up the newspaper or turn on the radio.

There's nothing I can do now, about that girl I saw. But there's one thing I can do—and I will. I'm not going into that shop any more. The sooner they go bust and get out of this neighbourhood, the better it's going to be for everyone.

I'll walk the extra hundred yards and buy my cigarettes in the Spar.

Twenty-Four

'It's not you,' Ashley said, repeating it to make herself take it in. 'You're not the stalker.'

The Hyena blinked across the counter at her. 'What stalker?'

Then he looked down at the things lying in front of him. Slowly his hands moved over the sutures of the skull and his fingers ran down the ugly black lines on the photographs. When he looked up again, his face was bleak.

'You thought . . . that I sent you these?'

Ashley's throat was dry. 'And I thought you were the person who telephoned me. And scratched on the drainpipe under my window. And chased me home in the dark.'

The Hyena's mouth twisted and he shuffled the pictures together. 'But I would never . . . how could you think—?'

Ashley couldn't look at him. 'There were clues, you see. Footprints in my garden, that matched your shoes. And that scarf.'

'I haven't— I don't wear a scarf.'

Ashley leaned forward to contradict him. To say that Annie had recognized the scarf. But just then a woman walked into the shop, to buy a bag of flour. By the time the Hyena had served her, he'd worked out which scarf Ashley meant.

'That scarf—I understand now.' He said it eagerly, wanting to explain. 'My grandfather knitted it. I couldn't possibly— It's not the sort of thing I could wear. But Granny likes to see it. So I keep it in the car. Ready for when I visit her.'

'In the car?' Ashley said slowly. 'You mean—the car that was stolen?'

A picture sharpened in her mind, swimming out of her memory. How could she have forgotten about it? It was perfectly clear now. She could see Sam crashing the Hyena's car into the garages and then jumping out. She saw her running through the Newenthal flats with a long scarf flapping round her neck.

And then she saw her collapsing against the wall of Toronto House, next to Spider Mo. And draping the scarf ceremoniously round Mo's neck.

A yellow scarf, with a black pattern.

'So what did you think?' she said faintly. 'When you got the scarf back?'

'My . . . um . . . my mother said some children had it. I didn't tell her it was in the car. She gets so—' The Hyena avoided Ashley's eyes. 'It's not good when she thinks about the car.'

'So it *was* your scarf I saw,' Ashley said slowly. 'But I don't know what happened to it after that. That's what I need to find out.'

She left the words hanging in the air and began to scoop the bones and all the other things back into her rucksack. Everything had sharpened suddenly, and she knew what she had to do.

'Ashley—' the Hyena said.

'Yes?' She fastened the pack and looked up. He was twisting his hands together.

'I . . . um . . . I mean . . . you don't still think—?'

His pasty face was pale and mournful, and there were strands of black hair slicked over his balding scalp. It would be easy to make fun of that face. If you didn't know. Ashley rested her backpack on the counter.

'I'm sorry,' she said awkwardly. 'It was a mistake. I wish I hadn't . . . I'm sorry. And . . . for everything else, as well.'

There was so much to apologize for that she didn't know where to start. She picked up the pack again and hooked it over one shoulder.

'But I'm going to find out what's going on.'

'You shouldn't go on your own,' the Hyena said. 'Do you want . . . um . . . shall I shut the shop and come with you?'

Ashley shook her head. 'That's really kind. But it's OK.'

'Well, if you're ever in trouble—'

'Thanks,' Ashley said. 'I'll remember that.'

Then she went out to look for Spider Mo.

It wasn't easy to track down Mo at that time of day. She wasn't an active beggar, like the people who loitered round the shopping centre, tootling on tin whistles. She spent most of her day shuffling round the town centre, from one bench to another. Ashley had seen her a hundred times, on one or another, but that day all the benches were empty.

A couple of old men were slumped on the pavement in one of the doorways along the Row, but Mo wasn't in any of the doorways. And she wasn't in the library.

In the end, Ashley asked the man who was selling the *Big Issue* outside Woolworths. He was there every day. He must know Mo.

'Sure I know her,' he said, but he didn't smile. He looked at Ashley as if she were an earwig. 'Why don't you kids leave her alone? You're always teasing her and knocking her about for no reason. She's harmless if you treat her all right.'

'I know,' Ashley said. 'Really. But I have to ask her something.'

'You're wasting your breath. She'll never remember.' The man smiled past her and reached over her shoulder to sell a copy of the paper.

Ashley caught at his sleeve. 'Look! I'm trying to do something good. Please believe me. But I can't do it unless I can find Mo. You don't have to tell me where she is, but please, *please* give me a clue where to look.'

The man dropped the coins into his pocket and looked down at her, examining her face. Then he said gruffly, 'It's pretty cold today. If Mo's got any money, she'll be having a warm drink somewhere. Where it's cheapest.'

'Oh,' Ashley said. 'Thanks.'

She began to walk away, running through the cheap cafés in her mind. Working out how long it would take to visit them all. When she'd taken half a dozen steps, the man called after her.

'Hey!'

She looked back at him, and he grinned.

'Try Popeye's Parlour.'

Ashley grinned back and set off there, through the covered market. When she arrived, she saw that the man was right. Popeye's tea was ten pence cheaper than anywhere else. And even through the steamy window she could see Mo, sitting up at the far end, where it was warmest.

Ashley pushed the door open and strolled up the café. As she passed Mo, she saw that her cup of tea was almost empty. She bought another and took it back to the table.

'Hi. Would you like this?'

Mo's eyes flicked up at her. Bright black. Suspicious. Then they flicked down to the table again. She ignored the cup of tea, as if it were a trap.

'It's OK,' Ashley said. 'I've bought you some tea because I want to talk to you. It's a trade.'

The eyes looked up again, and stayed on her face. Waiting.

'I want to ask you a question,' Ashley said. 'About . . . about Sam. You do know her?'

'Eddie's Sam?' Mo looked cautious. 'What do you want to know?'

Ashley pushed the tea with one finger, edging it across the table. 'I was with her the other night. A couple of weeks ago. We came through the estate with Joe and Doug. You were sleeping round the back of Toronto House. Remember?'

'I might.' Mo's fingers closed round the teacup. 'So what if I do?'

'And do you remember the scarf Sam gave you? It was yellow.'

Lifting the cup with two hands, Mo took a long swig of the tea. 'It was a good scarf,' she said. 'Warm.'

'And have you still got it?'

Mo was lifting the cup to her mouth. As she drank, she shook her head, and the tea spilled out and trickled down the sides of her chin.

Ashley tried not to look excited. 'Somebody took the scarf away? Who was that?'

She said it as gently as she could, but the effect was disastrous. Mo's face crumpled and she slammed the tea down on to the table, pushing it away so roughly that most of the rest of it spilt.

'No,' she said. 'NO!'

'Please!' Ashley knew she'd blown it, but she couldn't bear to give up. 'Please! You've *got* to tell me where that scarf is!'

'No! No!' Mo started to rock in her chair. 'There wasn't a scarf. I never had a scarf. No! No!'

Out of the corner of her eye, Ashley saw the man behind the counter turn to look at them. He was frowning. In a moment he would come and interfere. She hadn't got long.

'Please, Mo—'

But Mo was picking up her bags now. Gathering them together frantically, to make a getaway. Ashley stood up and leaned forward, trying to stop her. Knocking the bags out of the way.

She was so frantic that she didn't see the *Big Issue* salesman come into the café. She didn't notice him at all until he appeared beside her, tall and furious.

'Get out,' he said.

'But I'm not—' Ashley wanted to explain, but he didn't

give her a chance. He just glared, scornfully, until she picked up her backpack and sidled out of the shop.

What was she going to do now?

TOM

I thought she was OK. I really thought she was OK, that girl.

When you're out on the Row every day, there aren't many people you don't know. I'd seen that one going backwards and forwards to school, and doing her shopping, and I thought: she's OK. Never bought a paper, but I reckoned she was pretty short of cash. If she'd come up to me a couple of weeks ago and asked for Mo, I'd have told her without thinking twice.

But then there was all that weird stuff about old GG stalking her.

The story spread like measles. And no wonder. Eddie Beale's boys were all out, making sure everyone got it. And I saw Sam and her mother, too, chatting up the old ladies.

It wasn't obvious, mind. That's not Eddie's style. *You* wouldn't have noticed anything, if you were out shopping. But *I* noticed. I could feel the atmosphere on the Row thickening up like soup, and I didn't fancy it.

And when the girl turned up hunting for Mo, I didn't like that either. I told her where to look—didn't take much working out—but I took my coffee break early to keep an eye on things. Mo's a smelly old wreck, but it makes me sick the way people get at her.

And I was right. *Of* course. When I got to Popeye's, the girl was coming over really heavy. I don't know what she was after, but you could see Mo wasn't going to cough.

I watched until I was sure what was going on. And when I saw Mo start to rock, I went in and sorted out Little Miss Cindy Spray-can. (Oh yes, I know that too. I told you—I don't miss much.) I sent her off with a flea in her ear.

Then I stayed and had my coffee. I was trying to calm Mo down and tell her she was safe, so she wouldn't get flung out into the cold before she'd finished her tea. But I don't think she heard a word I was saying. I couldn't get any sense out of her at all.

Whatever that girl was asking, someone had beaten her to it. They'd really put the frighteners on Mo. She was still shaking when I left her and went back to my pitch. But all she would say was, *I didn't tell her. I didn't say a word.* Whatever she knows, there's someone who wants to be sure she won't tell. And I could have a pretty good guess at who it is.

There's only one person round here who frightens people that much.

Twenty-Five

So what now? Ashley walked back through the market, feeling angry and defeated. She couldn't bear to give up, but she didn't know where else to look.

As she came out on to the Row, Joe appeared beside her. She kept walking and he fell into step, with his big hands hanging loose and his long arms swinging.

'Heard you were looking for Mo,' he said.

Ashley blinked at him. 'Who told you that?'

'People.' Joe leered sideways at her, from under his bobble hat.

Then he hunched his shoulders and started to waddle, so that his whole body looked square. He swayed from side to side, toting imaginary carrier bags.

'Unnph,' he mumbled. 'Got to . . . Friday night . . . it's important . . . '

Ashley didn't smile. 'It's not funny. Mo's not funny.'

Joe's eyes hooded themselves and she felt him take in her expression and the tone of her voice. For the first time, it struck her that he wasn't just a clown. He was a bit of a video camera too. Whatever she did, whatever she said, he could play it back to someone else, later on. *It's not funny. Mo's not funny.* With a toss of the head and a little pinch of the lips, to make it ridiculous.

Imagining his performance, and the eyes that would watch it, she suddenly realized what she had to do next.

'I've got to see Eddie,' she said abruptly. 'Do you know where he is?'

Joe looked wary. 'Maybe. Why do you want him?'

'It's the Hyena—Mr Galt. He's not the stalker after all. I've got to see Eddie and make him tell people.'

Joe pushed his hands into his pockets and stopped. 'Nobody makes Eddie do anything.'

'I'll ask him, then. What difference does it make? There's been a dreadful mistake and we've got to put it right.'

She could feel Joe hesitate, and for one baffled moment she thought he was going to object. Then he shrugged.

'You might find him at Tricia's.'

'Where's that?'

'I'll show you.'

It was getting dark already, but Ashley was determined to do something useful before she went home. She followed Joe along to the far end of the Row, and then right, into Barham Place. Joe led her straight across the square and through a gap in the tall white terrace at the end. Beyond the old houses, there were three small blocks of modern flats, quite different from the Newenthal towers.

Tricia's flat was in the furthest block, at the far end of the walkway. Ashley guessed which flat it was from the white curtains, patterned with red poppies, and the ivy trailing over the balcony. Joe nodded up at it.

'I think Sam's having her hair done,' he muttered. 'So she'll be there, anyway. But she doesn't like being disturbed.'

'I'll risk it,' Ashley said.

They climbed the steps to the first floor and Joe took out a key and let himself in. When he opened the door, Ashley could see right through the flat and into the kitchen at the back.

Sam was sitting by the sink, with a mudpack on her face. Her wet hair was hanging in strings, and Tricia was busy ragging the ends with a pair of scissors. When Joe and Ashley walked in, Sam ignored them.

Tricia spoke without looking round. 'Put the kettle on, Joe. We're both gasping.'

'I've brought Ashley,' Joe said. He picked up the kettle and took it to the tap.

Tricia half-turned and waved the scissors. 'Pull up a chair, Ash. And pretend this mud monster is a total stranger. That way she won't bite you.'

'But I need to talk to her.' Ashley walked round Tricia and knelt down, looking up into Sam's face. 'Can you tell me where Eddie is, Sam? I've got to find him.'

Sam's eyes glittered ice blue in the middle of the mudpack, but her face didn't move. The mask was smooth and undisturbed.

Ashley tried again. 'I've got to tell him that we were wrong. About the stalker.'

Still no reaction. Except, maybe, a catch in Sam's breathing.

'How could you be wrong?' Tricia said. 'There were all those clues.'

'They're fakes!' Ashley said fiercely. 'Someone must have framed him! *He didn't do it!*'

The smooth grey surface of Sam's mask twitched once and then fractured suddenly into thousands of little cracks.

And then the doorbell rang.

'Oh *blast*!' Sam said loudly. The mask crumbled into fragments, and she stood up. 'He's early.'

Ashley thought it was Eddie at the door. Before anyone else could move, she ran down the hall and opened it. But it wasn't Eddie standing there. It was the most beautiful man she had ever seen. His hair was pale and smooth. The grey of his expensive, exquisite suit matched the precise grey of his big, lustrous eyes. And his shirt was open to the waist, showing a chest like ivory silk.

Ashley was sure she had never met him. *But he recognized her.*

She knew it from the way his eyes snapped and then flicked quickly sideways, avoiding her face. The way he started to smile and then wiped his face clean and blank as he remembered who she was. Somehow, he knew her.

Then Sam called from the kitchen.

'You're too early, Rick! You're a toad!'

Rick.

Ashley's mind lurched, and she heard Tricia's voice, babbling on to Pauline. *Rick's absolutely made Sam's career. You should see some of the pictures he's taken* . . .

Rick was a photographer.

And he was Eddie's friend.

Sickeningly, the pieces started sliding into place. Eddie had a friend who took photographs. And he knew who she was. Sam had had the scarf. And the scarf had turned up just when Eddie said she needed another clue.

Like the phone call that had come just as she got home from Eddie's party. Everything fitted too well.

And it all led back to Eddie in the end.

Furiously, she looked up at the man in the doorway. 'I know who you are!' she said, before she could stop herself. 'You took those horrible photographs!'

The moment she'd said it, she was ice-cold with terror, but there was no going back. Rick reached inside his perfect jacket and took out a tiny mobile phone. It was the same ivory white as his long, beautiful hands. Still watching Ashley, he tapped in a string of numbers and then raised the phone to his ear, holding it a fraction of an inch away, so that it didn't touch his skin.

'Eddie,' he said, 'I'd come round to Sam's if I were you. And bring a *huge* cork. The dam's struck a leak.'

RICK

It was bound to happen, of course. Eddie can't strong-arm the whole world into silence, even if he does think it's his own private circus. Sometimes the tightrope walker breaks out. And this one was way along her own wire. I'd never seen anyone so up and so tight. Believe me, the whole big top was *juddering*.

Sam came out of the kitchen with her hair wet and her face scrubbed clean. That little pulse was beating in her throat, the way it does when she's driving

163

too fast, or posing on top of a church steeple. She caught at the girl's arm and I almost fainted. I was terrified there was going to be some kind of *skirmish*.

But not a bit of it. Little Miss Tightrope Walker sat down in one of Tricia's appalling repro Louis XV chairs. Virtually chained herself to it. *Darling*, I wanted to say, *no one has the faintest desire to lay a finger on you. We'll leave that to Eddie*. But she wouldn't have heard. She was watching that door like a cat at a mousehole. She actually wanted him to come.

It was rather amusing, in a grim way.

When the bell rang she jumped up and faced the door, like a gladiator, but she didn't open it. Joe was left to play doorman. The girl stood on the other side of the hall, trembling like a guitar string.

Well, my darling, I thought, *we all learn by making mistakes. I bleed for you, I really do. But I think I'm going to enjoy this.*

I was looking forward to seeing what Eddie pulled out of the hat. To keep her in line.

Twenty-Six

Two heavies came through the door first. Big men in jeans and T-shirts. They stepped sideways, framing the entrance, and Eddie came after them, with his eyes on Ashley.

She was beyond thinking. Her mind had flashed like quicksilver to an answer she had never expected. All she could do was speak it out, and the words erupted, the moment she saw Eddie's face.

'You tricked me! The stalker was you! You sent people to take photographs, and push things through my door, and you tried to make me think it was Mr Galt!'

Eddie stepped into the hall, neat as a cat, and shut the door behind him. 'Well done,' he said. 'You worked it out. It took you long enough.'

'But why?' Ashley said. 'What's the point?'

'Maybe it was just for fun.' Eddie leaned back against the door. 'It's a good laugh, isn't it?'

If he'd tried to pretend, Ashley could have coped. If he'd told her she was mad, she would have known where she was. His calmness threw her right off balance.

Behind her back, she could hear Tricia whispering to Sam. The two heavies were smirking, and she could see Rick glancing over at Eddie, and Joe tracing shapes on the floor with his toe. They all knew more about what was going on than she did. She could feel the knowledge all round her, just out of reach. It was like being in a theatre before the play, watching muffled shapes move behind the curtains.

Her eyes darted round from face to face, trying to pick up some extra clue. But the only person who looked back at her was Eddie.

'What did you think was going on?' he said scornfully. 'Did you think I was going to all that trouble just to save you from a few loony letters?'

'I thought . . . you were being kind,' Ashley said slowly. 'People said—'

'Ye-es?' He tilted his head on one side, watching her. Amused.

Ashley spun round to Tricia. 'You told my mum he helped people!'

'He does,' Tricia said easily. 'Don't take any notice of what he says. He's got to talk tough, to keep people in order, but he's got a heart of gold. Look how he rescued Joe from that horrible Vince.' She ruffled Joe's hair and opened the kitchen door. 'I'm not listening to this stuff. When you've sorted it out, come through and have a drink.'

She went in and shut the door behind her. Very softly, under her breath, Sam said, 'That's Mum all over. Get out when things turn nasty.'

'And why not?' Joe said. His hand went up to his head, but it wasn't his own hair he was patting. It was Tricia's blonde candyfloss. 'Why do people want to look at the nasty things? What I say is—'

He wriggled his shoulders girlishly and his voice got shriller, going up a couple of notches, like a tape getting faster.

'—what I say is if you don't look on the bright side, you might as well be d—'

'Joe.'

Eddie's voice sliced through the chatter. Joe stopped halfway through the word, with his mouth open and his two eyes wide, like dark moons.

'Shut it,' Eddie said.

Slowly Joe's big mouth closed, and he folded up like an umbrella, squatting on the floor with his sharp knees under his chin.

'That's better,' Eddie said. He flicked his fingers at Sam.

'Go and tell Tricia we'll be through in a minute. She can get out some beers.'

Sam looked at him. Then she turned abruptly and went into the kitchen. Eddie nodded a signal and Joe leaped up and closed the door behind her.

'You see?' Eddie murmured. He glanced across at Ashley. 'Even Sam does what I say. It's the only way to be. Keep your mouth shut and your eyes closed. There are things it's better not to think about.'

'I can't do that,' Ashley said stubbornly. 'Not now I know what you're up to. You're trying to wreck Annie's shop, aren't you?'

Eddie jerked upright and took a step towards her. Suddenly, he pushed his face at her, and his eyes were like steel. 'Say that outside this flat, and you'll be sorry.'

'What do you mean?' Ashley edged backwards.

'It's slander, that's what I mean. You can't prove anything. The first whisper about stalking, or plotting against Fat Galt, and you're in trouble. And so's your mother.'

'But you can't—'

'You think I haven't got any solicitors?' Eddie sat back and looked at her, scornfully. 'You don't have a clue, do you? Look around. I've got Rick to take my photographs. Sam and Joe to keep me amused. Tricia to do home cooking if I fancy it. And . . . these.' He flicked his fingers at the men by the door. 'There's someone of mine in every street round here. In every pub and every block of flats. I'm the ringmaster and they all jump when I crack the whip.'

He looked round the hall, daring the others to answer. The heavies were expressionless, but Rick raised a rueful eyebrow and Joe dropped his head on to his knees.

Eddie laughed softly. 'I give them what they want. That's why they stick with me. And you're the same.'

'No I'm not.' Ashley clenched her fists. 'You can't buy me with a secondhand video.'

167

'Don't be silly,' Eddie said. He leaned sideways and snapped his fingers at Rick. 'Show her the photographs.'

Rick reached inside his jacket and took out a pale blue envelope. Suddenly, danger glittered in the air. The heavies leaned forward to see what was in the envelope, and Joe lifted his head and glanced at Ashley.

Rick slid a long finger under the flap. There were ten or fifteen photographs in the envelope and he fanned them out under Ashley's nose. She looked down, expecting to see more ugly pictures of herself.

But she was nowhere, and the pictures were beautiful. They showed two women laughing in an autumn wood. Their faces glowed among the scarlet and crimson and gold of the leaves.

Tricia and—

Rick pushed the pictures at Ashley, flicking through them so that Tricia seemed to rise and dance under the trees. In the last couple of pictures, the other woman was on her feet too, standing with her arms spread wide and her head flung back. She was laughing like a teenager.

'Mum,' Ashley said.

'That day they went out to look at the leaves.' Rick peered down at the pictures. 'Not bad, are they? Considering I had to get them without being seen.'

'Show her the other one,' Eddie said sharply. 'The one you took before.'

Ashley guessed what kind of picture he was talking about. But she didn't see how Rick could have taken one, until he pulled it out of the envelope and showed her. Then she caught her breath.

'That's our house!'

He must have been outside, looking in through the window. The picture showed the front room at its worst, with heaps of dirty clothes all over the floor. In the foreground was Pauline, sitting up in bed. She was grey-faced and her long hair—the old, untended hair—trailed into her coffee.

Ashley glared. 'You were spying!'

'Darling, it was dreadful!' Rick pulled a pathetic face. 'I couldn't get a really good shot. It's a pity when the others came out so well.'

'Never mind,' Eddie said smoothly. 'You'll be able to take a replacement. The lady's going to look like that again, when Tricia gives up visiting.'

Ashley stared down at the horrible, depressing picture. 'And suppose Tricia doesn't stop?'

Eddie pulled a face at her. Wide-eyed and innocent. 'Your mother won't want her to come, will she? Not when she knows it was all done out of pity. And Tricia thinks she's a boring old cow.'

'It's not true,' Ashley said. Fighting off the image of her mother hearing those words and shrinking back into her old, miserable self. Shrinking back too far for anyone to reach her. 'It's not true! Tricia wouldn't—'

'Tricia,' said Eddie, 'will do whatever I tell her to. She's no fool.'

'But they're friends! Tricia likes Mum! Ask Sam—'

'Sam?' said Eddie. Very softly. '*Sam?* You think *she's* going to argue with me?' His mouth started to twitch and he looked across at Joe, tilting his head slightly.

It was a signal. For a second, Ashley thought Joe was going to disobey. Then Eddie jerked a finger at him and he bounded up, long-legged and defiant, with his hands bunched. He held one fist under Eddie's nose and shook it.

'You don't tell *me* what to do! Maybe you can push all the others around, but not me. We're equals, aren't we, Eddie Beale?'

He had it, exactly. Even the way Sam stood, with her feet wide apart and one hip pushed forward, aggressively. Ashley saw him dissolving, in front of her eyes, giving way to an image of Sam, as crude and powerful as a cartoon.

Eddie's finger beckoned, slowly. It was Joe he drew towards him, but it wasn't Joe that the watchers saw. Not

Joe who moved forward, responding to that power, crumpling to the ground as Eddie pointed.

It was like seeing Sam on her knees in front of the dusty toes of Eddie's shoes. Joe leaned over them and stretched out his tongue, pretending to lick away the dust. And all the time he was waving his fist in the air, in a pantomime of independence.

No one else moved. No one made a sound.

'He's a real scream,' Eddie said, into the silence. 'Isn't he?' He glanced round sharply at the men by the door. 'Shaun? Dave?'

The men sniggered obediently and Eddie looked back at Rick and Ashley. Rick's face twisted into a sickening grin, but there was no smile in his eyes. Ashley turned her head away.

Eddie wasn't going to let her escape. He stepped sideways, so that she had to look at him. 'What's wrong with you? Got no sense of humour?'

'I—' Her voice caught in her throat.

'Everyone else thinks it's hilarious,' Eddie said smoothly. His mouth twitched again, and he looked past her, over her shoulder. *'Everyone.'*

Ashley spun round. The kitchen door was open. Sam was standing there, with a four-pack of lager in one hand. Beyond her was Tricia, breaking open a bag of crisps. Ashley could tell by their faces that they had seen Joe's imitation too.

'Laugh!' Eddie snapped.

There was a hair's-breadth pause, and then Tricia gave a forced, nervous cackle. When Ashley turned away, she met Eddie's eyes.

'You see?' he murmured. 'Tricia knows it's best to play things my way. If you don't, you might get—hurt.'

Ashley couldn't speak. She felt the air crowding in and the walls threatening her. Eddie nodded across at Rick.

'Give her the pictures.'

Rick pushed them into her hand, closing her fingers round them so that they didn't fall. She looked down and saw Pauline's grey face staring back at her.

'Think it over,' Eddie said. 'And remember, it's not going to help your mother if anything happens to you.'

They all stood and watched her as she stumbled across the hall and opened the front door. She stepped outside and glanced back once, as she pulled the door shut behind her. The last thing she saw in the flat was Sam's face. Sam's unreadable, ice-blue stare, following her as she walked away.

SHAUN

The funny thing was—*Sam* didn't laugh.

The girl went off down the stairs and we all stood there, listening to her feet.

'She'll come round,' Eddie said. 'When she's had time to think it over. Won't she, Sam?'

And he lifted his head, in that way he has. Looking for an answer. But Sam didn't say a word. She stood in the kitchen doorway with the lager hanging from her hand, and you couldn't tell what the hell she was thinking.

Usually, she has everything in her face. In those photos Rick takes, you can see exactly what she's thinking, *Out of my way, worm!* and *Get your hands off my leathers!* Stuff like that. It's great.

But just then there was nothing. She stared back at Eddie and she never answered him at all.

It was Joe who jumped up—for no reason, as far as I could see. He charged down the hall into his bedroom and shut the door. Slammed it. It could have been a nasty moment, but Tricia came out with the crisps and we all had a beer and went in to watch the match.

Twenty-Seven

Ashley didn't know what to do, so she went home. There was nowhere else to go.

She walked round the block for ten minutes, until her face was under control. Then she plastered a smile on it and let herself in.

'Hi, Mum. Sorry I was so long.' She strode into the front room. 'You know what it's like when Vikki and I get talking.' She could hear her voice sounding shrill and brittle and she smiled harder.

Pauline was sitting at the table, with a bag of sprouts in front of her, peeling them and dropping them into a bowl. She looked up, and her hands stopped moving, but she didn't say a word.

'I asked Vikki about that Cindy letter.' Ashley laughed brightly. 'But she hadn't got a clue who could have sent it—'

There was something unnerving about Pauline's expression. She was just letting the words wash over her, as if they had no importance.

Ashley faltered. 'Are you all right?'

Pauline pulled another leaf off the sprout she was holding. 'Ash, you don't have to keep on fooling me. I know.'

Ashley's heart lurched. 'What are you talking about?'

'I phoned Janet. She said the intruder was Mr Galt, and he's been stalking you for weeks. Why didn't you tell me?'

Ashley's brain churned. 'I . . . I didn't want to worry you.'

'Don't you think I was worried anyway?' Pauline picked at the sprout again. 'I *knew* there was something wrong.'

It was a sickening, black joke. Ashley felt the whole, tangled story swirl around her. *True/false, true/false, true/false.*

She'd struggled to stop Pauline finding out about the stalker and, now she did know, there was something worse to hide. The real truth.

And the threats.

Eddie's voice echoed in her mind. *Keep your mouth shut and your eyes closed. There are things it's better not to think about. It's the best way, if you want a quiet life. If you want me to look after things.* She had to get away and pull herself together.

'I'll go and make some tea,' she muttered. 'Do you want a cup?'

Pauline put the sprout down. 'No, I don't!' she said sharply. 'I want you to talk to me.'

'We can talk with the tea,' Ashley said briskly. 'I won't be long.'

She was almost through the door, when Pauline said, 'Don't go.'

It was quite soft. Ashley could have pretended not to hear, and carried on down the hall. But there was a firmness in Pauline's voice that made her stop. She turned round.

'What's hurting you?' Pauline said. Very gently.

Ashley felt the answer inside her like a lump of stone. She seemed to have been carrying it round all her life. Keeping it inside because the world would collapse around her if she ever let it out.

Pauline pulled herself on to her feet and lurched slowly across the room towards her, holding on to the furniture. When she stopped, they were near enough to touch.

'Tell me,' she said.

How can I? Ashley thought. She wanted to pour it all out. She wanted to fling herself into her mother's arms and yell and scream. But if she tried, both of them would fall over. And there was no one else to pull them up.

But even while she was remembering all that, she heard her own voice. Heard the lump of stone rolling out of her mouth.

'I don't know what to do. I'm in a mess and I just . . . can't *manage!*'

173

Then the words caught in her throat and choked her, and Pauline opened her arms. Ashley went into them and, as they closed round her, the two of them tottered and fell over, just as she'd known they would, crumpling into an untidy, undignified heap on the floor. But Pauline just laughed and sat up, keeping her arm tightly round Ashley's shoulders.

'Now tell me,' she said.

And Ashley did tell her, sitting there on the carpet. She told her everything, without trying to tidy it up or miss out the parts that would hurt. Every single thing, right from the beginning.

When she finished, Pauline sat very still, stroking her hand.

'Do you know something?' she said. 'That's the first time you've asked me for help, since you were seven.'

'Only because you've had enough to put up with. And because—'

'Because you had to cope.' Pauline nodded. 'I know. And you were afraid of what would happen if you didn't. It's frightening, isn't it? Well, now we've landed on the floor, and there's nowhere else to go.' She straightened her shoulders. 'So how can we tell people that Mr Galt is innocent?'

'Go to the police?' Ashley said.

'We haven't got any evidence. We have to sort it out ourselves.'

'But Eddie won't *let* us! I told you!'

'He can't stop us if we do it fast enough. We need to tell hundreds of people at once. Couldn't we call a meeting?'

Ashley pulled a face.

'We must do something!' Pauline said desperately. 'What about posters?'

Another poster? The empty shops were covered in them. People just didn't bother to read things like that.

Unless . . . A plan exploded suddenly in Ashley's brain, like fireworks in the sky. *Yes! That was how to get words across!* But would her mother—?

174

Pauline looked at her sharply. 'You've thought of something.'

Ashley hesitated, tempted to keep her idea secret. To fob Pauline off with a half-truth and pretend she was going to put up useless posters. She could do that—

But she wasn't going to. Not any more.

'Yes, I have thought of something,' she said steadily. 'It means climbing on to that roof again. But I won't do it unless you say it's all right.'

Pauline looked down at her fingers. 'Will it work?'

'I think so. Especially if Mr Galt helps me.'

Pauline took a deep breath. 'You're sure about him, are you, Ashie? You're sure he's not—'

'Certain,' Ashley said.

There was a long silence. Very slowly, Pauline nodded. 'You'd better phone him then, hadn't you? But take me into the kitchen first. I don't want to know the details.'

The Hyena wasn't easy to persuade. 'It's so . . . so dangerous,' he kept saying.

'But it'll work,' Ashley said. 'Won't it?'

'I . . . um . . . well, yes. I suppose so. But if you fall—'

'I *won't* fall. I've done it before.'

'But what about your mother?'

'She—' *What*? thought Ashley. Then the words came, and she knew they were true. 'Mum doesn't like it either, but she trusts me. She says yes.'

The Hyena swallowed noisily. 'Well, if she thinks . . . I suppose I can . . . um—'

When Ashley put the phone down, she found she was shaking.

She and Pauline both tried to sleep, but neither of them succeeded. At a quarter to two, Ashley picked up her backpack, padded downstairs and stuck her head round the front room door. Pauline's bedside light was on, and she was sitting up, waiting.

'I'm going now,' Ashley said.

'You will . . . be careful?'

'Yes. I promise.' Ashley slipped down the hall and out of the kitchen door. The grass in the back garden crunched frostily under her feet, and her fingers left black, melted patches on the fence.

Spider Mo was round at the side of Mrs Macdonald's, curled up among the dustbins. Ashley almost fell over her and Mo grunted and sat up for a second. There was a glint of light as she opened her eyes.

'Knock it off, Eddie,' she muttered. Then she slumped back against the dustbins and started snoring.

Out on the pavement, the litter was edged with frost, and the puddles had a rim of ice. Ashley walked lightly, trying to visualize what she was going to do.

The Hyena was standing at the end of the alley, watching out anxiously for her. He started whispering as soon as she was close enough to hear.

'I've been . . . um . . . looking at the roof. It's too dangerous. You can't possibly—' He bit at his lip. 'You really *can't*. Not in this weather. Let me—'

Ashley almost laughed, remembering how miserable he'd looked when he was up there painting the wall.

'I'll be fine. I've done it twice already, remember. But it would be good if you kept a lookout.'

For a second, she thought he wasn't going to let her into the yard. Then he stepped aside and she went through and took hold of the drainpipe.

'Whistle if you see anyone around,' she whispered. 'What can you whistle?'

'Er . . . ''God Save the Queen''?'

'Fine.' Ashley grinned at him and started to climb.

When she reached the top of the extension roof, she

looked down and saw the pale shape of his face, tipped up to watch her. Then he turned away and walked out of the yard, heading for the Row.

Ashley forgot about him, and concentrated on the roof in front of her. Thank goodness the Cavalieris hadn't insulated their loft. The frost had melted. Putting one foot on the windowsill, she hauled herself up.

When she reached the wall, she stopped, working out exactly what she was going to do with the space. This was the most important piece of writing she'd ever done and she had to make sure it could be read easily from down in the street. For several minutes she stood still, sizing up the space and working out how best to use it. Then her fingers started to get cold, and she pulled out the first can and began.

The letters spread across the wide white space.

STALKING

MONDAY 4PM

BE HERE!

When she had shaded them—from light, bright yellow at the top, to heavy crimson at the bottom—she added one more word.

CINDY.

No little drops of blood this time. Instead, she trailed a string of flowers from the crimson tail of the Y. Then she pushed the top on to her spray-can and started back to the ground.

There was not a sound. Not a movement in the air. She didn't even know where the Hyena was. As she held on to the gutter, lowering one leg towards the window, she felt like the only person in the world. Settling her foot on the windowsill, she lowered the other one to join it and then bent down, to grip the windowframe.

And she found herself staring into a huge white face, peering at her between the curtains.

Her foot slipped, scrabbling uselessly at the edge of the windowsill, and she felt the wood crack under her and give

177

way. She clutched at the windowframe, but her fingers couldn't find a hold and she went scraping down the wall of the building.

She didn't stop until her feet thudded on to the extension roof. For an instant she was right off balance, and she thought she was going to fall. Then she landed on her knees and threw herself towards the drainpipe, sliding down so fast that she burnt her hands. She was across the yard and almost through the gate when the Hyena appeared.

'What's the matter?' he whispered. 'I saw you coming down—'

Ashley caught at his arm. 'I've got to get away. There was a face. Tony Cavalieri—'

She pointed up at the window, but the curtains had fallen together again.

'It's all right,' the Hyena said. 'Tony's ... um ... he can't do anything, you know. But you don't have to ... let me make sure you get home all right.'

MRS CAVALIERI

Usually I sleep. With a life like mine, you sleep when your head hits the pillow. Flat out until the morning. But that night I woke up just after two o'clock.

There were movements. Someone was shuffling about at the back of the house.

I didn't waste time with trying to wake Pete—he'll have problems with the Last Trumpet. I slipped out of my bed and went to see.

And there was Tony, down at the end of the landing.

My heart! I thought it was a ghost. I was thinking he'd never move out of that room of his. Never again. It was two years he'd been lying there, or sitting in the chair, and I'd watched him bloating up, till—if you're a mother you'll know how I felt. If I didn't go to sleep so fast, I'd cry into my pillow every night.

But now there he was, in his wheelchair, gazing out of the back window. I was afraid to disturb him.

But he heard me and he spun the chair round. 'Here!' he said.

That's one thing he's never lost, my Tony. He's always been good at giving orders. I went down the landing and he pointed through the window.

'Take a look. Tell me what you see.'

I just caught a glimpse of them, before they disappeared down Railway Street. The last people you'd expect to see in the middle of the night.

It was Geoffrey from next door, with the girl there's been all the fuss about.

Mind you, I never believed it. All that stuff about stalking. Eddie's been out to get Annie ever since she refused to pay him off. There was bound to be trouble there sooner or later. There's always trouble if you cross Eddie.

We ought to know.

When Annie stopped paying, I told her, 'You're in for trouble.' But all she said was, 'I'll give him trouble! The first time my window's broken, or I'm burgled—he's had it. I'm straight round to the police and I'm camping there until they take him in.'

She should have known he wouldn't be so obvious. If Eddie wants to fix someone, he likes it to be a surprise. And when those stories started, about Geoffrey and the stalking, I said to Pete, 'Well. We know who's behind *that*!'

But the girl, with Geoffrey—now that was something different. I didn't know what that meant.

'So what's going on?' Tony said.

Oh, my heart again! That was the first question he'd asked since the fight. The first time he'd shown any interest in anything.

'It's a long story,' I said.

'So? We've got all night.'

Twenty-Eight

The writing was on the wall—but Eddie wasn't going to ignore it. Ashley knew he would try and find out what was going on. But she didn't guess how.

Not until Sunday afternoon.

She and Pauline were watching the television when the phone rang. Ashley jumped and snatched up the receiver.

Before she could say a word, Vikki started in.

'Ash, what are you up to? What's all this stuff about Monday at four o'clock?'

'You saw the wall?' Ashley said.

'Did I see it! I nearly fainted! And the minute I got home, Matt rang and said, "What's going on?" Mum said he'd rung three times already. What are you going to do?'

'I—' Ashley was about to blurt it all out. The words were already formed in her mind. But something, some extra alertness, kept Vikki's words sounding in her head. *Mum said he'd rung three times already.* That was weird. 'Why is Matt so interested in what I'm doing?' she said.

'Of course he's interested!' Vikki shrieked. 'He's your friend. And anyway, Ginger and Phil were on at him about it. Not that he'd tell them, of course, but—'

Ashley didn't hear the rest of what she said. Her brain was working at double speed. So that was how Eddie knew so much about her. Vikki told Matt, and Matt told his big sister Ginger.

Who was going out with Phil Carson.

Eddie's Phil.

Ashley closed her eyes. It was one thing to work out how your secrets leaked away. It was quite different to know for

180

sure. Well, if Eddie wanted information about what she was up to, he was going to get it.

'I'm going to make an announcement,' she said, picking her words. 'From up on the roof.'

She was sharply aware of Pauline, on the other side of the room.

Vikki gave a funny little squeak. 'The roof of the chippie?'

'Don't tell anyone,' Ashley said quickly. Thinking, *I'm sorry, Vik. I haven't told you a lie, but you'll think I did.*

'Of course I won't tell anyone!' Vikki was indignant. 'But what are you going to say?'

'Why don't you turn up and see? I don't want to spoil the surprise. Bye.' Ashley put the phone down and looked across the room at Pauline. 'Vikki,' she said. 'That's how Eddie knew I was Cindy. Because Vikki gossips.'

Pauline was looking pale. 'And you want her to gossip now?'

'She'd better!' Ashley said fiercely. 'I want Eddie to think I'm going up on the roof of the chippie. So he doesn't find me.'

That was easy to say, but it needed planning. She was going up on the cinema roof instead, and that was right opposite the chippie. She had to get there without being seen, by anyone. Eddie's words kept running over and over in her mind.

There's someone of mine in every street round here. In every pub and every block of flats. I'm the ringmaster and they all jump when I crack the whip.

The only way to be sure of beating him was to get up early. Ashley set her alarm for five o'clock in the morning. By quarter-past five she was down, carrying her backpack.

When she looked into the front room, Pauline pushed herself up on one elbow. Her eyes were dark from lack of sleep.

'Is this it?'

Ashley nodded.

'Do you have to go so early? It's cold out there.'

'I've got lots of clothes. And things to eat. Don't worry.'

'Don't *worry*?' Pauline dredged up a grin from somewhere. 'What do you want? A miracle?'

'It's OK,' Ashley said gently. 'There'll be hundreds of people there. Eddie won't be able to do a thing. I'll be back around half past four, to tell you all about it.' She waved and let herself out into the street, walking briskly up towards the Row.

As she reached the traffic lights, she glanced quickly over her shoulder. Fat Annie's was closed, but the lights were on, and she could see the Hyena, behind the security shutters. He raised a hand, wishing her luck, and she nodded back at him. Wondering if Annie had given him a bad time when he refused to paint the wall again.

Trying not to hurry, she walked down the side of the cinema, into the car park. It was deserted, but the security lights were very bright, lighting up the scrawled graffiti on the back wall. There were a couple of her own there and she was proud of them, but just now she wished she'd left the place alone. The manager had fought back, with long revolving spikes round all the drainpipes, and strands of barbed wire along the gutters. She hoped her extra piece of blanket would be thick enough to cope.

There was only one place where she could climb without being seen from Toronto House, and the wire was thickest there. She scratched her legs three times on the way up and one of the scratches wouldn't stop bleeding. When she reached the roof, she had to wind the tattered blanket round it and wait for it to stop.

By then, the sky was getting light and the Row was noisier. She crawled forward, along the flat roof, until she was hidden by the top of the ventilation shaft. Then she unpacked the warm clothes from her rucksack and pulled them on. After that, there was nothing to do except lie flat and wait. It was a long, cold, boring day.

At midday, she ate her sandwiches and drank a bottle of

water. The cinema was open now, and she didn't dare to move much, in case someone heard her. She flexed her muscles carefully, going over and over what she meant to say at four o'clock and checking the time every ten minutes or so. Four o'clock was very slow in coming, and there were lots of panicky thoughts to fight off.

What would she do if someone found her before she was ready? What if no one came to listen? And if people did come, what would she do after she'd spoken? She tried to make plans, but the answers were just stories, spun in her head. There was nothing real except the flat roof and the waiting.

At half-past three, she began to hear a buzz from down in the Row. Cautiously, she wriggled forward across the roof. In front of her, the huge false front of the cinema reared up in an elaborate curving wall. In the centre, it was three times as tall as she was, but at the sides it swept down to make a low parapet. She lifted her head just high enough to see over it.

Even though no one was back from school yet, the pavements were full of people loitering about and looking in shop windows. There was no mistaking why they were there. The way they kept looking at their watches gave it away and Ashley felt her heart beating harder. It was real. It was going to happen.

And there was no sign of Eddie.

At a quarter to four, the kids began to arrive from school, and the buzz grew louder. She peeped again, and saw people jostling each other off the edges of the pavement. There was a crowd of boys peering in at Fat Annie's window and jeering at the Hyena. Lisa was there too, and so were Vikki and Matt, with their arms around each other.

But still she couldn't see Eddie. Or any of his friends that she knew.

Most people had their backs to her. They were looking up at the painted wall, as if they expected someone—or something—to appear up there. It would take a very loud shout to turn them round. Ashley began to clear her throat, ready to stand up and yell over the parapet.

Was it going to be that easy? Was she going to do it without Eddie trying to stop her?

She was just beginning to believe that, when there was a burst of sound, coming from Shepherds Corner, so loud that it drowned the muttering from below. Circus music filled the air, as if the Row was about to fill up with lions and elephants, with white-faced clowns, in baggy trousers, and girls in sequins swinging high above the ground.

And now, before your very eyes . . .

Sheltering behind the parapet, Ashley stood up and looked along the Row. There was a procession approaching, moving slowly down the middle of the road.

Eddie was in front, driving a car with a loudspeaker strapped to the roof. He had the window down, and as he drove he was waving to people and calling their names.

Behind him, pulling another car on ropes, were Phil and Doug and the two heavies who had been in Tricia's flat. They were tugging at the ropes and making a performance of it. Every few yards, they stopped to pose and flex their muscles.

Sam was on top of the car, sitting on the roof. Her legs were curled under her and she was wearing one of her tiny, glittering dresses. Ashley could see boys waving and whistling, but she stared away over their heads, looking grand and remote.

Last of all came Joe. He was marching along behind Sam's car, grinning left and right and juggling four sticks with the ends wrapped in cloth, like the torch Sam had used at the party.

Eddie stopped outside Fat Annie's, still in the middle of the road, and got out of his car, leaving the music blaring. The men behind him dropped their ropes and Sam stretched and stood up on the roof of her car.

By now, the sound of the music was accompanied by

furious hooting from the trapped cars at the ends of the Row. Eddie ignored those. He stepped back, raising his arms to Sam, and the crowd surged forward to see what was going to happen.

It was impossible to hear anything, but Sam didn't need to speak. She bent down and took a bottle from Phil. Then she waited. Joe handed one of his torches to Doug, and Ashley saw the flicker of a cigarette lighter, and the flare as the cloth caught fire.

She looked at her watch. It was exactly four o'clock. What was she going to do? Everyone in the crowd was watching Sam, and she had no way of attracting people's attention. No one was going to hear her announcement.

She tried anyway. Stepping sideways, so that she was clearly visible above the lowest part of the parapet, she opened her mouth and yelled at the very top of her voice.

'Hey, everyone! Look up here!'

It was useless. Even while she was yelling, she could feel the wall of sound from below, swallowing her words and swamping her voice. The music battered her back and as far as the crowd was concerned she was invisible. Everyone was watching Sam as she raised the bottle to her lips.

Taking a swig from it, she lifted the lighted torch, paused dramatically, and then breathed out, sending a jet of flame down the road, right over Joe's head. Ashley couldn't hear the cheers, but she saw people clapping and yelling and she thought, *He's done it. He's beaten me.* As Sam raised the bottle again, she turned her head away in despair.

That was when she saw the huge, pale face across the road. Tony Cavalieri was staring at her, from the upstairs window of the chippie.

TONY CAVALIERI

Yeah, of course I spotted her. As soon as I heard the procession and wheeled myself to the window. I know how Eddie works, you see. If he comes down the road with a circus like that—all that music, and Sam doing her fire-eating bit—it's like he's saying *Look at this! Look over here!*

And that means he's probably hiding something. Trying to distract you from looking somewhere else.

So I ignored his stuff and concentrated on spotting the other thing. And the moment I saw that girl up on the cinema—well, it was obvious. When I saw her in the night, she must have been painting that notice on the wall, and now she was there to deliver. But Eddie had stuck his knife in.

No need to tell me about all that.

The thing you've got to understand about Eddie is, everything he does is for real. When we both had gangs, I got a kick out of trying to con him. It was all part of the game, and I thought he felt that way too—until the day when I finally did con him. That night, when I got home, there were six heavies waiting in the back yard.

No one could ever pin it on Eddie, but he's the one who put me in this chair. In the beginning, I used to sit and scream because of not being able to get back at him. I wanted to open the window and yell at the whole world, *It was Eddie Beale!* But there wasn't any way to make people listen. So when I saw that girl on the cinema, shouting her head off without being heard, it was like seeing myself.

Only this time—at last—there was something I could do to make it happen. I saw her up there, and I thought, *You can do it for me, sweetheart.* I didn't know what she had to say, of course, but I'd seen her with Geoff and that was good enough. Eddie's been out to smash Geoff and Annie's shop, ever since Annie stopped paying him off.

If that girl was on Geoff's side, I was going to see she got a hearing. And—after all those years of waiting—it was easy. I didn't need a gang. Or legs. All I had to do was open my window as wide as it would go, and push.

Twenty-Nine

Tony Cavalieri grinned and raised his hand. Ashley was still working out what he meant when he started to push the television on to the windowsill.

It was a small portable television, and it must have been standing on a shelf by the window. For a second it tottered on the sill. Then it tipped forward and fell, crashing on to the pavement in front of the chippie. The pavement was empty, because people there had crowded forward, towards Sam's car, but the crash was only inches away from some of them. They turned round furiously as the broken glass flew about, and shouted up at the window.

Tony shouted back in a frenzy, turning bright red and waving his fist. Ashley couldn't hear what he was saying—no one could have heard—but there was no mistaking what he meant. He was gesturing across the road with his whole body, waving his fist and leaning out of the window to make people turn the other way and look across the road.

At Ashley.

One by one, they did turn, until everyone was staring up at her. She saw Vikki and Matt. Lisa. Mrs Macdonald. People she had known all her life and total strangers. Sam spun round on the roof of the car and Joe put down his unlit torches. Suddenly, she was on stage, with people waiting to see what she was going to do.

But what could she do? Her only plan had been to bellow out a message, but that was out of the question.

She turned towards Eddie, with some crazy notion of pointing at him and hoping that people would guess what she meant. But the moment she saw him, the idea shrivelled. He was watching her with a faint, amused smile, enjoying her dilemma.

Slowly, he cocked one eyebrow, giving her that long, long stare that meant, *So? What are you going to do then? What's your trick?*

It was a taunt. He was daring her to put on a show. Well, if he wanted a performance, she was going to give him one. Defiantly, she stepped up on to the parapet.

Immediately, she felt the stillness. The loudspeaker went on blaring away, but the crowd stopped moving. Looking down, Ashley saw Lisa's eyes open wider and Vikki clutch at Matt's arm. Everyone was waiting to see what would happen.

The only person who moved was the Hyena. He came suddenly out of the shop and started pushing forward, past Vikki and Matt. His face was chalk white as he looked up.

From where Ashley stood, it was a sheer, vertical drop on to the pavement below. The wall was just wide enough for her feet to stand side by side, but there was no sloping roof to grab at. No second chances.

While the Hyena struggled to the front of the crowd, everyone watched her. But she still hadn't worked out how to speak to them. And already people were starting to get bored. They were glancing at Eddie, to see what the next entertainment would be.

She had to do something else, to keep their attention. And there was only one thing she could think of. The idea terrified her, but it was all there was.

Looking away from the crowd, she blanked them out of her mind and concentrated on what she was going to do. The world shrank round her. The people and the music disappeared. There was nothing but the bubble of space where she was facing the curved, narrow wall.

When she was quite steady, she went up on her hands and let her feet flop over, to balance her body. Then she began to climb, hands first, looking ahead for the next step and fighting the urge to glance down. All she could see was the top of the wall and the flaking paint that coloured the palms of her hands.

And the circus music went trumpeting on.

Now, the beautiful Miss Cindy will risk her life to bring you a daredevil display of balance and courage! Watch her climb to the roof, without a safety net!! Thrill to her death-defying ridge walk!!! Marvel at her calmness . . .

At the top of the wall, the curve flattened to form the base of a triangle that pointed down. As she reached it, Ashley went up on her hands again and flipped her legs over the other way. Then she stood triumphantly, with her arms spread.

The applause was so loud that she could hear it, even above the music, but it didn't mean anything. Because Eddie was smiling at her. A small, triumphant smile. And she saw that she hadn't done anything brave or independent. Eddie's face said it all.

You see? You're just part of my show.

Then he waved his hand, dismissing her. It was finished. Her trick was over. He turned his back on the cinema and signalled to Sam, calling up another burst of flame. And the crowd turned too, following where he pointed.

From the roof of the car, Sam gave him a long look. Then she lifted her head to look up at Ashley. Their eyes met, but Ashley couldn't read that ice-blue stare. Not even when Sam raised the bottle, turning on the roof of the car as she opened her mouth. Not even when she tilted her head back and brought the torch towards it.

When it happened, it was a shock as sudden as the burst of flame itself. As Sam breathed out, she jerked her head down sharply. Aiming her jet of fire at the top of Eddie's car. The flames roared and wrapped themselves round the loudspeaker, and there was an ugly, sizzling crackle. And a flash.

And then silence.

But it was only silent for a heartbeat, while Ashley realized what had happened. What Sam had done for her. Then she took in a huge breath and yelled into the silence, yelled, with every atom of breath in her lungs, every scrap of energy in her body.

'THE STALKER ISN'T MR GALT! HE'S INNOCENT! THE STALKER IS—!'

Her voice caught in her throat. What was Eddie's threat? *Say that outside this flat, and you'll be sorry. It's slander. You can't prove anything. The first whisper about stalking and you're in trouble.*

She was in enough trouble already. How could she cope with any more? But—someone had to say it. As long as people whispered and trembled and kept their mouths shut, Eddie would go on being the ringmaster. Someone had to take the risk.

'IT'S NOT MR GALT, IT'S—'

Her voice cracked again. But this time another voice broke in. A cold voice, as sharp as steel.

'Say that out loud, and you'll be sorry. It's slander. You can't prove anything. I've got solicitors!'

For a second, she thought it really was Eddie. Then she saw Sam bending down to haul Joe on to the roof of her car. He scrambled up beside her and for two or three seconds, he didn't say a word. He held the crowd in suspense, controlling them by the way he stood, by the tilt of his head and his arrogant, scornful stare.

Then he spoke again.

'No one puts me down, because you all jump when I crack the whip. I can do what I like on the Row, and no one touches me. Try it, and you'll suffer!'

He half-closed his eyes and pushed his face forward at Sam. Abruptly. Dangerously.

It was only a tiny movement. Ashley hadn't even noticed it particularly when Eddie did it. But the moment Joe mimicked it, she saw that it was Eddie to the life. Eddie blown up into a grotesque cartoon.

Everyone saw it. All round the car, people began to laugh, looking at Joe and then glancing sideways at the real Eddie, as if they were checking the resemblance. Joe played up to the laughter, picking up every little movement Eddie made and guying it, as if he had been practising for years.

Yes! Ashley thought, triumphantly. *Yes, yes, yes!* They'd done it. All of them together. They'd made people understand what Eddie was like and what he did. He was beaten!

She looked sideways, to see how he was taking it—and all her triumph fell away.

He was utterly still. There was no sign of anger on his face, no flinching. He didn't look beaten at all. He was standing in the middle of the crowd, silently watching Joe. Waiting for him to finish his turn.

His stillness started to affect people. One by one, they stopped laughing and edged away, until Eddie stood by himself in a circle of empty space. As the laughter disappeared, Joe's voice faltered, too. Finally, it died away and, for a second, the whole crowd seemed to hold its breath.

Then Eddie spoke, crisp and clear, into the silence.

'Oh dear, Joe,' he said. 'Oh dear, dear, *dear*. I thought you were my friend. But I was wrong, wasn't I?'

His voice was almost without expression, but Ashley had never felt such a sense of menace. Joe's pale clown-face turned dead white and his shoulders flagged as if he'd been beaten. Whatever Eddie was threatening him with, it didn't need to be spelt out. Ashley could feel the fear from where she stood.

And not only Joe's fear. The crowd faltered too. People began glancing at each other. Edging away from the cars. To Ashley, high on the cinema roof, it was like seeing Eddie tighten his grip on the Row. Fearless as a lion tamer, he was facing down a whole crowd. Splitting the wild, dangerous pack that had been ranged against him into separate, threatened individuals.

In another second, the whole crowd would have dispersed. But in the last, precarious instant, Ashley heard a soft footstep on the roof behind her.

And Tony Cavalieri leaned out of his window again, flapping his arms and yelling.

'Look out on the cinema! It's Eddie's men on the roof! Look out!'

Turning, automatically, Ashley saw Doug and another man only a few feet away, creeping past the ventilation shaft. They were hidden from the crowd by the high front wall, but she could see they were heading straight for her.

The shock of it was too much for her balance. She tried to keep her footing, but there was nothing to grab at. Her foot slipped and she knew she couldn't save herself.

As she fell, she heard the crowd roar.

LISA

She went off the top, and I started to scream. You can't help yourself. It's like a physical thing. Everyone was screaming and pushing backwards, so she wouldn't smash into them. And I was pushing back too, even though Ashley's one of my friends. I could feel Vikki doing it too, and Matt, and everyone. It was like a disaster movie erupting suddenly in the middle of your real life. Everyone wanted to get out of the way.

Except the Hyena.

He didn't even hesitate. The moment she slipped, he raced forward, pushing people out of his way. He stood at the bottom of the wall with his arms held out for Ashley, as if he thought he could catch her.

Anyone could see it wouldn't work. There was no way he was going to be strong enough. But even though she went through his hands, he broke her fall. Instead of smashing straight into the tarmac, head first, she hit his shoulder and spun over. Her feet cracked him in the skull, which slowed her down even more and she hit the ground legs first, and crumpled and rolled.

You think I can't remember all that? I'm telling you—I could draw it, frame by frame. I dreamt the whole thing, over and over again, for weeks afterwards, and the worst of it wasn't the moment when she hit the ground. It was the next moment, when we all realized that we'd pulled back. We'd left her to die.

There was a horrible quietness.

Then someone said, 'It was Eddie's men!' and it swept over me like a great wave.

It was Eddie's fault! Everything. *Eddie did it.*

The whole crowd roared, out loud, and we started pushing towards Eddie's car. But he was too quick for us. He jumped into the car and drove off, going up on the pavement to get past the other cars. We chased him to the end of the Row, but he wasn't stopping. He'd have run over anyone who got in the way. He didn't even pull over to the left till he saw the ambulance coming for Ashley and the Hyena.

Of course, *I* never believed all that stuff about the Hyena stalking Ashley. I mean, anyone could see it was one of Eddie's little plots.

I can't think how he fooled people so long. Everyone always used to make out he was so good, fixing things for people, and that sort of stuff. The way they talked, you'd have thought he was some kind of fairy godmother.

Huh! Some fairy godmother. You should hear the tales that are going round the Row now that people know it's safe to tell. Every time I go into Annie's, there's someone else in there, letting another cat out of the bag, and they're always nasty little stories.

Mrs Macdonald's taking up a collection for the Hyena, and Annie puts up a notice every day, to say how he's doing. She says he's got so many flowers the hospital's going crazy.

If only he could see them . . .

Thirty

Ashley opened her eyes and saw a white room. Hospital equipment. Flowers.

And Pauline in a wheelchair beside the bed.

Pauline took a quick breath and reached for her hand. 'Ashie? Can you hear me?'

'Of course,' Ashley tried to sit up. 'I'm perfectly—'

Then she lost the rest of the sentence and fell asleep.

The next time she came round, there were two nurses by her bed, busy with a drip. But Pauline was there too. Ashley blinked drowsily.

'The Hyena —'

'Mr Galt,' Pauline said.

'Yes, him. What happened? He hit me, or I kicked him, or something—'

'It was all my fault,' Pauline said. 'I should never have let you—'

Her face blurred, and Ashley let it go. She couldn't think about all that yet..

She couldn't think about anything much. For almost a week, she drifted in and out of sleep, without really remembering, trying to piece little bits together and giving up because the effort was exhausting. Faces flickered past her eyes—Janet, Vikki, Lisa—and she heard her voice mumbling to them. But when she looked at the flowers by her bed, and the cards and the grapes and the magazines, she couldn't remember who had brought them.

The only constant person was Pauline. She came every day in the wheelchair. Sometimes it was Janet and Frank who pushed her in, and sometimes it was another woman, with an unfamiliar face.

'That's Penny,' Pauline said, every time Ashley asked. 'She comes in to help me get up and go to bed. She's very nice. You'll like having her around.'

The first time she said it—and the second, and the third—the idea was so strange that Ashley forgot it. But gradually it stuck. Penny was coming in to look after her mother, and that was all right. She didn't have to worry. She could just let it happen.

'Janet kept on at me,' Pauline said. 'She said I had to get some help from the doctor and the Social Services. I didn't want to, but Tricia told me not to be an idiot.'

Tricia? There was something surprising about that, but Ashley couldn't work out what it was. She kept wondering about it, and forgetting, and then remembering again.

Until the morning when she woke up and found that her mind was completely clear. And she knew why she'd been surprised.

She sat up as far as she could. 'Did you say *Tricia* had been to see you?'

Pauline nodded. 'And Joe. It's helped me a lot, talking to them.'

'But what about Eddie? He said—'

Pauline hesitated, finding the words. 'People like Eddie have . . . lots of things going. They don't have to hang around if it gets difficult. He's moved on.'

'You mean . . . he's gone?' Ashley tried to get her brain round it. 'But what about his people? He told me he had people in every street.'

'Tricia says it's all changed. Phil's the one everybody's talking about now. Sam's going out with him, and Tricia says he's brilliant. He's really taking charge of things.'

Ashley felt strange. 'She used to think Eddie was brilliant.'

'Till he made fun of Sam, in front of everyone. And made Tricia laugh at it. That was his big mistake. She said it was really cruel.' Pauline squeezed Ashley's hand. 'Tricia's like me, you see. She thinks the world of her daughter.'

So that was what had swung it. After all the threats and the violence, it was a joke that had brought Eddie down.

And now Tricia was looking for a new fixer. Phil. Someone else to solve everyone's problems like magic. Was that better or worse?

Ashley concentrated on the things she could understand.

'At least Mr Galt's all right. Everyone knows he wasn't the stalker. He'll be fine now, won't he?'

'He—' Pauline's hand squeezed harder. 'Everyone thinks he's wonderful. They're calling him a hero in the Row.'

'So he doesn't mind any more? About me accusing him?'

'He—' Pauline stopped.

Even a day before, Ashley would have been too muzzy to wonder about that, but now her mind was working. 'There's something wrong, isn't there?' she said sharply. What she was thinking was too awful to say.

Pauline bit her lip. 'He's not dead. But he's still unconscious, and they're getting worried. His mother talked to him for an hour yesterday, to see if he'd respond to her voice, but it was no use.'

'So why don't they try someone else?'

'It's got to be a voice he'd recognize. Someone he cares about.'

Ashley linked her hands on top of the sheet and looked down at them. There was a dark bruise on the back of the right hand, turning an ugly yellow now. She thought about the Hyena dashing forward to catch her. About her feet, hitting the side of his head. And his bleak, unhappy face staring across the counter at her. *You mustn't be Cindy.*

'Can I go and talk to him?' she said.

It took two days to convince the doctors that it was worth organizing. Ashley was better, but she was still too weak to walk to the Neuro-Surgical Unit. One of the nurses had to take her in a wheelchair.

And when she was there, beside the Hyena's bed, she didn't know what to do. She sat helplessly, looking down at his face, which was even paler now. There was no mark on it, not a bruise or a scratch, but there was no sign of life, either. He was as still as a waxwork, pasty and middle-aged.

How could anything she said possibly make any difference to . . . that stranger?

'Don't worry,' the nurse said cheerfully. 'You haven't got to say anything earth-shaking. Just chat to him, the way you'd normally do.'

Oh, great, Ashley thought. *What do I say? How about: I'm sick of being chased and phoned and persecuted? Or: Why don't you stop stalking me?*

'No need to be shy.' The Hyena's nurse joined in. 'Be yourself.'

But that was the trouble. If she'd been like Joe, with a hundred different voices to call on, she could have launched into a fantastic speech. If they'd given her spray-cans, she could have decorated the bare walls with black and yellow horses. She could even have turned cartwheels down the corridor, if it hadn't been for the plaster.

But she had nothing. She couldn't even run away.

Eddie had gone. The circus was over. There was nothing except the Hyena, lying there unconscious. And her voice.

She started to talk.

'The writing on your wall—it wasn't meant to be horrible. I know it sparked everything off, but I didn't do it to annoy

197

you. I just wanted to climb up there and leave my mark. I wanted to be special . . .'

GEOFFREY

I can't say when I started hearing her voice, because in a way it was there all the time. I was dipping in and out of a grey mist, and her voice was whispering in my head. All sorts of things, coming back in a jumble.

LOOK! ARE YOU PROUD OF SENDING THAT TO ME?????
. . . halfapoundofcookingonionsplease . . .
THE STALKER ISN'T MR GALT! HE'S INNOCENT HE'S . . . *three cooking apples and a bag of sugar* . . .

Coming and going, round and round. I wanted to tell her it was all right, I wanted to say I understood, but my eyes wouldn't open and my voice wouldn't work. All the words in my head were hers.

. . . *You're not my father. My father's dead* . . .
YOU'RE NOT THE STALKER . . .
. . . pleasemayIhaveaboxofmatches . . .

Her face kept drifting through my mind, like a ghost's face. Coming into focus and then blowing away. Not real, just a Cinderella in my head, twisting and dissolving and slipping away. I knew I had to catch the real Ashley—the one who shouted at me and painted on the wall—but whenever I tried to see her face, there was such a pain. Such a miserable, wrenching pain . . .

. . . the writing . . . wasn't meant to be horrible . . .
. . . *I just wanted to . . . leave my mark* . . .
. . . I wanted to be special . . .

The voice pushed its way in, until I couldn't believe it was just in my mind. But how could it be anywhere else? I'd seen her fall. I'd seen her hit the ground.

I meant to help her, the way I always wanted to. I meant to race in and catch her, like some kind of magician, flying to the rescue. But it was no use.

198

She went through my hands like a thunderbolt, and I just keeled over. So when I heard her real voice—

I was scared to open my eyes in case I was making it up.

But you can't hide out in the dark for ever. If you do, you end up like Tony Cavalieri, wasting your life away. In the end, the real world's better, however bad it is. So I made myself look.

And she was there. She was sitting next to me, with half her hair cut off and a line of stitches across her scalp. She'd got stitches over one eyebrow, too, and her arm in plaster. The moment I saw all that, I knew she was real.

She'd survived without a magician.

But she didn't know what to say. I could see that in her face. She's only a child, after all.

So I helped her out with a little joke. 'Are there any pens around?' The words were croaky, because my voice was out of practice. 'It's my turn to do a bit of graffiti.'

She didn't get it at first. Not until one of the nurses passed her a handful of felt tips. Then she grinned and held out her arm.

'You'd better leave a bit of room,' she said. 'My sisters'll kill me if they can't fit their names on.'

'They can have the other side,' I said.

And I wrote my name along her arm, in three different colours. With shading.

LIBRARY
ISLINGTON SIXTH FORM CENTRE
ANNETTE ROAD
LONDON N7 6EX

LIBRARY
ASTON SIXTH FORM CENTRE
LINNETTE ROAD
LONDON N9 8EX